Pete
Thanks for all your he
I hope the kn

Caught

on

Camera

by
Adrian Spalding

Contents

In memory of Vernon Campbell Walker
22 Nov 1961 –23 March 2022

Other books by Adrian Spalding

The Reluctant Detective
The Reluctant Detective Goes South
The Reluctant Detective Under Pressure

Sleeping Malice

The Night You Murder

Preface

Becky held the burgundy chiffon evening dress against her body and smiled. She recalled the last time she had worn the garment, remembering the hem swirling as she enthusiastically danced with her husband. It was at the celebration event for their tenth wedding anniversary. There was no way she was going to leave the dress behind; it was her favourite outfit. If there were going to be any formal gatherings, then this would be her preferred attire.

Even as Becky carefully folded the dress into her suitcase, she started to wonder. Would there be any formal events where she was going? Her husband had not mentioned evening wear. The only urgent guidelines he had given her were to pack one suitcase, no more, pack only essentials. Well, Becky decided, the burgundy dress was essential, especially if it meant she could leave behind some boring, practical everyday garments.

It was not as if they were going to the back of beyond. There would be shops there. Not that she knew exactly where in Spain her husband had planned to take her, but she trusted him. He had always made the big decisions in their lives and so far, they had turned out to be the right judgements.

She hoped there would be dress shops, or a department store not too far away. She was excited by the possibility of spending a few days shopping, even if it was in a foreign country.

She only wished her husband had given her a little more warning that they were leaving today. They had been talking about going to Spain to settle down for months. Now in their late fifties, they had no ties here in the UK. No children to hold them back. No close relatives to be cared for. They were free agents. The attraction of better weather and cheaper housing was a real draw. Sensibly, they both agreed that first they should spend six months in Spain to make sure it was where they wanted to go. Only if it was the right area would they sell their English house and live abroad for the rest of their lives.

This morning all those practical and sensible plans had changed. He had rushed into the kitchen as she was washing the breakfast dishes, telling her to pack. He said he had ferry tickets for that evening. The sudden change of plan put Becky out, she now had lots to do. You can't just walk out of your house and spend six months abroad, it takes planning. As she tried to explain this to her husband, she sought a good reason as to why he wanted to leave immediately. He refused to explain. All he said was she had to trust him. He knew what was best for the two of them and leaving the country tonight was their only option. The consequences of staying would be dire he told her, without any further explanation.

Becky was never one to argue. She hated raised voices and always believed there was a compromise to be found. The other fact was that her husband was resolute, even to the point of calling her Rebecca, something he only did when he was angry or exasperated. She had dried her hands, put the dishes on the side and agreed. Deep down she knew the day would fly by as she gathered her thoughts, her possessions and her sanity.

At the back of her mind, she wondered just what he was thinking. He had altered over the last few months. He snapped at her more often. Went out less. Called her every few hours when he was at work. Every time she questioned his change of mood and his unusual behaviour, he told her she was imagining things. She knew it was not her imagination, but a change in him.

It was soon after they had been burgled that his mood had changed still further. Nothing much had been stolen, just a CD player, an obsolete mobile phone and a handful of DVDs. The damage to the back door was the biggest expense. The burglar or burglars had just prised the door out of its frame. In the end they bought a whole new door and frame. Her husband had insisted on additional locks and a reinforced frame.

After that he became overly security minded. Doors always had to be locked, windows closed. They changed their shopping routine each week. Dutifully Becky did exactly as she was instructed, without any sort of explanation.

Now as well as her treasured garments, she also managed to squeeze in a couple of photographs. Their wedding day, the time they walked to the summit of Mount Snowdon, only to be enveloped in fog and could not see a thing. The picture of the two of them at the Acropolis. An old man had offered to take the photograph, then asked for ten euros as he handed the camera back. Her husband wanted to refuse, but she was more charitable and gave the man his money with a smile.

She looked around the room. Everything else, all their belongings and furniture would either follow them, or in six months she would be back here in their bedroom unpacking. Deep down she knew they both wanted to make it work and live in Spain until their lives ended. She heard a noise downstairs, was it the doorbell? Most likely her husband had returned. She had not expected him back so soon.

3

He had not told her where he was going or who he was visiting, but that did not matter anymore. She was now about to close her suitcase, grab a lightweight coat and join him downstairs to begin their trip.

Her nose reacted, a tingle. She smelt something unusual. Something was burning. A smoky acrid odour Becky could not recognise. She thought she had heard the front door close earlier. Doug must be back; he could have called up, maybe he did, with the bedroom door closed she might not have heard him. She hoped her husband had not come back and decided to have one last fry-up before going, that would be so like him. She looked around the bedroom one final time. Did her eyes detect a slight blue haze in the room, mutating the colour of the wallpaper, or was it the light bulb playing up? Maybe she was tired, it had been a busy day. The stench was getting worse. Leaving the suitcase on the bed, she opened the bedroom door intending to call down to her husband, 'What have you burnt now, dear?'

The words would not come out. Her breath was stolen from her by a rush of lung-scorching heat and eye-watering black smoke, which barged into the bedroom. She slammed the door shut. Not in her wildest dreams did she ever think that she would have to contend with her house being alight. And today of all days.

What should she do? Call the fire brigade, what else? Her phone was downstairs. Becky had always wanted a phone by the bed, but hubby had always said no. She now wished she had been more insistent. Could she dash through the smoke? Go downstairs to safety? She opened the door carefully, just a crack, more hot smoke forced its way into the room. She closed the door. Even so, smoke was

4

now leeching in over the top of the door, finding every gap around the frame.

The window. Jump to safety. It was locked. Of course, it was. Her husband's security obsession. Becky anxiously looked around the window. The key had to be nearby. He would have left it close to the window, of course he would. Why wouldn't he? She scrabbled around the windowsill; the chest of drawers next to it. She extended the radius of her search. All the while the smoke thickened and hindered her vision, irritating her lungs as she tried to control her breathing.

She was now wildly emptying boxes, jars, vases, anywhere that the key might be. There was no longer any rationale to her actions. Terror clouded her thoughts. Break the window! She grabbed her vanity stool, an old retro one that she had found in a flea market and lovingly restored. She had spent hours re-upholstering the seat in a material that matched the curtains. Regardless, she threw it towards the glass with her failing strength. Pathetically it struck the toughened glass then fell to the ground. Not even a crack in the window.

Becky was now almost blinded by the smoke. With every breath she took she felt pain from the heat drying out her lungs, the fire stealing her oxygen. Her mind was failing, her thoughts confused. She was no longer able to work out a plan of escape from this inferno. Her knees gave up first, she collapsed to the floor. There the air was clearer, more life-giving. Just giving enough oxygen to clear her mind, to recognise the inescapable fact that she was about to die.

Two years later

How hard could it be? All that Tony was asked to write was one hundred simple words. A regular filler news story about a couple celebrating their sixtieth wedding anniversary. There was even going to be a picture of the happy old couple chinking glasses of champagne. Tony guessed the photographer would have taken the remainder of the bottle home. A simple one hundred words and Tony was struggling to even start.

That was always the way. Tony was not a reporter. Well, technically he was employed as a reporter, yet he had never considered himself to be a journalist. He was a lot older than the young guns around him, productively tapping away at their keyboards. Also, he had never been or even considered being a journalist in all his working life. Whatever Tony thought did not matter in the slightest. He had to write one hundred words and have them on the desk of his sub-editor within the next thirty minutes.

Tony had spoken to the couple in their cluttered home. As a result he now had enough material about their lives together to fill a book, a book he did not have to complete. All he needed to write was a single column to fit under a photograph. Time was ticking away.

When his phone rang, he was happy to answer; a distraction was exactly what he needed.

"Kent Herald! How can I help?"

Even after a year, Tony still felt uncomfortable answering the telephone. It was not so much the act of conversing that bothered him, it was his position as a regional newspaper reporter. He had never planned to be a news reporter. At school he had been successfully inept at

English. Apart from being described as a poor speller in junior school, when it came to English grammar, the mystery had deepened further, as had his fear of the subject.

He did try to understand conjunctions, syntax and the construction of sentences. There were rare times when he saw the light at the end of the grammar tunnel. Then it was time for English Literature and Shakespeare, who in Tony's teenage view, spoke a different language to the one his teachers were trying to instil in him. He much preferred art classes and chemistry, as a mature man he still occasionally picked up a stick of charcoal and sketched out an abstract landscape.

"Hi Dad, I'm home." His daughter, Isobel, sounded buoyant.

"Hi darling, how was school?"

"Good. I managed a 'B' in maths. Do you want me to cook tonight?"

Did he want her to cook? Yes, he did. Tonight was Isobel's martial arts training, which meant he would get home to find a simple plate of pasta and sauce waiting on the table as she was not interested in cooking anything more complex. He never complained though. All other nights, Tony oversaw meal preparation while Isobel finished her homework. They would eat together before she retired to her bedroom to do what teenage girls do. He was not too sure what she did but knew most of her time was spent talking to friends through one or more of the many channels of communication available nowadays.

What she did regularly each day, was to call him as soon as she arrived home from school. Tony worried about having a thirteen-year-old schoolgirl as a daughter leaving school with her friends, who gradually peeled off until she was left walking alone. He knew from bitter experience there were a lot of evil people on the streets. He did not impose too many draconian rules on his daughter but calling him as soon as she arrived home was one of them.

"Can we pick up Judy on the way to karate and then bring her home? Her dad is working away for a couple of days."

"No problem. It's all very quiet today, so I'll be home on time and we can swing by her place on the way."

It was not often that Tony worked late. Although he was forty years old, he was looked upon as the junior reporter in the office. He dealt with the soft filler stories that normally ended up deep in the paper. Jumble sales, church events, anniversaries, charity fund-raising, were his staple diet for work. Part of him liked the idea of being home every evening and weekend, it enabled him to manage the many housekeeping chores: washing, cleaning, shopping and still have time to spend with Isobel.

Before he could leave, he had to finish typing up his copious notes from the happy couple. One hundred bloody words, he thought. Sixty years of marriage, children, grandchildren, hardship, happiness and sadness, were all included in the pages of notes he had. Now he needed to condense their life into just one hundred words.

Maybe he should focus on one event in their lives, keep it quite simple. After all, he considered, did anyone care that this couple of old people had spent sixty years of marriage together? It just made those who had managed only six years before getting a divorce look bad. Finally, he started, 'a daily cuddle is just the thing to make your marriage last'.

That was exactly what they had told him. But it sounded rubbish as a start and already he had used thirteen of his one-hundred-word allocation. 'If I leave her, she'd kill me, so I thought I had better stay'.

Fourteen words this time, a lot more dramatic, but not what was said. Although Tony did get the impression that the wife would have done exactly that had her husband even looked at another female.

Thankfully, his typing was interrupted again by the ringing of his desk telephone.

"Kent Herald! How can I help you?"

"Hi mate, it's George here, been a while. How're you doing?"

For an instant Tony could not quite place the voice. He knew a few Georges, but there was only one to call him 'mate' and that was George Stevens, born and bred in south London. Tony had known George for the best part of ten years, possibly longer. He was one of those people who only ever seemed to contact you when they wanted a favour. Even so, Tony still had a lot of time for George. He was likeable, always had a joke to brighten the day and lived his life with a good splash of optimism.

"I'm good, thanks. To what do I owe the honour of this call."

"Well, I heard through the grapevine you're some sort of reporter now, a bit of a change I must say. Anyway, thought being as you work for a newspaper you might be able to help me out."

"It depends on what sort of help you want?" Tony spoke cautiously, knowing full well that George was a local character who frequently ended up on the wrong side of the law.

"One of me tenants popped his clogs, leaving me with a room full of stuff which ain't mine. I have no idea if he has any family. I got to wondering if you could put a bit in your rag, see if anyone knows the guy. I can't rent out the place till his stuff has been cleared. I want shot of it all, one way or another."

"I thought your places were all holiday lets? There can only be a few personal possessions, which I'm sure you can store somewhere."

George Stevens had for some years let out three holiday chalets that he had built himself on spare land attached to the house he currently owned in New Ash Green. He had bought the house soon after leaving prison, which raised a few eyebrows and questions as to just how he could afford such a place. Five-bedroomed house with a sizeable chunk of land, which still had a large farm hangar on it, as well as more than enough space for three one-bedroomed chalets. The police did poke into his finances but were unable to prove there was any illegality in the way he acquired the money to buy it. The excuse George had and stubbornly stuck to, was as soon as he had been sentenced, he sold his building business. This netted him a substantial amount of money, which was wisely invested to enable him to buy Green Lane Farm. Many, including Tony, were suspicious of this explanation.

"Nah, this guy wanted to stay long term, I did him a good deal, paid every month, cash on the nail. Nice little earner, especially through the winter season. Course I let him have some of his own stuff, sofas, tellies, all that sort of thing. Nice bloke. Became a bit of a mate, so I don't want to just throw all the stuff out. Come down and we can go through it together, might be a few clues to any of his relations there. I know you're good at sorting that legal sort of stuff."

Tony sighed, "I'll pop along tomorrow morning."

'Childhood sweethearts, Jessie and John, pleaded with their parents to let them marry. They were both sweet sixteen and all their parents doubted it would last. Sixty years later, Jessie and John both 76, have proved their parents wrong as they joined their fourteen grandchildren and six great-grandchildren to celebrate their diamond wedding anniversary.

Jessie and John Harris from Downham have put their long marriage down to never telling lies and always 'having a daily kiss and cuddle' they admitted, with a twinkle in their eyes. John added, 'always agree with the wife, it makes life so much easier'".

Tony read back his hundred words for one final check then sent the file to his sub-editor. It was not going to win him any journalistic prize, but it did mean he could leave the office and go home to his daughter.

Chapter 1

The next morning George greeted Tony with a broad smile and a friendly slap on the back as he showed him into his home. Even though George was almost twenty years older than Tony, he still had a youthful look to his face and eyes that sparkled with a natural mischief. The house was impressive in its size and architecture. Built back in the early nineteenth century, the weathered Flemish brickwork belonged to a time far removed from modern living. The slave-merchant who had originally commissioned and built the house would be turning in his grave knowing that a common criminal such as George now owned his prestigious home, even though modern society considered George's misdemeanours less hideous than the merchants. Located along a long, quiet country lane sparsely lined with individually built modern luxury houses, it was a polar opposite to the council estate where George had grown up. Tony imagined that the current neighbours were not too pleased to have George in their neighbourhood. The big downside of George was his hoarding disorder. The house, which Tony had visited before, was cluttered with peculiar boxes, car parts, broken radios awaiting repair, picture frames that needed a lot of love and attention. Tony stopped at doing a full stocktake of the house contents in his mind, he knew it would be too much to take in.

George did not end at hoarding in the house, he also extended his obsession to the front garden, where three cars and a small van required parts and repair. The large farm hangar which came with the house, contained the odd valuable car, metallic signs from decades gone by, as well as a chaotic mix of machines and paraphernalia from bygone eras, including a complete Shell petrol pump, which would have worked perfectly if George could have acquired a large, garage-sized petrol tank from somewhere. Tony did not put it outside the realms of possibility that George was looking for such an item.

By way of alleviating the pressure on the house, as he was reluctant to throw anything away, George did regularly have a stall in Chatham Antiques market and sold many of the random belongings he had accumulated over time. This venture did make him a handsome profit as he had an eye for a valuable item as well as a grasp on the relative value of any article that might be of interest to a more focused collector. However, the profits from the stall were in the main ploughed back into purchasing other collectables to replace those he had sold.

For all his foibles, George was a nice bloke who wanted to help wherever he could. He loved a chat, which Tony imagined was the real reason for the construction of three self-contained cabins to be let out to holiday makers. The holiday homes would give him the chance to make a few extra pounds as well as have a constant flow of new faces to talk to.

Tony and George walked out of the kitchen, which was situated at the back of the main house, ambled across a garden that just happened to be in the middle of a refurbishment that had started five years earlier, then took a few steps up to a gravelled parking area fronting a block of three brick-built single storey homes. Each cabin had one bedroom, a fully fitted kitchen, a living area, a toilet and shower. The middle home was adapted for disabled use. George was unhappy to spend extra money to have a walk-in shower and disabled access toilet, until it was pointed out by the local planning officer that he had no choice and so George reluctantly built one as required.

Building and decorating had been George's trade for many years, although Tony was also more than aware that he had several sidelines, both legal and illegal.

They walked into the cabin on the left which was number one and stepped straight into the kitchen area with its clean smart cupboards and stainless-steel sink unit located beside the door, under the front-facing window. In the centre was a small pine table with four chairs. The living area was not divided from the kitchen by a wall but continued from the table towards the back of the cabin. Tony could see evidence of the personalising the cabin had undergone. There was a large flat-screen television opposite a comfortable-looking reclining single-person chair, just the one, so the person who lived here did not have many, if any, visitors and a stylish looking stereo unit, with a pile of CDs next to it. On the back wall, in which was located another window and a door leading out to the communal grassed play area, was a glass-doored cupboard, in which Tony could see a large collection of single malt whisky bottles at various stages of consumption.

George sat down at the pine table, opened a blue folder and beckoned Tony to join him.

"Okay, George, tell me all about your man whose relatives you want to find."

Tony guessed that the deceased occupier of this cabin must have been a good friend to George. Otherwise, knowing him as Tony did, he would have expected that George would have simply taken out everything of value and sold it. Alternatively, he might have left it all in place and put a surcharge on the number one cabin for future hirers.

"I'll start at the very beginning; that's a very good place to start." George laughed at his own droll joke. Tony waited with pen and notepad poised.

"A couple of years ago this bloke calls me interested in renting out one of me cabins long term, asked if I offer discounts. How long do yer want? I ask. 'Until I die,' he says. Well, at the time I didn't know how old he was, but it sounded like he wanted the place for a long time. I gave him a good deal and he moved in. He was no bother, paid his rent on time, always in cash. Helped me out once in a while for the odd building job I did. Occasionally had a drink with him. All in all, a quality bloke."

"Then he dies. Natural causes?"

"He was 'bout the same age as me, which you know is just on the verge of the big six oh. It wasn't bad health. He was repairing his car. Nice little Morris eleven hundred, good condition, real classic, the Vanden Plas model. He picked it up cheap, got a good deal for cash. Anyway, he was doing something under the car when the jack gave way and crushed him. The oil sump flattened his head on the ground. A real mess, I can tell you.

"It was up at the barn, so I had no idea what had happened until I was about to settle down for the night and saw the barn light on and wondered what was going on. Took a stroll up there and saw his legs poking out from under the car. Really did me in. I tried to move the car, but they are heavy things. He was no doubt dead. I came back to the house, called the ambulance, not that they could do much, and had a stiff drink, I can tell you."

"If he died in an accident, didn't the police try and trace his next of kin?"

"I think they tried but no luck. In the end, the coroner called it accidental death. I paid for the funeral and stuff. Well, he had paid up front for the rent, so I thought it only right and proper. The Old Bill then said as he has no relatives, it's up to me to sort out his stuff. I still reckon he must have some people out there. Everyone has someone surely. My best guess? He was hiding from someone or something, but I never asked. Fag?"

George offered Tony a cigarette from a packet of Benson and Hedges with all the health warnings clearly printed in French. Most likely it was part of an illegally imported batch of tobacco that George had been involved with.

"You know I don't smoke. What was the guy's name?"

"Doug. Here's some of his stuff, but I found just about nothing worthwhile in it. No bank statements, nothing medical, no address book, nothing to point to where he might have come from."

George spread out an assortment of semi-official-looking papers which Tony glanced over. Instructions for the TV, a cash receipt for a pay-as-you-go mobile phone, a logbook for the Morris car which in the end killed him, as well as a small booklet which noted the dates he had paid George the rent.

"Well, nothing here; anything anywhere else?"

"I haven't found anything of interest. I wondered with your experience if you might well be able to find something. Have a good look around. I done the drawers and stuff; you might have some other ideas." George waved his hand towards the rest of the cabin, causing the smoke from his cigarette to swirl in the rays of sunshine coming in through the window.

"What about the cash George?"

"Cash! What d'yer mean?" his voice became defensive.

"What I mean is, he had no bank statements, yet he still bought stuff, so I would imagine he had some cash lying around. You said he paid cash for the car that killed him. If there was no cash found after his death, then maybe it was a robbery that went wrong. Just the sort of thing the police should know about."

George flicked the ash from his cigarette into his hand, walked over to the sink and emptied his hand. He turned, leaning back against the sink. "There's no need to call the police back. There was some cash. It wasn't like I was thievin' it, I got to sort his stuff out and get this cabin all cleaned out. Plus, the blood stains in the barn, can't have them there for the rest of eternity. I took the cash on account, so to speak."

"How much?"

"It covered all the costs I've just mentioned."

"How much?" Tony repeated.

"Four thousand," George admitted unwillingly.

"Covered your costs with plenty left over. You'll never change will you?"

"God looks after those who look after themselves."

"Your morals are yours to live with. What made you think he was hiding from someone?"

"He never wanted to talk much about what he did before arriving here. Every time I tried to pry, he changed the subject or just clammed up. But it was him dying under a car which really has spooked me. Doug was a careful bloke, real careful, I mean safety gone mad. Any building job we had to have the ladders fixed, hard hat, wires all kept tidy and in good nick. I can't imagine him going under a car with just one jack. He would have had at least a couple of axle stands, just to be sure."

"You think he was murdered? What did the police say?" The allegation surprised Tony. He had arrived expecting to be writing up another soft story. Now, George was making the allegation of a murder having been committed, yet he appeared very calm.

"I never told them. You know what they're like, make that suggestion when they're planning to write it up as an accident, they'll be all over this place and 'ave me as top suspect. All I'm saying is that I thought it was funny he had no axle stands."

"They also might ask if he had any cash lying around that might make it look like a robbery."

"Alright, point taken. You know I don't like the Old Bill. I'm thinking he might have hidden something away that might help work out a little bit more about his past. That's why I asked you and no one else. I trust you, you're a diamond bloke."

Accepting the compliment, Tony started in the kitchen. Every cupboard he opened, the contents pulled out: the saucepans, frying pans, colanders, jugs and jars of various shapes and sizes, everything examined and returned. Drawers were pulled out, the rear void investigated, cutlery trays lifted, cooking foil rolls opened and replaced.

Then it was into the living area. Not many possible places to conceal something, depending on what that something might be. Even so, Tony ran his hands between the leather cushions of the reclining chair to see if a letter or document was hidden. He turned the chair on its side, looking for traces of coverings having been removed and replaced. He pulled out the malt whisky bottles and looked behind each and every one of them. None of them were cheap bottles, Doug must have been a connoisseur of the single malts.

The first time Tony stepped into the bedroom; he noticed a slightly damp smell. In the corner were tell-tale signs of black mould. He would mention it to George later. The wardrobe was his first area of interest. Only a few coats were hanging up, tee shirts lay in a pile. Obviously, this Doug was not one for going out dressed formally or smartly. Tony dug deep into each coat pocket, nothing but a packet of Polo mints. He looked to the very back of the wardrobe, there, behind a pile of dirty work jeans, he spotted a box file, the type you might find in any office, but not often in a wardrobe. He pulled it out and opened the hard lid.

The box was full of sales invoices from a malt whisky company based in Loch Lomond that Tony had never heard of. The customer was Mr D. Halifax. Tony read the note on each invoice which seemed to be a handwritten opinion that the deceased Doug, no doubt, made to appraise the single malt he had bought. Tony recognised some of the brands from the cupboard he had just searched.

"George, what was Doug's surname?" Tony called out.

"Halifax, like the place," George replied from the kitchen, where he was on his phone buying a Victorian brass bed warmer from eBay.

After closing the wardrobe door, Tony glanced around the room. Next to the bed was a modest occasional pine table on which was a small lamp and an old-fashioned radio alarm clock with red digital numbers. On the floor, just under the table, lay a pile of magazines. Tony picked one up and flicked through the pages. It was last month's copy of 'Prestige Cars', expensive exclusive cars which Tony guessed might be beyond Doug's budget. Amongst the glossy photographs of dream cars were scribbled random numbers and letters, the meaning of which eluded Tony.

Tony walked back into the kitchen, placed the invoices and one magazine on the table in front of George, then showed him the invoices.

"Maybe Doug was a secret shopper for malt whisky?"

"He did like a dram or two. Nothing else?"

"How did he pay for it? By mail order, I mean, if he only used cash."

"Postal orders, you know, the old-fashioned way."

"I didn't know you could still get postal orders. And the dream cars?" Tony pointed to the magazine.

George flicked through the pages, seemingly ignoring the notations. "We all wish to have a flashy car. I'd love one, just lack of cash stopping me."

Tony ignored the temptation to point out George had at least four thousand pounds towards his dream car. "Those numbers mean anything?"

"How would I know?"

Tony sat down next to George, scribbled the deceased Doug's name on his pad and took one more look around the kitchen. If you are going to hide something, kitchens are the best place. Lots of nooks and crannies as well as empty voids to hide contraband. He looked down at the plinth that was fitted under the kitchen base units. He had forgotten about kitchen plinths; it had been a while since he had officially searched a house.

"Are they screwed in?" Tony asked, pointing towards the white base.

"Nah, from IKEA, they sort of clip in."

Tony left his chair and knelt beside the base units. He first removed the plinth that spanned the width of the kitchen sink cupboard using a knife to flick the board away from the legs it was clipped to. As he pulled it away, he investigated the dark void using his phone torch and concluded, "You got a leak under the hot water pipe."

"What? Are you a plumber as well as a reporter now."

Tony moved onto the next plinth, which encompassed two base units, one, a double, the other housed the cooker. Once again, he flipped the plinth off and turned on his torch to examine the void. He stretched his arm into the dusty space and pulled out a brown hard–backed envelope; he blew a fine cobweb from it.

Sitting on the floor, Tony looked inside the envelope and pulled out a United Kingdom passport. "Well, you'll be pleased to learn that you did not leave the IKEA instructions under there. Is this your Douglas?"

Tony held the photo page of the passport towards George, who leaned forward on his chair, squinted a little and confirmed it was the Douglas who lived in the cabin.

"Well, Halifax was not his name. According to this, he is a Douglas Wright from London. And this," Tony said, as he opened a second passport he found in the envelope, "must be his wife, Rebecca Wright, also from London."

***

Together they emptied the contents of the envelope onto the kitchen table, to begin examining the incongruous selection of items it contained. The passports revealed that Douglas Wright was the same age as George, with Rebecca two years younger. Both had been born in London. The next of kin pages at the back of both passports had not been filled in. Not a lot of help there.

Slipped inside each passport was a travel ticket for an overnight ferry crossing to Calais more than two years out of date. Several euro bank notes were neatly wrapped in a plastic band. George counted one thousand euros in total, his eyebrows rose in surprise as he laid the neat pile of notes on the table. He then turned to the next items, two ten by eight inch black and white photographs, very similar in their subject.

Each photo showed three men in what appeared to be a second-hand car lot. The faces of two of the men were clearly visible. The third was a part profile, the hair, one ear and just the tip of his nose was discernible. The only change in the second photograph was the two identifiable men were shaking hands. Tony looked beyond the van they were standing next to, trying to judge the age of the print from the types of cars that were on sale. From what he could make out, he guessed perhaps the late eighties or early nineties.

George next picked up a roll of thirty-five millimetre black and white film, unrolled part of it and held it up to the light, squinting to try to make out the images.

"They all look to be of the same place, the three guys are in most of them. Then a couple of close ups of one who I think is the car dealer, plus a few wider views of the whole car dealership. I know this place. It's on New Cross Road. It's still there, different owner, I would guess."

As George was still looking up into the light making out the images, Tony picked up a folded newspaper cutting. Slightly browned with age, the main photograph accompanying the story was the same as the print with the car dealer shaking hands. There were two other photographs in the cutting, one plainly showing the row of cars for sale, with prices on their windscreens which proved they were years old. The broad signage on the gantry above gave the name: 'New Cross Cars'; George was right. There was no date on the clipping that Tony read. A telephone number and name, Marcus Young, was written on the back. Once he had read through the story, he handed the frail newsprint to George summarising the article.

"Well, according to that press cutting, which must be a good few years old now, the owner of 'New Cross Cars', Mickey Ross, was a bit of a lad. Picking up stolen cars and selling them on with false paperwork, getting written-off cars rebuilt with dubious safety or any regard for the new owners. He also seemed to be a favourite amongst villains to get a car with false paperwork. A good bit of investigative journalism, I'd say."

There was a brief silence between the two men as they took in the allegations the newspaper had made many years ago.

"The nineties, which was your era, you must have known this car dealer given the nature of your work back then?" Tony asked.

George did not answer at once, he seemed to be distracted by rolling up the film. Thinking back, or more likely, making an excuse, Tony guessed.

"Well, I knew of him and his dodgy dealings, but never knew him as such. All I recall is that he never dabbled in car sales after the Old Bill had cracked down on him. He got a suspended sentence but had learnt his lesson, I guess. I wonder why Doug had these prints and this cutting? Didn't think he had any connections to the area."

Tony looked at the abstract items strewn over the kitchen table as George once again unrolled the film and carefully re-examined the small negatives. Passports and tickets, went together, as did the euros. That little group, Tony compartmentalised in his logic, it made sense and he could understand why Douglas had them, even though they were hidden. He undoubtedly did not want to advertise his real identity.

The prints, the negatives and the press cutting. Once again, Tony could see the way they fitted together like a jigsaw. What he could not understand was the reason that Douglas might have them hidden alongside documents from his own life.

"Your Doug, he never mentioned a wife or possibly living or working around New Cross?"

"Not a dickie bird. He never mentioned 'aving a wife and told me he originally came from Nottingham, although he never had much of a northern accent. Sounded a southerner to me, which he must have been. He just kept himself to himself. Every time I mentioned what he did in the past, he just glanced over it and changed the subject."

"Well, at least we have a phone number," Tony said, as he dialled the central London number on the back of the press cutting.

"Good morning, Daily Mirror," a young female voice answered in an efficient tone.

Tony had not expected a newspaper. He had assumed the telephone number would be the personal number, not a switchboard.

"Marcus Young, please." There was a brief silence.

"I'm sorry, Mr Young no longer works here."

"Do you know how I may contact him?"

"I'm sorry, we have no contact details for Mr Young. Is there someone else who might be able to help you?"

"Was Mr Young a reporter at the Mirror?"

"No sir, he was the editor a few years ago."

"And there is no way that I can contact him? Would you know if he is still in the newspaper industry?"

"I really have no idea. What was the nature of your query?"

24

Tony did not wish to share the reason for his call so politely he thanked her and ended the call.

"Odd having the Mirror's editor's details written down. There must have been a reason for it. Let's look again at your Douglas Wright; find out if he was hiding from something. I'll Google his name, see if anything stands out amongst the millions of hits it might get." Tony opened his phone and tapped the name Douglas Wright into the search engine.

There might have been five million results mentioned, luckily for Tony, it was the third search result down, a news headline and the same passport photograph he had just seen.

'Husband sought after tragic fire.'

Tony opened the link which took him to a news story from the Maidstone Times published two years earlier. He read it, then read it once more, to make sure it was not another Douglas Wright.

"Your Douglas Wright is wanted by the police to help them with their inquiries. According to this newspaper report, following a fire at the family home in which his wife, Rebecca, died. No wonder he was hiding, sounds to me like he murdered his wife."

***

George read the news article, shaking his head in disbelief. The Doug that had rented one of his cabins, shared his whisky, helped out with building work, was not a killer, of that George was sure.

In his life, picking up crumbs of living on the outer fringes of the criminal world, George had met all types, murderers included. He could not see Doug being in that category, even when Tony suggested that sometimes rage and arguments could lead to people doing things they

25

would not normally do. There could be several reasons that had driven Doug to kill his wife. George remained steadfast in his opinion: Doug was not a killer.

"Let's see if this Marcus Young appears anywhere."

This time there were no news stories, in fact, very little, which surprised Tony. An editor of a national newspaper he would have assumed would have multiple snippets on Google. The closest that Tony could find was a Facebook link, a Marcus Young who described himself as an ex-journalist now travelling the country looking for enlightenment and the perfect ale.

"Looks like a hippy," George commented when Tony showed him the Facebook profile of Marcus.

"It's a long shot but ex-journalist, worth a punt. I'll slip him a message later. See if he has heard of Douglas Wright.

"Anyway, it's not for us to worry too much about. I'll pop this stuff into the police station and let them sort it out. They're the ones who get paid to make investigations."

"Whoa! Whoa! mate, hang on, why bother handing it over? He's dead, it's not as if they can nick him now. Can't we just leave it all as it was? They just get left with an open case."

"What's it to you? For all we know they might have had kids or family who are wanting justice, or at least closure on the tragedy which would, no doubt, have blighted their lives. Plus, the police get to close a case and move on. You know what people are like when they talk about open cases, the police aren't doing enough, being lazy, not bothering. I can drop it in and that will be the end of it."

"They won't want to come and re-examine the way he died?"

"Look George, I am sure you were having kittens while police officers were walking round your place looking into how Doug died. I'm guessing you would have hidden anything that they should not see. They've done their job. I guarantee, they'll enter a few details on their computer, and the case gets closed, next of kin told, then they can move onto the next case. A nice easy win, trust me, that's what they like best, easy wins."

"You know what the Old Bill are like, re-opening the case, digging around even more. Can't we just leave it, Tony?"

"No, George, we can't just leave it. They have the wrong name on a body buried somewhere and that needs to be put right."

"Well, just give them the passports. The newspaper story and the photographs have nothing to do with him killing his wife, we'll hang onto them."

"Is there anything you're not telling me, George? Because if there is something, I'd rather know now than later down the line."

"Nothing, honest. It's just that if they start digging around an old news story, who knows what they might turn up. And Doug is dead after all, no harm done. I'd hate to think of his memory being tarnished."

"He murdered his wife, George, it doesn't come more tarnished than that, does it."

"Just the passports and tickets, Tony, I reckon that will be enough to clear his name. He was no killer of that I would swear on me mother's grave."

Tony ignored the plea and gathered up everything, replacing it all in the envelope, citing that if they wanted to look at the photographs, he'd have them, then there would be even less reason for the police to visit George.

Tony checked his watch, he needed to get home urgently. He had an important appointment.

Chapter 2

Rita Taylor was short and plump with wiry grey hair pulled back into a tight French bun. She had long ago given up worrying about her weight. No longer concerned about finding a soulmate; living alone with her cat was just as enjoyable. If Mr Right did happen to come along, then he would just have to take her as he found her, overweight.

Things were different years ago. Rita had given in to the so-called helpful advice, which was really peer pressure, to slim down a bit. 'You'd look so much better. Have a stylish hair do. Pick out some slinky clothes and the fellows will be fighting over you' was the vision and the promise made.

Rita did all that. Yes, she did attract the men. However, none of them wanted her for her intellect or views on politics. They just wanted sex. That made Rita feel uncomfortable when after a couple of dates, she had not allowed any of the men to sleep with her. A simple goodnight kiss was as far as she would go. She had never envisaged having sex before marriage, no matter how outdated that concept might be to her peer group. The men in her life quickly left to find women with a more relaxed attitude to physical interaction. Was she wrong? Should she go to bed with a man as soon as she had found out his middle name? It depressed and worried her.

Then there was the constant, unrelenting attention to what she was eating. Was it helping or hindering her rigid diet to ensure she maintained her target weight? It darkened her mood, not being able to eat the food that she liked and enjoyed. She looked good, everyone agreed on that, it was just that they did not see the inner darkness that was consuming her.

One day she woke up deciding that enough was enough. She might become plump after ditching her diet but at least she would be happier. That was the important thing. If being a few pounds overweight was her only problem, then she was lucky, unlike her clients.

Having spent the last seven years as a social worker, she knew that weight or how you looked was not that important. There were far worse circumstances that could befall you. She had seen many tragic families in her time, had done her best to help them but she had not always been the solution to their problems. Sometimes when a family came to her attention, they had travelled too long in the wrong direction, the journey back was hard.

Tony Vercoe and his daughter Isobel were different. Officially, it had started as a simple case, one that Rita had volunteered for. The mother no longer around, working father needing to look after his teenage daughter. It should have been just a case of keeping them on the straight and narrow, offering advice, signposting them in the right direction for support. Rita did not see it like that. Today's visit was going to be uncomfortable for Mr Vercoe.

It was not helped by the room she was sitting in with Mr Vercoe. His house was a large contrast to many of the squalid homes she often found herself in. Apart from being a well-maintained semi-detached house on the edge of Croydon, the road was smart and fashionable. She doubted that any social worker had visited this street in its one-hundred-year history. The fixtures and furnishings inside were not luxurious in an ostentatious way; they were trendy and expensive. The fabric sofa almost swallowed her plump frame, forcing her to sit forward to ensure her feet remained on the Persian rug that just about covered the whole room.

She looked at Mr Vercoe. His tall, slender body had no trouble sitting back on the matching sofa opposite her, his feet firmly planted on the carpet. She felt resentment towards him in his posh middle-class house. She had already refused the offer of any refreshments, which was standard practice when she was working.

"Mr Vercoe," Even though they had met face to face many times, she still addressed him formally. Tony had, in the early days of their interaction, encouraged her to call him Tony, however, she would not budge in her refusal to call him anything but Mr Vercoe. That was the way she liked to deal with her clients, always keeping a professional barrier up.

"As you know, in the little over two years in which we have supported you, Isobel has always remained the focus of our support and encouragement in order to develop her into a well-balanced young lady. It was, as you know, a concern to us when we saw her schoolwork decline, though not unexpected given the circumstances of her mother. However, the decline has continued; I'm sure you are aware of this."

Tony nodded in agreement. He had tried his best to encourage and help Isobel with her schoolwork, yet however hard he tried, she seemed to be becoming disheartened with education and consequently losing interest in obtaining good results.

Rita continued, "The school called me earlier this week with another concern they have identified about Isobel that's related to her lacklustre results. She threatened to stab another pupil."

"What? And I'm only being told about it now!" Tony ranted.

"It sounds a lot worse than it was. Isobel threatened to stab another pupil using a ruler, saying, 'if this was a knife, I'd do you'. The school took it as just an argument between two girls at first. When they investigated it more, it would seem that your daughter has been threatening several pupils over the last couple of months, which is in line with her decline in educational results. The school knowing that I am assigned to her case, decided that it might be better if I deal with the matter."

Tony made no comment. He was trying to digest why his daughter would even consider being a bully; it was something she had never shown any sign of before.

"Nothing is being made official or written down, as they understand the stress that Isobel must be going through with her mother being away. All the school has asked me is that you have a word with your daughter. The school wants what is best for Isobel."

"And why have they asked you to interfere when they could have just called me in? Does it require the interference of a social worker?"

"I am not interfering, as you put it Mr Vercoe, I am your social worker. I am doing my job, which is to ensure that given the circumstances of your family, Isobel is not disadvantaged. Being a working parent is never easy, it's even harder for a man bringing up a teenage daughter, who would normally look towards another older female in the house for guidance. There are, no doubt, things that she feels uncomfortable talking to you about."

"What is that supposed to mean?" Tony asked, trying not to sound irritated, which he was every time Rita Taylor decided to pay him a visit and gleefully point out that men cannot make good mothers.

He wondered just why ever since she had been involved in his family's lives, she had taken every opportunity to put him down. He suspected it was a lot about jealousy. Rita, with her glasses perched on the end of her fleshy nose, looked down at you as if you were a little bit of dirt that needed to be tidied-up. He imagined a lot of the families that she, so-called helped, would look upon her as some sort of authority, whose word was gospel and who had the answer to all the problems of the family. Tony did not think of Rita in that way. He thought of her as an interfering little lady, whose professional qualifications did not give her the right to tell Tony he was a bad father. He knew he was not.

"As you're now a reporter, I imagine that Isobel is often left alone to her own ends while you're finishing stories at work. This can lead to boredom and fantasising that other families are more cohesive. That is when feelings of jealousy well up. It's to be expected, you're a man after all, and you do have a career to carve out."

"I am the new boy on the paper with little experience of being a reporter, hence I get all the easy stories which enables me to be home most evenings to look after my daughter."

"As you say, most evenings."

"A late evening for me is being home by half past six. Now I know a lot of workers might be finished by the early afternoon, but I'm not one of those fortunate people." He guessed that Rita might be one of those workers who looked upon an afternoon appointment as an opportunity to skive home afterwards.

"The fact of the matter remains. You will need to have a word with your daughter, unless you would prefer not to, in which case, I can speak to her. Whichever way you want to play this, this behaviour must stop in its tracks. If not, I will need to take this issue further."

"Are you dealing with a case of bullying by being a bully yourself?"

"That's not the case, Mr Vercoe. But if things are not contained now, there will come a point when I have to suggest that Isobel is cared for elsewhere."

"Take her away from me? What's wrong with you people? You leave poor kids with drug addicts, living in conditions I wouldn't keep a cat in, yet as soon as a rumour rises up, you want to take my daughter away from me."

"I'm just saying our priority is the welfare of the child."

**

Tony looked across the table at his daughter as she eagerly consumed the macaroni cheese he had prepared for her. She was like her mother in so many ways. In looks, she had the high cheek bones, the wide eyes, brunette hair, and that sharp thin nose. As well as her natural beauty, she had some of her mother's spirit and the same rebellious attitude to life. Isobel had said she wanted to be a tattooist, she liked the combination of drawing and earning a regular income. It was just that she did not want to have any form of art placed on her own skin. It was pointed out to her, during previous conversations, that such a stance might reduce the confidence of potential customers.

Having put the tattoo shop to one side, Isobel then decided that she wanted to design petrol garages of the future. Not that they would be for petrol at all, she admitted, but places to recharge and replenish motor vehicles in the future. She wanted to put her design skills to use and make garages pleasant places to visit.

Combining shops and restaurants instead of the normal convenience garage shop and coffee machine. She wanted to see a petite shopping centre attached to charging stations for cars, pleasant areas to relax and enjoy a break while your car is being charged, acknowledging that a car battery takes longer to charge than a petrol tank to fill.

"Rita called in today," Tony started the conversation.

"What did that old biddy want?" There was a whiff of disdain in her voice.

"She's there to help us, that's the point of social workers." Tony would not normally defend social workers, for whom he had a natural aversion. He defended Rita because that was the right thing for an adult to do.

Isobel finished her plate and wiped her mouth, then looked across at her father. "She just likes to get people to do as they are told, worse than some teachers I know."

"She tells me that you have been fighting and intimidating other pupils, being a bully."

"Did she tell you the other girls are being mean to me? Going on about Mother. Everyone knows as it was all over the papers. They're always ribbing me, bullying me, to put it bluntly."

"We all need to put up with being bullied in some form or other, it's part of life. I'm not saying bullying is good, all I'm saying is that there's banter which can be mistaken for bullying. Threatening to stab someone with a ruler isn't banter or the way to react to taunts."

"Dad, I try to be calm and ignore them, but sometimes the constant hurtful words get to me. I think I'm defending Mum more than myself. I didn't think the school were that bothered, they seemed to have taken my special circumstances into account and just accepted it. They did say I should be careful. But when that old biddy popped in..."

"You mean Rita," Tony corrected her.

"She was the one who got up on her high horse when the school told her about the couple of times I..." Isobel hesitated, "...got into a bit of a fight."

"I presume you used your martial arts skills to calm yourself and not hurt the other party."

"A bit of both."

"But the school were happy to deal with it internally until Rita was told about it?"

"That was the way I understood it. Mum always said I should stick up for myself. She would have told me to stand up to the name callers."

"This has nothing to do with your mother. You need to control your feelings. You're now a teenager; you need to start making your own sensible decisions."

"Dad," Isobel sounded calm despite feeling as if she wanted to scream loudly from the highest peak, "it has everything to do with Mum. She might be back in a couple of years, but you know our family will never be the same."

She was right, Tony knew that, even though he did not want to admit it out loud, family life was never going to be what it had been before his wife was sentenced. From the day she had been arrested, the Vercoe family began to crumble. Tony had done all he could to find out the real facts, he knew his wife was not a criminal, his daughter knew it too. Friends did not believe it either, yet the proof seemed indisputable. The jury had accepted the evidence, his wife was sentenced and now serving time in prison.

Relationships were not helped by her refusal to see her daughter while in prison, but she was adamant. As much as she was missing her daughter, she did not want to expose

Isobel to the demeaning prison environment. However hard Tony tried to convince his wife, she would not budge.

The only positive was Tony had good contacts within the prison service and was allowed generous visiting rights. He saw her most weeks as she was being held not far from Croydon. The downside was the constant pleading from Isobel to see her mother.

Putting his thoughts aside, Tony answered his daughter, "Yes, I know, but we both know that your mother was innocent of every allegation. It's been a miscarriage of justice, but until we have concrete evidence, we need to stay firm and fight for her."
Isobel shrugged, gathered up the dirty plates from the table and stood beside her father.

"I want to go out with some of the girls this weekend. I'd like to have a new dress and shoes, please."

"You know that we don't have so much money now. We have to be careful if we are to keep this house, there's a mortgage to pay."

Isobel left the room to wash the dishes. She did not take the trouble to stay and argue, discuss or even plead, she had tried it many times before. Her father was maintaining an extremely strict budget, constraints on the house worse than the austerity everyone talked about on the news. There was no austerity when Mum was around, how she missed her mother.

Chapter 3

"Well, if it isn't Tony Vercoe, God's gift to journalism. What headline-grabbing scoop brings you into our humble police station?"

Tony looked up from the chair he had been offered earlier after being shown into a cramped box officially described as a witness discussion room. Tony knew it had been originally designed by the architect as a large cleaning cupboard. During the late nineties, it had been converted into a space where members of the public could discuss their problems, complaints or crime reports in relative privacy. What happened to the cleaning materials originally stored, no one ever asked. Looking around, Tony suspected they had dispensed with both the cleaner and their materials.

"No uniform, Pete, when did they make you a detective?"

"Took my D.C. papers and passed with flying colours. Gets me off the street and now doing real crimes. The front desk told me you have some information about a deceased Doug Halifax. Funnily enough, my first investigation in plain clothes. Come on, what you got for me, or are you just after a story?"

"Sorry to disappoint you, this being your first detective case and all that, you got the wrong name on the death certificate." Tony slid both passports across the table.

The police detective picked them up, examined each carefully spending enough time to read the information contained several times before he asked, "How is this Douglas Wright and his wife connected to my deceased Douglas?"

"They're one and the same. I found them at George's place, you know where your Doug was staying. Both passports were hidden behind a kitchen plinth. George tells me that the photo looks exactly like dead Doug, making your surname wrong and my one correct," Tony smirked, which did nothing to lighten the expression on Pete's face.

Pete threw the passports down onto the small graffiti-strewn desk, not believing a word of what he was being told.

"Did you ever meet this Douglas person?" Pete asked as he once again picked up and flipped through both passports.

Tony just shook his head. "Long dead when I came on the scene."

"Thought as much. So, you never actually met this Douglas before he died, but were happy to take George's word for it that the Douglas in this passport is the same bloke who ended up under a car, which crushed his face. You disappoint me, you of all people should know that George is not exactly a tower of morality."

"Douglas Wright is apparently wanted by you guys for allegedly killing his wife in a house fire. Have a look on your system, it would explain why he was living under an assumed name. Plus, I can't see George having any reason to lie about his tenant. You weren't to know. Unless it's because it's your first case, you got a little too excited and forgot to do some basic checks. I doubt Doug's false name had a National Insurance number." Tony smiled, he knew he should not have made that snide comment, it would only provoke the detective. Even so, he wanted to point out that Pete might not have been as meticulous as he should have been.

"Let's see if your Douglas Wright is wanted as you say. It would be here on our system and there will even be a photo with a bit of luck." Pete began entering information into the computer in front of him. He stopped typing, waited a moment, then his expression changed.

"Hmmm, Douglas Wright, wanted in connection with the death of his wife in a fire."

"And the photo?"

Ignoring the question, Pete grabbed the two passports and his yellow pad, then stood up. "I've got to make a call." He nodded in the direction of the computer screen. "Apparently someone else has an interest in him. Don't go away." Pete left the room, almost slamming the door closed behind him.

The converted cleaning cupboard had just enough space to accommodate two chairs and a dull tiny square desk. As Tony had not been dismissed, he waited patiently in the stuffy room which had no space for an air conditioning vent. Tony wondered who Pete might need to call. The obvious was Kent Police who were looking for Douglas in connection with the fire occurring in their jurisdiction. He doubted anyone else would be interested, yet Pete did not say he was going to call Kent Police, just he had to make a call. Was someone else interested in Douglas? It really was none of Tony's business.

Out of habit, he leaned forward to peer at the screen for any information it might hold. Pete had been circumspect; the screen was locked into a Met Police emblem.

It still rankled Tony, why George was so keen to pass on the possessions of Douglas Wright to any next of kin. The George that Tony had known for years would not normally have handed over anything he could sell, or in the case of the single malts, drink.

He ignored his thoughts and took the opportunity to text his daughter, hoping her day was going well. He wondered if he should allow her some extra cash to buy shoes and an outfit for the weekend. Part of him wanted to, but the other part of him viewed it as spoiling her because he was a pseudo-single parent trying to make up for her absent mother. His thoughts were interrupted as a rush of cool air accompanied Pete's return to the room.

"Well, you're right, Douglas Wright is a person of interest in the fire that killed Mrs Wright. It's why I should take your word, and worse still George's word, that the dead Doug and the wanted Doug are one and the same person. Let's be honest, Tony, I can see a lot of advantages in Doug faking his death. He'd be off the radar. Got any other proof?"

"Well, didn't you take any other notes for identification, fingerprints, morgue face photos, dental records? That's what good detectives do."

"You're the reporter, I'm the detective, hence I get to ask the questions."

"Actually, we both ask questions, but I'm happy to help if you have any you want to ask. Like what's George doing these days? What scams is he involved with? Why did he have a wanted man living with him? Oh, before you ask, I have no idea, plus, I don't really care anymore."

"Alright, smart arse, all I'm thinking is that George has some form working fraud around cars. If the car that crushed Doug was a newer model, I would have suspected he was under there helping George file off the chassis number. Instead, it looks like he was doing some sort of inspection on an old banger with rusted jacking points.

"We can compare what we have on record. Yes, I do have fingerprints and some old scars on his belly to confirm the identity one way or another. Plus, all I need to do is pass it on. By the way, was there anything else with the passports that he had hidden? You know personal stuff relating to his previous life: keys, letters, notes, anything to hint why he might have killed his wife, maybe a press cutting of her reported death?"

From previous experience, Tony knew very well that Pete was not the sharpest officer in the force, plus he had a habit of blurting out the wrong word at the wrong time. Tony suspected that he had done just that.

"Why would he have press cuttings? Do you think he had a scrap book of what he did to his wife? And keys, pointless having his old front door key, I read the house was burnt down."

"They're just examples, evidence comes in all shapes and sizes. Was there anything else hidden with the passports?"

"Yes, but you might not want to hear. He had two ferry tickets for a sailing the night of the fire." Tony pulled them from the envelope and offered them to Pete who snatched them with a concerned frown on his face. "As you can see, both Mr and Mrs Wright were planning an overnight ferry to France, with their car. Do you think Doug might have killed his wife and burnt the house down because she was taking too long to pack?" Tony was pleased that the derision in his voice was received loud and clear.

"Husbands do all sorts of funny things without good reason, so do wives, as you know full well."

Tony ignored the comment aimed at his own circumstances and asked his own question to change the subject. "Who was so interested in Douglas Wright, the Kent force?"

The answer did not come straight away. Pete gathered up the passports and ferry tickets before he answered, "No, the number I had to call was I think part of National Security, the shadowy department that lurks behind every corner."

"MI5?"

"Spooks, dumbledorks, spies, call them what you will, they who must be obeyed."

"How come they have an interest in Mr Wright?"

"You know as well as I do, they never share information with us common law enforcers. They just swallow the intelligence that we painstakingly gather for them and take all the credit. I guess we'll never know. But at least when the Kent constabulary hears about this, they will get to close one of their cases."

As Tony stepped out into the refreshing air of the car exhaust–fume–filled street, he wondered just what had happened in there. It was fortunate that Pete was hopeless at his job and loved to take notes. When he had returned from his phone call, he had laid his notepad down on the desk. The words might have been upside down, but Tony had no trouble reading the name Douglas Wright, his date of birth, the case number, and the words, all underlined, 'photos, press cuttings, keys, a lockup', then several exclamation marks. All made little sense, but it further sparked Tony's inquisitiveness. Just what was MI5's interest in Douglas Wright?

That could be why Tony had on the spur of the moment decided not to hand over the photographs or the press cutting. Maybe he was becoming a true journalist, sensing a story.

**

Tony knew there was a small coffee bar in a parade of shops that abutted the police station. He decided to go in and ask for a latte and a warm croissant. He wanted time to clear his mind and order his currently muddled thoughts. He had a sixth sense when it came to crime; he could sense when something was not plausible. That sense had not alerted him to his wife, but Douglas Wright, that was another matter.

The consensus assumed that Douglas Wright killed his wife in a house fire, this troubled him. If you have a great desire to kill your wife, why destroy your home at the same time? It did not make sense, unless, at the time, Douglas was no longer living in the family home and his wife had a new live-in lover. He read the press cutting once more; there was no indication of that scenario.

Now if Douglas had killed his wife, or at least was suspected of killing her, he would have become a wanted man. Therefore, he moved away from the area, changed his name, and ended up living at George's, now calling himself Douglas Halifax. First off, how did he pay for the rent? George was no charity and would have wanted his money in cash each month on the dot. There was only a brief mention of helping George with building work for cash. Douglas, even if he did have a job, would have needed a bank account, hard to get without identification. No bank cards, no credit cards, cash only would be all Douglas would have worked with. This would lead Tony to think that the best way to earn simple cash was by doing things illegally. Living alongside George, Tony suspected there would have been enough opportunities for such work in this shady sector. Hence the wad of cash that George had commandeered from Douglas's.

An interest in cars was something that both George and Douglas shared, which brought Tony to the press cutting. A news story printed almost thirty years ago. Tony could imagine that George would have been around such crooked car dealers back then, but why would Douglas have hidden the cutting? Was he using something in the article as a lever over George?

Maybe Tony should have asked if Douglas Wright had any sort of criminal record, not that he would have been given any answer from Pete, no matter how politely he asked. That was how police treated reporters whoever they might be.

Then there were the car magazines with odd notations that Tony did not understand. What he did understand was that if Douglas wanted to steal a high-value car, he might need to undertake some homework to find the best way of driving one away without the owner's permission.

Once again, Tony looked at the photographs. He had learnt since becoming a reporter that having a press cutting, some prints and the negatives all together was unusual, especially almost thirty years after the event. Someone had collated them, kept them, and in Douglas's case, hidden them. They must have some significance which at present Tony could not grasp.

Another dilemma for Tony was the ferry tickets for both Douglas and his wife. The night of the fire, they were planning to leave the country, to where and for how long Tony had no idea. Nothing seemed to make sense. Especially the interest that MI5 now appeared to have in Douglas and his belongings.

Every long journey starts with a single step was how the saying went. His first step was going to be a long shot. The photographs and article originated from a local paper which had offices a short drive away. There was the slimmest chance the reporter who wrote the story might still be there, or at least someone might know where he is now.

Within thirty minutes, Tony was showing the yellowed press cutting to Luke Campbell, news editor of 'The Comet', a direct competitor to Tony's Kent Herald, which Luke happily put to one side. He read the article, noted the reporter's by-line, then looked at the two black and white photographs before handing them back to Tony.

"It's good to meet you Tony, I always like to know who the 'other reporters' are. I have this strange habit of when a story breaks, trying to imagine which rival reporter will be assigned, that kind of helps me decide who to send. You've not been there long, have you? Straight in as a mature reporter without going through any form of journalism school. A lucky break for you?"

Tony guessed it was a jibe being sent his way, which he ignored. It was not the first or he doubted the last time people would point out the way he joined the paper. 'Without being a professionally trained journalist', was the most common taunt he had endured. Tony was the first to admit to his editor that English was not his best subject. It was a deficiency he had worked hard at overcoming and in the main had coped with in his previous job. But a reporter, that was going to be a mountain to climb. Even so his editor supported him, pointing out that, 'before your story gets printed onto newsprint, there's a computer spellcheck, a sub-editor and a proof-reader to sort out your grammar. You just need to make sure you're writing the truth in the first place. I don't want lies in my paper; however grammatically correct they might be.'

"Well, we all have to get lucky sometimes in our lives. The reporter who wrote that, I guess he is long gone, but would you know where he might be nowadays?"

Luke smiled. "I was about a year old when this was written. The named reporter I have never worked with or ever met at any social occasion when new hacks and old hacks come together. That, by the way, is when we young hacks get told how much better things were back in the old days. I guess I'll be saying the same thing when I have retired.

"I have heard stories of Archie Walker," Luke said as he pointed to the by-line on the article. "By all accounts, nice guy, liked to dig into the shady side of living, hence I guess that article about a crooked car dealer. Bread and butter stuff for Archie, I would guess. All I know is that a good few years ago he ended up in some sort of care home. Problems of the mind, as it was politely described. Pretty young so I hear, about my age when it happened. Where he is now or even if he is still alive, I have no idea. Maybe some of the older hacks at your place might know. All our guys here are young guns, eager to make a name for themselves."

Chapter 4

"Is he around?" Neal asked. He looked down at Rupert Bell's secretary sitting at her desk, being as efficient as she looked. Although as he was cleaning his glasses with a small black cloth, she appeared to be not much more than a blur. Neal, since a child, had extremely poor eyesight. Without moving her gaze from her screen, she continued to type at great speed as she answered.

"He's up on the roof." She stopped typing to hand Neal a security pass. "Here, borrow my pass, you'll need it to get up on the roof."

"Can't you just change my access rights, so I can use my own card?"

"He said no when I asked him. He's very fussy about who has unfettered access to the roof. He views it as an extension of his office. You can always wait for him to return if you wish." She left the security pass on the desk and continued typing, ignoring Neal as he replaced his glasses.

He snatched the card from the desk, walked out of the office and took the lift to the sixth floor. There were no offices on the sixth floor, just whirling machinery, air conditioning units plus other equipment that Neal had little interest in. He turned right, proceeding along a low narrow corridor that was painted a very mundane olive green. He used the secretary's security pass on the door marked, 'Roof, restricted access', opened the door and walked up the short flight of metal-framed stairs, before going through another door which led him out onto the blustery roof of the building. He looked around and spotted Rupert Bell standing against a waist-high wall that marked the edge of the roof. Rupert was looking over the hazy London skyline smoking his pipe. The woody aroma entered Neal's nostrils as he approached his manager, avoiding the jumble of air vents and ventilation ducts. The biggest threat to his health up here were the thin wires stretched across the area in various directions, as they held the tall aerials which were such a feature of the roof.

Rupert sensed the approaching person. Without turning, he instinctively knew who it was. Neal, the only person with enough confidence to interrupt his roof top breaks.

"Is that coffee you're drinking?" Neal nodded towards the insulated cup Rupert was holding. The pair had worked together for many years, allowing, at times, Neal to be less formal. He stood beside his boss, his senior in both age and rank. Rupert now approaching sixty, his thin, besuited frame dwarfed by Neal's younger, muscular body.

"You know very well I don't drink coffee; it's a simple gin and tonic. Now, what is the reason for this intrusion?" Rupert drew deeply on his pipe, turned from examining the London skyline and watched as Neal withdrew a notebook from his pocket, flipped through the first few pages and began.

"I had a call from a local detective. They've located our person of interest, Douglas Wright, or to be more precise, your person of interest. Mr Wright was found dead under a car, tragic accident involving a rusty old car and a rickety carjack. His head was squashed well out of shape by the oil sump."

"Sounds like one of your scenarios. I do hope you did not instigate the accident without asking a few questions."

"No, I had nothing to do with it. But it's an interesting method, which the local police just accepted as being an accident. I did refer to your notes on the case and asked if they had recovered any keys to a lock-up, safe deposit keys, old photographs, press cuttings or any other such related items. All they have is his passport, his wife's passport and some ferry tickets. The thing is they had him down as a Douglas Halifax at first. It was a reporter who brought their attention to the real identity of Douglas and highlighted that he was living under an assumed name."

"A reporter?" Rupert sounded surprised. "What was his connection to all this?"

"Not sure. The landlord wanted to trace the deceased's relatives to return belongings to the family and seems to have asked for his help. They found the passports hidden under a kitchen unit; it appears Douglas has no next of kin."

As Rupert exhaled, he shrouded himself in a plume of light blue tobacco smoke. Neal had taken the precaution of standing up wind from him, to avoid the fumes.

"I would offer you a taste of my G and T, however, I know you never touch the stuff. You need to pay the reporter and the landlord a visit, see what other belongings Douglas left behind. The photographs and press cutting could still be amongst them."

"Even now that Douglas Wright is dead you want me to carry on? I thought that his death would mean case closed."

"You are paid to do, not think. Arrange a visit to the landlord and reporter, be discreet about the way you ask your questions. Also, make a call on the local constabulary, a polite visit and have a good look through the autopsy report. If it was a murder, I need to know. You had best get on before Mr Wright's belongings are listed on eBay."

Neal, aware that he was being dismissed, navigated the obstacle course of the roof before disappearing back through the stairwell door.

Rupert leisurely finished his drink; it helped him make the difficult decisions he often faced. He hated making them. Choices that you made sent you in a direction, in which you never anticipate the final consequences. Rupert had made a choice thirty years ago; at the time it seemed a simple decision. He had made it to benefit himself, further his career. His career did flourish, as it would have even without that decision. What it had created was a sword hovering over his head, hanging there, ever present for the past thirty years. During some sleepless nights he dreamt of it crashing down through his chest. There was no pain in the dream, yet he knew that should that sword fall on him in real life, it would cost him his job, his reputation and maybe his life.

He prayed that the incriminating evidence had died alongside Mrs Wright, burnt and withered up, but until he could be one hundred per cent sure, the breeze from the sword swinging above him continued to chill his body. It had been thirty years. He hoped the sword would not fall just yet; it was only going to be a matter of months before he would no longer care.

Rupert tapped out his pipe on the wall, the warm ashes joined the cold ashes from his regular visits to the roof. With a sigh, he turned and followed Neal's steps back to his office.

Chapter 5

A grey early morning mist diluted the normally bright pastel colours of the semi-detached houses along Viking Road. Tony blew into his hands in a vain attempt to warm them. He had only walked a few yards from his parked car, yet in that short time the dampness of the air had swamped his hands. He looked for number twenty-three. He could see a house ahead of him covered in scaffolding, which appeared to be fenced off from the rest of the street. That had to be Doug's house.

Swiftly he strode along the road, acknowledged a lone dog walker, her Golden Labrador interested to make buddies with this stranger. Tony ignored the dog's eagerness and continued until he was standing outside what was no more than a blackened shell. He peered through the wire-linked fence that had been erected around it, a Russian Vine from the once cared-for garden now wound its way across the fence. In the garden were the charred remains of household furniture and belongings that were now no more than lava-like shaped globules deformed beyond recognition.

The uPVC-framed window had melted and cooled into abstract sculptures that no artist would put their name to. Peering through the downstairs windows he could see the blackened ceilings and the smoke-damaged walls. Towards the bottom he could just make out the wallpaper, rose flower pattern. From what he could see of the upstairs, the damage appeared to be greater. Numerous tiles were missing from the roof, the void they left was blackened around the edges. He was not a forensic officer so the house could not offer any clues or theories for him, those might come from the neighbours. He decided to knock on the door of the other half of the semi-detached house. If the current residents were there when the fire started, he was sure they would have a hard time forgetting that night.

The door of number twenty-one was opened soon after Tony pressed the doorbell and an elderly gentleman appeared from behind a chain that allowed the door to open while still secure. He was smartly attired with neatly pressed trousers, a dark blue woollen jumper over a clean white shirt and the knot of a tie visible within the vee-neck of the jumper. Tony guessed he could be in his seventies. He was clean shaven with a thin head of greying hair, which had been greased to lay flat on his head. Maybe even at his age, he still had trouble controlling his hair.

"Are you from the insurance company?" The old man asked with a firm voice that bristled with confidence.

"No," was all Tony could say before the old man continued.

"Ah! Thought you might be the insurance company; I saw you looking at number twenty-three and hoped it was going to get sorted out. As you're not from the insurance company, what can I do for you?"

"Well, I am interested in what happened next door. I'm a journalist trying to uncover what occurred. Were you living here when it happened?"

"Best come in. Looks like you could use a warming cup of tea." He released the chain and opened the door fully.

Tony welcomed the generous invitation and settled himself in the warmer surroundings of the gentleman's kitchen. The strong tea thawed his hands and heated his core temperature to a more acceptable level, which enabled him to open his notepad and hold his pen firmly in readiness to hear the story of that fateful night.

"You said you were living here at the time of next door's fire?"

"Yes indeed young man, moved here way back in 1961, two years after I married Mrs Robinson. Lived here ever since, seen some changes, I can tell you. Back in those days the telephone had a party-line with next door, nowadays with the internet and things, a party-line has a totally different meaning," he smirked.

Tony looked around the kitchen, it was a hint of life from many decades ago. Mr Robinson was no doubt one to spend his money on sensible long-lasting merchandise. There was a cream-coloured fridge with a brand label: *Prestcold*, that Tony did not recognise. He did know the *Tupperware* tea, sugar and coffee caddies that were lined neatly beside a *Swan* chrome kettle, much like the one that his parents owned when he was a child. The room would not have been out of place in a heritage museum.

"Mrs Robinson passed away three years ago, so now I'm waiting to join her in heaven. At 82, I hope I don't have too much longer to wait. Still, if this is heaven's waiting room, then I am sure there are a lot worse places to wait for the grim reaper."

"I'm sorry to hear about your wife. So, you were alone on the night of the fire. When did you first know that your adjoining house was alight?"

"Billy from across the road alerted me. We go to the same bowls club, an enjoyable form of exercise for a chap my age. He banged on the door, shouting, 'Next door is on fire, best get out'. Well, he was concerned the fire would spread. I slipped my raincoat on and joined him outside. There was already a crowd gathering. All neighbours, no gawkers, we're not that sort of neighbourhood. There was thick black smoke coming out of next door's downstairs windows. Upstairs, I think it was their spare bedroom, we could see Becky, Mrs Wright, at the window banging on the glass and looking terrified, well, of course you would be, all that smoke and stuff.

"Chris, he lives at number thirty, young chap, opened the front door only to see a wall of flames. There was no way he could get in without killing himself. Doug's car wasn't parked outside, so we thought he must be out. A couple of minutes later, the fire brigade turned up. They get their breathing apparatus on and two of them go in. By now Mrs Wright was nowhere to be seen, but we told the firemen where she was.

"Then more fire engines turned up and they all started working on the fire. A few minutes later they carried out Mrs Wright. She didn't look good, so it was no surprise when we heard she had died, smoke inhalation they said.

"Some firemen went into my house and kept an eye on the place. They went up into the loft. There was smoke coming through, a few bricks had been removed up there and not replaced. Then they took some tiles off my roof to let the smoke out, they told me. Never knew the firemen were such good builders. I would have liked to ask them to clear my gutters while they were up there." He laughed and took a bite of his biscuit.

"But Doug was not in the house at the time?"

"No, Doug was not in there, thankfully. I think the firemen at first thought they might find him in the house burnt to death, but they never found anyone else there. I got back to my house later. My electrics and stuff had to be checked. I stayed with Billy across the road for the rest of the evening. Got back in the house at about eleven that night. Pretty tired out and strange, the party walls were eerily warm and I felt sad that Becky had died. She was too young to lose her life, with me here waiting for it to happen."

"The guy, Chris, who tried to get in, you said he opened the front door, wasn't it locked?"

Mr Robinson pondered the question, recalling the night, before he concluded, "No, it couldn't have been locked, he just turned the handle and tried to walk in. Never really thought about it before. That was odd, as they always kept their doors locked. There had been some sort of break-in a few months earlier. Doug was very fussy after that about locking doors and windows. We think that was why she couldn't get the window open. Must have been terrifying having to search around for a key to the double-glazed window. That's why I have stuck to my old-fashioned wooden sash windows. More of a pain to look after, but I enjoy getting out there and painting them once a year in the fine weather. Keeps me occupied."

"How well did you know Doug and Becky?"

Mr Robinson offered a plate of digestive biscuits to Tony who refused the offer, for no better reason than he did not want to make a mess in a very orderly kitchen.

"I wouldn't say I knew them well. Pleasant enough couple, they moved in about ten years before the fire. Bought the place after old man Stokes died. Strange man, never married, but had a lot of male friends if you get my drift."

Tony nodded that he did get the drift before leading Mr Robinson back to Doug and his wife.

"As a couple they weren't overly friendly. We always passed the time of day in the street or across the garden fence. He helped out when I had a problem with the plumbing. Had a new washing machine plumbed in, just the workman was not the sharpest knife in the drawer.

Doug came in and fixed it all. Saved creating a total mess on the kitchen floor.

"It was a shock to hear that after the fire the police were looking for him to help with their enquiries, as they say. In other words, they thought he did it. Well, he was never seen after that night. Such a blow, I never took him to be the murdering kind. I shouldn't be surprised when you have lived as long as I have, there's not much that can shock you."

Tony noted the words as Mr Robinson spoke, before asking, "Did he have any family or relations?"

He finished his tea before revealing. "Neither of them ever mentioned any and I never asked. Didn't want to appear the nosy kind. How I regret that now. No relatives and her being dead and him missing. The house is in a sort of limbo, giving the insurance companies plenty of excuses to delay any pay-outs, which is what they do best.

"They used to have a few friends around from time to time. Oh, maybe you would be better off speaking to someone he worked with on the building sites, name of Frank, lives not far away. The two of them were often seen together. He might even know where Doug is now."

"I'm sad to say that Doug was located recently after being killed in a tragic accident."

"Ironic and maybe justice in the end. Well, that's the end of a chapter and now perhaps I can get that wreck next door tidied up. None of us residents are happy with an eyesore that has been hanging around for the last couple of years. I can't tell you Frank's address, but I know the name of the road and it is the only house painted a very loud shade of red, you won't miss it."

***

It was exactly as Mr Robinson had described it, a very loud shade of red that stood out in the street of terraced houses like a nasty gnat bite on pale skin. It also had a large, weathered Union Jack hanging from the top window. St George's day was still a long way off. Thankfully, the sun had now decided to break through the early morning low clouds sending shafts of light along the street and creating much-needed warmth.

Frank Adams was a large man wearing an ill-fitting tee shirt which accentuated his belly spilling out from under it over the top of his loose jogging bottoms. Suitable clothing was the closest he ever came to exercise. He resembled the bulldog that now sniffed around Tony's shoes.

"Don't mind him. Come in and have a seat. You said you want to talk about Dougie Wright, good bloke."

Tony started his visit by informing Frank that his former work colleague had been located following a fatal accident, before moving on to ask about the times they worked together on the building sites. It soon emerged that Mr Robinson was not as accurate as he made out, which was not surprising for an 82-year-old.

"Dougie and me were not builders. Of late, we worked on demolition. We decided knocking places down is much easier and more enjoyable than building them up in the first place. I retired last year, breathing problems, summat to do with all the brick dust and crap I breathed in over the years." Frank pointed to the obvious small clear tube that entered his nostrils to deliver extra oxygen to his lungs.

"Dougie might have been a demolition man all his life, but I doubt it. He knew a lot about building work. I always figured he was some sort of plumber, but he never actually said."

"Did he talk at all about his work before coming to work with you?"

"Nah, very shy about his past. Just described himself as a general labourer, but I could tell, been around blokes long enough to know a general labourer when I see one, and he was not a labourer. Trade worker maybe but not someone's lackey."

"Baron!" Frank shouted, "leave the man alone." The bulldog stopped trying to breed with Tony's trouser leg and crept timidly towards a well-worn cushion in front of the television where he settled down.

"Do you know anything about the fire in which Mrs Wright died?"

"Well yes, I can tell you a lot, most of it I told the police, but they weren't interested. First I heard was the next morning on the radio, fire in Viking Street, well it's only around the corner, so gets on the blower to Dougie, you know, bit of excitement in his road. No reply. I thought he must already be on the boat, in my car."

"What do you mean by your car?"

"I'd better start earlier, well, in fact, a few weeks before. Dougie told me that he and Becky, his Missus, were planning to go to live in Spain. They were going to stay for six months before deciding if they would move permanently. I was jealous, always fancied a place in the sun. I thought it was just chit-chat, you know, blokes talking over a pint.

"That morning, the day his place burnt down, he arrived here at my door a little bit cranky. Says they were bringing their plans forward and he was preparing to leave the next day for Spain. Asks me to tell the foreman he wasn't coming back. Then he makes the oddest request, says can we swap cars as he doesn't want to turn up in Spain with a flash car. He asked if we could do a straight swap, no money, just keys and documents.

"Well part of me thought, bloody cheek, running down my car. Then I thought, well straight swap, I get shot of my boring Ford Focus and get a flashy Lexus in its place. Of course, I swallowed my pride and told him, yeah, why not. The plan was he would come round later and we would do the exchange. I was pretty pleased with that, couldn't wait to take it for a spin and see what sort of birds I could pull with it."

Tony scribbled away as Frank revealed the story. Listening and watching him, Tony could understand why Frank was still single. Then he asked, "Moving forward, the next you heard was the fire had killed his wife?"

"Nah, he called round in the evening to swap cars and asked if he could leave a suitcase here, 'course he could, we were mates. Said he would be back later with the wife, collect the case and then they would be off. Well, no more than an hour later he's back, grabs the case, all in a rush, told me he was sorry and I never heard hide nor hair of him again. Well, till you told me about him popping his clogs."

Frank burst open a can of beer, took a large swig and wiped his mouth with his wrist before he continued. "I just thought, crazy bloke, but what did I care I had a nice new Lexus sitting outside. That is until I heard the news and the police wanted to talk to him. I thought, bugger, there goes my Lexus. Sure enough, next day the police turn up, so I told them everything, no point in lying. It would seem that the Lexus still legally belonged to him even though we had a gentleman's agreement. Apparently, that doesn't count. They took the Lexus away and found my car in a side street in Lambeth, all in one piece, so I got the old Ford back. Although at least I'm still alive, poor old Dougie."

"The suitcase, do you have any idea what might have been in it?"

"Nah, it just sat there in the hall till he took it that night. He was a mate, so I wasn't going to poke around in his stuff."

If the case was all Doug left with, then the passports and tickets must have been in it, possibly along with the press cuttings, negatives and prints. Tony pulled them all out of the envelope he had brought with him. First, he showed Frank the photocopies of the passports, Frank confirmed, as had Mr Robinson, that the two people in them were Doug and Becky, but Mr Robinson had never seen the car dealer photographs before. Tony showed Frank the black and white prints.

"Have you ever seen these before?"

Frank studied the photographs; it did not take him long to decide.

"Yeah, they're Dougie's, he found them."

"How do you mean found them? What's the story behind them?"

"Well, not just them, as I recall there was a roll of film and some sort of newspaper article. We found them a few years back. We were working on a building in London, Kingsway it was, a big turn of the century office building. We weren't knocking it down, but doing a strip out, taking the whole place back to its structure. It was being modernised, a full refurb. Anyway, me and Dougie were on the top floor taking off this cheap plastic cladding from the walls. It had been fitted to about halfway up, desk height, I suppose, hid loads of wiring and stuff.

"Well, behind the plastic cladding was this really good wood panelling, and I mean good. Might even have been the original stuff. Dark wood. Well, me and Doug think, we got a result here, this sort of stuff goes for a pretty penny with those reclaim depots selling old stuff, so popular nowadays. The plan was to strip it out, get a van and make a few bob. Course we had to clear it with the site governor, he agreed in exchange for a cut of the profits.

"We got a van at the weekend, came in, started stripping it out and loading it on the van. Anyway, you want to know about the stuff he found. Every few feet there was a brass grill, some sort of vent thing – we had some of that as well, brass is worth a few quid. Behind one of these grills Doug finds an envelope, plain brown and inside are a couple of photographs. These," he waved the prints around before giving them back to Tony and continuing his saga, "a roll of film and a bit of a newspaper. It was some sort of story about a bent car dealer. Well, I wasn't interested in them, so Dougie kept them. We got a good drink for the wood panel stuff and the brass, one of the perks of the job."

"What sort of offices were they, newspaper offices?"

"No idea, by the time we go in you just can't tell."

"And you never saw the stuff he found again?"

"No, never." Frank hesitated, talking about it once again was a catalyst, jogging his memory of what he had considered junk. "Never saw them, but Dougie did mention them again, said they might be worth something. He was going to have a word with a newspaper 'bout them. Didn't say any more, and I didn't ask, forgot all about them, to be honest. Anyway, I trusted him, if he'd got a few quid for the stuff, I knew he'd share it with me, a decent bloke that way."

"Did he tell if it worked out with the newspaper?"

"He never mentioned it again. Baron, get back!"

The dog had moved slowly off its cushion hoping to get a little closer to Tony's leg, but the ploy had failed.

Tony left with more knowledge and less understanding. Importantly, he had an address. It had taken a little while to obtain it, but with the help of Google Street View coupled with Frank's hazy recall of the journey he had made to the building, Tony was now certain they had correctly identified it as seventy-one, Kingsway. He just had to find out a little more about who occupied the building before the refurbishment.

Chapter 6

Police stations were never Neal's favourite places to be hanging around. He always had this irrational fear that he would be invited into an office to be unceremoniously handcuffed and imprisoned for some small misdemeanour such as double parking or being late paying his rates, both of which he never did. Oddly, not once did he ever consider that he would be incarcerated for doing shady work on behalf of the government, for which, if he was ever compromised and found himself arrested, they would see to it that all charges were dropped. At least, that was his hope, although some members of his department had been thrown to the lions, so to speak.

For now, Neal sat in a room where the walls were so close together, when sitting down he could stretch out both arms and touch the walls on either side. He was not so much claustrophobic, just overheating in the cramped airless surroundings.

"I'm DC Pete Lewer. I hear you have an interest in one of our cases." The young man threw a large brown envelope and a buff file onto the table before taking his seat opposite Neal. Neither man smiled. "What's this Douglas Wright been up to, to warrant the interest of our security services? I presume that's who you're with?"

If he was going to be truthful which he had no intention of being, Neal would have told this young detective constable that it was of no concern to an obscure local detective. Instead, he chose to simply say, "Regard me as a secure courier with no knowledge of the case or the offences involved. I just need to collect all the property that was handed over by the reporter."

Pete tipped out the contents of the brown envelope over the table. "That's all he gave us, a couple of passports and a couple of ferry tickets for the perpetrator and victim. Do you want the autopsy report?"

"No, just tell me the highlights. I'm not concerned if he had an ingrowing toenail or a fifty-year-old operation scar." From experience, Neal knew that autopsy reports are boring and, in most cases, far too detailed. He had learnt that when he was a young detective constable himself, many years ago. He recalled the stench of the mortuary and the amount of concentration he needed as he watched over post-mortems to avoid fainting or throwing up.

"Please yourself." Pete opened the buff folder and read the relevant bits.

"Douglas Wright, 60, died from catastrophic injuries to the back of the head. I say head, there is a technical term written down here, but to you and me, not being doctors, we'll keep it to head. Sustained by the oil sump of a car he was working on. It's believed the wheel jack had not been attached correctly and gave way. He was three times over the drink drive limit, which we think contributed to him setting the wheel jack incorrectly. Death was estimated to have occurred about an hour before the emergency call was made by George Stevens, his landlord. No suspicious circumstances, Verdict: accidental death. Enough for you or do you want to know how enlarged his prostate was?"

"No thank you, injuries to the back of the head you say. Was he face down?" Neal asked. If this was a murder, then that was an error. If he had been responsible for the alleged accident, then he would have made sure the victim was face up. Face down would have been a schoolboy error to his mind.

"Yes, if the oil sump had not killed him, then being pressed down into the concrete floor would have hindered his breathing greatly. You not taking notes?"

"I have an exceptionally good memory, which at times can be my downfall. I will be taking the tickets and passports. The report you just read, you said it was Douglas Wright, but you couldn't have known that was who he was back then. Wasn't it a reporter who flagged it up to you?"

"Yes, but we have the correct name on the reports now, so everyone is happy."

"One minor thing. When it first happened, didn't you run a fingerprint or national insurance check to establish just who the dead guy was? Verify who he was as opposed to taking some landlord's word for it?"

Loudly, Pete slammed the buff folder back onto the table before he replied with a high proportion of anger in his voice, "If you're just a courier, take the stuff back to your bosses. Messengers don't get to ask questions."

Police stations might not have been Neal's favourite places, but they were the best to irritate young detectives.

**

Standing in a very jumbled kitchen, Tony had to move what looked like the workings of an incredibly old eight-track cassette player. He used the space he had cleared to put his cup of coffee down. He wanted to gesticulate with his hands, something he did when he was getting frustrated, in this case because George was not answering his questions.

"It's a simple question. How did Doug earn enough to pay his way and still have some very fancy stuff in his place as well as an ancient yet valuable car? Oh, and let's not forget the roll of cash he had."

66

"The Morris was not pricey. The floor pan was well rusted, that's why the jacking point gave way. Now my Austin 1100 that I have under covers is in prime condition and worth a pretty penny."

"I don't care about you; it's Doug I'm asking about. Where did his money come from?"

George took a final deep draw on his cigarette before stubbing it out on a saucer. "Is this what the police asked you? I told you to let sleeping dogs lie, once they start, they…"

"It's my question. They're just happy to have found their suspect. I want to know how he obtained his money."

George continued to unscrew the cover of an old, dusty-looking Crown cassette player that he had been in the process of dismantling when Tony arrived.

"I told you, he helped me out on a few odd jobs. We did a bit of painting and decorating occasionally. But where he made his bucks, I'm his landlord, not his friggin' mother."

"Not any thieving or shady deals?"

"Come on Tony, I gave that stuff up years ago. I'm too old to run around the streets carving out a living. All guys my age do now is buy cars and radios from our youth because it helps us remember when we were young and rheumatism free."

Tony showed George the car dealer's photograph again. "And him, you sure you don't know him?"

"I told you, I knew the geezer years ago, everyone did. If you wanted a bent car, or had a car to get shot of, he was your man. I haven't seen him in years. We're all old men now, tired of dodging the law and too afraid to go head-to-head with these new gangs on the streets nowadays with all their guns and stuff. Not a place for old blokes who had a gentlemen's understanding. We all had a common

67

enemy, the Old Bill, so we worked together not against each other. How Doug collected all that cash, I don't know, I don't care."

In his frustration Tony threw the remainder of his coffee down the sink, adding the empty mug to the pile already cluttering the stainless–steel bowl.

"Well, I do care." Tony took a deep breath. "And I'm sure you recall I have a habit of getting to the bottom of things."

Chapter 7

Now in the sanctuary of his sensibly organised home, (that was his opinion, not his daughter's) Tony relaxed on the sofa with a chilled glass of San Miguel. The last twenty-four hours had been strange. Uncovering a fugitive from the law felt just like old times and in the end maybe that was all there was to it. Although he remained unconvinced by George's explanation, he was certain that George had been a bad boy in his younger days, yet now as he neared sixty, maybe he had finally retired from the criminal world he had once inhabited.

Tony wondered if he was trying to make something out of nothing, attempting to be a real reporter so that he could prove himself to the others at the office. Well, he consoled himself, at least uncovering a wanted murderer on his patch was a lot stronger than the mayor handing over a cheque to the local boys' club. The doorbell interrupted his thoughts.

He answered the door expecting to see one of Isobel's friends standing in the doorway, instead it was a man who looked vaguely familiar. He was taller than Tony, about six-three. His receding hairline accentuated what was already a high forehead which, as well as being frownless, had a baby smoothness about it. Tony would describe the whole face as soft and rounded. His jawline was on the edge of becoming a double chin, his nose triangular. His eyes appeared squashed between his forehead and plump cheeks. Tony recalled who the man reminded him of – the children's TV character, Mr Tumble – only the one standing on Tony's doorstep was wearing rimless glasses and did not have any painted freckles.

"Mr Vercoe? I'm Neal Matthews from the passport office. I wanted to have a quick word with you about the passports you handed into the police. May I come in?"

"Identification?" Tony asked, never understanding why anyone would invite a stranger into their house whoever they said they might be, not even if they did look like a children's comedian.

Neal first fumbled in his jacket pocket, a corduroy jacket, the like of which Tony had not seen in years. Then the visitor delved into his trouser pocket and pulled out a small photo identity card attached to a lanyard, both of which he handed to Tony with a smile.

Neal sat on the same sofa where Rita had previously sat, took out a small black notebook which he consulted, purely for effect. Before beginning with his questions he promised there were only a couple to clear up any misunderstanding around the passports.

"We all now know that the passports you found were the genuine article and the deceased man was in fact Douglas Wright. Did he have any other type of identification on him, either in his real name or the assumed name that he was using?"

"When I looked around his rented premises with the landlord, we found nothing else at all."

"But you did find some tickets with the passports, for both him and his wife?"

"Yes, I told the police what I found hidden under some kitchen cupboards."

"But nothing else, odd that, don't you think?"

"I have no opinion on the matter. I never knew the man, I was only there as a journalist at the request of the landlord, who wanted to try and find any relatives he might have had."

"All I was wondering was, well, two things. How did the man survive without any sort of bank account to pay his bills? Plus, don't you think it was odd that he had a ticket to take his wife away on the night he kills her?"

Tony looked at the pseudo children's character sitting opposite him and wondered just why the passport office might be asking such questions. In all his experience, he had never come across the passport office doing investigations. Immigration officers did the dirty work on the ground, passport office workers, in the main, stayed in their offices.

He recalled that when Pete had the true identity of Douglas Wright in his possession, he had to make a call. What was it he said, National Security, MI5, the spooks? Now they do ask questions.

"As I said, I had no interest in the man. As for his wife's ticket, I have no idea what was on his mind. He might not even have killed her; the police only alleged he did. He never had his day in court in front of a jury. There might be another explanation for the wife's death. Or another story entirely."

That gained Neal's attention. He looked up from his notebook, where he had been scribbling a type of shorthand that only he could understand, mostly symbols and doodles about the inside of the room that he was sitting in. Notes about the window locks, the level of security, the passive detection unit in the corner above the bookcase. The alarm panel to the left of the front door looked dead and unused.

"You have another theory?"

"I have a theory that you're not from the passport office. A theory that you're from the same office that had to be called the moment Douglas Wright was located, alive or dead. National Security? As if you'd admit such a thing. The other story could be Douglas Wright wasn't only wanted for killing his wife, which he might not have done, but was also wanted by some branch of the UK Security Services, meaning he must have done something pretty bad."

"I'm afraid I don't know about that, but rest assured, working for any of those departments you mentioned would be far too scary for me. Simple administration and passports fulfil that need for me. I see you have a Blackstone's manual up there." Neal pointed to a bookcase in the centre of the wall behind Tony. The thought had not crossed his mind until now. He recalled something that the young detective constable had said earlier which he had dismissed, taking it as a surplus comment, 'Tony Vercoe knows our procedures too well'. It was a bit late, yet Neal wished he had carried out a brief check on the reporter that he was going to talk to. Normally, it would be the first thing he did, to try and understand just who the person was that he was going to speak to. It was his annoyance that Rupert Bell wanted to continue searching for these stupid photographs. Prints that he was convinced had been destroyed in the fire that killed Mrs Wright. To Neal, all this was a waste of his valuable time, although he could not refuse to do as his boss requested.

Without looking at the book, Tony knew exactly what he was referring to. He answered, "I'm a journalist, I need to know what I can and can't do legally."

"There are better books out there for journalists, that one is designed for police officers. Did you work with that young hopeless detective constable who got the wrong name on the death certificate? When I say work, I mean as a fellow police officer, not a reporter."

It was a bit of a gamble for Neal, a small harmless shot in the dark. He wanted to know before he got back to his office just who Tony Vercoe was, a journalist asking questions, or an ex-copper asking questions. Any answers that he gave would need to be dealt with differently depending on who Tony Vercoe was.

"I'm an ex-uniformed officer. Pete was still in a uniform when I last worked with him professionally."

As Tony answered, Neal made a point of looking around the room as if he was searching for something. He had no need to, he already knew the answer from his constant surveillance.

"Not a single photograph of you in uniform, I find that odd. I too am ex-job. Many years ago, I gave up the uniform, too much excitement, yet I still have a photograph of my passing out parade. A special day, three months of training and the young teenager who entered Hendon Police training school came out a man, ready to clear the streets of villains and law breakers." Neal had not meant to sound so sentimental; it just came out that way.

"My police days are in the past; I like to look forward not back. Yet I would have thought someone like you, from National Security, would have known my background."

A wry smile broke across Neal's face. "Generally it's not such a good idea to be up front with my work, passport officer suffices in the main. If I'd known you were ex-job, I would have been up front with you in the first place. I was certainly not going to introduce myself to a journalist as MI5, it would get them too excited. They would start thinking I carry guns and spying devices, when in fact I'm only a pen pusher at a related department. I like being boring and predictable. The thing is, Douglas is a very low priority person of interest and now he's dead, puts everything to bed. Case closed, as they say."

73

"Is that what they say? So just why was he a person of interest to MI5?"

"I wouldn't share that with a serving police officer let alone an ex-copper who now bats for the other side. All I am doing is tidying up the loose ends. Doing the department's paperwork, which I'm good at if I say so myself.

"For example, the ferry tickets have turned the police theory on its head. Unless there's a third woman in the picture. Our Douglas Wright might have been having an affair and planning to take the other woman away with a false passport, which is why I am asking if there was anything else with the passports. There wasn't a third passport or you would have handed it in. But were there any other addresses or names on scraps of paper, telephone numbers, or even a photo of another woman? I would find that helpful, so I can dot the i's and cross the t's"

"Nothing else at all," Tony repeated conclusively.

"Come on, he must have had other belongings in his lodgings."

"Well yes, but as an ex-officer, nothing which I would consider of any interest."

"That's for me to decide. Take me, step by step, through the morning when you found the passports hidden under the kitchen cupboard, then I'll decide what is and is not of interest."

Tony did as he was asked, starting with the telephone call that he had received from George. As he spoke, he observed the eyes of Neal Matthews, who appeared to be taking short notes in his book, yet was looking around the room, studying the books on the bookcase, looking at the family photographs that were on the wall. Noting the make of the TV, examining the condition of the fixture and fittings. His actions were unsettling Tony, not unduly, he had often in his previous job, found himself in a stranger's house looking around, yet not with the intensity the eyes of Neal contained as they darted around the room.

"Maybe you're right, nothing else of interest. Well, thank you for your time. It has been most helpful chatting with you and it allows me to close the case file, leaving the complex bit to the police. Always the best thing to do."

Neither man spoke until they were both standing in the hallway. Tony had already opened the door encouraging the exit of Neal when Neal decided to ask another question.

"It must be exciting being a newspaper reporter. Who's the most famous person you have met?"

The question was not an unusual one, Tony had heard it many times before. It was just, as he answered, he could see Neal's eyes once again darting around the hallway as if he was committing to memory every item in the narrow corridor. More importantly, he was hovering a little too long over the door locks. He was not taking much interest in Tony's reply.

Once Tony had closed the door on his guest, he walked back into the kitchen, pulled some tins out of a tall wall cupboard and grabbed the envelopes secreted behind them. He took out the prints, the press cutting and the roll of film. These seemingly innocent items, that he had spread out on the kitchen table, had a story to tell, a story that MI5 was involved with.

***

"What are you doing?" Isobel asked, hugging her father from behind and looking over his shoulder at the laptop screen. She inhaled his familiar aftershave, the one she had bought him last Christmas and every previous Christmas,

75

since she was able to hand over a few coins, with her mother's help, to the man in the chemist.

Her father had spent the evening reading as many news reports of the fire in which Douglas Wright's wife had died. He only managed to find six on-line, four of them written the day after the fire giving the barest facts. There had been a house fire in which a fifty-six-year-old woman had died; she was not identified. In those early reports the police had stated they had an open mind about the cause of the fire. The last two news reports, both from the local paper, confirmed the name of the woman as Mrs Wright and that the police were keen to speak to her husband, who they were now trying to trace.

Tony could not find any newspaper report stating the police thought the fire was started deliberately and they were searching for the husband who they suspected was guilty of at least starting the fire. Although the implications of the news reports, or at least, the briefings the police gave, pointed to the fact that they believed Douglas Wright had killed his wife.

Tony played out several scenarios in his mind as to why Douglas might want to kill his wife. He considered perhaps Douglas had not intended to kill her, but she had died during an attempt to claim the insurance on their house, or if it was an accidental death after all. He wondered if there had been an argument over lovers, greed, stolen money, an argument that ended in murder. Tony thought through as many possibilities as he could. None of them could he align with the hidden negatives and the press cutting, or the interest of MI5 in the life and death of Douglas.

The neighbour had described Douglas as a pleasant quiet person who kept himself to himself. His work colleagues trusted him. But, yes, there was a but. The man with the randy bulldog had said he suspected that Douglas was a true tradesman, not a general labourer, which prompted Tony to speculate that Douglas was not as forthcoming about his past with his work colleagues as he might have been. An ambiguity as to his previous work or life, which followed through to his arrival at George's holiday cabin. Douglas, a person Tony never knew in life, was beginning to show his true colours in death. Douglas was shy about his past. Was that the reason for the interest MI5 had in him? Had he worked for them at some time? Carried out work that meant he learnt secrets that the agency only felt safe about once they knew of his death.

What was it that Neal had said, 'now he's dead puts everything to bed' yes, that was it. Tony felt he was beginning to get a handle on this. Douglas, at one time, worked for MI5, in what capacity, he had no idea. Yet during that time, he learnt something and was from then on a fugitive, with the government agents like Neal on his tail, chasing him and hunting him down. Only his death had brought everything to a conclusion.

That led Tony towards the inevitable question. Was it an accident or was it a contrived murder?

On the whole Tony was a persona non grata at his old police station. Few officers would give him the time of day, let alone help him look at a file. However, there was one young officer who had always been sympathetic to his plight, Janne Pihlblad, of Swedish origin. Janne had arrived on a police international exchange trip and ended up staying, falling in love, and then marrying a young English girl. Without any reservations, Janne got onto the Kent Police database and extracted the initial report of the fire at Twenty-three Viking Road as a favour to Tony.

The cause of the fire was an overturned paraffin heater at the bottom of the stairs. The oil had spilt over the carpet, the fire quickly taking hold and engulfing the stairs, trapping the wife in her bedroom.

The fire brigade had arrived and removed the unconscious Mrs Wright from the smoke-filled house. She was pronounced dead at the scene. The investigation concluded that on the burnt bed, which had been consumed by the fire leaving only a charred metal frame and the interior springs from the mattress, was a suitcase, or at least the ashes of one, which the forensic scientist believed she might have been packing at the time.

This led the police to suppose that she was in the process of leaving her husband. Although they had no evidence, their first theory was a domestic disagreement that got out of hand. Their preferred scenario was he kicked over the paraffin heater causing the oil to spill and catch light. It was found that the heater, whose safety features should have prevented such a tragedy, had been repaired badly at some time. Douglas was not only a person of interest he was also the prime suspect.

Two days after the fire, the report also mentioned that when Douglas Wright was eventually located a Neal Matthews should be contacted. He was described as an interested party for another official security organisation. No mention of his involvement should be made to Mr Wright who should be held until Mr Matthews either agrees to his release or arranges further remand.

This confirmed that MI5 had a big interest in Mr Wright. What that interest was eluded Tony, but it had to have something to do with the photographs that Douglas was going to take with him to Spain.

Tony looked at his daughter. "It's a story I'm working on. I'm trying to find the truth behind these headlines; I might not succeed but at least I will have tried. Any fights today?"

"No, honest I am trying, Dad, but it's so hard to just let them say what they like. Maybe it's best if I make all my mistakes as a teenager rather than waiting 'till I'm an adult. Look at Mum, after her mistake she will never get her job back again, will she? All her hard work at university, a total waste of time."

"Throughout our lives we often make mistakes, that's what being human is all about. Sometimes mistakes are when people just make bad choices because at the time, they think they're for the best. It's often hard to truly understand what the consequences of your actions might be. Just stick with it darling. We'll get through this together, helping each other."

"Do you still love Mum?"

"Of course, I do," Tony answered, he thought maybe a little too quickly. Even as he heard the words escape from his lips, he doubted the truth in them. It was a question that often transferred from his unconscious to his conscious mind, and where he tried to find an answer before pushing it back for consideration later. There was still time, yet he knew full well that there would come a moment when he would have to answer the question. Could he ever love his wife again? After what she did?

He wanted to love her. He wanted to start over again, but things could never go back to where they had been. 'We're all the sum of our experiences', she often told him. Well now that sum had a different result. Their relationship would never be the same again. He had no idea what it might be but did not want to confront those gremlins now.

For the time being, he wanted to find out more about Douglas and discover more about the crooked car dealer from Southeast London.

Isobel left her father to begin her homework, reassured that her mother and father still loved each other and permitting Tony to ponder the fatal fire, the death of the alleged perpetrator, the interest that MI5 had in the mystery. Finally, what would happen when his wife returned?

Chapter 8

It was extraordinary, Neal could not believe what he was reading, yet it had to be true. It was, after all, an official file on Tony Vercoe, chronicling his police career from the moment he began his training until his resignation. His was a promising start to what should have been a lifelong career in the police. Amongst the top twenty of his training cohort and with glowing reports from his tutors before entering into the real world, where his ability as a police officer able to sympathise with the community in which he worked showed through. A little over three years ago a black mark, a stain on the immaculate record appeared. Neal thought back to his own short time in the force and could understand things like that happen in the heat of the moment. Making split-second decisions is what a police officer is trained to do. Unfortunately, if that decision goes wrong, superiors and lawyers can take weeks, sometimes months, dissecting it and gathering a mountain of reasons to show it was the wrong course of action.

As bad as it might have been Tony was only lightly reprimanded, to save the faces of his superiors and satisfy public interest. When he was a police officer, Neal did not care about public interest and even less about the opinion of his superiors.

It was about a year later that Tony resigned from the force. The reason Neal could not understand, it made no sense. He needed more information. He searched through another database and pulled up the record of Mrs Vercoe.

He read her story with interest. Even if it had been fiction he could not have imagined it to be plausible, he would have put it down to the wild imagination of the writer. But he was reading official facts, correlated and recorded, this was the truth as the authorities saw it. Neal was not so sure; it was frankly too unbelievable. He searched another database and found the name Mrs Vercoe.

It was no wonder Tony had to resign; his position in the force had become untenable. No doubt pushed, unofficially, by his superiors who now saw him as a liability to the public image they were trying to construct around the force. Neal always knew that there would be bad apples in any large organisation. The boy scouts had their share of sexual predators. Financial services, plenty of fraudsters are attracted to that industry. The police, are just the same, if you try to reflect all of society, then you'll get bad people. Yet in Neal's humble opinion, bad apples fall from bad trees. He could not see a bad tree anywhere near Tony or his wife. Something was not right. Neal wanted to know more, but now was not the time or the place. He closed his computer and went in search of Rupert Bell.

***

"Is he around?" Neal asked, knowing he would not get a straightforward answer from Rupert's secretary. She was at best obstructive, at worst a bloody pain. Yet for some reason unknown to all the staff who worked under Rupert Bell, he had kept the same insufferable secretary for the past ten years. The most common theory was that her attitude encouraged you not to trouble the boss.

"Is who around?" she asked without looking up to see who was standing in front of her. She gave everyone the same treatment, even famously one day the Home Secretary, who incredibly walked timidly away and said he would come back later.

"Mr Bell, your boss, the person to whom you do secretary things for."

"I provide administrative support to not only Mr Bell, so you need to be clearer in your request." Still looking at her keyboard, she now knew from the voice she was talking to Neal Matthews.

"Mr Rupert Bell, CBE. Senior Policy Advisor, Her Majesty's Government."

"Actually, his title is Senior Policy and Strategic Advisor. Why do you want to see him?"

"I'm going to ask for permission to kill his secretary, who is generally uncooperative and supremely able in delaying the progress of governmental work, which seems to be the only reason she was put on this earth."

She stopped typing, looked up at Neal, smirked, she always found his face to be humorous, then opened a large leather-bound diary beside her. Looking at the entries, she ran her finger down the page and then returned her gaze to Neal. "I'm sorry, you will have to join a long list of staff who wish to kill me. You might be better off dropping him an email request which comes through me first." She smiled broadly.

Derision undoubtedly did not work when fighting Rupert's secretary. Fortunately, fate played a part as Rupert stepped out of his office, placed a buff folder beside his secretary and looked at Neal.

"Any news?"

"Yes, do you have a few moments?"

"Come in and close the door."

Neal followed his boss into the office, childishly he poked his tongue out at the secretary as she went back to her typing.

Both men settled into their respective seats, Rupert his luxury leather chair behind a large imposing desk cluttered with piles of papers, Neal, a small mahogany chair with a tartan cover.

"Well," Rupert sounded impatient and tetchy, not a good sign Neal thought.

"This reporter, Mr Vercoe, isn't what he seems. He is ex-job and has a chequered background in the police."

"Why are you sharing information that I already know? Or would it be that you, thinking my concerns were frankly tiresome, omitted to do a background check on a person you were going to visit?"

Neal was not going to answer that question and admit his failings. Instead, he simply continued with, "His wife has an unusual history as well."

Slowly, Rupert picked up a silver letter opener twisting it around with his fingers. He scowled at Neal wishing to apply unspoken pressure; he wanted to get to the bottom of the missing photographs. As much as he knew Neal to be sceptical about what was put in front of him, Rupert had total faith that if he asked Neal to do something, anything, no matter how bad, Neal would accept the request and carry it out. It was getting his attention and holding it that was the problem.

"Now that you have done your homework, you will see that Tony Vercoe being anywhere near this situation has the potential for it to go pear-shaped. Does he have any knowledge of a car dealer being photographed?"

"I didn't want to ask that direct question, but as we both know he was a copper, he would have handed over everything he found, of that, I'm sure."

"I am glad you're confident. I don't share your optimism. We have a photograph of a car dealer, or to be precise we don't have the photographs, we just know they exist. Douglas was also a car thief of sorts as was his landlord, George Stevens, but I am sure you know that, having fully looked into the background of these people.

"Too many people in this scenario have connections to the car industry, which to my mind suggests they could all be in collusion with each other. Tony, not a car thief, yet no doubt holds a grudge with the authorities. You need to dig deeper and find out conclusively if any of them have the photographs. Also was Douglas murdered?"

"If he was, there were a couple of simple errors that could have suggested it wasn't an accident. I am surprised the police wrote it up so quickly as one. I would have thought there were sufficient circumstances for them to question it further. But the investigating officer is not the best copper in the pack, of that, I am sure."

"This has the potential of getting out of hand unless you get a total grip and manage the situation. I should point out, Neal, that I don't want this situation to get out of hand and you certainly don't because you will be dragged down in the shit if these photographs are in the wrong hands and are allowed into the public domain."

"Sir, with all due respect, I know just about zero regarding what these photographs mean. Having a better understanding would help me. I would also point out that we have talked about a press cutting, so technically the photographs are already in the public domain."

In an act of anger Rupert lunged forward and stabbed his desk with a letter opener, leaving it impaled through the inlaid leather top. The action took Neal aback.

"Don't try to be clever with me Neal. Visit the landlord. Go back and see Tony Vercoe if you must, knowing what you now know. Visit his house when he's not there. Do whatever you need to do, but you and I both need to find those photographs. So, unless you already have irrefutable proof that they have been destroyed in a certain fire you know a lot about, get out of this office and get cracking."

Neal left knowing that arguing was going to get him nowhere. He had to go out onto the streets and search for some photographs without knowing why they meant so much to Rupert Bell. Try as he might, and he had often tried, he still could not fathom the reason they were so important.

On the other hand, Rupert Bell knew exactly their importance. He regretted letting his feelings get the better of him as he extracted the letter opener from his desk. He needed to calm down. If the photographs had not been destroyed, he would get them back one way or another. It was just the situation was becoming, he felt, slightly out of hand and things could deteriorate further.

Across the city in north London, a young man was sorting through the belongings of his recently deceased grandfather, a man he loved and respected. Things for Rupert Bell were about to get a whole lot worse.

Chapter 9

There are many ways into journalism; a one-size-fits-all does not apply to those wishing to become writers of newsprint. Old industry sages suggest that perhaps the best way is a degree course in something other than journalism, followed by a postgraduate course in a key skill such as media law.

Ignoring advice from seasoned professionals, Jane Ward followed her individual route, while she worked at Tesco as a full-time supermarket cashier. She scanned and smiled, she talked to customers about their day, the weather, lack of tinned lentils, tasty beef casseroles that made your mouth water. Regulars often sought her out to scan their shopping and chat about family matters.

At night, she transformed those conversations into a daily online blog reflecting the sadness, frustration and joys of ordinary shoppers. She also touched on and shared those personal tragedies and celebrations she had been told about, always carefully ensuring her subjects could not be identified from her stories. Subscribers to her blog grew and grew, enabling her to get a steady, although modest, income from the digital adverts on her site.

After a year at Tesco, Jane was ready to present herself to local newspapers across London. She sent an email containing a link to her blog to every editor, as well as a short news feature about the habits of shoppers. Within a week she had three job offers. After the editor of the Kent Herald told her, 'I want drive and passion, not fancy degrees and silver spoons' she knew she was going to be at home there.

It was the challenge Jane liked and as she sharpened her reporting skills, she was always the first to offer support and assistance to other reporters. Consequently, when Tony took her to one side and asked if she could help him with a bit of research, she was more than willing.

Being only five feet tall, she had to look up to Tony as they stood in the communal kitchen waiting for a battered Russell Hobbs kettle to boil.

"I wouldn't know where to begin," Tony admitted, throwing himself at her mercy. "I have an address; I just need to know who has used the offices there since 1990. I am guessing there could have been a number of companies. I also want to know what refurbishments have taken place since then, there can't be too many."

"Kingsway, London is out of our area you know," she pointed out as she poured water into their cups.

"It's linked with a story of a wanted man hiding out in our area, that's the connection."

"Always need a connection to the area." She smiled, her teeth perfect to the point of probably looking as though they were false, which they were not. Her long dark hair draped over her shoulders with her glasses slipping down her nose as she stirred her herbal teabag. "Why 1990?"

"Why do you always stir your tea bags? Shouldn't you just let it rest and brew?"

"It's a bad habit, I know. I am an impatient person. Why 1990?" she repeated.

"I have a press cutting dated for that year. It was hidden behind some panelling, so it can't have been concealed there before that date. All I want to know is which company or companies occupied those offices. That might lead to the person who squirrelled it away, well, I hope so."

A male voice joined the conversation, "1990, I recall I was young back then." It was Alistair Johnson, their editor, bringing his large tea mug into the kitchen to be re-filled. He smiled at his two employees and began rinsing his 'I'm the Boss' mug. "Why the '90s? Are you two taking part in a history lesson?"

"Old story," Tony admitted, "but has a connection to the one I'm doing about the alleged wife killer who was hiding out on our patch." Tony offered the press cutting to Alistair, who dried his hands on a tatty tea towel before taking the yellowed paper from Tony, adjusted his glasses and read the article.

The two reporters stood in silence like school pupils waiting for their homework to be given a grading by teacher. Alistair was far from being a teacher. Now as he was approaching retirement, he was laid back, slowing down, letting others, including his deputy, take the strain of running the newspaper. He now saw himself as a figurehead, a sage, offering snippets of wise advice from his years of experience.

"Archie Walker, I haven't seen that name in a good few years. Very much his sort of story, he loved the undercover investigating part of our job."

"Did you know him?" Tony asked, realising, even though he knew Alistair very well, he did not have any knowledge of Alistair's early career in journalism.

"Yes, we worked together as junior reporters. He was always one to dig down and search out conspiracies. Not that there were many on our patch in south London, but it was an interesting area. Sharp guy, always had a nose for when someone was telling him a pack of lies and would not be shy about pointing that fact out to them."

"Is he still working or is he on the verge of retiring like yourself?"

"Sad story actually. Could only be a couple of years after this story was published that he suffered from carbon monoxide poisoning that almost killed him. He had been found in his garage with the car engine still running. No one could work out just what he was doing in there, which led to a lot of speculation. The consensus suspected he wanted to commit suicide. I never really believed that, but you can't tell sometimes what is going on in peoples' lives. Anyway, after the accident, or whatever it was, he was no more than a shell of a man. He spent a few years at a nursing home before he died when he was barely thirty, such a waste."

"What about one of the people he'd exposed? A revenge killing?"

"There was of course that theory, given the number of people he'd upset. The thing is the type of people he normally upset were everyday villains who would shoot, stab or beat the living daylights out of you. Most of them wouldn't even know what carbon monoxide was, let alone know how to use it in a crime.

"On another note. Tony, when you've finished here, can you pop in my office please, I need a quick word."

***

Alistair had worked relentlessly to get behind the editor's desk of the local newspaper. The first thing he did when he was appointed was to order a larger desk, as well as a huge imposing leather swivel chair. Today, behind the desk, framed headlines from his era would ensure the next editor knew what he had to beat.

Besuited as he always was, Alistair gestured for Tony, who had brought his tea in, to take a seat. At first Alistair recounted some stories from Archie's life as a junior reporter, which Tony found to be mildly interesting. He was used to Alistair, who could both tell and write a story, picking over the numerous incidents and scoops that he had been part of over the years.

Finally, Alistair got around to the reason he wanted to speak to Tony. "Anyway, that's enough of me reminiscing about the good old days. I just wanted to tell you that your social worker has been on to me. Lovely Rita, who is not a meter maid but worse, spent about twenty minutes on the phone talking about you, Isobel and how she thinks you are a terrible father for allowing her to get into fights. She even hinted that Isobel might be better off in care. The woman is a bloody idiot! How can any daughter be better off in care when her father is still around, especially as he's a good father?"

"It's got to do with Isobel getting into fights and verbal confrontations with the other girls, about her mother. Rita has already spoken to me. The best part of it is, the school was not that bothered, only when Rita stuck her nose in did the whole thing become an issue."

"She really seems to have it in for you. You haven't upset her or written a damaging story about her, have you? Because she's nothing like I expect a social worker to be. You do know that she asked specifically to handle your case when it came up?"

Tony frowned, that information was news to him and a little disconcerting. He, as far as he knew, had never met Rita Taylor until he was about three weeks into being a single parent and she turned up at his door, introduced herself and appeared to be both concerned and caring. Neither trait seemed to have survived that first meeting.

"How did you find that out?"

"A couple of weeks ago, at some boring council meeting of people who think they are important. One chap there mentioned how one of his social workers had volunteered to deal with the case of the policeman's wife who was imprisoned. Well, there aren't too many of them, are there? I just earwigged a bit and didn't own up to the fact they were talking about your wife.

"Anyway, whatever her motives are, I thought you should be warned that the woman seems to have a sharp set of kitchen knives out for you. Any time off, arrivals in the morning, early finishes, just do it. Until this is all over, I am happy for you to be as flexible as you want to be regarding caring for Isobel."

A telephone rang inside Tony's pocket; the sudden vibration startled him for a moment. He looked at the caller display.

"It's Isobel checking in, to let me know she has arrived home safe and sound."

"You know I'm so proud of my granddaughter. Whatever Rita says, I know she is becoming a very mature and sensible young lady," Alistair pointed out as he listened to Tony talking.

"Hello darling.... What? No, stay outside... you have already checked the house? That was stupid, you should have called me first... don't worry, I'm leaving now. Go and stay with Kim next door. I'll see you soon."

"What's happened?" Alistair's voice reflected the concern he felt having listened to one side of what was clearly a fraught telephone conversation.

"It seems we've been burgled. I'll call you later."

Tony took immediate advantage of the working flexibility he had been offered and left the office to get home as quickly as possible.

Chapter 10

"You do realise this house is a mess?" Neal was always blunt; it was his normal approach.

"It's the way I like to live. I no longer have a wife to moan about my house full of treasures, I'm my own man. Anyway, you're here to talk about Doug, not give me housekeeping tips." George tried to sound defiant, but Neal sensed a defensive tone in his voice. It did not surprise him in the slightest that George had no wife; he couldn't see any woman staying long in such chaos.

"True," Neal replied, as he lay the two passports and two ferry tickets on the kitchen worktop, having first moved a motorcycle battery to one side. Earlier, he had spent a while in front of the police national database looking to see what exactly the police had on George; he was not surprised to discover the list was long.

George had first appeared in front of the magistrates whilst in his teens, after stealing a Vespa scooter. From then on, he became a regular at the courts for petty crimes linked to motor vehicles. It was becoming clear to those in the judicial system that George was mapping out a career path for himself. He was nineteen and driving a stolen car without insurance and without a licence, his blood full of alcohol, which took him into his first custodial sentence.

The casual observer would have concluded that the young George learnt much from being in prison. Over the next ten years he was suspected of carrying out many crimes, yet there was never enough evidence to prosecute. In his thirties he was a little sloppier, serving three years for supplying counterfeit MOT test certificates. He also had a concurrent sentence for selling a stolen car.

For the next couple of decades George avoided being caught, whilst he, according to police intelligence, went about adding covert storage space to cars. When he was finally caught, he pleaded that he did not know that the cars would be employed for hiding drugs. He believed the cars were going to be used by sales representatives in the jewellery business to ensure their valuable samples were secure. The only person who believed him appeared to be the judge, who gave George a minimal two-year sentence. It only came out years later that at one time George, under the guise of his painting and decorating business, had painted the outside of the judge's London residence.

"Four items, is that all you found under the kitchen cupboards?"

"Apart from a water leak, that was it."

An answer Neal did not believe. He guessed that any answer George gave to a question would include some sort of lie. In his experience, villains spent so much time lying, they had a built-in ability to not tell the truth, whoever might be asking.

"And Douglas Wright never once mentioned his past to you?"

"Blokes don't gossip. If he wanted to tell he would have done, but he didn't. It was up to him. As long as he paid the rent, I couldn't care less what he did before he came here."

Neal decided it might be worth messing with George. It could be interesting to test him out, see how shrewd he truly was. He knew that George had been in front of police officers all his life trying to get out of situations, so he would know how not to answer questions. Now at sixty, he might be a little less sharp than in his younger years.

"What if I told you the reporter mentioned some other items."

"I don't know what he told you. I know he was bemused and interested in all the single malts Douglas had, as well as the invoices for them, but they weren't found under the kitchen units. Oh, there was a magazine, but again, by his bed, not in the kitchen."

It was obvious that George was still sharp. Neal was seriously doubting that the photographs Rupert craved were ever here in the first place. It seemed obvious that the reporter would have taken everything they found to the police station. There was no reason for him not to hand over any photographs.

A cursory look around the reporter's house this morning had turned up nothing. It had surprised him that an ex-copper's house would be so easy to break into. Neal wasn't complaining, just observing. He had searched most of the rooms and the obvious places where someone might hide items of interest. His hunt had been unproductive. No sign of the photographs. He did look around at some of the other personal items around the house. Some family albums, bank statements, then there were the drawers, where Mrs Vercoe's clothes still waited for her return. The more he looked the more he convinced himself that the story surrounding Mrs Vercoe was wrong. She might be in prison serving a sentence, yet Neal, using years of experience, concluded that she would never have committed the crime she was accused of unless she had been forced to. He left Tony's house without the photographs but was overloaded with many questions he wanted answering about Mrs Vercoe.

"I'm not interested in any magazines that a man might have by his bed." It was a passing comment from Neal to give him some space before he thought about another relevant question.

"Wasn't dirty, it was a car magazine."

An innocent reply, which sparked Neal's suspicion. Of course, Douglas might well have a car magazine by his bed. Lots of men are interested in cars. Douglas had dabbled in car crime as a young man, maybe that interest had continued. He was even killed by one. Neal knew from George's record that he had a long interest in cars, albeit an illegal one. But two men with a common interest under the same roof.

"Show me."

"What, the magazine?"

"Yeah, show me." Neal sensed a reluctance.

"It's only a magazine."

"I still want to see it."

"Why would the authorities be interested in a boring car magazine?" George now regretted mentioning the publication in the first place.

Without pausing for breath Neal replied, "We suspect that he was about to elope with another woman who would travel under his wife's name. I'm looking for a passport in the name of Mrs Wright with someone else's photograph in it. The magazine might hold a clue." Neal did not care if he was believed or not, he just wanted to look at the magazine.

As he flipped through the pages, he was surprised that it was not a classic car publication, given that Douglas bought and died under an old Morris. The photographs were of high-value marques, Land Rover, BMW, Audi, Honda R type, all out of the financial catchment of Douglas. What really took Neal's attention were the numbers and notations alongside some of the photographs. Neal would have liked to ask about them, though he knew he would be lied to, but he did not want to draw attention to what he

97

was looking at, or warn George that his suspicions had been raised exponentially.

***

"George, this isn't a good time," Tony pleaded, as he looked around his hallway. He promised to call him back later.

His hallway had not looked so well ordered in years. In times gone by there would have been a selection of shoes, boots and trainers all in disarray on an overloaded shoe rack behind the front door. Above that rack, a small window with an even smaller wooden shelf, that buckled under the weight of all the mail rejected at the point of arrival. Takeaway menus, charity mailshots, offers of interest-free credit cards, all piled high on the shelf. The wooden coat rack on the left of the hallway, of late, had been neater for the simple reason that his wife was no longer around. There was now just one of her coats hanging on a peg. All the others belonged to Tony or Isobel. More often than not, there would be one or two parcels on the floor along the right-hand wall, with its large circular mirror, strategically positioned for one final attire check before leaving the house. The regular appearance of parcels had often led to a trip hazard and Tony protesting that they should be put somewhere else.

Today there were no parcels on the right-hand wall. There were still obstacles that could form a risk for anyone rushing in through the front door. Tony looked at the neatly stacked electrical goods, his belongings, television, two laptops, a tower PC, one satellite TV box, a DVD player. A selection of remote controls was neatly laid on the top of a record deck. Two speakers, wires neatly wrapped around them and a combined amplifier and radio that Tony had paid a small fortune for. The burglar or burglars might have been about to decant this neat pile into a waiting vehicle when his daughter coming through the front door made them rapidly alter their plans.

"I thought you were moving out and not telling me at first." Isobel sounded genuinely concerned, as her father comforted her with a strong arm about her shoulder.

"When you decided they had been stacked too neatly, what did you do then?"

"Well, I called out, 'Hello'. If anyone was upstairs, I wanted them to know I was around. I popped my head into each of the ground floor rooms to check but they were empty. In the kitchen, I saw the door was open and the handle didn't look too clever, so I guessed that was how they came in. Then I popped upstairs; if they were up there when I arrived, then at least they might have had the common sense to slip out through the front door while I was searching the ground floor. When I checked upstairs, that was empty as well. Then I called you."

"You did well, young lady. But next time, the first thing you should do is to step out of the house, stand in the street and call the police. I know you are a tough little girl, but these villains often have weapons on them. So just in case, next time, if there is a next time, get help."

"Do you think they will come back?"

Tony pulled his daughter closer, reassuring her, "I very much doubt it, they got spooked and look upon us now as a jinxed house. I'll give the police a call and let them know, but I doubt if they'll be able to do much. Okay, let's go and look at the back door, sounds as if we will need to get a locksmith to sort it out. I guess we'll be relying on Uber Eats tonight, what do you fancy?"

"Mexican," Isobel replied without hesitation.

Together they examined the lock on the kitchen door. The chrome handle spun around uselessly; the door frame cracked and split. Leaving Isobel to unpack her schoolbooks, shower and change, Tony checked the remainder of the house. Apart from the dusty voids where the electronics needed to be returned to, there was little evidence of any intruder.

The contents of drawers and cupboards were not arranged as Tony remembered them. Not that he made a point of ensuring that anything hidden behind a drawer front or cupboard door was tidy, but he had an idea of the kind of mess that he would describe as normal. The contents were no longer his mess, they had all been rummaged through. In Tony's experience, burglars would be looking for small valuable items: cash, watches, mobile phones, jewellery. He consoled himself that they had not simply pulled everything out and left it littered over the floor. Nothing appeared to be missing. Even his own bedside cupboard still contained his spare watches. He could only guess that they were upstairs when they had been disturbed and exited silently through the front door, empty-handed.

Isobel came out of the shower in her oversized, soft pink dressing gown that had a small rose pattern. She poked her head around her father's door to see him checking her mother's jewellery box. He looked sad as he caressed a white gold necklace that he had bought for Mother on their wedding anniversary.

"Dad, why did the robbers pile all the stuff in the hallway? They wouldn't just take it out of the front door, would they?"

Tony carefully replaced the necklace and closed the lid. He patted the bed to encourage his daughter to sit next to him.

"They might have broken in through the kitchen door. I guess they came along the back alley, over our fence across the garden and into the kitchen. But when they want to leave with all their swag, that route is onerous, so they take it out the front door. Which sounds a little brazen I know, but being brazen often removes any suspicion from their actions. I would imagine once they'd decided they had enough of our stuff, they would bring their van, normally white, around to the front, and then simply load it up. Anyone passing by might think someone's moving or shifting rubbish and that it must be okay as they're going in and out of the front door."

"But if Kim next door saw what they were doing, she'd have known we weren't moving."

"They would have a fall-back plan. Think of all the post, addressed to Mr Vercoe, that we leave hanging around the front door. Kim comes along and asks what they're doing. They say, 'Mr Vercoe is donating this stuff to the local charity or has asked us to move it to a friend in need. They'll think of a plausible excuse, so Kim will be placated."

"I never imagined criminals as being clever people."

"Oh, they are, they need to be very resourceful. Just because someone is a criminal doesn't mean they are stupid. Criminals who set out to break the law are often intelligent and ingenious."

"But you called Mother stupid for doing what she did."

"True. All criminals are stupid in a way, or at least lack enough good judgment, to break the law in the first place. There's never a good reason to break the law. If they do, then they must be foolish, but it doesn't always automatically follow that they lack intelligence. Some I know are very clever, or devious might be a better description. Let's not forget, your mother is innocent, she told us and I believe her as I am sure you do.

"The main thing is you're okay. Your arrival made them flee and we've nothing missing. The only bad thing is it has shown I don't dust behind the television enough! Now, let's get ourselves a locksmith and then we'll order our Mexican and I'll call George back."

He watched his daughter leave the room. He was pleased that she seemed to be coping well with her mother being imprisoned. Many teenagers in her situation might well have rebelled, gone off the rails. Isobel, apart from a small aberration at school, seemed to have accepted the current family circumstances. He was pleased and proud of her.

The burglary was a worry. He recalled Douglas's neighbour, the old man, mentioning a burglary which had sent Douglas into a frenzy of security. Was it just a coincidence, Tony wondered? People get burgled every day around the country. His own house, in a pleasant affluent area, would attract burglars looking for easy pickings. A target high on their list.

He opened his work rucksack, pulled out a hard-backed envelope in which he had placed the black and white photographic prints from decades ago, then just stared at them. The prints that Douglas no doubt had in his possession when he was burgled. A pile of electrical goods in the hallway screams robbery. Rummaged drawers with small easily carried items left in place screams someone searching for something specific. The photographs?

***

"Thanks for calling back, Tony. I've had a visit from someone who is not who he says he is. He said he was a government official, no way he was. I'm thinking police of some sort. He was asking all sorts of questions about Doug. Asked about photographs too."

"You didn't tell him, did you?" Tony interrupted; he need not have worried.

"Course not, you know me."

"Short, fat man, glasses, rounded face?"

"Yeah, that's the bloke. Do you know him?"

"He paid me a visit yesterday. He's a sort of copper, think of special branch plus. They appear to have an interest in the photographs that we found; the ones you didn't want anyone else to see. George, is there anything about Doug that you are holding out on? Because if you are, I'd rather know now, than later down the road when there is no turning back."

George thought about the question. He did know a bit more, but he couldn't share it with anyone. In fact, he knew a lot more about Doug and how he earned his money. That was the dilemma George found himself in. He had known Tony for many years and trusted him. He was a good bloke, always wanting the best for everyone. Sometimes even turning a blind eye to a bit of naughty business knowing such things go on and he'd never be able to stop them. So, he felt it best to let them continue, that way he knew who the bad guys were and could put them in check when needed.

But he could not share this with Tony; it was all too risky and complex. If he told Tony even a small amount, it would spark his interest; he remembered what Tony was like when he was in uniform. Then George feared he might end up the same way as Doug and the one thing George valued above everything else was his own skin.

"Honest, I've told you everything," George lied.

Chapter 11

Everything about New Barn in Kent was large. The houses, even the smallest homes, were above average. They all had immaculate gardens that extended many yards in front and behind them (the residents preferred imperial measurements, shunning the new modern metric system). They needed large gardens, every self-respecting resident of the small village had either a swimming pool, tennis court or, at the very least, an outdoor hot tub. Four of the very largest houses had all these items in their garden. There was never any on-road parking, everyone had enough gravelled driveway to accommodate their own cars, large BMWs, Jaguars, low sporty Porsches. Personalised number plates appeared to be mandatory. Driveways were large enough to accommodate both residents and guest cars.

It was not the sort of area that Tony had expected to find a disgraced car dealer. Yet, this is where his enquiries had led him. The press cutting had named Mickey Ross as the criminal car dealer working out of his premises on New Cross Road. That was where Tony had started, the car showroom still existed, albeit under new management. Showroom was a little of an overstatement, it was still a simple car sales lot, with an ageing grey portable cabin in one corner where the deals were finalised, and the current owner ran his business.

Luckily, Mickey Ross did and still had a reputation with local car dealers.

"Everyone knows Mickey, still see him around once in a while – absolute legend!" Tony was reliably informed by the current owner of Mickey's Used Car Sales. He did not receive an exact address, just that he lived in New Barn. Fortunately, there were not too many homes in the village and a brief conversation with the local grocery store-cum-post office enabled Tony to identify the house he needed to visit. Hopefully he would get some answers there.

Tony parked his Ford Ka on the semi-circular driveway, his car dwarfed by the large black Range Rover Vogue he was parked next to. There was another car on the drive a, small one-year-old Vauxhall Corsa, perhaps the wife's car.

The house had a large façade. In the centre was a grand wooden door enclosed by two large pillars, reminding Tony of a Georgian house. Either side of the entrance were large bay windows which continued, resembling columns, upwards to the upper floor. Wisteria clung to the wall of the house on the right-hand side. Above the front door, a tall rectangular stained-glass window, he could not make out the design, the ostentatious coloured glass distracted from it.

The door was answered by a smartly dressed lady, her blonde hair permed in a beehive style, which Tony had not seen for years. Her wrinkled skin did indicate that she was born many decades ago, yet she stood upright, had a shrewd look about her and spoke with a firm high-pitched voice. Tony imagined that she could still be described as attractive by fellow pensioners. In fact, she was still waiting to receive her State Pension as she was still only in her fifties. Her aged looks could be put down to the stressful life she had led with her husband and his criminal cronies.

"Can I help you?"

"I'm here to see Mickey," Tony tried to sound friendly, almost as if he was a comrade of Mickey's. He was sure if he had asked to see Mr Ross, he would not now be following someone he assumed was a senior citizen through a wide hall with tacky white statues, down a short corridor with crass reproduction framed paintings, through the kitchen, which was the biggest he had ever seen and crammed with every sort of kitchen gadget you could imagine. They continued out into the garden, where his guide stopped and pointed towards a large greenhouse in one corner, beyond a covered swimming pool.

"He's playing with his plants. I'm doing him tea in a bit; do you fancy a cup?" Her voice might have been firm, but it was not eloquent, she sounded south London through and through.

The humid heat was for a few brief moments overpowering, catching Tony's breath as he walked in. The long rectangular greenhouse was lined with shelves on both sides. Neatly spaced out were rows of cactus plants of various shapes and sizes, some with small pretty flowers, others with large threatening spikes. All this glass house needed now was a couple of tons of sand on the floor to transform it into a piece of desert.

The short man in front of him was wearing oversized rubber gloves as he went about repotting a very spiky-looking cactus. The man stared at the intruder to his desert haven with a look of distrust in his eyes. Automatically, his hand moved towards a small trowel he could use as a weapon.

"Who are you?" The tone was not in the least inviting.

"Tony, I'm a reporter, I wanted a brief word with you."

"Piss off! I don't talk to newspaper people." He turned his attention back to the spiked cactus, carefully compressing the fine soil with his fingers.

"George Stevens sent me; said you might help."

This produced a different reaction, a more cautious, less confrontational manner. He put the cactus down, took off his gloves and stepped towards Tony.

"George should know better than to send people to me, I'm not the helpful type."

Mickey Ross stood close to Tony, wiping his hands on a grubby purple towel. Recalling the newspaper photograph, Mickey had aged well. He was now bald, his head the perfect shape and size to be used as a basketball, but for the fact it was attached to a short, slightly overweight body. He still sported the same neat thin moustache he was pictured with in the news clipping. He wore a red Cotton Traders Polo shirt, which had smears of soil on the front. His eyes were blue and mean looking, Tony could easily believe that this man flourished well in the underworld of criminality all those years ago.

"One of his tenants died leaving a newspaper clipping from many years ago featuring you, but George reckoned you didn't know him, I just wanted to make sure." Tony unfolded the newspaper article from his pocket and tried to hand it to Mickey who took one brief look.

"I did read it at the time. One of his tenants had it, you say."

"Douglas Wright, but you might have known him by the name he was using: Douglas Halifax. The guy with his back to the camera, I was wondering if that might have been him."

"I don't socialise with any of George's tenants, so I can't help you."

Tony then presented the passport picture he had of Douglas. Mickey gave the black and white photocopy barely a glance before deciding he did not know the man. But he did put in the caveat that he had met lots of people in his

108

time, so that it was not to say that he hadn't stood in the same room as him. Then carefully, he placed the newly potted cactus on the lower of the shelves in front of him.

The inclusion of that caveat intrigued Tony.

"This Douglas Wright, which is his real name, was on the run from the police having burnt his wife to death. I'm just trying to get some background on him and hoping to find out why he had your photo in his pile of treasured belongings."

"Killed his wife?"

Tony picked up on the tone of the reply. There was a hint of surprise, no more than that. Tony took it to mean he might well have known or met Douglas, not just stood in the same room. Surprised that Douglas would be a killer? Much the same conclusion the work colleague had. Maybe Tony was reading too much into his instinct. He always doubted his feelings and intuition in the first instance even though it had never let him down before.

"If you didn't know him and he wasn't one of those in the news photograph, why do you think he kept the press cutting?"

"How should I know? Maybe he was a fan of mine," the belligerent tone had returned. Mickey had regrouped his thoughts; his defences were once again intact.

"Teatime." Mrs Ross appeared at the door, a tray with ornate handles in her hands. She had prepared a generous afternoon tea with biscuits for her husband and his guest, no doubt one of his many business associates. She had used the Royal Albert's Old Country Roses tea set, her favourite that her sister had bought Mickey and her for their recent thirtieth wedding anniversary. Only when either Mickey asked, or she thought the guest was special, did it come out. This young man looked as if he was important, he had an air of confidence about him.

"Not now Dolly, you stupid woman, we're talking business. Put the tray down and leave us in peace."

Sheepishly Dolly put the tray down, doing as she was told, something she always did, life was easier that way. Quietly she closed the door behind her, she knew Mickey was funny about keeping the temperature in the greenhouse at a perfect level.

"What about that transaction? The one you were doing in the photograph, what were the guys buying?"

"It was thirty-odd years ago. I sold loads of bloody cars; how should I know?"

"Because that photograph brought you down, cost you, no doubt, a lucrative career of crime. If the two of them weren't the regular villains you worked with, then I bet you spent many a restless night wondering just who they were, maybe they worked for the paper setting you up. I suspect you know what they bought and what they paid for it."

Mickey took a Bunny Eared cactus from the shelf, examined it and then returned it to its rightful place where it dwarfed its neighbour, a Red Ball cactus. He took off his gloves and moved beside Tony, pouring the tea and offering one of the chocolate biscuits that Dolly had added to the tray.

"Interesting. Maybe you'll come across them as you research your story. Never knew them, they just turned up one day wanting a van, offering cash and not wanting me to ask too many questions, which I never did. As clearly stated in the article, I was not fussy about the paperwork. It was the Ford Transit we are all standing next to in the photo that they bought. They gave me the cash and drove it off the same day.

"Of course, when the newspaper contacted me to ask if I wanted to add any comments to the story, they were writing about me, I thought they were bluffing. I told them, 'No comment'. Then the story came out and yes, I tried to find out if it was the paper that bought the Transit to trap me. Never could prove it, ironically, because there was a lack of paperwork with real names on, I couldn't find them. I suspect it was the newspaper, making sure they got photographs of me doing a dodgy deal. There you are, happy now. If they're still alive, I'd love to meet them and ask them personally just what they were up to."

"That kind of circumnavigates my next question about checking back on your records."

"All those records have gone now. Once the paper published, the Old Bill turned me over and charged me with a load of stuff. I think they were pleased to get something on me at last. Then the tax man turned up, took all the records for that year."

"Didn't the police take all the previous years as well as evidence? They surely looked at all your previous transactions, linking crimes, tax evasion, building the case against you."

"They weren't that interested. It was put to me that they had overwhelming evidence anyway and suggested that if I pleaded guilty, they would go easy on me. So course I pleaded and got seven months suspended sentence. My Dolly was relieved, it would have broken her heart, as she would never go near a prison even if she wanted to visit me."

"Correct me if I'm wrong, but I got the impression from the newspaper and some police that I have spoken to, that you were something of a celebrated criminal. If a villain wanted a motor, you were the go-to man."

111

"I'd agree, but I'm too modest."

"Yet you got off very lightly. I would have thought they would have slammed you up for a couple of years at least."

"Thought so as well. Course, I lost everything, just find the odd car for friends and family now, not in the business anymore. After I got my sentence, I gave it all up, burnt all my records just in case and stepped away from the twilight world of dodgy motors. No point, the Old Bill would have their eye on me, waiting for me to put a step wrong."

"If you lost it all, this isn't a bad place to spend your poverty–stricken retirement. Who pays for all this?"

"It's all Dolly's money, I'm a kept man," Mickey laughed as he poured himself another cup of tea.

"Just one other question, the reporter who wrote that story might have tried to commit suicide, it went wrong, but he died a few years later. Could that have been you, somehow trying to get revenge?"

"I knew the guy, for Christ's sake his name was plastered all over the story. Yeah, I would have liked to punch his lights out, mess up his face somewhat, why wouldn't I? But if I had done, then I would be the prime suspect and banged up for a good few years. I'm not that bloody stupid. But if he tried to top himself well, don't expect me to shed any tears."

Tony drove away. Dolly waved him goodbye from the door like some adoring auntie sorry to see her nephew leave. However sweet she appeared to be Tony doubted that she had ever been the breadwinner in their marriage. Mickey was and still is, in Tony's opinion, a career criminal and they never move away from breaking the law to make their money. Mickey was one of the smart ones; his profits were always beyond the reach of the law, constantly changing and evolving his methods as the enforcement agencies encircled him. Mickey was a good liar, but Tony did not for one minute imagine Dolly had the cash. In the same way, he did not believe that Mickey had not seen George recently and he sure as hell had met Douglas before.

Tony weaved his way through the traffic towards his home. He looked at the cars around him, they were the common denominator through all this, motor vehicles.

Thirty years ago, Mickey was dealing in dodgy cars. Today, Tony would bet a week's wages that he was still involved in some sort of shady dealing with cars. George was a villain, open to any opportunity to make a few pounds here and there. Douglas had a car magazine enigmatically marked, he also died under a car. Tony needed to work out how Karl Benz's invention connected all three, only then might he find the truth behind the photographs.

***

"I'm going onto the roof for a smoke. If anyone decides that they need to speak to me, tell them to either wait or use telepathy," Rupert informed his secretary as he strode past her desk. He ignored her disapproving eyes that he could feel burning into the back of his neck.

Rupert was now of an age and seniority that did not require him to worry about what people thought of him. There was a time, many years ago, when he did care, but that was at the point he was clinging to the lower rungs of the Civil Service career ladder. As he climbed the ladder, the thinner air at the top took away his need for peer approval.

Walking through the long, carpeted corridor, colleagues nodded respectfully as he passed by them. He knew it was an open secret that at 11am and 3pm each day he would be on his way up to the roof to have a smoke along with the gin and tonic he concealed in an insulated cup. They also knew that Rupert, or Mr Bell if they addressed him to his face, would not tolerate anyone disturbing him during his time on the roof. Only the onset of a nuclear attack might be considered a valid reason for an interruption to his break.

On the roof amongst the whirling ventilator motors, with the noise of the wind playing melodies on the taut wires supporting the communication towers, Rupert could be alone with his thoughts. His staff knew it was his meditation time to help ease the stress of his post, a position that required him to decide the fate of people's lives.

Rupert bore the responsibilities of his post with ease. It had never bothered him that if he made the wrong decision someone might die. It was added to the fact he often had to order the death of certain individuals. He had no need to seek solace, his work never caused him to lose sleep. A different topic hindered his sleep pattern; a choice he had made many years ago. He had gone along with a decision that the younger him knew to be wrong. It was his craving to be considered the right stuff for promotion which had seen him meekly agree with his seniors.

Rupert sensed another person on the roof. He turned; it was Neal.

"Did that irritating secretary of mine give you her pass again? I told her I wanted to be alone."

"We all know you want to be alone up here unless the realm is under nuclear attack. But you know as well as I do there will never be a nuclear war. A man in a suicide vest can bring a government to its knees for a fraction of the cost of a nuclear warhead. Plus, I know you don't like talking about certain photographs in the earshot of anyone else."

"Any good news on that front?" Rupert took a large gulp from his insulated cup, it caught his throat, today he had added a little too much gin.

"That depends on what you consider this news to be when you hear it. Will you take it to be good or bad?"

"Why is it everyone has aspirations to be a clown?" Rupert snapped. "I blame social media; it recycles rubbish jokes. People share the stupid things they do in the vain hope they will get a smiley-face reaction. Or else they are bragging about what a great time they're having living a dream life. It's about time someone toned the whole thing down, have some depressing posts where people admit they are in a dark place, need the support of others. Social media should reflect the whole of society, not just the extroverts and phonies. Photographs, do you have them, yes or no?"

Neal was taken aback by the rant. He knew too well that Rupert could be cantankerous. He often described new recruits as politically correct and scared of getting their hands dirty. But normally, he was subtler in his rebukes. Today was a bad rant day. It was going to be wise for Neal to stick to the facts as he gave his verbal report to Rupert.

"I did as you asked and broke into Tony's house..."

"You did what?" Rupert exclaimed. "To be clear, Neal, I told you to visit Tony when he was out, not break in."

There was no point in trying to defend your case when Rupert was in such a bad mood. Nothing would mollify him. Most of what you did was going to be wrong. The only way to get through this was to speak in bullet-point phrases that contained just facts and little opinion.

Starting with the search of Tony's house, which Neal judiciously pointed out had been on his own initiative without any departmental authorisation, had produced nothing of value. Well, not for the department, although it had heightened the interest Neal had in the reasons Tony's wife was now serving a three-year prison sentence.

Then he moved on to his meeting with George Stevens, the landlord, addressing the utter chaos of the man's house and his total disregard for authority. Neal did not believe a word the man had said. In the end there was no indication that there was any incriminating evidence at George's house and even if there had been, Neal suggested it would easily have been lost.

"You're telling me you found nothing at all. A result which supports your hypothesis of the tragic fire having destroyed the items I want to find."

"Nothing you wanted was there. I do think that Douglas was murdered. He was found face down under his car. Everyone I know who decides to wriggle under a jacked-up car tend to lie on their back. Plus, he had no tools near him. There's more. Without any visible means of supporting himself financially, I began to wonder how he managed to pay his way so did exactly as you asked, you'll be pleased to hear, I dug around the backgrounds of Douglas and George. Both, as you mentioned before, have in the past been dab hands at stealing cars. Both have convictions but have never been together in the same prison at the same time.

"Douglas had a magazine full of high-value cars with notations I recognised written alongside them. Codes for getting into those cars are as easy as if he had a key. Both were nicking and selling cars, that's where my money is going. And I would be looking very closely at George Stevens as a potential killer. All I need is a motive for him to kill his partner, I suspect greed."

"All very well," Rupert said as he tapped the white ash from his pipe onto the concrete floor. The ash swirled, caught up in one of the mini vortexes that inhabited the roof. "You're getting paid to find some black and white prints and their associated negatives. Her Majesty's government is not paying you to act like bloody Colombo and solve murders. I have no interest whatsoever in who killed Douglas or what the reason might have been. I want those negatives. Do you understand?"

The reprimand took Neal aback. "But if he was murdered..."

"I told you, I have no interest. Have you located the negatives, yes, or no?"

"No," was the curt reply.

"Do you think you will ever be able to find them?"

"No," Neal sounded like a child who had been reprimanded by a parent, "because I think if Douglas had them, they would have been destroyed in the fire at his house."

"As I have asked you on many occasions when you have offered that theory, what proof do you have?"

Neal took a moment to arrange his thoughts. He did not really want to reveal them to Rupert, who was obviously still in a mood, but there was going to be no other way to end the cycle that Neal found himself trapped in.

"I preface this with the simple fact that I have no understanding of why you have such an interest in these negatives and photographs. I think they were destroyed in the fire, but just suppose, for a moment, they weren't. Then what do we have.

"A fugitive from the law being accused of killing his wife in the most horrific circumstances, who has in his possession an item that he knows you're very interested in getting your hands on. I presume he has some idea why you want them back. He knows you are powerful and able

117

to twist the arm of the law. If he had them, he would have contacted you to strike a deal. He knows he didn't kill his wife; you know he didn't kill his wife. He could get off, only be questioned and released. The tragedy would have been written up as some unfortunate accident, which it was always meant to be. But he did none of those things because he never had them after the fire. He had lost any leverage that he might have had and needed to lay low, never living under his true name again."

Rupert took a sip from his drink. Listening to Neal reminded him of why he had taken Neal onto his special team in the first place. A disillusioned police officer, who had an elephant's memory and a sharp incisive logic when it came to ordering facts. Plus, he did things, dark things, without question. Already Neal had gathered some facts and had woven a story not too far from the truth.

It had been an editor who had first alerted Rupert to the fact that Douglas had the photographs of two men buying a transit van. A throwaway comment at some informal meeting, where government ministers were trying to whip into line some of the national papers who were becoming too vocal.

The editor mentioned someone who had been trying to sell him some old photographs, the editor had turned him down saying they were no longer news, public interest in them would be just about zero. Sensibly the editor had suggested that Douglas contact MI5, hand them the photographs, it was evidence they might be interested in. Douglas never contacted the department, but the editor was happy to hand over all the contact details he had for Douglas.

"What if George knew they, the negatives that is, had some sort of intrinsic value. That could be your motive for him killing Douglas." Rupert proposed his own theory.

"No, he called a reporter in to help him find relatives. It was the reporter who found the passports, if he had uncovered the photographs as well, he would have innocently handed them in with the passports."

Rupert nodded; he could see what Neal was saying. Yet he felt that if Douglas was hiding the photographs and negatives, he would have hidden them with the passports that revealed his true identity.

Keeping Neal in the dark had worked so far. Maybe the fire had destroyed everything after all. Rupert was just being obsessive about the whole episode that had haunted him throughout his time in the department. A couple more months and it would all be over.

"Reluctantly, I find myself agreeing with you. We'll now assume the matter of the lost photographs is now fully closed. Time to get back to more mundane pieces of work."

"What about the fact that Douglas might have been murdered?"

"I told you, it's of no interest to me, or to you, for that matter. Step away, have a few days off and then we can see what other work we can find for you to get your teeth into."

Neal turned to leave his boss to the gentle breeze that combed the roof, then he thought of something, stopped and turned back towards Rupert.

"You've been in the department for a long time."

"Too many years, some would say, why?"

"I got a call today from someone asking for a Brigadier Howard Harvey. Well, I've never heard of him, asked around but no one knew the name. But then Graham on the main desk thought the name rang a bell, something to do with Kingsway House, an old building we were in once, so I'm told. Anyway, I said to the guy we didn't have such a brigadier working here. The caller, who had a light Irish accent, became a little agitated to say the least, called us a bunch of British bastards then hung up. You haven't heard of this Howard Harvey, have you?"

"No, the name doesn't ring any bells."

Chapter 12

If he closed his eyes, Liam could still make himself
believe that his grandfather was in the room wearing those
chocolate corduroy trousers with the well-worn leather
belt. They were the only trousers that Liam ever saw him
wear. Then there were his chequered shirts, either black
check or red check, it was always one or the other. His
grandfather liked to keep things simple.

Having been brought up in poverty in a small Irish
village which relied on the weather and a strong harvest to
feed the citizens throughout the hard winter. Grandad was
shrewd with his money. Clothes were a luxury, 'you can
only wear one shirt at a time', he would often tell Liam
when he showed off his latest fashionable shirt to his
grandfather.

Liam knew his grandfather was not there. The musky
odour of his aftershave lingered, as did the memories, but
sadly his body had been buried just three long days ago.

The colour had faded on an old glossy square
photograph, taken probably more than forty years ago. The
edges were split, one corner was dog-eared but for all its
imperfections, the photograph still warmed the heart of
Liam Connor.

The photograph was of a bare-chested man, strong
arms folded, a wide smile of contentment on his face. He
was sitting on the bonnet of a blue car, that Liam did not
recognise. He did know the man, his grandfather, a
younger version of the one he loved and always would.
Even though death had now taken him away, Liam would
forever hold memories of the man closest to his heart.

Ancestrally, he was a grandfather. Yet in the realities of Liam's life, he was the only father figure he ever knew. Liam was four years old when his father died. If he dug deep into his childhood memories, he did have a hazy recall of a man whose hand he held when walking around the meadows of his birthplace.

In later years, Liam learnt that they moved away from the green fields of Ireland soon after his father died. Liam moved to England with his mother and grandfather, a tall robust man who took the place of Liam's deceased father.

As Liam grew up, both his mother and grandfather were happy to tell stories of his father, hoping to nurture some sort of bond that he could feel with his deceased father. But Liam was never very interested in a man that he never knew. What was the point? He already had a father figure, so had no need to know what his father was like or what he did. But for his accent, Liam considered himself to be English and Ireland was no more than the landscape for stories about how his mother and father came together and how toddler, Liam, explored the lush grassy meadows.

Sitting on his grandfather's bed, Liam began the depressing task of sorting through the old man's personal belongings. He knew some things would need to be thrown away, cast aside and forgotten. But what should he keep? What should be disposed of? That was his dilemma. Every time he asked his mother about something, she just held the object in question to her chest and started crying. At least she had her own father for many more years than Liam had his, he thought unsympathetically.

Liam was more of a practical person, there was no need to keep every photograph of Grandad. His clothes could not be kept forever, they needed to be packed up and given to charity. It was the small, personal items that Liam struggled with. A wallet, frayed, yet still practical, containing a five-pound note. His glasses, smeared without a case. A cheap Casio watch with a plastic strap, low on value, high on sentimentality.

Liam sat on the bed amongst a selection of photographs that his grandfather had kept in a special box, a memory box Liam would describe it as. A wedding photograph of Grandad and Nan, looking so young. Photographs, creased, black and white photographs of Liam's great grandparents. His mother as a baby, a toddler, her first communion picture, dressed in white, so young, so sweet.

Then there were the newspaper cuttings, wedding banns, obituaries, a long one about his nan, who Grandad loved so much. A faded printed article of Liam's mother winning a bonny baby competition. A family history in a collection of yellowed and withered snippets.

Then there were the unidentifiable items. The things people keep but never explain to anyone why. A crucifix with a broken gold chain. A single mother-of-pearl cufflink. A twenty-year-old entry pass to the paddock at Sandown Racecourse. A press cutting of a crooked car dealer in south London. Liam stopped, looked closer at the picture in the press cutting. One of the men looked familiar, could it be his father? He had seen images of his father, shown to him at various intervals when he had come up in conversation. He wasn't sure. He called his mother, who strolled into the room and sat beside him on the bed. She looked at the photograph, read enough of the article to get the general drift of the story, then frowned.

"Well, it looks like your dad, I'd say that much. But it can't be, he never came here to England, ever. Hated the thought of leaving the Emerald Isle. It must be a man who looked like your dad."

"Then why did Grandad have this amongst his belongings?"

His mother brushed some imaginary dust from her pinafore and shrugged her shoulders, she did not have an answer.

"I wish your grandad were here to tell us. He would know the answer, as he always did, but he's no longer with us. It will end up being one of those mysteries that families can never answer. There are always questions we never think of or know to ask before someone passes away. Maybe it's for the best."

Liam noticed the indentation of writing on the reverse of the newspaper cutting. He turned it over and saw the handwritten words, 'Brigadier Howard Harvey – MI5', followed by a telephone number and extension. He showed the name to his mother, who showed no reaction.

Her only comment was, "Do you think that's MI5, like the security force?"

"I don't know. Do you know the name, Brigadier Howard Harvey?" Liam asked.

"No, never heard of him. I have no idea who he is. Maybe we should just throw it away, any meaning it might have had will no longer be useful. It's a mystery from the past, which might be the best place for it to stay."

Liam thought she sounded a little flustered, or was it just the grief within her voice? He protested, "But that's Grandad's writing, he must have written the name on the back for a reason, he must have known something."

"It's all history, I'm sure Grandad knew what he was doing at the time, and I guess he had a good reason. But whatever it was, nothing must have come of it or else I would have known about it. I'm just getting your dinner;

it'll be ready in about a quarter of an hour." She stood up and left Liam alone with the mystery.

His father died, that had been the only account his mother ever gave him. No mention of any illness or accident. He died. That was the only explanation Liam had been given by his mother.

In his teens, he began to ask more questions about his father, but he was met with the flimsiest of reasons from his mother. 'He died suddenly, let's not talk about it, our talking can't change things' was the only answer she would ever give.

His grandfather when he thought Liam was of a correct age was more forthcoming, 'The British Army killed him, in the troubles, like they killed so many of our brothers.' Even then his grandfather would go no further. His strong Irish brogue, which he refused to give up, rebutted any request that Liam made for more information. 'He died a hero for the cause. That's all you need to know son.'

Teenager Liam became distracted by love and good times. His father, a stranger to him, was dead, he was not coming back, so what did it matter? He had been a victim of the troubles in Northern Ireland like so many had. But now, Liam wanted to know more. Was that really his father in the picture? His mother denied it; his grandfather was no longer around to ask. He had to call the number and ask, find out for himself.

Chapter 13

The last person that Tony wanted to see standing on his doorstep was the short, rotund figure of Rita Taylor. The scowl on her face did little to ease the disappointment he felt.

"Mr Vercoe, we need to talk about the circumstances and consequences of your recent burglary."

Tempted as he was to say, 'I don't think we need to talk' and close the door, he knew that would be a waste of time. Rita was not the sort of person to walk away meekly. She was a warrior as well as a pain to Tony.

"Come in and tell me more about the consequences." He hoped the sarcasm in his voice was appreciated.

Rita sat down on the long settee, unzipped her coat but left it on. Opening her slim briefcase she withdrew a blue folder and flipped through several pages. She looked up at Tony and began to speak,

"I understand that your house was burgled yesterday. A crime which your daughter stumbled across when she returned home from school alone."

"Well, you have the general idea, but your interpretation is not mine. Someone did break into our house yesterday, but nothing in the end was stolen. Yes, my daughter was the first one back and she called me. It's normal for her to arrive home alone from school. What has this to do with social services or are you expanding your remit to include crime investigation?"

"My concern is that the context of the burglary is directly connected to the activities of your wife. Your home could become a target for unscrupulous people hoping to find valuable items in your house."

"Such as?"

"I think that yesterday's attack on your home was carried out by someone believing that there might well be drugs or large amounts of money on the premises. Your wife is a convicted drug dealer and it's not unusual for other dealers to ransack the homes of other dealers to collect contraband."

Tony was in general a placid person, but he was finding that peaceful attitude hard to hang onto as Rita threw her allegations and wild theories around. He knew full well from past meetings that she did not like the idea of Isobel staying with her father. Rita would prefer to see his daughter in the care of Social Services. He was sure that he was not the first husband to have a wife in prison and be left to look after the children.

"I'm not sure what you watch on TV but what you have just stated is the biggest load of tosh I have heard in a while. Now if the burglar yesterday was after illegal drugs and cash, that would imply I am dealing drugs as well. Is that what you are saying?"

"No, I'm not accusing you of anything like that. I am saying that your home is a target because of the crime your wife committed."

"Let's get things straight in your crooked mind, Ms Taylor. My wife was stopped by police because of reports of a similar car dealing drugs on a nearby housing estate. I would remind you that the officers never said exactly where that information came from when they were questioned in court. When they searched her car, they found eleven hundred pounds in cash and a few ounces of cocaine. She was arrested, charged and in the end found guilty of PWITS. Which as you might or might not know is 'possession with intent to supply'.

127

"She never had so much as a parking ticket let alone any sort of criminal record. Her phone was never searched to see what sort of supposed deals she had been making using it. The police never showed who she might be selling to. There wasn't even any suggestion as to where she got her drugs from. I know my wife better than anyone, she isn't a drug dealer. I'm aware that her daughter knows that too. In my opinion, whether you like it or not, someone for some purpose framed her."

"Mr Vercoe, I deal in facts. Your wife was convicted. My priority is your daughter. What you are doing now I only take into account when I think about the welfare of your daughter and at this time, I am very concerned that she isn't in the best place not only for her mental wellbeing, but also her safety is of concern to me."

Tony leaned forward pointing his finger in a clearly aggressive manner which he was not worried about showing. "And do you know what concerns me, Ms Taylor, how come you're here so quickly? Within twenty-four hours of my reporting a crime, you're down here spouting off crap and allegations, none of which I would imagine you have a shred of evidence for. If you want to take my daughter, get the court order. Otherwise leave now, you're no longer welcome."

Rita huffed and puffed. She closed her blue folder and replaced it in her briefcase. She stood as tall as she could, given her limited height then spoke. "This isn't over Mr Vercoe." Then she turned and walked out without adding anything further. All Tony could do was slam the door loudly as she walked down the path towards the street.

Tony flopped down onto a chair with two questions buzzing around his head. How did she find out so quickly about the burglary? Why had she volunteered to deal with the Vercoe family in the first place?

***

Tony had managed to calm himself down. He focused on his work in the kitchen which was the perfect place for him when working from home. He had a large table, giving him enough space for his laptop, numerous sheets of paper, and still oodles of space left over for a cup of coffee and bacon sandwich on a plate. The room was generally warm, full of pleasing odours and handy for replenishing his coffee cup and taking in the occasional snack.

He had found the living room to be the worst place to work. There were just too many distractions: television, radio, music player, plus rows of books. Also, when sitting with a laptop on your knee there are few areas which are suitable to place the aforesaid cup and plate as well as the numerous papers that he usually accumulated around him while researching the news story he was to write.

He had for the moment put to one side Douglas Wright, the fugitive. Instead, he was grappling with a news story he was assigned. It involved tracking down a local councillor who was supporting planning permission for a large shopping centre. It had attracted a lot of bad feelings from local retailers afraid that such a development would hit their businesses. All Tony wanted was some quotes from the official putting his point of view to balance out the hostile shopkeepers. The councillor was being elusive.

When Tony's phone rang part of him hoped it might be the councillor. However, his hope was dashed when Jane Ward greeted him.

"I thought you might want to know what I've found out concerning that office block you were asking me about."

"Fire away Jane, my pen and pad are at the ready."

129

"First up, a potted history. All the original buildings along Kingsway were built between 1903 and 1905. Good old-fashioned stone-built structures in lots of different styles including neoclassical and neo-Baroque, not that I'd know what either of those two looked like. As I recall they're majestic-looking buildings along that road, whatever style they're in.

"Anyway, you wanted to know about one in particular. For most of its life it was a bank with related offices upstairs. Back in the eighties, the whole building was taken over by the government who leased the ground floor back to the bank, they, the bank that is, used it as a local branch. The government used the building up until two thousand and sixteen when it was sold to a private investment company. No doubt part of some cutbacks to save a few pounds here and there.

"Right, now into the detail from the nineties that you were asking about. The inland revenue used floors one, two and three. They were not so much tax inspectors, more those who formulate policy and stuff, backroom staff. The fourth floor was at the time Customs and Excise, the VAT men to you and me. It seems they were VAT inspectors and enforcement teams who investigated fraud and the like."

"Like car dealers avoiding VAT?" Tony interrupted.

"Maybe, I would think that was the sort of thing they got up to. The fifth floor is more of a mystery.

"I managed to get hold of some floor plans from the local planning office as well as some details from the national archives. The fifth floor was clearly used by a government department, but there's no indication of what that department was. The floor plans I dug up from National Archives have all sorts of information: desk positions, where different grades sat, who had private offices and so on.

"The fifth-floor blueprint is very much a technical plan, the sort of thing given to the builders: where to put the phone points, where desks and cupboards go. But nothing to indicate what department used it or the grades of staff that sat there.

"There is only one clue, a handwritten note in the margin, someone wrote 'CHINIC 8' whatever that means. I'll dig around for you to see what I can find, but it's a bit of a needle in a haystack."

As Jane spoke, Tony made notes on his pad listing the key points. He wrote down the word 'chinic' then the number '8'. It was a long shot, yet feasible he thought, did Neal have connections to this chinic? He added the following: 'Neal', 'MI5', 'Kingsway'.

"On to refurbishments. When the government took over the place, they of course modified it to suit their purposes. All floors underwent another upgrade during 1998 and 1999. The next upgrade came when the government sold the building and new owners took it over. They gutted the whole building in 2017, preparing it for smaller offices and companies who were permitted to rent half or a quarter of a floor."

"Wow, you certainly dig deep, Jane! I think I told you the stuff I showed you had been found on the fifth floor. Could that floor and this CHINIC8 have been some sort of covert team of VAT inspectors, you know top secret?"

"Could well be. The car dealer might have been under investigation for a while, maybe that was why the news cutting was found up there, left behind, some evidence that they'd mislaid. It's possible that was the reason for him just getting a suspended sentence, as they cocked up the prosecution evidence. I presume you know all about Douglas Wright, the guy on the run from the police?"

"I might do," Tony answered cautiously as he added to his list, 'VAT fraud'. It would make sense for the Revenue and Customs to investigate the creative accounting of Mickey Ross and his car sales.

"What do you know about Douglas?" he asked.

"Well, you know that once I start, I can't stop digging and researching. That's why I have my family history going back to seventeen-ninety."

"That's a lot of research," Tony commented. One Sunday, when he was bored, he had started to research his family history and only got as far as his great-grandparents before losing interest.

"I guess with your background you'd have found out that Douglas has a criminal record. He did time for stealing cars when he was in his twenties. Nothing after that though, until he supposedly killed his wife."

"I do have to admit I didn't know that or think to ask that question. A car thief! Thanks Jane, things are now beginning to make sense."

Chapter 14

His mother was not going to like what he was doing, but there again, there were few things that she did like about Liam. The way he dressed was one thing, 'too flamboyant', she would say. She also did not approve of his textured cropped hair, whereas he loved it, as did his boyfriend, which was something else she did not approve of.

He dialled the number and asked for the extension his grandfather had written down. The phone rang three times before a man answered it, "Matthews."

With a dry throat, Liam asked, "Can I speak to Brigadier Howard Harvey, please?"

"You sure you have the right department, we're a government office, nothing to do with the military."

"It's the number I was given."

"Hang on, let me ask."

Mundane music played into Liam's ear as he held on for the reply. He did not wait long.

"Sorry, no one here of that name."

"But you're MI5, I know that the Brigadier told me," Liam lied, knowing MI5 would lie to him without any remorse.

"You're mistaken, I work in a boring department. Maybe the man you're looking for was a little boastful about his job."

"I know you British lie all the time. I want to speak to the Brigadier, I need to ask him some questions."

"Look I told you, you're mistaken, you must have the wrong number."

His grandfather had told him on many occasions about the dubious practices and treachery the English soldiers brought to Northern Ireland. 'They will keep the north at all costs' he used to say, 'no matter how many lives they lose, or our brave freedom fighters have to die'. They cannot be humiliated: they will lie and cheat. Never trust the British Government. Now Liam was experiencing it first-hand. He could easily believe that Brigadier Howard Harvey was sitting listening to his call, laughing and smirking.

"You're just a bunch of lying bastards! I'll find him, don't you worry!" Liam cut off the call and threw his phone down onto his bed in anger. His grandfather had always told him, 'You're a Catholic living in Northern Ireland, you'll have to fight until your dying day or just be a slave.'

Liam had no intention of being a slave, he was going to find the Brigadier at any cost.

***

Mickey Ross had been sitting comfortably in his wicker chair. The sun had at last broken through morning clouds and was now warming his bare liver-spotted hands. There was a gentle breeze cutting across the garden as the noisy blue tits were bouncing around the tall shrubs that ensured his privacy. Today he wanted to take things easy, just sit and enjoy his garden. Watch Daniel, his gardener, tidy up the lawn and the bushes, as well as an hour or so deadheading some of the more colourful plants that lined the borders. Mickey considered himself a cactus person, not a gardener, which was why he employed Daniel to make sure the garden always looked neat and pristine. It was also the expected thing in the village. Everyone had a gardener to do the messy work and allow them to enjoy the fruits of someone else's labour.

In his younger days when they had a smaller garden, Mickey enjoyed tinkering around with things horticultural.

Now he was older, pushing even a powered petrol mower around was something he could not be bothered to do. Standing in the warm greenhouse, tending and caring for small slow growing cacti was a far more appealing excuse to avoid sitting down and talking to his wife.

He watched as Daniel stood on a small step ladder and used a petrol hedge trimmer to straighten the tops of a privet hedge that Mickey had inherited when he bought the place. He was always amazed at how Daniel could maintain such a clean horizontal cut. Mickey often wondered if gardeners had built-in spirit levels somewhere in their bodies.

"There's a man here to see you."

Dolly appeared beside him; she had an uncanny way of doing so without any sort of warning. He wondered if she had died years ago and only remained to haunt and annoy him.

"What does he want?"

"He didn't say. Nice, sweet-looking young man."

"Dolly, you find all young men sweet and attractive, don't think I haven't noticed. Does this sweet man have a name?"

"Liam Connor. I think he might be Irish, not that he has a strong accent, but a bit like cousin Hazel."

"Cousin Hazel comes from Liverpool."

"Hmm, maybe he's from there then. Anyway, he wants to see you. Shall I ask him what he wants?"

"Does he look like he is going to kill me?"

"Oh no, he looks...."

"Sweet, yes, you told me. Send him through and we'll see what he wants. And don't bring any tea out either." Mickey sounded exasperated as he stood up from his comfy position ready to receive the sweet young man.

135

Sweet was not how he would have described the young man who followed Dolly into the garden. Liam Conner stood around six feet tall, with one of those modern haircuts which Mickey thought looked stupid. He was not excessively muscular, but there again he looked as if he could handle himself in any bar room brawl. His face was stretched, ending in a long, pointed chin reminding Mickey of Bruce Forsyth. What he did notice was that this man, maybe in his thirties, looked nervous as he took the seat offered. That always worried Mickey, he had learnt from bitter experience that sometimes a person may look nervous, not because they are scared of you, but because they know they are about to stick a knife into you. Cautiously, Mickey sat down and asked the young man why he was here.

"I wanted to ask you about a newspaper story that you appeared in many years ago." Liam handed the press cutting to the older man. He was surprised that Mickey barely looked at the cutting, only glancing at both sides and handing it back to him with a question.

"How did you find me?"

"The bloke who runs the car place you once owned told me where you lived. I just had to ask around a bit and here I am."

"Enterprising. Were you even born when that appeared?" Mickey indicated the paper with his head.

"Yes, I was a toddler at that time. It's just that I think it's my father in the picture."

"I presume you are referring to one of the customers and not me as being your father."

Liam failed to understand the humour in Mickey's voice. Frowning, he at once corrected himself, "Sorry, I wasn't saying you were my father. He's the customer shaking your hand, well, I think he is. My mother says that he never came to England, yet I am sure that's him from the photographs I have seen of him. I wondered if you had some sort of record of the transaction which might confirm that it's my father."

"From what you're saying it sounds like your dad's not around to ask. Where is he?"

"He died when I was a young boy, so I never really knew him, but I do have pictures of him. I can show you one if you want, then you can judge."

"If that was your dad, then I shook hands with him over thirty years ago. I don't recall his name and I have no records going back that far. I have been out of the motor trade for many years now. What I will say is that you're not the first person recently to ask me about this news article, which has made me think back. Although my memory is hazy, I do vaguely recall that the man I was shaking hands with had an Irish accent. You also have a very diluted, yet distinctive Irish accent, am I right?"

"Yes, I was born in Ireland. After my father died my mother and I moved to Kilburn where we've lived ever since."

Liam did not stop there, he went on to speak about his grandfather living with them and how he had uncovered the newspaper article amongst his grandfather's belongings. He wanted some answers, he was just not sure of the questions he should ask. When Mickey inquired, he confessed that he did not know exactly how his father died. All he had ever been told was that his father was killed during the troubles and that there was no reason to drag up old conflicts now, that peace appeared to have descended on Northern Ireland.

Sympathy for other people was not something that Mickey often felt. Maybe it was because he had never had a son of his own, but Mickey did feel sorry for Liam. Innocently asking questions of his mother about a father he never really knew, only to find that she was not inclined to share much with him at all.

"Look Liam, I'm not sure exactly what you have made of that article or me, but I just want to make it clear that I was no ordinary car salesman. I sold cars in the main to villains. As I said I have been thinking about that transaction since the day I was asked and odd scraps of facts come to mind.

"That could be your father, I've no idea if he was Irish, but I thought he had that accent. He wanted a white van, wasn't fussy about the make, and he had cash. Someone had told him I could cut him a good deal without asking many questions. He gave me cash, a name, and an address, I gave him the van, everyone was happy. Once that article was published, I was turned over by the Old Bill and the name and address that your father, if he was your father, had given me was false. I wasn't surprised in the least.

"All I am saying is that you seem like a nice chap. If that was your father, then he was up to no good. Knowing what the Irish were like at the time, he was no doubt about to rob a bank or a security van.

"Take some advice from someone who has conducted business with criminals for most of his working life. If your dad was about to do a bank and a couple of years later, he dies and your mother doesn't want to talk about it, I would suggest you let sleeping dogs lie. The answers might not be the ones you want to hear."

"What about this name?" Liam turned over the press cutting and showed Mickey the name.

Mickey let out a low whistle, the MI5 did not endear him to say too much more. Maybe Liam's father had been more than just a bank robber.

"Sorry, never heard of him."

In silence Liam thought about the warning he had been given. Possibly this old man was right, maybe his father did commit crime, even so if he was the victim of a gangland killing, Liam wanted to know. It was only right, that he should know who his father really was and not some image concocted by his mother to protect his feelings.

"You said I'm not the first person to ask you about the story recently, who was the other?"

This young chap was not going to give up on finding out the truth about his father, which part of Mickey regretted. He feared it would not end well. He already had doubts about Tony being a real reporter, he could still smell a rat. Then there was the writing on the back of the press cutting, which only served to stoke his fears. But who was he to thwart someone's personal quest to find the truth?

Not that Mickey was being charitable, there was going to be something in it for him, there always was an angle. After Tony Vercoe had left, there was something about the guy which bugged and worried him. Cautiously he had asked some questions, dug a little deeper, spoken to a couple of friends. Now he knew more about Mr Vercoe, just not enough.

At that point, he had not been sure what he should do, maybe just leave things, forget about the press cutting and the nosy reporter. Now with young Liam in front of him, there was an opportunity, an opportunity that he was not going to miss out on.

"A reporter called around with the same press cutting as you have, asking questions. Not that I could give him any answers. I have his phone number that I am happy to give you. He might have some answers for you, he might have some additional information or perhaps nothing, I have no idea. I have a word of warning for you, I don't think he is a real reporter, too formal. I can smell out potential trouble and I'm not often wrong."

Mickey wrote out the phone number of Tony Vercoe and handed it to the young man with a warning. "Be on your guard." He hoped Liam was listening.

Chapter 15

"Aren't darkrooms a thing of the past?" Tony asked, as he peered over the shoulder of a truly short man, who had to stand on a small stool to reach the photographic enlarger.

"They are really. You must know, all newspapers now have digital cameras and standing in a chemical-filled room, only lit by very dim red light, does not sit well with modern-day health and safety," Robert replied from the stool that made him almost eye level with Tony. "But they indulge me and have let me keep this dinosaur of a room so I can play with negatives and old black and white prints when I like."

Discovering the room had been a revelation to Tony, having worked at the newspaper for a couple of years, he never imagined there was such a place deep in the basement of the building. It was only when he asked his editor where the best place was to get old 35mm black and white negatives printed did his boss laugh and reply, "You need to speak to Basement Bob."

Tony had heard of Basement Bob but had only met him once, when searching for some background on a story. Basement Bob, or to use his correct name Robert Marsh, oversaw old file copies of the paper, an archivist, as he liked to call himself. With fewer and fewer editions and physical copies of the newspaper, he was also awarded the chore of maintaining all paperwork that needed to be stored to comply with company and accounting laws. Robert spent his days in the artificially lit basement, occasionally entertaining reporters who needed information. On the whole, his working life was close to that of a hermit.

The arrival of Tony so near to the time he was to go home at first annoyed Robert. He often thought that reporters had little regard for anyone else. Just because they chose to work odd hours did not mean he should deviate from his regular nine-to-five job.

His mood changed when he saw the roll of black and white negatives. He beamed at Tony as if his horse had just won the Epsom Derby. It might now be after five, but Basement Bob liked darkroom printing.

Unbeknown to most of the staff, Basement Bob had an arrangement with the editor. As well as shelves and shelves of newspaper copies, he also looked after boxes and boxes of old press negatives taken years before the advent of electronic photography. In his spare time, and at his own expense, he stocked the photographic darkroom with all the materials needed to produce black and white prints. Robert had never taken photographs himself; he was far too shy. Yet, in the isolation of a darkroom, he revelled in the process of producing images from the past, pictures he tried to make as perfect as possible. He had as a young boy wanted to be a darkroom technician, however photography had moved on before he could start. In the basement he could indulge himself in his childhood dream.

He unrolled the film and held it up to the dim red light. "Just one ten by eight print of each negative, is that right?"

"Depends on what we see in each print. If there is something I want a closer look at, then I'll have an enlargement of that one."

"Right, let's get to work."

Once more on his stool, Robert carefully fed the film strip into the enlarger, lining up the projected image onto the masking board. Skilfully, he adjusted the focus, then turned off the lamp. A sheet of photographic paper was placed into the masking board. He turned the enlarger lamp on for a few seconds before transferring the exposed paper into a dish of developer. Together he and Tony watched as an image gradually appeared. When Robert judged it to be right, he pulled it out of that dish and put it into the fixer dish. The process was then followed by a wash before he turned on the normal lighting and together, they looked at the first result.

"Looks good to me," Tony commented, only to be slapped down by Robert.

"Could do with a bit more contrast, I don't like wishy-washy shadows. I think I'll use a grade three paper this time, we'll get better results."

Tony did not understand a word, he just let Robert get on with doing his thing.

Soon Tony was able to follow the process and was confident enough to help with the production of the thirty-six prints. Swishing the exposed paper in the developer, then, once Robert had confirmed it to be okay, he used the tongs to move the print into the fix, then finally he added the print to the others already in the wash tank.

Bent over the focusing glass, Robert spoke, his voice slightly muffled, "Always a bit sad printing old photographs, I always think of the photographer who took them. Working out the exposure, thinking about the composition, wondering if he should wait a bit longer or just go for it. These I guess, being candid photos, Clive would have been firing them off every time the guys in the picture faced the camera. Even so, he never managed to get them all facing the camera, that would have been a tall order."

"Did you know Clive Shenton, the photographer whose by-line is on the press cutting?"

"Never knew him exactly," Robert admitted as he adjusted the focus once more, "knew of him. He was a well-respected snapper, took some good pictures for the paper, like these. Had a knack of hiding in plain sight and getting great photos. He might have been working for our rivals, but you could not deny his talent, such a waste."

"How do you mean?"

"You're relatively new here, so, I guess you would not have heard, it's a bit of a folklore story amongst photographers. He died in a darkroom, just like this. One of the film-developing tanks had some faulty wiring on the heating element. He walked in one day, unloaded his film in total darkness, felt his way to the metal tank and as soon as he touched it, it killed him in one big flash. Ruined the film and ruined his life; he died instantly."

"Isn't any of this wiring ever checked?"

"Back in the day, things were a little more cavalier. Of course, there were all sorts of rules and regulations. The COSHH regs were just coming in. But photographers, especially press photographers, liked the danger and the excitement of their job. Worrying about the fumes from chemicals or getting electricity near water wasn't something they ever worried about."

"A tragic accident and he was no more. When was this?"

"His death: October, ninety-one, about a year after these photographs were taken. Big funeral and a big centre spread in his paper, even we carried the news in a respectful sort of way. It wasn't the time to cry out about poor safety as our news rag was in the same situation. At least things were tightened up after that. I always think it also accelerated the change to digital photography."

"There was no question it was anything but an accident?"

This caused Robert to stop what he was doing and step down from his perch which meant he had to look up to Tony who was still moving an emerging print through the chemicals.

"You mean the photographer dying in the October and two months later the reporter on this story trying to kill himself. That question was asked at the time, but nothing came to light that linked either the two accidents or any story they were working on. Too long ago to worry about it now." Robert checked the developing print, gestured his approval and stepped back up onto his stool and exposed another print for Tony to develop.

"You said accidents, I thought the reporter, Archie Walker, tried to commit suicide."

"That's what it looked like, not that I knew the man. But several times I have heard people saying if he was going to top himself, which no one believed he would even consider, then he wouldn't have wasted petrol running his car to suffocate himself. He would have just jumped off a bridge, a lot cheaper. But you should know more than anyone what journalists are like for gossip and hearsay."

They worked in silence, alone with their thoughts, before Tony had a bundle of black and white photographic prints he began to examine.

"What exactly are you looking for?" Robert asked, as he replenished the developer tray with more chemicals.

"I don't really know what I am looking for in these photographs, I just know there must be something in them." Tony stopped at the sixth one, then looked at the seventh one, then back to the sixth one. He compared the two to all the others and bingo, he found a clue.

"Frames six and seven, can we blow them up, this bit of the background beside the office area? There's a bloke who appears and then disappears from the other photographs."

Robert looked, then went through the other prints. "He's only in these two," he confirmed, "I'll blow them up for you. Hopefully they are sharp enough to get a reasonable image of the face."

Ten minutes later, together in the darkroom, they turned on the white light to examine the freshly enlarged prints. "Not the best exposure I've ever done, very grainy, but I suppose you can make out the main features of the man, although he might have changed since he was caught in these photographs. I wonder if he's still in the area?"

"Oh yes he is," Tony asserted, "I know exactly where to find him."

Chapter 16

"You're hurting me!"

Which was exactly what Tony meant to do. He had one hand squeezing George's neck and pinning him against the entrance hallway. A framed print of some dull-coloured landscape had fallen to the floor and broken as George's body hit the wall. Tony's other hand slammed the door shut; he wanted no prying eyes watching him intimidate George.

"You were at Mickey's car lot the day he was photographed. Now you had better tell me the truth, the whole truth and nothing but the truth, or so help me God, I will break every bone in your body if I even get a whiff you are lying. What was going on that day?"

Without waiting for an answer, Tony dragged George into his cluttered kitchen, threw him onto a chair, which recoiled from the impact and hit the table, knocking a pile of model railway magazines to the floor.

"Well?" Tony stood over the slumped figure of George, who was rubbing his neck.

"Alright, alright, just calm down. Back in the old days, I did a lot of ducking and diving. Earnt a few quid here, a few quid there, times were hard..."

"Cut the Dickens' hard life crap. Why were you there, at Mickey's car lot, that particular day?"

George quickly capitulated. He knew he had no choice or enough time to concoct a story that Tony might believe. "Two Irish guys I met in a pub wanted a van, were paying cash and didn't want it traced. I told them I knew a guy and took them round to see Mickey. I sat in the office while they did their deal. Mickey gave me a 'pony' for my trouble.

The tight-fisted Irish didn't even buy me a drink. They just drove off in their white van. I went back to the pub. It's that simple."

"Nothing is that simple. Why not mention it to me the first time you saw the press cutting? You must have known you were there on that day. When the paper was published and Mickey got turned over, you would have known through the grapevine that it was the same day you took the Irish."

"I forgot."

Without warning, Tony lunged forward and grabbed George's throat again. "Let me help you remember. You're still working for Mickey, aren't you? Up to no good? I want the whole truth now!"

"Odd jobs, that's all," George gasped the words, trying with both his hands to release some of the pressure on his throat to no avail. Tony was younger and fitter, his hand remained firmly in place.

"Mickey sells bent cars, you steal cars. Doug, I understand, did the same. He was, so you told me, unemployed, yet had four grand in his drawer. What were you all doing?" Tony released his grip.

"Alright, alright, just don't hurt me. Doug and I were chatting one night over a drink or two. Talking about old times, this and that. He said a couple of things that made me think he'd been inside. Little clues, little things only ex-cons say. Anyway, I ask him outright. He admits he was inside for car crime, which I thought was ironic, me also dabbling in cars from time to time. But you know that.

"We chatted about this and that. The old days of easy alarms, soft door locks and how things have changed with hi-tech alarms making our job tough. Not that we were planning to do anything at the time. But the more we talked, the more I could see he had a real interest in cars and the technology that makes them work or at least how to get into them.

"I knew Mickey was doing some part-time stuff around getting high-value cars for some of his better-off clients. I figured with Doug's tech skills we could help Mickey get his stock. We all had a drink round Mickey's house one night. He liked Doug, liked the idea and two weeks later we got our first job, he wanted an Audi R8. We went out and got one for him and got a good payday. Happy days."

"Just the one car?"

"What do you think? Once a week, sometimes twice, or nothing for a couple of weeks. When Mickey had an order for a car, he called us, told us the make, the model, and the year he wanted, preferred colour too. Often, he even told us which driveway it could be found on. It was a nice little earner."

"Your partner in crime then dies under a car, the police write it off as an accident and everyone is happy. You have lost a useful partner, but at least the police aren't snooping around. Why ask me to help find his relatives, when I bet, he told you he wasn't who he said he was. What's my part in this scam?"

George took a packet of cigarettes out of his pocket dragging heavily on the smoke as he lit it. He looked at Tony. Maybe considering just what he should say, what he might say, or what he had to say. Judging by the mood that Tony had shown so far, there was not much leeway to embellish or conceal. It was going to have to be the truth, something he preferred to avoid. In the past, he had found telling the pure truth came back to bite him.

"I didn't honestly care about any relatives even if he had any. I told you that to get you involved. When you

149

found the stuff about his wife and him being the killer, that was a total surprise to me and something I never imagined of him."

Tony sat down and tapped his fingers on the table. "I'm getting bored. Why did you call me then, if it wasn't to find out about his relatives?"

"I couldn't tell the police, they would have dug deeper, no doubt stumbled into my little arrangement with Mickey. I couldn't risk that, so I thought with your background you would be the best person to help me. To be honest, Tony, I think Doug was murdered. I wasn't going to tell the police that. But he didn't die in an accident, of that I'm certain."

"Explain and let's just stick to bullet points, not go around the houses."

"Doug was safety mad. You might not know it, but he worked in demolition, you had to be careful else a wall would end up on top of you. I never saw him work on a car without axle stands. He would never have gone under a car with just a wheel jack holding it or work on a car after drinking. Someone put him under there, I know it. Maybe he was dead before they dropped the car on him. I don't know, but someone killed him. I was thinking, you being an ex-copper, might be able to help, ask around a bit, see if my worst fear is correct."

"Why didn't you just come out and ask me in the first place?"

"You might have reported my suspicions to the police. You know the same way that as soon as you found out he was wanted you went rushing down to them."

"So, you thought, reel me in gently, feed me a few facts at a time, hook my interest."

"Sort of, but the thing with his wife, well, that all went out of the window."

"If he was hiding out here, who would want to kill him?"

"Blowed if I know, that's the strange thing. He only really knew me and Mickey and we were doing well, had no reason to do him in, we were all making plenty of cash. I was thinking, maybe something caught up with him from his past."

"What about Mickey, would he have any reason to kill Doug?"

The answer did not come at once, George thought about it as though he was weighing up a body of evidence.

"I don't know of any reason. That's the bit that scares me, if it wasn't me or Mickey, then who wants to have poor old Doug killed?"

Back in his car, Tony paused before driving off. He needed time to rearrange some facts, re-order the theories he had been building. Nothing made much sense. The photographer dies in an accident, the reporter tries to kill himself. Doug dies in another so-called accident. Now he has these photographs, he has had a visit from a so-called security service man and a burglary. Tony needed to choose a pathway. The photographs had a value to someone, why and who? Was it in connection with the cars or something else? Cars were not logical, over thirty years had passed since the photo was taken. VAT frauds, stolen cars, aftermath from such crimes do not linger over decades, things are forgotten, times change. Tony added the accidental death of Doug's wife, another victim. The photographs, they were the toxic part of this. They had something in them that someone wanted to hide. Something that still, all these years later, could hurt somebody. Tony needed to examine the photographs and the press cutting once more, the answer had to be in there somewhere.

As he turned the ignition key his phone rang. Leaving the motor running he answered, but before he could speak, he heard,

"Hello, my name is Liam."

Chapter 17

They had always been a poor family. The young Liam lived with his parents in a small cottage on the edge of Nutt's Corner, west of Belfast, where his father worked as a casual labourer on the farms and small holdings around the area. His mother cleaned other people's bigger houses, while young Liam played on strangers' floors.

The countryside seemed to go on forever when Liam was young, playing in fields, scaring the cows, chasing pigeons, running from crows. He loved and missed the open spaces of his childhood. Now sitting on the cool, damp grass of Blackheath he felt at ease, relaxed. Part of him wanted to stay here forever with space to breathe, space to run, space to shout at the top of his voice. Liam wanted to be Liam. He also wanted to know more about his father. He now sought answers to questions he had never thought of before.

Even though they appeared poor when in Ireland, after his father died they had the money to come to England and buy a compact flat in Kilburn. Liam now realised that the money his mother and grandfather had spent on that tiny flat could have bought them a house and several acres of land back in Nutt's Corner.

Maybe Mr Ross was right, if his father had robbed a bank and double-crossed his accomplices, it would explain a lot. Neither his mother nor his grandfather ever clearly explained just how they managed to afford the move to Britain.

As he looked at the phone number he had been given, Liam felt a sense of unease about what he was on the edge of. The car dealer, by his own admission, was a crook.

There was, according to Mr Ross, a doubt over this Tony who said he was a reporter but might be something else. Then there was the name of the Brigadier on the reverse of the cutting that his grandfather had written down, with the term MI5. Liam had read about the way the I.R.A. bankrolled their fight by robbing banks, and that would no doubt attract the attention of MI5.

There was far too much information. Liam had never managed to handle even small scraps of information with the ease of his peer group. At school he always struggled with what his teachers believed to be easy concepts. During each year of his education, he fell further and further behind the rest of the class. The school did try, offering one-to-one lessons, which did help him a little but not enough.

Now, in the big wide world, Liam had a choice to make for himself. He could either get back into his van and continue laying carpets for the rest of his life, holding onto an enchanting image of his father that had been painted for him by his mother, or he could step into the unknown, asking strangers questions to get to the truth. His concern was just what that truth might look like and whose path he would need to cross to get at the facts of who his father really was. In the end would his own congenial version of his father be shattered beyond repair; he had no way of knowing.

He twiddled with the scrap of paper in his hand, hesitating. He needed to speak to Brigadier Howard Harvey. He, if he was still alive, would have the answer. Thinking of what his grandfather would do, Liam made up his mind. He had to be tough and ruthless, not that he had ever shown any such traits, but he would have to if he was going to get anywhere near the truth. With a sense of purpose, he got back into his van and called Tony Vercoe.

"Hello, my name is Liam. Is that Tony Vercoe?"

"Yes," the voice sounded tentative.

"I have spoken to a car dealer by the name of Mickey Ross about a press cutting in which he featured. I understand that you have the same press cutting and wondered if we might meet up and see what else we have in common."

A little too enthusiastically, Liam thought, the invitation was accepted. Tony offered his address, suggesting they meet in about an hour. As Liam started his van, he wondered just who this Tony Vercoe was, to be so confident and eager as to invite a stranger into his house. His mother would not approve, she was always wary of strangers.

***

Liam was not going to lie to himself, he was nervous as Tony ushered him into a kitchen which resembled a temporary office. There was the odour of burnt toast lingering in the air that made him feel hungry, he had not eaten since breakfast.

The cause of the cooking aroma was a teenage girl spreading a thick layer of Nutella on her burnt toast, no doubt a post-school snack. She was introduced to Liam as Isobel, Tony's daughter, and then encouraged by her father to leave them alone. She smiled and complied with his request taking with her a slice of toast on a plate and another firmly fixed in her mouth.

"I hope you don't mind the mess and being in the kitchen, all my notes are here. Grab a seat."

Liam's sense of unease increased as he sat down at the kitchen table. He glanced across at the laptop, the notes, the slips of paper and a pad with odd words on, including

155

'MI5'. The car dealer had mentioned that Tony might not be a reporter and had suggested he could be something more. Maybe he was wrong to meet Tony, maybe Tony was there to deter him, or worse ensure he did not ask too many questions. His grandfather had mentioned 'the missing' when he talked about the troubles, those who, just disappeared without a trace.

"I see you're a carpet layer," Tony casually commented as he settled down at the table.

At once Liam became defensive, this showed Tony must have been researching him, possibly from the moment he had called the department. They would have tracked his call, found out who he was. They would guess he would try and seek out the car dealer, of course they would. No doubt Tony was primed to expect him. He thought it had been strange that Tony was so quick to consent to meeting without knowing him, but if he had been expecting him, then that would explain it.

He wanted to get up and walk away. That would be the easiest option, but in his heart, he knew he had to find out the truth about his father. It was what his grandfather would have wanted, 'whatever the cost' as he had often quoted. There again maybe he might just not understand what was going on. That was an accusation that was often levelled at him. His teachers often pointed at him saying he lived in a fantasy world and was just dreaming, much easier than learning.

"Yes, I go around houses ripping out the old and laying the new," Liam coyly admitted.

"I could do with some new carpet along the hallway and up the stairs, but you're not from round here are you?"

There it was again, this MI5 agent knew all about him, his work, where he lived, no doubt about his upbringing too. He wondered if he knew about his father. If he did, would he tell the son, or leave him ignorant forever. No, the British always kept their dirty secrets, which was what his grandfather had told him.

"No, North London," Liam replied. "Kilburn obviously, an Irish enclave." Liam regretted using the word 'enclave', did it make him sound like a terrorist fighting for his homeland? His heart was beating faster than it should; his thoughts were becoming jumbled.

"It's funny how us Londoners are either north of the river or south of the river. It's almost as if London is composed of two separate cities, south London and north London. I doubt you come south of the river much, if you did, I might have seen your van around."

"My van?"

"Yes, the one you have parked outside."

It was as if his whole body deflated and called him stupid. The van. Of course, the van that he had driven here today and parked right outside Tony's front door. The van was branded, 'Liam, Carpet Fitter' with a north London telephone number on it. Liam relaxed; he had been silly making up such wild stories in his head, although there was still a small seed of disquiet in his mind. He suspected, he was dealing with an agent of the British security services and they could be quite canny at times, his grandfather told him, together with the advice, 'Always be wary of the British'.

"Right, business. I understand that you have a copy of this press cutting," Tony said as he laid his own yellowed clipping on the table.

Liam picked it up. "Yes, the self-same one." He turned over the clipping. "But a different name and number on the back though."

"So I see," Tony admitted as he read the name on the back of Liam's press cutting with its torn edges. Tony confessed to not knowing the name as he pulled some of the newly printed photographs from a hardbacked envelope, "it does seem to be the thing to do with this story, stick a name and a number on the back. I am still hoping to contact the person on the back of my clipping, a newspaper editor. Any luck with your name?"

"None at all."

"But you want to see if it's your father in the picture, I hope these might help." He laid out the ten by eight prints on the kitchen table for Liam to look at.

Liam's big disadvantage was he could not fully recall his father. He had only a hazy distant memory of what he looked like. The only real evidence that he had was old family photographs, faded and fuzzy. His father was not, so he was told, ever keen to have his photograph taken. The only other failproof way was through his mother. But of course, she had taken little interest when he had shown her the cutting, and in the same way, she had little interest in telling him about his father. It was almost as if she wanted to strike their time together from her history.

Liam offered what photographic evidence he could, four faded, dog-eared photographs. Tony studied each one. A proud father holding his newly born son. Three men, each holding a large carp they had caught. A group of men at a bar, pints in hand, cigarettes in mouths. The final one was yet another group, this time holding the Irish flag, five men looking very serious and determined.

Holding them side by side, Tony tried to make out if the man in the black and white newsprint photo was the same as the one in Liam's collection of pictures.

"I'm not convinced Liam, there are similar features, but I just can't be sure. Are these the only photographs you have of your father? Anymore with him on his own? The one where he's holding, I guess, you as a baby, he's looking down at you and not so much at the camera."

"That's all. When I was younger, I asked about my father and if there were any photographs. Mother said that was all she had, and my father was not one for the camera. Grandfather said there had been others, but Mother threw them out after he died. He told me it was one of those things women do when they are in the deepest of despair. Maybe this Brigadier Harvey, if I can find him, might be able to help."

"He might not even be alive now and even if he is, if MI5 don't want you to speak to him then you'll have to point a gun at them to make them change their minds. Why is it so important that you find out if this is your father? Didn't you say your mother told you he never came to England?"

"Yes, but why did Grandfather keep this?" Liam pointed to the newspaper article. "There must have been a reason. I'm just sorry he didn't tell me while he was alive."

"Maybe he didn't want to tell you. Maybe you don't want to find out the story behind this picture. If you say your father died in the troubles, then he could have been on the wrong side of the law. Sometimes the past, if we tease it, it bites back."

"Wrong side of the law! You mean the wrong side of the British law, which was what the troubles were all about. I want to know if my father died a hero or a villain and which one depends on which side of the fence you might be on. Are you able to arrange for me to meet this brigadier?"

"I'm a reporter, I have no sway."

159

Automatically Liam started to wring his hands as if he was dry washing them. It was something he did when he was nervous. It was a habit that the bullies at school picked on him for, well at least one of the habits he was ridiculed for. He decided it was time for him to ask the questions.

"What interest do you have in this car dealer?"

The answer did not come straight away as Tony had looked up to the ceiling while he considered just why he was interested in the story. Liam took this to be a moment that Tony was taking to make up some fiction.

"The press clipping and photographs were concealed by a man who was hiding out from the law. In the end he died, so I can't ask him why he had the cutting, in the same way that you can't ask your father, if it was your father, why he was buying a van in south London. Maybe I am looking for an answer, just like you, so that I can compartmentalise just why Douglas Wright, the guy this stuff belonged to who died under a car, had the cutting in the first place."

"He died as well?"

"Yes, but we know that it was, or at least it appeared to be, an accident. The troubling thing is there have been some other deaths around this story. Possibly that is the reason I want an answer. Why is this story so toxic?"

"But there have been no deaths on my side."

As he spoke Liam realised the meaning of what he was saying, no one he knew connected with the press cutting had died. But his father had died during the troubles, was the press cutting to blame? Then Liam admitted to himself, that the press cutting in his custody had lain buried in his grandfather's possessions for the last thirty years. No one knew he had it until... until he called MI5 asking about Brigadier Harvey. Liam felt afraid. Was he now a target? Questions, Liam hated questions. That was the reason he

160

hated school, too many questions that he had no answer for.

"Maybe not, but the two press cuttings are the same. They must, using logic, present the same danger to whoever thinks they're a threat."

He was in the tiger's den, Liam was convinced. MI5 now knew he was looking for answers that the press cutting might have. This guy in front of him, Tony, had just told him that people die because of the press cutting. Liam was now cornered, or so he thought. Had Tony issued a veiled threat? A reporter or not a reporter, Liam was taking no chances, he stood.

"If you can't help me, then I'd best be off."

"Don't go yet, maybe if we pool our resources, we can get to the bottom of this."

Yes, there it was. Liam could see it now, Tony working for MI5, an agent of the British. He wanted to make sure he stayed close to Liam, so they could track him, feed him false information. That was not going to happen.

"On my own, I'll do this on my own," Liam's voice could not hide his panic.

Scared he left the kitchen without waiting to be shown out. He left gripping the yellowing press cutting. He needed to stay clear of anyone who might be with the Security Services, he was now convinced, however mild Tony seemed, he was working for the British Government.

***

Liam parked in a street in south London, outside a house that he was currently laying carpet following a refurbishment. He squatted, rocking gently, in the back of the van, amongst the gripper rods and carpet off-cuts, away from the driver's seat. He had no plans to be a sitting target and wanted to clear his thoughts and decide what he should do next. He felt threatened and vulnerable.

All he was asking for was the truth. Could that be so bad? What was his father doing at a car sales plot in south London when his mother denied he had ever been to England? Why had his grandfather written down the name of a MI5 brigadier? Where was the connection? They must have the answers but have no need to give them. His grandfather had always been right when it came to the way the British act. 'They couldn't care less about a young man from Northern Ireland who's Catholic. They just don't care.' He was also right when he told a young Liam that the only way to get the government to listen is to be dramatic. Even Tony, one of their own agents, touched on it, 'you have to point a gun at their head'. Yes, he was right. Do something spectacular to get them to sit up and take note.

His grandfather had told him stories of the escapades of the republicans during the troubles. Brave men who fought for what they believed in and were prepared to lay down their lives for. Liam imagined he came from that same stock. He had to take a risk, make them listen. In his jumbled thoughts he could see a plan, just the thing to make them sit up and listen to him.

***

The best thing about working for the Government Security Services, in particular working for Rupert Bell, was the identification you could carry. It allowed Neal to waltz into just about any government or official building he wanted to. It was especially handy when he was on a case, like today, visiting Croydon Police Station. He flashed his credentials, asked to see DC Pete Lewer and he was politely shown through the double security doors and directed to the third floor where the person in question was working.

There were other advantages of a culinary nature. Every government building in Westminster had its own canteen as Neal still liked to call it, the civil servants preferring to refer to it as a staff restaurant. Normally, you would be confined to the staff restaurant in the building you worked in, not so Neal, he could enter any government owned office block and have lunch at the best canteen His Majesty's Government had to offer. Currently that accolade was held by the Foreign Office which ranked top of the charts in Neal's thinking. He spent as many lunchtimes there as possible, plus the walk, he liked to think, did him good.

Once on the third floor amongst the crammed overloaded desks, Neal could see Pete beside a corner window in a deep conversation on his mobile. Slowly Neal walked towards him, he wanted to make a bit of an impression to start with. The shocked look on Pete's face when he saw who was approaching justified the stagecraft that Neal had employed.

Casually, without waiting to be invited, Neal drew up a chair and sat at Pete's desk, waiting for the call to finish. It was not long before Pete's attention turned to his visitor.

"How come they let a friggin' courier into the building? You're meant to wait downstairs until I collect you. What is it now, another errand for your boss?"

"Oh, too many questions for such a young inexperienced detective. They let me in because today I'm not a courier, I'm an investigator, a bit like you, just better qualified and with stronger credentials. I want a word about an ex-colleague of yours, Tony Vercoe. Well, to be accurate, I want to learn a little more about the circumstances under which his wife was arrested and handed over to the courts."

"Can't help you with that," Pete answered instantly, absently gathering some files from his desk and placing them in a pile on the floor. "It wasn't my case, uniformed picked her up and dealt with it."

"That was what the report said, and that was what the uniformed officer who carried out the stop and arrested her told me. He also told me that it was an anonymous tip-off that led to the car being stopped and the subsequent arrest. He added that when he returned with Mrs Vercoe in cuffs, you were on hand to give advice. Tell me, just what made you so good at offering advice in this case? Given how badly you performed in the investigation into the death of Douglas Halifax, oh sorry, Douglas Wright, the real victim."

"You're not my boss, you're not stationed here, I don't give a shit what you think. But to be clear, police officers often help each other. The young officer who brought in Mrs Vercoe, who we all knew was Tony's wife, felt out of his depth after nicking a fellow officer's wife. I gave him support, in that no matter who you arrest, upholding the law is still our paramount reason. And why should you be so interested in a convicted drug dealer?"

Neal smiled, infuriating the young detective. He knew that the law was the overarching reason a police officer becomes a holder of the Queen's Warrant. Neal also knew, that when one of your own comes in, or the wife, then there will be a sense of disbelief and questions asked. They would not stop the law from taking place, but there would not be an assumption that the person was guilty.

"She had never featured on any local intel, no previous, no real proof," Neal pointed out, "yet she was still arrested, charged and found guilty."

"Why does that surprise you? When she was stopped, she was carrying over one thousand pounds in cash and seven wraps of heroin. Not what you would expect a police officer's wife to have, unless of course, you consider her connection to us and no doubt her knowledge of the way we work. She was below the radar, low profile, avoiding detection, until she no doubt upset one of her fellow dealers who called in and told us to pick her up."

He did not want to admit that what Pete had sketched out was a plausible explanation, not unheard of in the annals of drug dealing history. He still had one question.

"A woman married to a serving police officer, with a daughter, and holding down a job as a data analyst is not a typical drug dealer CV."

That had been bothering Neal ever since he had learnt that Mrs Vercoe was arrested, charged and found guilty of PWITS. She was nothing like the average criminal drug dealer, she didn't even have a parking fine or a speeding ticket in her name. She was not brought up on some rough estate, where drugs were being traded day in day out. She had no contact with that part of society. From what he could see he doubted that she even dabbled in drugs while at university.

Families like Mr and Mrs Vercoe, if they decide that the drugs trade is the place to make money, will have the intellect, the cunning and the education as well as the family facade to be a high-level dealer. The sort of person who goes nowhere near the drugs. Always keeping things at arm's length. They do not dirty themselves by dealing on the street. Something was wrong and Neal did not like things being wrong when the justice system is involved.

"People get greedy, they want more and selling drugs in that way, gets them more money than they can imagine. Anyway, what has this all got to do with anything, she was caught, and she is doing her time, why are the Security Service so interested in a two-bit drug dealer?"

"This might surprise you, I think there's a connection between her conviction and the death of Douglas Wright, you know, the Mr Halifax you found under a car."

"That's a wild guess," Pete mocked with a smile. "George, Douglas and their cohorts are more into stealing cars than selling drugs. Never knew much about the deceased Douglas, but George has been around for years, very much old school when it comes to crime. Avoids drug dealing, too many of the younger and fitter generation in it for his liking. To be truthful, can't see a connection."

"If we're being truthful, I'm not asking you to find a connection. I'm the one investigating and looking to have some questions answered."

He would have added, 'annoying young detective' but thought that would be a little too cruel and should have been obvious in the first place. Even so, he could see that Pete was concerned that someone was connecting Mrs Vercoe to a death. Was that for the simple reason that there was an actual connection, Neal did not really think so. Was her arrest suspicious, yes, Neal thought, that was the real question he wanted answered. He also had a gut feeling that Pete knew more than he was prepared to say.

There were not going to be any easy answers for Neal here. He would need to look elsewhere, gather some firm facts and come back to Pete, perhaps then he might be more inclined to share his knowledge.

"Then you had better get out on the street and do some investigating," Pete responded, as his mobile phone rang. He was more than happy to ignore Neal and answered the call.

"Hold on, Tony, just slow down..."

***

Thirty-six recently printed black and white prints were spread over the desk. Jane Ward examined each one thoroughly. "This is the stuff that was found in that building you had me research?"

"Yes, together with a press cutting. There is something in the photographs or the story, I just can't see what."

"Tony, maybe there is nothing. For each questionable event you have told me about, there's a logical explanation. Possibly that's why you cannot see anything, there's nothing," Jane pointed out, in an unhelpful, yet straightforward way.

This was what Tony had asked for, an alternative viewpoint, another examination by an independent person, Jane was that person. Now, as she spoke, Tony began to wonder if the answers she was giving were the ones he wanted.

"Why did Doug keep them, hide them away? There must be a reason."

Jane sighed, sometimes she felt certain reporters just looked for a story where there wasn't one. They badly wanted to be on the edge of a great conspiracy which they were going to reveal and win accolades and admiration from their peers.

"Let's start at the beginning," Jane waved her hand over the prints as if she were going to begin some special magic trick that would make the truth jump out. "The story, a newspaper reveals a car dealer is breaking the law. He's arrested and sentenced. One of his crimes is VAT avoidance. The photos and cutting are found behind a wall in a building which once housed VAT inspectors."

"Is that what the CHINIC thing was?"

167

"Not sure, still poking around, but I guess it will be in the end. So, it should be no surprise to you that the photos and newspaper cutting were at a VAT office. They were simply left behind when they moved. The case would have been closed, so no need for the stuff."

Jane continued. "Next, the Irish guys buying a van. Well, the fact they wanted an unrecorded van would suggest they were up to no good. Don't forget most of this car dealer's customers were villains. And I did a quick search online and I can tell you two months after this picture was taken there was a bank robbery at the Hither Green Branch of Barclays bank. Two men, one with an Irish accent, masked, pulled a gun on the poor old security guard, grabbed the cash – just over ten grand – and drove off in a white van which was later found abandoned and burnt out in Downham. No one was ever charged with the robbery. But it works for what we have in front of us."

"You're telling me I'm coming to the wrong conclusion about this?"

"I'm saying you don't have a conclusion or much of a theory. What I've just told you makes a lot more sense. We live in the real world, which in the main is boring." Jane started to gather up the photographs. "I'll let you know if I find out what CHINIC 8 is, but I suspect it will be some dull government department"

"Maybe you're right." Just as Tony replied, his phone rang.

The display showed that it was Isobel calling. Tony was expecting her to ring, as yesterday she had telephoned exactly as he had asked when she left the school grounds, and once again when she got home. Today she was late, he guessed she had left class and begun chatting to her friends before leaving the school premises. He knew his daughter too well, her excuse would be she called late, she would say, as technically she had only just left the school grounds.

"Mr Vercoe?" The voice was not Isobel's, it was a deep masculine voice with a lilt that sounded Irish. It was familiar.

"Who are you? Why are you using my daughter's phone?"

"It's not who I am, it's who I want to see and you are going to make it happen."

"What are you talking about, where's my daughter?"

"Listen carefully Mr Vercoe, I am going to say this once and then I'm ending the call. I want to speak to Brigadier Howard Harvey about my dead father. I want you to arrange a meeting for me with him. Once I have spoken to him, I will release your daughter without harm. I'll call you tomorrow so you can tell me when I can meet with him."

"Liam, I told you yesterday, I don't know any Howard Harvey," Tony spoke rapidly, he did not want the call to stop just yet.

"You work for the government at MI5, you must know him or know how to contact him. Check your internal directory. I want to speak to him."

"I don't work for MI5, I'm a journalist. You've got this all wrong."

"The British always lie. Get him to see me and your daughter will not be harmed."

"Wait, I can make a call. I might have a way in, but there's no guarantee."

"See, I knew you were lying. Tell him Liam Connor wants a word." The phone went silent.

Tony had trouble focusing his thoughts. There were too many abstract subjects shifting around too fast in his mind to enable him to fully understand just what was happening in his life.

Yesterday he had invited a shy young man into his house, tried to be helpful. Was that the same person on the end of the phone saying he had abducted his daughter.

Kidnap, abduction, strangers in his house, burglaries, press cuttings, black and white photographs, car dealers, murder, government departments, however, he tried to arrange the jigsaw of shards in his head, nothing presented a clear picture, he needed help, and he knew where he was going to get it.

"What was that about?" Jane asked having heard Tony on his mobile.

"If I knew that, I'd know the significance of these photographs."

Chapter 18

"I've got officers knocking on his door as we speak. We'll soon have your daughter back," Pete asserted comfortingly as he joined Tony who had been waiting impatiently in the small cupboard–like room at the police station.

"And you think he'll be there? Waiting at home for us to pay him a visit."

"You know as well as I do, if he's there then he will qualify as the most stupid kidnapper in history. Visiting you the day before, then asking the same question about this brigadier bloke, kind of ties him in before we even start. So he isn't that sharp. Even so, to be honest, Tony, I doubt if he will be there, but always worth a try."

"What about this brigadier person he wants to speak to? MI5 paid me a visit about Douglas Wright; Liam wants to speak to MI5. Give me a number and I'll make a call."

Pete leaned back in his chair and cupped his hands behind his head. "You're a scummy journalist now, all you need to know is that I'll act upon all the information you've presented me. The police will deal with this."

"Pete, you're going to tell me exactly who you called. After finding your wanted man for you, I get an odd visit from someone who first claimed to be from the passport office before admitting he was MI5. I have also been burgled and now my daughter's been kidnapped. To secure her release, this Irishman has demanded that I arrange a meeting with some brigadier from MI5, which even you are aware I have no connection with. You must have instructions in the case file to tell someone about Douglas Wright, I want to know who you told. And before you get all smart acting the detective, you know me well and I am currently running on a very short fuse. Who did you tell?"

The atmosphere in the room darkened in an instant. Pete sat forward, his elbows on the desk, his face so close to Tony that each man could feel the other's breath. The threat and the tension invisibly tied them together.

"You don't get to tell me what to do anymore. You lost that privilege when you resigned from the force. Without a warrant card you have diddly squat over me. Just remember that Mr Vercoe," Pete spat the name out.

"I will remember that in the same way I recall that I was in the force for a lot longer than you have been. I know more procedures and people than you. I would also add that I'm a journalist with an intimate knowledge of some of your indiscretions from the past. They would make good headlines, not to mention losing your job and your wife. Who did you call?"

"It would be your word against mine and for someone who has lost their wife, well, I doubt anyone would bother listening to you," Pete retorted, feeling he had the upper hand in the telling stories stakes. Yes, he was a naughty boy, occasionally lifting cash from drug dealers to help fund his lifestyle, but he didn't think Tony would know about that. Then a seed of doubt germinated in his mind when he recalled just why Tony had left the force, perhaps he did know about the dirty money.

"I need to know who you called. I'll speak to them; I imagine they will have more pull than a bunch of local bobbies."

Cautiously to protect himself, Pete compromised. "It will be better if I call them as part of the investigation. I'll give them the heads up, then I guess they'll be in touch.

That way I'm not sharing confidential information with a journalist. Win-win as I see it."

The threat that Tony had made he knew was not very strong, even so it seemed to have worked. He could try and write a story about how Pete had become a little too friendly with a female victim of domestic violence, spending most shifts at her house. Then there were the periods he spent hours sitting in a café avoiding the real world. Yes, he could try, but he knew at the back of his mind that his editor would not take too kindly to contentious stories that were based on hearsay and Tony's word. As ex-police, maybe he should have gone down the old colleague route, that might have been a lot more productive even with someone as pretentious as Pete. If Pete was going to call his bluff, then Tony would be at his beck and call.

As he gathered his notes, Pete spoke without looking at Tony. "You might be a total prick and not my best mate, but I'm doing this for your daughter, not for you, understood?"

Tony nodded, he knew as he was no longer a police officer, he could do little else.

Chapter 19

The refurbishment of the office was long overdue. Built in the 1950s it had changed little since then, apart from the very occasional coat of a muted colour paint that only added to the dismal atmosphere. The last time the painters had visited Elizabeth recalled, was about five years ago. Now the walls were disfigured with the remains of dried Sellotape and pin holes from the numerous maps that had been displayed. There was also the red wine stain from the Christmas party three years ago when Elizabeth celebrated her promotion with her colleagues in Social Services.

She looked around her dreary office, like her, it was tired. Being in middle management was not all it was cracked up to be. For her it was no longer much about helping people, more about making annual cuts to the budget, trimming back on staff, deciding who she could or could not afford to help. Then there was the constant need to motivate staff in her team, all of them overworked, doing more hours than they should, all driven by the simple mantra of wanting to help people.

In winter Elizabeth froze at her desk. The cast iron radiators might be big and now fashionable, but they only managed to pump out a tepid warmth that never reached hot. In summer she suffocated as the wooden sash cord windows had been carelessly painted over, locking them closed. Even after countless requests to the maintenance department, she had yet to see a man in blue overalls arrive to free the frames.

She straightened the numerous buff folders on her desk, clearing some space in front of her. She had only just arrived at her desk when the call had come from Rita insisting on an immediate meeting. Reluctantly, Elizabeth agreed. Rita was on her way.

Not all staff were like Rita. Most of them were reasonable and understood that Elizabeth had to balance budgets, pacify the directors above her and still do her best for her staff. Rita did not see things with such a practical outlook. Rita was a social worker who saw a family that she wanted to defend and then defended them tirelessly until another family came along whose needs seemed to be better, then the first family would be pushed to one side. Staff like Rita were the ones that made Elizabeth's life difficult. Blunt, to the point, brash and belligerent, was Rita all over. An early morning meeting could only mean trouble.

Rita strode in purposefully, clutching a thick file and wad of papers, she had a frown across her forehead and a resolve in her eyes. Elizabeth wished she had taken today as annual leave.

"It's the Vercoe family. I understand from the police that the daughter has been abducted by some criminal. I think it's high time that we start procedures to get the daughter, Isobel, into our care. I am sure Mr Vercoe will not agree to us taking care of Isobel, so it will need to be a care order. I am happy to start the process with your approval."

Sometimes it was best to sit back and speak slowly to Rita. That was the only way Elizabeth had learnt to deal with her unbridled enthusiasm, an eagerness that had often led her Social Services team into murky waters that resulted in harsh criticism of their work.

"Firstly, Rita, it might be better to wait until she is released from her captives. Let the police get on and do their job. It will be hard to place her in a safe environment until she's both safe and free."

The sarcasm was lost on Rita.

"Then once she has been released and we can fully understand the circumstances of her abduction, it may well exonerate Mr Vercoe of any blame. This isn't the time to rush off to the courts for a care order."

"Wouldn't it make sense to put the care order in place, so that as soon as she is released, we can act on it?"

When Rita had a bee in her bonnet, she was like a terrier nipping away at someone's ankles, would not give up. Just why she was so fixated with Mr Vercoe, Elizabeth could not comprehend, nor could she get a reason out of Rita.

"Look at it this way, Rita. Suppose I agree to you going and getting your care order so that you can snatch Isobel away from her father the moment she is released. Apart from not being the most appropriate time, I just wonder what happens if things don't go well with the abduction. Imagine, God forbid, that something terrible happens to Isobel, but supposing it does, then there will be questions about our involvement. Some will no doubt say, 'why did we wait until she had been abducted before we sought a care order?' We will all be in the dock and as ever it will be our fault for not acting fast enough. Let's wait, once she has been released and we know the reasons, then come back and we'll talk about a care order."

Rita gathered up her papers, sighed loudly in a disapproving way and walked out of the office without a word. Another round to me, Elizabeth thought, she wondered how many more rounds she could survive.

Chapter 20

Victoria Tower Gardens South overlooks the River Thames. Abutting the House of Lords, the gardens are a tranquil setting for office workers to eat their lunch or stretch their desk-fatigued legs. Situated in the middle of the Government Security Zone, it is surrounded by ministerial buildings, government department hubs and the constant ebb and flow of high-ranking civil servants. Walk or drive along any street within the security zone and you'll notice the cameras tracking and watching you. Nothing goes unnoticed.

That was just how the area had been planned, a constant eye watching over those important people who make decisions that affect our daily lives, ensuring their safety. Yet, there were some high-ranking personnel, including some members of parliament, who did not want to be watched all the time. They did not want everything tracked and recorded. Where else could they carry on their love affairs, meet lobbyists they should not be seen meeting or talk with accomplices to plot and manipulate political shenanigans. It was agreed, for those in the know, that Victoria Tower Gardens South would be a haven for such activities.

No camera ever spied on those moving around the gardens. Once you stepped off the pavement and onto the lush grass, you were off the grid. There was no evidence to indicate what you were doing in the gardens, who you were meeting, or who you might be kissing.

Sitting on a bench overlooking the Thames was Neal Matthews. He knew the significance of this green space as Rupert had once told him. The first time Rupert had wanted a special one-to-one meeting with him, he arranged a rendezvous in these gardens, which had surprised Neal into asking, 'What is wrong with just popping into your office?' Rupert had been firm when he articulately replied, 'In our line of work there are at times special, very important tasks that we have to carry out. We perform these based on a raft of often sensitive information. Not everyone would understand or even agree to some of our duties, yet we carry them out regardless. The fewer people involved, the easier it is to deal with complex situations.' For Neal a simple, 'this meeting must not go on the record' would have sufficed just as easily.

Neal sat relaxed knowing he was not being watched and when Rupert sat down next to him, to onlookers they would just appear to be two gentlemen passing the time of day in gentle conversation. He was concerned about what he was going to be asked to do.

"Another job?" Neal queried, without looking at his park bench companion.

"Before I start, can you explain to me why you're wearing shorts with a hideous pattern on them and flip-flops on your feet, foot attire which I would consider dangerous on the streets of London. Plus, why the Willy Wonka t-shirt? Are you on holiday nearby?"

"You sent me a text less than an hour ago, 'Urgent meet, VTGS, ASAP?' I am on leave today, yet lucky for you I was nearby, so here we are. If you prefer me to dress for the occasion, I could pop back to my home, change and return in say three hours. Would that suit you better or am I embarrassing you sitting here?"

"I'll cope. Another job, you asked. I would describe it as an addendum to a previous piece of work: Tony Vercoe."

"What's he done now?"

"Not so much the man, more the daughter. She has found herself to be the subject of a kidnapping and is currently being held at an unknown location. The local bobbies called our department with the feeble excuse that as we wanted to know about the late Douglas Wright, they thought we might be interested. Jumping to conclusions as normal, connecting my department to this kidnapping. They have woven this link because Tony Vercoe reported the death of Douglas and now his daughter has been kidnapped. The kidnapper wants to speak to a person in MI5, so they have assumed, by some flawed logic, that we are MI5. All they had was a phone number, local police do jump to conclusions."

"MI5, what a silly notion," Neal's voice hid the fact that he had in a way admitted to Tony the department he worked for. He reflected on the irony that he knew very well that Rupert did not work for the 'Policy and Enforcement Review Team' as his job description indicated.

"Exactly my thoughts Neal. I'm glad we are seeing eye to eye on the matter. Nevertheless, it's prudent that we help Mr Vercoe with the safe recovery of his daughter, which I would prefer to do without the help of the local bobbies. Hence, we are sitting here on a very pleasant afternoon having a discussion. You will oversee investigations. I want you to go back and see Tony Vercoe and work with him to get his daughter back and find out a lot more about this representative of the Connor family. The Irish culprits who want to speak with a brigadier."

Neal considered the task and was slightly concerned that his first impression of the whole thing appeared to be a little messy. It also mystified him as to why Rupert appeared very concerned regarding the Irish connection.

He quickly pointed out his concerns to Rupert, "We're not dealing with some fool in Mr Vercoe. He was a serving police officer and is now a journalist. I can't turn up having already told him I am from the passport office, and now tell him I am going to help with his problem and by the way, Mr Vercoe, the local police are off the case. He's either not going to believe me or think the world has gone mad. Can't you arrange for the police to be on the sidelines? I'll be there as some sort of negotiator because maybe the Irish guy is an illegal of some sort."

As Neal turned to look at Rupert, a thick plume of pipe smoke engulfed him catching his breath. Once Rupert had exhaled all the smoke he spoke as he continued to look out over the Thames.

"If Mr Connor, our Irish needle in the side, wants to speak to MI5, then that's who you will be representing. It will also be the reason the local bobbies aren't involved. He's Irish, hint there is a terrorism threat here. We might have the Good Friday Agreement; we do not have a full peace just yet. Even the wary Mr Vercoe will believe that version of events and if he doesn't then make him. Given the fact that he thinks you're from the passport office, well, he'll understand that we need to be discreet in our line of work. I am sure you can work your magic on him. He is, I am sure, more concerned with getting his daughter back than which department of the government you're working for. If he hasn't already worked out who you are."

"If I need additional resources, do I hire them?"

"No, any resources you might need I will provide you with, if appropriate. I suggest if things get too messy, you work with Simon. I don't want to have any connection to this kidnapping. If it goes wrong and the girl ends up dead, then you and Simon will be taking the flack."

Neal knew Simon all too well and did not want to work with him again.

Two years ago, Neal had worked a case on behalf of Rupert. A simple case of a civil servant passing on sensitive information to the Guardian newspaper. That leak not only embarrassed the government of the time but also led to the resignation of a high-ranking minister. Neal had worked independently of an internal investigation which sat on its hands until he had the whistle-blower's name. Everything had pointed to an advisor who believed the government were morally wrong. Neal sympathised with his view and secretly thought the guy had done a good thing. However, as instructed, he handed everything he had over to Simon, thinking that he had performed well in uncovering the perpetrator of the leak until he saw a headline ten days later. The advisor was found dead hanging from a tree in a forest. The news story implied that the internal investigation planned to question him over the leak. The poor man had taken his own life. What Neal knew of the advisor, and he knew a lot, did not make him believe anything close to suicide would have crossed his mind. But he could imagine and believe a scenario where Simon arranged every detail to make the entire thing look like a suicide.

Yes, Neal knew Simon was capable of anything. He was very wary of him being anywhere near anything he might be doing.

"I'd rather not work with Simon, if that is okay with you. Not the right attitude for this case."

"Well ensure you work with very few, very trusted operatives, who need to know nothing about the whole operation."

"Who does this Connor man want to speak to? You mentioned a brigadier."

"A Brigadier Harvey, but you can leave that bit to me."

"The same name that was asked for over the telephone. And are the photographs still something you are interested in?"

"That should go without saying. I am hopeful that once you have recovered Mr Vercoe's daughter, alive hopefully, then as you try and ascertain just why his daughter was picked on, Mr Vercoe might well reveal the location of those photographs and, equally important, the negatives."

"What about this Brigadier Harvey, do you want me to trace him as well?"

"I told you," Rupert sounded irritated, "leave that to me. I am confident that I can bring him into negotiations and resolve this whole ugly business. All you need to do is get this irritating Irish man to come to the negotiating table."

As Neal walked away, Rupert tapped his pipe against the metal leg of the bench, clearing the warm ashes out onto the pathway. Looking for thirty-year-old photographs was one thing, but the arrival of an Irish man into the equation was just the sort of thing he had always feared.

There were more than just one Connor family residing in Britain, some were Irish, some were not. There was, Rupert knew, one particular family called Connor who would also know of the existence of Brigadier Howard Harvey. The older members of that family knew part of the story. They had remained silent over the past decades exactly as they had promised.

Rupert recalled a young boy, too young at the time to understand what was going on. A mental calculation placed that boy being now in his early thirties, that dangerous time when they start to ask questions of the past. He could now be seeking answers to why his father had not been around to bring him up.

Three months was all Rupert wanted. It had haunted him for thirty-odd years, why now when he could see the finishing line ahead of him. Why did the Connor's boy want to speak to the Brigadier now? Rupert had to find a way of delaying the inevitable questions that would be asked. If the boy had not taken the daughter, then there would have been a chance of kicking the can down the road. Three months more was all Rupert needed. With a young teenage girl being held hostage, he knew that he would not now get the three months he needed. With that in mind, he called Simon to make him aware of the situation and what might be required.

Chapter 21

Tony did not appreciate being told to 'stay calm', how could he? His daughter was locked away in some unknown place held captive by a man making demands on him that he could not fulfil alone. He was being forced to rely on others, something he hated doing. The night had been a long agonising one for Tony. Fitful periods of restless sleep between calls to the police station, pleading for news. The only response from Pete was, 'relax we are all over this like a rash'. The casual response did nothing to allay his fears, he no longer had much faith in the police. Solving crimes seemed to have taken second place to producing favourable statistics. They had visited Liam's home and spoken to his mother who informed them, unsurprisingly, that Liam was not there. The police had no new ideas, they could only wait to see if he called again.

He tried willing his phone to ring, that did not work. The kidnapper remained silent, waiting for something from Tony that he did not know how to give. He had no connections to MI5 and did not know anyone called Howard Harvey, with or without a military rank.

Tony's phone did eventually ring. He hoped Pete had some good news.

"Knowing how much you despise us down here at the nick," Pete sounded tired, "you'll be pleased to know we're no longer on the case. As I promised, I did speak to the specialist crime group, or whoever they are, and told them about the kidnap and the demand for a conversation with the Brigadier. Now they're in charge of the case."

"You've just handed over the case to a bloke on the phone who you have only spoken to twice! How the hell do you know he's not a crank? Do you have a name?"

"I'm not important enough to know who they are. I called the guy, gave him the details, the same people that I told Douglas had died. They thanked me and told me they would get back to me."

"And you put the phone down," Tony interjected.

"I haven't finished yet; you need to take a breath. Twenty minutes later, I get a call from my Chief Inspector. I am told and reassured that another department has taken over the investigation and they would be contacting you. There you have it."

"When are they going to contact me?" Tony snapped.

"That's not for me to say. I guess they do their own thing and will be calling you sometime this morning. How should I know? I'm off the case and off to grab some sleep. Have a nice day," came Pete's sarcastic comment.

The phone went dead meaning Tony did not have the chance to ask any more questions. He felt he was now in a worse place than he had been before Pete's phone call. At least then he had a number and a person he could harass, now he had nothing.

During the next two hours he tried to occupy himself. Googling names, car thief rings, kidnaps, anything that made him feel he was contributing something to finding his daughter. Nothing he did seemed useful. He called on his land line as many of Isobel's friends as he could. He did not have that many numbers and those he did call did not answer, no doubt at school learning as his daughter should have been. Now she could be anywhere. The doorbell interrupted his chaotic, anxious thoughts.

Tony opened the door, not that surprised to see Neal Matthews standing there, the so-called passport man, with a half-smile across his face.

"I understand you have an issue that I might be able to help you with; can I come in?"

"What the bloody hell has this to do with you?"

"Let's go inside, sit down and I will explain everything frankly to you. You need to stay calm."

"Why is everyone telling me to stay calm? I can't stay calm; my daughter's in danger."

"We don't know that yet; let's talk with the door closed."

Neal sat down, relaxed, and looked around the room to see what had changed since he last sat on Tony's comfortable settee. All around was the debris of a man who had spent the night without any or with very little sleep: cups and mugs, plates with half-eaten sandwiches on them and one piled with empty crisp packets. Neal noted that Tony was evidently a salt and vinegar man, odd, he had him down as a smoky bacon kind of guy. Tony remained standing, scowling at his visitor.

"You really ought to sit down and rest a while. There's little we can do until your Irish friend calls again."

"What's all this about, has his passport run out?" Tony queried in a sarcastic voice. "Don't tell me, I can guess, government cutbacks, MI5 has been disbanded and you guys have taken over police work."

"Sarcasm does not flatter you, Mr Vercoe. Do you mind if I call you Tony? I guess we will be working closely together over the next few days?"

Tony did not answer. He remained standing with his arms crossed.

186

"Well, Tony, officially I'm allowed to tell you our Irish friend, who goes by the name of Connor, is somewhat of an illegal immigrant, not in the cross-channel variety, it's just he has several passports which don't belong to him. For a reason we have yet to ascertain, he has picked on your daughter as some sort of leverage to force our hands, but that isn't going to happen."

"That makes no sense at all."

"Few things do in this world; you must know that being an ex-police officer. You also know from our previous meeting, the passport office is not my, how shall I say, prime employer. The periphery of human behaviour is an unfathomable place so I'm here to be a lighthouse in the fog of confusion to guide your daughter safely home. What department I'm from is irrelevant, what you should be asking is can I help you and the answer is, yes, I can."

"Why would someone sounding like Bob the Builder want to help me?"

"Because this Bob the Builder, as you put it, wants to help and bring this matter to a satisfactory conclusion. Can I have a tea or coffee while we are waiting for your phone to ring?"

"But you admitted you don't like excitement, or the danger of front-line work, so why has the passport office, or whoever you work for, sent you?"

"You are correct, more of an admin man, but I do have good skills, if I say so myself, in negotiating. Hence my presence."

Neal listened as Tony banged about in the kitchen making tea for his uninvited guest. He doubted that Tony would believe any cover story he gave. Police officers, by nature, tend to be suspicious people. They spent their careers interacting with criminals who mostly tell lies to cover their illegal activities. That meant police officers were distrusting, cynical people, who only believed what you have told them once they have carried out extensive investigations and proved it. He hoped what he had shared with Tony was sufficient for the two of them to work together, that Tony would trust him.

Neal knew just how sceptical police officers could be, he had spent time in uniform himself. Not only did he find the uniform constricting and hot, but he also grew to hate the job. It was sold to him as a vocation, helping people, rehabilitating those unfortunates who strayed over the line, finding themselves on the wrong side of the law. The truth was he was rushing from crisis to crisis, pulling apart drunks, watching bruised wives take back their battering husbands, searching youths who had no future, all the time being decried by the public and senior officers for not doing it the right way.

Even when he became a plain clothes detective it did not help, in fact it was worse. His colleagues lampooned him, his body shape, his highly efficient memory. They ignored his detecting skills and local approach to crime. They just wanted to do as little as possible themselves and make fun of him. Since the day he handed his warrant card back, he had had no regrets, his life had turned around and he began to enjoy it.

Enjoyment was something that could not be said about the intermittent, stilted conversation that dragged on between the two men. Tony used short, tense phrases; Neal applied flowery drawn-out descriptions of his interest in county borders. It was not as if Neal did not try, pointing out the many family photographs that lined the room. He asked with an interested voice who the people were, where they were taken. The only replies he received were blunt and to the point. Plainly Tony was not happy about sharing any family history with him.

During a period of tense silence, Neal inspected the bookshelves from his seated position, seeing an old yet fitting book for Tony given his previous profession.

"Mind if I look through your books?"

"Go ahead." The tone was indifferent.

Slowly, Neal got up and took the three steps to the tall bookcase and pulled out one slim, tatty paperback that he had in his sights.

"A Policeman's Progress by Harry Cole. I read this years ago, a mild, yet informative insight into the mind of an old-fashioned copper, if there ever was such a person. A present, given your ex-career?" Neal flicked through the yellowed pages, reading the handwritten dedication, 'Is this what you get up to? Love Janice xx'. Neal knew the answer he was going to be given, it was a present from Tony's wife. No doubt it was a silly gift given at Christmas or a birthday. Even a present for no better reason than it made them both smile.

"A present from my wife."

There was no smile on Tony's face, Neal noticed, no emotion or warmth. Maybe it was because of Janice's actions toward her husband, or that Tony was still too pre-occupied with the fate of his daughter.

After replacing the paperback, Neal continued to peruse the books that lined the shelves. There was nothing of great interest, general fiction, some true crime stories, plus some reference books on passing police exams.

"Who are you actually working for? Are you MI5, as you hinted the last time you were here?"

"Does it matter?" Neal replied, as he casually flipped through the pages of a book of war memoirs.

"I think it does, for all I know you could be a plumber."

Neal replaced the book and turned towards Tony. It was going to be pointless masquerading as something he was not. Tony was an ex-copper, so was Neal. There is always going to be a time to lay your cards on the table, especially if you were on the same side, or at least fighting the same foe, but now was not that time.

"Must have been a shock for you, your wife drug-dealing right under your nose and you being a copper," he said, attempting to change the subject.

Tony had expected the question. After all, this Neal person was not from the passport office but had something to do with the security services. One of the many branches that exist within that department.

It was strange, but Tony had sensed a caring tone in the question, almost as if Neal was sincerely concerned about the circumstances that surrounded the Vercoe family. An empathy he did not often see in connection with his drug-dealing wife, as outsiders liked to refer to her. As a result, he had not spoken to another adult about his feelings.

"Nothing was right about it. She knew zero about the drugs or the money found in her car. She is not and never has been a drug dealer."

"The jury still found her guilty. There must have been compelling evidence. And you haven't appealed against the conviction either," Neal added. The bluntness of his view was almost that of a child, just expressing exactly what he was thinking.

"Innocent people do get caught up in the justice system who can come out with the wrong conclusion. I could see the evidence was slim and tenuous. Of course, we talked about appealing. We talked about it a lot. The problem is money. I earnt too much at the time to qualify for any form of legal aid but didn't earn enough for a competent barrister. She said it would be better to serve the sentence, a couple of years at best in prison before being let out on licence or parole. At least she would still have a house to come back to."

"How's that working out? She's on suicide watch, so I hear."

"You're very well informed." Tony wanted to raise the tone of his voice, express the anger he felt beginning to rise inside of him. He held back. "We're dealing with her situation the best way we can. She's in good hands; they're keeping her safe."

"You don't sound that concerned, I would have thought you would have been making a hue and cry about her precarious situation. Ah, no wait," Neal held his hand up as if he was quieting a gaggle of noisy school children. He looked down at Tony. "Suicide watch, there are advantages to being a police officer, you know the system. I hear she spent her remand here at home with an electronic tag, which is better than being in prison and it still counted towards her sentence. Now, she's on suicide watch, very sneaky. Plead fear and terror, self-harm, she ends up on suicide watch in the prison hospital. I hear it's a lot better than being stuck on a wing with real criminals. Making the best of it for your wife, I'm pleased, that's what a husband should do."

This time Tony could not hold back, deciding he had been wrong about Neal being sympathetic. "I don't give a flying toss what you think. All I care about is getting my daughter back and if I have no other choice than to work with your arrogant attitude then I'll swallow my pride."

"Us at the office are always questioning things. Do you know what, having read about your wife's misdemeanour, your colleagues were the ones who built the case around her. They could have toned the whole thing down, I would think. They knew you and might well have known her. She didn't have a lot of heroin on her."

"Maybe you and your friends at the office are more corrupt than the officers where I worked. I did the right thing, I stood to one side and let them do their job. To try and interfere would not have helped at all. Doing the right thing was the reason I handed in my warrant card. The system is there for everyone, no matter what your role is in it."

That was not the way Neal recalled his colleagues and work practices at the police station he had worked at. Most of them looked upon bending the rule of law as their version of staff discount. Drink driving was prevalent among them as well as taking a backhander to turn the occasional blind eye. On one occasion there was a colleague whose wife was having an affair, so her lover found himself a person of interest to the police and ended up with a criminal record. Maybe his team were a little too arrogant and that was what had driven him out of the force, that, and the constant jibes he received for the way he looked. Looking back, they were not a good bunch to work with.

Then there was Tony, sticking to his role, adhering to all the rules and standing up for good against evil even when that evil appeared in the form of his wife. Neal had known drug dealers before, seen their houses. There were the low-life dealers working street corners. And then there were the others at a higher level in the pyramid of drug dealing, nice houses, clean living, they were not caught with a few grams of coke in their pocket, they dealt in kilos.

Having read the whole case file, Neal was less than convinced of Mrs Vercoe's guilt. He began to wonder about

Tony's then colleagues, especially Pete. There was something more behind the conviction his wife was now serving time for. That was Neal's biggest weakness, he could become easily distracted. A question would emerge in his overactive mind and he would chase it like a cat chasing a reflection.

"You never left the force over the other incident, did you?"

"I was exonerated, it wasn't my fault."

"Yet, you're a parent, I bet you wouldn't be happy, would you? A copper killing your kid."

Tony stood up and leaned over Neal, he was about to grab him, he wanted to punch him hard in the face, stop him talking. The past still haunted Tony every time he heard a siren echoing across the neighbourhood.

"I read the official version, what's yours?" Even though Neal was expecting to have to defend his face from a fist, his voice sounded calm.

Tony flopped back into his chair.

"I doubt that it will be much different. I was in a car on my own delivering some evidence when I saw the little urchin. Harry Hobbs, a thirteen-year-old kid who came from a family of career villains: his brothers, sisters, cousins, parents. Deport them and crime will halve in the area. Nothing major, just minor stuff which made them a few pounds here and there, that ensured if they ever were banged up, it would only be for a few months at a time."

"So, this Harry, what was he up to?"

"You've read the report, riding a motor bike without a helmet and no insurance. Oh, he was also banned from riding as he was underage. I flashed my blues and twos at him wanting him to stop. The kid just opened up the throttle and rode off. Well, my lights were still on, but I wasn't going to chase him, I knew where he lived, it wasn't worth the effort."

"But the kid was still going fast."

"Fast enough to ignore the red lights and not see the lorry that flattened him. Killed him instantly."

The sound of Tony's mobile phone interrupted them.

***

The penetrating electronic tinny sound shattered the tense atmosphere as Tony's mobile called out for attention. His daughter's name was on the screen.

"Is the Brigadier there?" Tony heard the question.

"No Liam, the Brigadier isn't here. Is my daughter alright?"

"Yes, well looked after. The Brigadier, where is he?"

Neal reached out his hand indicating he wanted to take control of the mobile. As much as Tony did not want to, he handed the phone to the odd-looking man he did not trust to do the right thing by his daughter. The whole truth soon became apparent.

"Mr Connor, my name is Neal Matthews. I understand that you wish to speak to a person called Brigadier Howard Harvey, late of MI5, is that correct?" Neal's voice was solid and precise, nothing like the soft tone he had used while talking to Tony.

The Irish twang in the affirmative reply was apparent to Neal. "Good, I'm glad we're clear on that. First, you have taken a young teenager hostage in order to achieve your goal. You should have first approached MI5 directly, they have a website you know. What you've done is to commit a serious crime. If this all ends happily then there is the high possibility that you could be let off very lightly. But if Isobel is harmed in any way whatsoever, then you will feel the full force of the law come crashing down on your head. Am I making myself clear?"

Neal had been told a fair amount about who the potential kidnapper might be. Rupert had explained earlier that he knew of the Brigadier, and he had heard of the Connor family. It was therefore not a giant leap of faith to imagine that the young Connor was the perpetrator. Rupert said he was also sure the young Liam had never been regarded as the sharpest knife in the drawer. All this was information Neal was making full use of in trying to make himself sound like a headmaster. The other question was how Rupert appeared to know so much about the Connor family, but he had to put that question to one side for now.

"Firstly, I want to speak to Isobel now," Neal commanded.

A moment later a breathless female voice answered. Without a word, Neal handed the phone to Tony, who grabbed it and spoke to his daughter, reassuring himself that she was alive and well, just frightened and confused. Father and daughter spoke briefly before Liam came back on the line. Tony handed the phone back to Neal.

"Okay Liam let's get down to business. You want me to arrange a meeting with you and Brigadier Howard Harvey to talk about your dead father. It's going to help me a lot if you tell me as much as you can about the reasons you want to speak to the Brigadier, the sort of questions and information you want?"

"I just want to speak to him and only him, face to face."

"That will be arranged, but I need some more information as to why."

"If you can't help, I'm ending this call."

"Come on Liam, be reasonable, you must be looking for answers and I can help but..."

195

"No more buts. Do I see him or not?"

The voice had changed, Neal still would not describe it as forceful, more like desperate. No matter how Liam sounded, Neal could not risk the line going dead without some sort of arrangement.

"Isobel will know the Walnut Shopping Centre, in the car park, Level Five." As soon as Neal had given the time the line went dead.

Before Tony had a chance to speak, a ringing tone emitted from the pocket of Neal's corduroy jacket that was folded neatly beside him.

"Any luck? Okay, we're all set for later as planned."

Neal returned his phone to his jacket and handed back Tony's phone.

"We were hoping to get a location for your daughter's phone, sadly not long enough and now our friend Liam Connor has turned it off. He's not entirely stupid."

"What does he want, do you know?" Tony sounded a little less tense, he had spoken to his daughter which had helped his anxiety a little.

"Not exactly, I guess when we meet face to face, he'll tell us more. The question I am struggling to understand is just why he would contact you to speak to someone in the security services. Why you of all people?" Another question Neal found he needed an answer for.

"I have no idea?" Tony lied. He had no intention of telling everything to this Neal person whose motives were unclear. All the time that he was kept in the dark, it would make things easier for Tony, or at least that was what he believed.

"Really, you have no idea why he asked for your help to find the Brigadier? Not any understanding why he might think you are MI5? Even though on the notepad over there you have written MI5, CHINIC 8. What story are you working on?"

Tony looked down at the incriminating evidence and realised the words: 'Douglas, Demo Man, VAT fraud' were also clearly visible amongst his scribbled notes.

"It's a nothing story. Just some thoughts about the deceased Douglas Wright you were so interested in."

As sceptical as he was, Neal did not want to pursue it just yet, he needed the daughter back and the Brigadier to meet Liam.

"It might be worth casting your mind back over the last few days, somewhere you have crossed paths with Liam Connor. Depending on how things go we might need to know just how that occurred. But for now, you and I need to get to the Walnuts Car Park and get ourselves ready."

Chapter 22

Carefully Pete made his way towards the table. He tried his best, but some strongly brewed tea slopped into the saucer as he brushed against a large builder whose attention was focused on what to order for breakfast. Once he reached his table, he put the two cups and saucers down, grabbed a tissue from the cutlery rack on the table, avoiding the sauce bottles with their gummed-up necks, then carefully dried each saucer.

"I'd never make a waiter with these skills, would I?" He lamely joked hoping to lighten the mood, his companion did not smile.

"Be thankful that they weren't mugs and then the tea would be all over the floor," Rita pointed out as she pulled her hot drink towards her, poured what Pete considered to be an avalanche of sugar into it, then vigorously stirred the mixture.

Even before Pete had settled into his chair, Rita began her tirade, in the main focused on her manager refusing point blank to agree to a care order for Isobel. Pete half listened, slowly stirring his own tea. He switched off to what she was saying as sometimes that was the best thing to do when she was having a rant. During her outbursts there was very little chance of getting a word in. If by some miracle you managed to interject, then whatever you said would be dismissed unless, of course, you were agreeing with her. Pete was not surprised she was still single.

He had other things on his mind. Just why was Isobel kidnapped? He had been surprised when he was first told of the abduction. While Tony was sitting in front of him pleading for help, he was tempted to tell him kidnapping and the like is often a side effect of working with drug dealers, but that would have been pointless. Had Tony, after handing in his warrant card, gone after a drug dealer who might have entrapped his wife? His snooping around such matters would most certainly stir things up to the point that his daughter might be used as some sort of bargaining tool.

What Pete could not figure out was just where Douglas fitted into all this. Douglas was involved with the illegal side of cars, not dealing drugs on any scale as far as he could see. If this was anything to do with him, then he would have thought the National Crime Agency would be leading the investigation, but they were not. Instead, Pete had found out that it was some section of the National Security Secretariat who were interested in Douglas and who were now dealing with the kidnap. Just what else was Douglas into? And what was Tony getting himself into? More importantly, was he potentially under threat by just being on the sidelines?

"Are you listening to me?" Rita hissed at him.

Pete looked up. "Just absorbing your wise words. It's just maybe you should not push too hard for a care order."

That went down like a lead balloon. She took three word-filled minutes to tell Pete what she could have achieved simply by telling him, "I disagree, I'm going for it."

Returning to his previous concerns, Pete pondered the Irish voice that Tony had described, he added that to MI5, mixed a bit of kidnap in the recipe and pulled out of the oven of his mind the IRA. That was one subject he did not want to get even close to. It was not so much the Republican Army he was concerned about; it was the involvement of MI5 and their ability to dig deep into anything and everything, something that Pete did not want to happen. As the investigating officer in the death of Douglas Wright, he could find himself in a lot of trouble. The less Rita stirred things up the better, it was convincing her that would be the problem.

He waited for Rita to pause, then began, "Rita, trying to get Isobel into care is not something I am comfortable with. It was never meant to go this far. Taking Isobel into care will hurt her parents, but more importantly it will impact on her own life with consequences for her we can't imagine at this moment in time."

"Are you going soft?"

"No, it's just not what I signed up for."

Back when this had all started, Pete could see the logic. The turn of events that Rita had planned was acceptable in both the outcome and the fact that Pete was able to make a fair wad of cash out of it. Somehow things had changed without him noticing. Maybe he just was not paying attention, but he was paying attention now. Rita appeared to be on some sort of crusade with the single goal of tearing the Vercoe family to pieces and leaving them scattered and broken across the urban landscape.

Pete rarely regretted getting involved with scams, but now he was beginning to rue the day he had agreed to help Rita.

"This is not bloody Weight Watchers; you can't just walk away when you feel like it."

"No, but I can stop when I've had enough." He wanted to add, 'something you should consider' but stopped himself. No point in darkening her mood further. "There have been changes, events at the station which you're not aware of, but you had better take them into account or else this thing will blow up in our faces."

"You're spineless! What's changed, nothing. The burglary, this kidnap all points to Mr Vercoe being a hopeless father so for her own good Isobel needs to be taken into care."

This was going to be harder than he thought. Pete had hoped to be soft, a little diplomatic about the next stage, but that was not going to wash.

"Rita, I have a national security department all over this kidnap. They are also asking questions about the corpse under the car. Plus, now this is the part you need to take in, they're asking about Janice Vercoe's arrest and subsequent prison sentence."

"The court convicted her; what more do they want?"

"I don't know, maybe not the truth, but if they are around ruffling feathers, I don't want to be close to the action. Let's just stop where we are, pause for a while, not draw attention to ourselves and see where we end up."

"I was told you were a wimp. Yes, that's what I was warned, speak to Pete, he's happy to take your money but weak when threatened. No balls, I think I would describe you as."

The frustration was in Pete's dry voice, the tea failing to lubricate the tension out of his throat.

"Rita, listen to me, National Security, an Irish man, a kidnap. There is a vortex developing and we, if we are not careful, are about to get drawn in and drowning will be a distinct possibility. You do what you want, I am having nothing more to do with you until this is over."

"That's the problem for you, isn't it? If I go down, so do you."

Chapter 23

The bland grey concrete car park built over the Walnuts Shopping Centre could have done with a good clean, better lighting, clearer signage and a reduction in the exorbitant parking charges. None of these elements encouraged shoppers to visit the centre and were the prime reasons for the numerous empty shop units.

None of this concerned Tony in the slightest. The dim lighting, the odour of urine, the graffiti-covered walls he glossed over as he waited anxiously for Liam to appear. Ten minutes passed while he stood beside Neal's car. Neal leant nonchalantly on the bonnet glancing up occasionally from his phone and scanning the parked cars around them before returning his eyes to the screen. Tony wondered how he could be so calm when he was anything but. However much he pressed Neal as to what the plan was, Neal just rebuffed him with a simple unsympathetic, 'leave this to me and my staff, we're professionals'.

Tony had plenty of questions. If Liam brings Isobel, will we take him down, save my daughter? What if he does not show up? Are there others from Neal's team around to secure the area? Every question was met with no direct answer, just a straightforward reassurance that everything was in hand. Tony did not feel so confident.

A car appeared from the up ramp to their left, both men stiffened and then relaxed when the driver was a young female shopper, not the kidnapper. A moment later a van appeared on the parking level where Tony and Neal waited, a sign-written van for a carpet fitter.

"He's used his own bloody van," Neal observed, "he's more of an amateur than I imagined."

The van stopped six parking bays away. They watched as Liam exited his van. He walked alone towards the two men, surveying his surroundings warily. He stopped some twenty feet from them.

Tony spoke first, "Where's Isobel?"

"She's fine, well-fed, and she's safe. I was not going to be stupid enough to bring her along. Well, the Brigadier, where is he, when do I get to meet him?"

"Okay, Liam," Neal said with a calm authority in his voice, "I'm sure you're keeping Isobel safe and well, she's your only bargaining tool. I'm just a little surprised that someone with your intelligence would have decided to kidnap an innocent young girl, there are other ways that are perfectly legal to get into contact with members of our staff."

"The British are good at stonewalling people. I thought this would be the best and quickest way to get the attention of Brigadier Howard Harvey. When do I get to see him?"

Neal shook his head. "If only it was that easy. Tell me just why you want to speak to this Mr Harvey. We have a lot of staff in our departments. Can you tell me a little more about him?"

"The father I never knew as a child is on this press cutting." Liam waved a yellowed piece of newsprint at them; Tony and Neal could not make out much of it from the distance they were away. "He never went to England in his life, that's what my family told me. But it's him in the picture, I'm sure. The car dealer said the man in the picture was Irish, like my father. On the back of it is written the name of the Brigadier. I want answers."

"You said yourself that you never knew your father. Maybe your family did not want to say he had been to

England. Back then the troubles created all manner of stories and secrets in families."

"My father would never have got involved with the English is what my grandfather told me, yet the name of someone from MI5 is on the back of this cutting. What's this all about? The English have never liked the truth but I want to find it."

"What did your father do in the troubles? I am guessing he was supportive of the Republicans?"

Liam stabbed the press cutting back into the pocket of his jeans. Nervously he looked around the dimly lit car park. He waited for a car to drive past and watched it disappear down the exit ramp. "I have never been told what he did, no one wanted to tell me. All I do know is that my father was killed in the troubles by the British invaders. He died a hero my grandfather told me. The same grandfather wrote the name Brigadier Howard Harvey MI5 on the back of this press cutting. I just want the truth about what happened. If you can't help me now, I'll give you one more chance, after that I take my revenge out on a young English girl. She might be innocent, but so were many of the thousands who died in the troubles."

"What if he has died, the Brigadier?" Neal asked calmly as he grabbed Tony's arm, sensing the father was about to rush Liam and beat a confession out of him as to where Isobel was being held.

"Then there will be records. When you have the man I want to speak to, message my Facebook page. You have until tomorrow." Without waiting for a response, Liam turned and ran back to his van, jumped in and sped out of the car park.

"Is that it?" Tony almost screamed at Neal, as the carpet fitter's van flew past them.

"Worry not, I have this in hand," Neal spoke as his phone rang and he answered the call.

"What!" The exclamation echoed around the car park level. "Dropped off... oh... for fuck's sake." He turned to Tony offering an explanation. "This is what happens when we employ dickheads and at the same time cut the training budget." He resumed the call. "Get onto the ANPR cameras and track him... It's a bloody sign-written van it shouldn't be too hard even for arseholes like you."

The call was abruptly ended. Neal turned back to Tony; his eyes appealed for forgiveness. "The tracker that was meant to be fixed to the underside of the van fell off as it moved. It's meant to be fool proof, clearly it's not stupid proof. Don't worry, with the plethora of CCTV and ANPR cameras we have, we can still track him."

"And if not?"

"I had better find the Brigadier, or at least pray he's still alive. Let's get back to your place."

After he had started the engine, Neal looked through the windscreen without seeing anything, his mind was elsewhere. He sat, holding the steering wheel for a few seconds then turned towards Tony, who, seat belt already in place, waited impatiently for the car to move.

"Something is bothering me, something that just does not fit," his voice dragged, tempting Tony to speak, it worked.

"What do you mean doesn't fit, he has Isobel, we need to get what he wants."

"Something is wrong," Neal repeated. "We both spoke to Liam on the phone yesterday. He drove into the car park as planned, arrived at the level we agreed to meet, but he didn't hesitate to approach us when he shouldn't have known what we look like. It was as if he recognised us."

Neal slipped the car into gear and pulled away as he waited for an answer. Tony did not rush. He was not planning to admit just yet that Liam had visited his house and seen Isobel.

"I would guess that he was expecting to meet two men on that level. I didn't see any others, did you? You said he was naïve, that was a stupid error."

"He would only expect to see me here."

"Well, he took a chance and it worked out, he got lucky. Either that or he was watching us both from a distance. It's not important."

"Maybe not important to you, but to me these things are. What if you had met Liam before, planned the whole thing? The two of you working together on a story, tricking MI5 into giving something they would rather not give up. Your daughter might be held hostage to ensure we hand over whatever you are after, not that I can imagine what that might be. Those notes on your desk, a nothing story, I think you said. I suspect you're trying to take us for a ride. Maybe I should call your bluff, tell you Isobel is dispensable, nothing to do with us. That would put you and your story in a difficult position."

"Intriguing, yet a wild hypothesis. I never imagined there was a story in this, but Liam has a press cutting which you find very interesting. I suspect that whatever story that snippet from decades ago holds is even more important to you than Isobel."

"Touché"

Chapter 24

It was not often that Neal ever felt put upon. All his adult life he had been an achiever in the workplace. One of those employees who took orders, carried them out to the best of their ability and for their trouble took home a reasonable wage. He never wanted to get involved in the politics of the country, or even the department. He did not, and never intended to make strategic decisions that might affect others. He just wanted to carry out his tasks, do his job and live his life. That was after all what being alive was about. No one was ever able to do exactly as they wished, if that had been the case, Neal would have travelled the world recording and photographing signs that plotted the man-made lines on the earth, the borders and boundaries. Those imaginary lines, that decide politics, living conditions and how happy you might be. Instead, he had to work, be at someone else's beck and call, which he had never minded until now. Now he felt he was being taken for a ride, both by Tony and by Rupert. He was between two people whose own agendas were well concealed from him.

"How do I find this elusive brigadier that's named on the back of the press cutting?" From the moment Neal had seen the press cutting in Liam's hand, he wanted to ask what the connection was between it and the photographs that he had been tracking for what seemed like years. If he did ask outright, he knew the answer would be fudged, so instead he nibbled around the edges of the subject.

"Why isn't it possible to use the full force and resources of our department to find where he's hiding out, scoop up the girl then arrest this Liam person? After all, he's no more than some young Irishman whose intellect is not up to that of a below-average criminal. That way we will have no need to spend our time searching for the elusive Howard Harvey."

Sunlight falling through the office window reflected off the silver letter opener that Rupert was fidgeting with. Neal wondered if it was nerves or just the need for a gin and tonic. Whatever the reason, Neal continued.

"He's more adept than we might think. He was shrewd enough to remove the tracker as he got into the van," Neal lied, knowing Rupert would not be aware of the real reason it was dislodged. "He has a press cutting, the press cutting," he emphasised, "and I suspect he knows exactly why it's so important to MI5." In reality, Neal guessed that Liam did not have the foggiest idea why MI5 was so interested in an ancient news story, in the same way that even he, although on the inside, had no idea of the true significance of it. Yet they both wanted to find out and this was going to be Neal's best chance. The suggestion that Liam might know the true meaning of the press cutting caused Rupert's eyebrows to rise.

"What about we present someone," Rupert suggested, "anyone and call them Howard Harvey, this stupid boy would not know any different. He'll ask some questions and he'll receive some banal answers. The girl is returned, he goes back to laying carpets and we have nothing to worry about. How does that sound?"

Maybe it was exactly something that Neal might have subscribed to if he had little interest in the whole thing, but his curiosity was now fully alert. 'Nothing to worry about', Rupert had said. Now was the time to add a little more pressure on his boss.

"The thing is Rupert, it could be that the reporter, Isobel's father, and this Liam are working in tandem, and they already have more information and are just looking for a way to confirm it all before they go public."

"If they're bluffing, then we just leave them to it."

"If we do and the girl dies, we'll have more than just egg on our faces. Is it so bad to tell them the truth about Liam's father? If he had connections with MI5 and he was also in the IRA, then even to my simple brain that shouts British spy. Now if that's the case, we'll have some information to give to Liam, whatever he might feel about his father working for the British."

If there was one place that Rupert hated to be, it was in a corner, trapped and surrounded by the lies he had woven over the years working for the department. He knew that he was caught and had few choices. Tell Neal all and work with him? No, he did not want to burden anyone else with the knowledge he had. Leaders hold all the cards and play them, not always in the way that suits the player. He had to offer something.

"Do you think this reporter is working with Liam?" He asked.

"If not working together, I'm sure they've been in contact. From what I suspect Tony has also seen the news story of the car dealer. If he had seen it for the first time in Liam's hand, he would have asked me questions about it, of that, I'm sure. We need to act. We need to locate the Brigadier, talk to him, get him to meet Liam. Then we might have a better idea of how to deal with this whole situation. It might help me, if I knew everything about why this story about a bent car dealer is so important to you."

"That isn't the first time you have asked that question and I sense it will not be the last time. Either way I have no plans to enlighten you."

That had always been the stock answer Neal received. Each time he had asked, he was told it was no concern of his, he did not need to know, it was unimportant. Today, he began to suspect what might be behind the news story: a British spy embedded in the IRA. Nothing uncommon in that, he knew there were dozens recruited during the troubles. Why was this one different? Neal also had another snippet of information, something he had seen on Tony's notepad, a word he had never seen in relation to the department.

"What is CHINIC 8?"

The atmosphere in the room chilled dramatically. Neal sensed what he had just uttered was as good as turning a key in a lock. He had yet to see if it was being unlocked or locked.

The letter opener was slammed down onto the desk. Rupert leaned forward, opened a large drawer beside him, took out a gin bottle and a glass. His doctor was always going on about how many units he drank each week, encouraging him to cut back, reduce his alcohol intake, lead a healthier lifestyle. Well, Rupert thought, I need these units, whatever the government are saying about drinking sensibly. The government burdened me with a secret that I never wanted in the first place. The government has no right to tell me what I can and cannot swallow. I drink to help the pressure. I drink to forget the past. I drink to numb the pain of all the hard decisions I took all those years ago. He finally admitted to himself that he also drank because he liked the taste.

Rupert poured a large measure, which he swallowed in one mouthful.

"Give me an hour, I'll have a location and time where Liam can meet his beloved Brigadier. You will need to be there as well; you have always wanted to know just why that news story is important to me. I also want Isobel there, as the Irish boy is not getting any information unless she's there and close to freedom. Plus, I want the reporter, her father, there. Finally I want nothing to go wrong."

"What about the Brigadier?"

"Rest assured I can get him there as well."

Chapter 25

It had stood in the same spot for almost one hundred years, long before Ronald MacDonald was born, longer than the Joe Lyons cafes that once populated urban areas. The Blackheath Tea Hut was not just a hut, it was an institution. It was a haven for bikers, police officers, night workers and a wide spectrum of passing motorists and tourists. Open twenty-four hours a day, it was the one place in southeast London you could rely on getting a mug of tea and a bacon roll whenever you wanted to.

Tony spotted Jane beside the tea hut biting into a thick sandwich. She waved awkwardly as she saw him coming towards her. Once Neal had dropped him at home, Tony had driven at breakneck speed to meet Jane. She had news.

"How did you get on?" Tony asked, refusing an offer of refreshments.

"I've got the address, it's just around the corner. He went straight there after meeting you guys. Who was the weird guy you were with?"

"I'm not sure he knows who he is really, perhaps an intelligence officer, spy, call him what you want. I won't be telling him."

As he watched Jane wipe a small trace of brown sauce from her lip, he felt pleased with himself for having a better plan than the national intelligence agency, who had totally failed in their attempt to track Liam when he left the Walnuts Car Park.

The plan had been simple. Jane was to drive to the car park level where the meeting was going to take place, wait for Liam to turn up, then move her car down a couple of levels and wait for him to exit. After that it was a simple matter of following him. Beforehand Jane admitted that she had never followed anyone in a car before and was not sure how good she would be at it. But one thing about Jane was that she was always ready to take on a challenge.

"It was pretty easy. It's not as if it was some production line Ford with hundreds on the street. It was a conspicuous van that I couldn't easily lose, even in traffic I could easily keep track of it. I think I would make a good spy. Shall we go?"

"You're not coming with me."

"I'll be your lookout, wing-person, or whatever the correct parlance might be during a rescue bid."

"No, I need to do this alone. If I haven't called you by this evening, then do something. Get the police round there, I don't know, whatever you think is best. But rest assured, I'll be back!" Tony laughed. It was not often that he made such jokes. Then again it was not often he had to rescue his daughter.

***

The address that Jane had given took him to a Victorian semi-detached house in the back streets of Greenwich. An affluent area where at least fifty per cent of the houses appeared to be having some sort of building work or renovation refurbishment. In front of this one was a large skip filled with building debris. The external brickwork had newly been re-pointed. The window frames and a large door appeared freshly painted. The house looked empty and there was no sign of Liam's van. If Jane had followed him back here, clearly he had now left. Had he taken Isobel with him or was she inside? The trail could be leading to a dead end and Isobel was being held somewhere else, but he had to check here first.

He slipped quietly into the front garden, edged his way down the righthand side of the house, making his approach to the rear of the property and concealment from prying eyes along the street. The long, narrow garden was full of untidy shrubs and a lawn that was overgrown, all waiting for some care. There was no extension at the back, just a simple half-glazed door and a large window. He peered in to see a kitchen full of new modern units, most still with a protective covering over them. The inhabitants were not yet in residence, presumably waiting for the builders to complete the works.

Unsurprisingly the back door was locked. He wondered just how many keys might be in circulation with plumbers, electrician, builders, carpet layers, all wanting to gain access. He looked around the garden and saw a garden gnome fishing carp in an overgrown terracotta tub which looked out of place and out of character. He lifted the gnome to reveal a key.

Carefully he opened the kitchen door and stepped inside. The newness of the space gave a sterile atmosphere to the room. He could hear no sounds above the beating of his anxious heart, apart from the distant murmur of traffic a few streets away. He longed for signs of Isobel but there was no indication of anyone living here, no pieces of food, glasses, or plates. If she was being held here, Liam was being very careful to conceal her. The hallway was ahead, a wide corridor, with a beige deep-pile carpet with a protective layer of clear plastic over it. If this was Liam's work, he looked good at his job. Tony stopped there, he had no plans to befriend Liam, however good a carpet layer he might be. The man had taken his daughter and was holding her captive somewhere. Tony prayed it was here, however unlikely it now seemed.

He checked the downstairs rooms pushing each door open slowly and cautiously. His heart sank, no furniture, no possessions, no Isobel. Treading with care, he inched his way up the stairs. Still the house remained silent apart from the occasional creak as the wood moved and cooled. The daylight began to subside. Four doors led off the landing. He could not explain why but he started with the back room first; the room which would face out over the rear garden. He pushed open the door, it moved easily. The room was not empty, as in the middle of it a figure, with a face he could not see, was sitting in a high-backed chair. The person was strapped to it, their hands taped behind to the framework.

"Isobel?" Tony asked anxiously, his heart racing still more. He knew it had to be Isobel. The girl mumbled.

Quickly, he moved in front of her and hugged her, more out of relief than practicality. Her mouth was covered with carpet tape. He pulled at it as gently, yet firmly, as he could. Finally, it came away from her mouth.

"Dad!" Isobel exclaimed, sounding surprised that it was her father that had walked into the room, and not Liam who she was expecting to see.

"Are you okay? Has he hurt you?" He tried releasing the bindings.

"No, but I am glad to see you, I have been so scared. He's been kind enough to me, but for these bindings and the tape so that I couldn't call for help. I couldn't keep track of the time and when he wasn't here, I was so bored, and it seemed to go on for an eternity. I am so pleased you found me. I really could do with a decent bowl of cereal. How did you find me?" Her words came out in a rush as though she had been quiet for such a long time and now could not stop talking.

"Let's talk when we get out, I have no idea if he's coming back."

"He won't be long. He only popped out to get some food. Dad, hurry," her voice became more urgent now as it dawned on her that Liam was coming back soon. He had only gone to the local store to collect some provisions for her. She had no idea where he stayed, as he left her alone for most of the day, only appearing at mealtimes. She hoped her father would not smell the urine on her as she had had to relieve her bladder. As trapped as she was, pissing herself was still an embarrassment for her.

"Christ, this tape is tough. I'll try and use a key, the kitchen looked empty of anything sharp."

Tony moved behind his daughter, sawing at the tape that bound her hands, wearing it away layer by layer. "Almost...." He had no idea of the cause of the pain. All he knew was it was a sharp intense painful stabbing sensation at the back of his head. His vision stuttered and faded away, followed by his hearing and finally his muscles gave up as darkness overcame his falling body.

***

The blackness began to wash away as light permeated Tony's pupils. The ache was coming from the other side of his head. His eyes flickered. The room was darker than he recalled. Sprawled out on the floor, he cautiously began to move his limbs, so far, they appeared to be attached correctly and mobile. As his eyes cleared so did his thoughts, Isobel. He rolled over and looked at the empty chair.

Hanging onto the chair, he hauled himself up. His body was still not fully recovered, he fell back onto the carpet as his arm gave way. Dispirited, he sighed. The ache was still pulsating through his skull. He moved his hand behind his head to feel the source of the pain. His hand felt what might have been some sort of tissue stuck to his head with tape.

"Don't pull it off," Neal's voice chastised him, "it might not look pretty but it has stopped the bleeding."

Tony rolled onto his back. It was not the best thing to do, his neck still had no strength and his head bumped on the floor. Even the thick carpet could not stop him from wincing.

"I'd say don't make a mess on the carpet, but you have already bled all over it. I presume this is Liam's handy work, both the carpet and that nasty bang on the head you have there?"

"How did you find me?" Tony asked, still lying on the floor and staring up at the ceiling.

"Ah, good question. I imagine you were so pleased with yourself, getting the address where your daughter was being held. As ever ex-job think they can do everything on their own, getting one over on us Security Service types. I bet you were feeling smug. Not so superior now though, are you?"

Tony rolled onto his front, drew up his knees and pushed upwards with his arms. At least he managed to get upright now and was able to look around the room. His balance was still adjusting, so he held onto the chair to steady himself.

"I guess you were too late to stop Liam from escaping with Isobel?"

"Too late. Me, too late. That's rich coming from a man on his knees with a head injury. You're lucky I got here in the first place. You were the one who let your daughter slip through your fingers. If you had shared with me what you were up to, then between us we would have your daughter back and I would have Liam in custody. As it is, we're just two blokes in a stranger's house."

"How did you find me?"

"I was going to ask you the same thing, well, how you worked out this address. Then I recalled, back in the car park, a young woman drove in, parked, but never got out of her car. She then drove out after Liam arrived. Fellow reporter? Waiting to follow him as he left? You should have shared that with me."

"Then how did you find me?" Tony repeated as he stood up, with one hand holding onto the chair to maintain his balance while the other pawed the dressing on the back of his head.

"Don't mess around with my handiwork, it should only be regarded as a temporary dressing. Lucky for you I had some clean tissues on me, plus there was some carpet tape handy."

"I'll ask again...."

"Alright, alright, I'm tracking your phone, as all good security officers should do. I was surprised when you left your house as soon as I'd gone. You then trailed over to Blackheath before arriving here. I was interested to see what you were up to. And before you ask, I'm tracking you because I still think it's not beyond the bounds of possibility that you're working with Liam, just to wheedle some hair-brained story out of all this. Although, I am starting to come around to the idea that you're not in cahoots with him, as you needed an associate to find out where he was holding Isobel."

Finally, Tony could stand without assistance from the chair. He shivered, was he cold, or was it just shock? He put it down to the latter, he had experienced the feeling before.

"That's very magnanimous of you. So, what now? I presume you have no idea where Isobel might be."

"No, but we have sent him a Facebook message with details of where we should all meet tomorrow morning. We've told him he gets to see his mysterious Brigadier, or so I am dependably informed. I'll have a car pick you up at about nine. I'm sure you want to be there."

Chapter 26

"What did I say?" Jane asked as she nursed a mug of coffee in Tony's kitchen. "Let me come along, be your wingman. But oh no, macho man Tony can handle anything. Well, all I will say is that if that knock on your head still hurts, it serves you right."

"Thank you for your sympathy, is that the reason for your visit, gloating over my mistakes?"

"Well, it's not the main reason just a handy bonus. The main reason is I have found out what the enigmatic CHINIC 8 is. Hence my visit to your humble abode."

Still holding a cold compress to the back of his head, Tony looked up from the pile of papers that she had presented to him. "How did you find out where I lived?"

"Where you reside was a lot easier to uncover than the history of a turn of the century building in Kingsway and its occupants. And a total doddle compared to de-coding the word CHINIC. You must give me more credit for digging out information and making the right calls, like offering to help you on a rescue mission."

Suitably berated Tony admitted, "Okay I should have listened to you. If I had done, it could well be that Isobel would be safe and well in bed tonight instead of still in the hands of that Irish fellow."

"I'm sorry, I shouldn't have made so light of the situation."

"Forget it, just tell me what CHINIC 8 is all about. I'm in no mood to read piles of old papers." Tony referred to the pile of yellowed and dusty documents that Jane had brought with her.

She did not get straight to the point, she wanted to make it clear just how deeply they had been buried in a damp Whitehall basement. So instead, she described all the steps she had to make to uncover the meaning of CHINIC.

Her first step was with Google, as it always was when she had a question. That was fruitless, only suggesting that possibly it was some sort of acid, but that seemed very tenuous. Nothing turned up searching abbreviations. Putting aside a general search she then turned her attention to financial terms, basing the assumption on the fact that the VAT offices seemed to be the main department using the building. She spent hours looking at terms used and sifting through the numerous departments and committees that are related to Revenue and Customs, even moving her search through Treasury terms and groups. In short, she was getting nowhere.

Her next step was to look at the company that Douglas worked for when he originally stripped the building out to see if that would give her any clues. Luckily the commercial director at the time was the site manager on the Kingsway building. He recalled that floor well. Over an all–day breakfast, she questioned him. Apart from too many anecdotes and boasting about other buildings he had proudly knocked down, she eventually managed to focus his thoughts on the fifth floor of the Kingsway building.

It had given him the most grief during the whole operation. He wanted to start on that floor and work down the building. The staff had left but the fifth floor had remained firmly locked for the first two weeks. Men were coming and going with all sorts of odd equipment. Finally, his workmen were allowed in. It was a maze of small offices; each with a strong keylock on, plus an access code lock. The telephone equipment had been removed from this floor whereas that had not happened with the others. Even the toilets had been dismantled, all of this surprised the demolition man. Jane asked him if he thought that the offices were part of the other floors, the same VAT department.

Jane put her mug down, leaned over to pull something out from her large handbag before she smiled at Tony and continued, "The bloke said to me, between mouthfuls of baked beans, that he knew it was not the same department. He looked smug and gave me this." Jane passed the sepia-coloured sheet to Tony, who straightaway noticed the large 'Top Secret' stamp at the top of the page.

"He was as pleased as punch," Jane continued, "when he heard I was interested in the building he made sure he had that with him. In the same way Douglas found the press cutting and negatives, Mr Demolition man found that document stuffed in a mouse hole in one of the offices."

Tony read the secret document, which went into detail about a well-known UK union leader corresponding with an American union boss who was planning a strike. In 2003 about 20,000 employees of the General Electric company at 48 plants across 33 states went on strike. It was the first against the company in 33 years, it was over the company's plan to shift more health care costs to employees and retirees. The memo also noted that the UK union leader was prepared to instruct his members to black-leg any General Electric merchandise should it arrive in the UK.

"What's this got to do with us?" Tony asked, unsure if the knock on his head was causing him to miss the point.

"Top secret, not VAT related, investigating a union leader? That office had to be either a covert Police department or a department of national security. I leant towards MI5 and their offshoots, then dug some more.

After a little research, I visited a nice, eccentric old man who lives in a flat stuffed full of old papers and with a mist of pipe smoke hanging in the air. An expert in the defence of the realm was how he was billed.

"I showed him the plan I had of the office and the notations. He did not recall what CHINIC was at first, but he dug around the piles of papers which inhabited the flat and dug these out," she pointed to the papers in front of Tony. "I think he lent those to me so I would have to go back and talk some more with him, or rather listen to him as he spent most of the time reminiscing about his days in the Ministry of Defence."

Tony shuffled through the yellowed papers and pulled out a cover for a report.

"Covert Human Intelligence Northern Ireland Cohort, is that what CHINIC stands for?"

"Yes," Jane replied. "Kingsway, according to the old man, housed cohorts one to eight. There was also a nine and ten, but they were at the Lambeth Bridge building. A grand title but really, they just dealt with IRA informants, passed on information and looked after their every whim including ensuring they were paid. There you have it, the Fifth Floor of Kingsway House housed MI5 officers."

"There is still the question as to why the photographs were on that fifth floor, hidden away."

"Why not ask your MI5 friends tomorrow?" Jane asked without expecting an answer.

Chapter 27

'The Hoo Hundred' was an odd name for a house was Tony's opinion as he was driven along the narrow-overgrown driveway. The period building with its seven bedrooms, four bathrooms and cellar kitchen had not hosted a domestic family of any description since the end of the Second World War. Located just outside St Mary Hoo, the house was almost in the centre of the Hoo Peninsular. As mentioned in the Domesday Book, much of the area was part of the Saxon Hundred of Hoo, hence the name of the house.

The unkempt driveway led off a main road. Most motorists passed by the unobtrusive entrance without a second thought, it looked no more than a break in the scruffy hedge that bordered the road. Others knew that it was some sort of narrow lane but had not bothered to investigate. Few locals, the older generation in the main, knew of the existence of 'The Hundred'.

Ever since the Second World War, 'The Hoo Hundred' had been used intermittently by several UK security services for various reasons. By and large it had been used as a remote location for high-ranking officials to escape the pressures of their London offices, plan future strategies and identify potential threats. It also afforded them the opportunity to escape their wives and drink fine wine late into the night. At other times it had been utilised as a location for spies that were about to be exchanged or double agents to be questioned at length.

Today the house was going to be the discreet rendezvous point for an Irish abductor to meet with the enigmatic Brigadier. Even though it was mid-morning,

Tony felt an apprehensive chill as he stepped out of the mud-splattered car and walked towards Neal, already standing on the gravel drive, hands in pockets, talking to an older man.

"Is this it?" Tony asked, expecting a raft of activity while they were waiting for Liam Connor to arrive. As the car he'd been brought in drove towards the back of the house, there remained just the three of them.

"What did you expect, the Household Cavalry?" The sarcasm was not lost on Tony. "This is Rupert Bell, my boss and mentor. Rupert, this is the Tony we have talked about."

Rupert, holding his insulated cup, looked Tony up and down as if he was about to make a bid on him at some sort of slave auction.

"I am sorry that it has come to this. Your daughter, as well as your family, have become caught up in the delusional aspirations of a young man who no doubt is still grieving for his dead father, hence his poor decision-making. But do rest assured that we will deliver your daughter back to you, safe and sound."

The words might have been spoken firmly, but Tony did not think they were sincere. He swatted an annoying fly from his face. "What about this brigadier he has been asking for? When does he get here?"

"Please don't concern yourself with the logistics of this exercise," Rupert assured him, "we have it all in hand. Your role is just to be here when your daughter is released. The young man should arrive within the next few minutes. Your daughter, I can confirm, is with him you'll be pleased to hear. Thus far, he's adhering to our instructions."

"How do you know she is with him?"

"The stupid boy drives a sign-written van. Some of my team have driven past it and she's in the front passenger seat looking calm." Rupert smiled, then added, "When he arrives, I don't want to hear a single word from you, Neal and I will do all the talking. You will need to remain completely silent, whatever happens. I have managed this sort of operation on numerous occasions. If you do decide to put your unwelcome pennyworth in, then I will not be responsible for anything that might happen to your daughter, so silence in this case will very much be golden. A couple of minutes and he should be here."

The three men stood together on the gravel as if they were waiting for some important guest to arrive. He might not be a VIP, but Liam was a person of value.

"But what about the Brigadier?" Tony asked again. Rupert put him down at once.

"No words Mr Vercoe, no words, remember."

In the grey sky, a group of four black-headed gulls were flying, fighting over a scrap of bread that one carried in its beak, squawking, and swooping like disgruntled siblings fighting over a precious toy. The men stood in tense silence. They did not cast any shadows; such was the gloom of the muted daylight. It was as if the sun had not risen, and the wind had decided to have the day off. They waited, backs to the house, patiently watching the long narrow lane.

They heard the noise of a motor vehicle becoming louder as it approached the house. They saw the sign-written van pull up well short of them. Liam got out of the driver's door, looked around suspiciously, before approaching the passenger door. He opened the door and roughly pulled Isobel out of the van, then held her in front of him like a shield. Holding one arm around her neck, his other hand was in his pocket, where he appeared to have a concealed weapon which was pointing at her thigh. He looked scared and jittery.

Liam, with Isobel, took four steps forward, then stopped at least one hundred feet from the three men staring at him. Tony wanted to call out to Isobel, but he could feel Rupert's glaring stare burning into him and stayed quiet.

"Good morning Liam, thank you for coming," Rupert greeted their visitor as if he had just popped along for a coffee and planned to spend the morning chatting about the price of wholesale milk or the latest trends in root-crop growing. Liam remained silent, his eyes darting around the house, the grounds, the gravel, he was looking for anything that might tell him it was a trap. Nothing seemed to indicate that it was, but even so he wanted to remain cautious.

"There is no need to hang onto Isobel quite so tightly, she's not going anywhere, and we're here to help you. Trust us and give her some breathing room."

"I came to see Brigadier Howard Harvey. Where is he?" Liam's voice was breathless, anxious, and with a hint of fear, just as Rupert had hoped.

"You're talking to him Liam. I am Brigadier Howard Harvey."

Instantly Neal turned to look at his boss. It was a reaction that he had sought to contain but still failed. Was his boss lying to pacify Liam or was he the mysterious Brigadier? Neal knew it was not the time to ask that question. He returned his gaze to Liam.

"How do I know you are really him?"

Tony, and especially Neal, waited for the answer with interest.

"I do understand Liam, you never knew your father and you obviously never knew me. You only have a name. Talking of names, you do know that you were not born Liam Connor. Your family changed their names when they came to England. I helped smooth that process after your father died. Paved the way for you, your mother, and your grandfather to come to England to escape the clutches of the IRA. In fact, that is the reason I would imagine, that my name is on that press cutting; written there by your grandfather with whom I liaised. There is nothing sinister, I was just a member of the government tasked to help you and your family."

"Then why was my father in England? It's him in the news story buying a van. My mother told me he never came to England, why should she lie? You lying would seem the better bet."

"Look, Liam, I have no reason to lie. Your father was killed in the troubles. Maybe the IRA killed him, I never knew. All I was expected to do was to get you and your family into England and settled, and that's exactly what I did. Maybe your father was involved with the IRA, I have no idea. Back then, Liam, you must understand that government officials like myself were kept pretty much in the dark about things, the less we knew the less risk of us leaking secrets. It was a war, Liam, I'm sure you understand that."

"And my grandfather? If you had been so kind to him, why did he hate the British and all they stood for? He never trusted the British or the RUC."

"He always trusted us when we were helping him. You're looking for answers to questions that I cannot help you with."

"My grandfather told me that the British killed my father. He laid the blame at your door. There's no death certificate for my father, no evidence, no paperwork. To me that sounds like a conspiracy."

Tony looked at his daughter, he felt helpless. He could see that she was shivering either from the cold or fear or probably a mixture of the two. He half listened to the conversation Liam and Rupert were having. If Rupert was Brigadier Howard Harvey whom Liam sought, he was not getting much information from him. Tony wondered if that indicated that he was not who he was saying he was and only masquerading as the Brigadier.

"What I can do for you Liam, is obtain a copy of your father's death certificate, which I am sure will show that he died as a result of IRA activity. It might not be what your grandfather told you, but as I have already said, the troubles split many families."

"A lie, the British killed my father. The death certificate will just show me another lie. And what did my grandfather mean when he said my father pleaded with your government to come to England? He told me that he appealed and begged to be relocated and the British government refused."

Tony looked at Rupert, for the first time in this conversation he seemed to be faltering, clearly thinking about his response.

"You have not mentioned that before. Have you just made it up to help you justify holding an innocent young woman hostage?"

"You killed my father, you and the soldiers, as you killed everyone who fought for a united Ireland."

Once again there was an uncomfortable silence between the two protagonists as they stared at each other across the weed-infested gravel. Tony had listened many times to criminals telling a story that they believed to be true. They would swear on their mother's life that was exactly what had happened, yet in the end it was always different, totally different. As a police officer, Tony's role was to sift through their account to try to get at the truth. As he listened to the two men, he had a sense that Liam was telling the truth as he knew it. He was repeating what he had been told without fully understanding what he was looking for or what the real questions were.

As he listened to Rupert speak, Tony believed that he sounded as though he was holding something back, only telling what he thought he could not avoid admitting.

There was more to this story, a lot more. Tony believed that Rupert knew the whole truth, it was just that he had no intention of revealing it. Muddying the waters, misrepresenting the facts and drip-feeding parts of what he knew into a petri-dish that Liam was holding. Liam, eager to uncover the truth about his father's life, was being led down a narrow path leading to a brick wall.

"Liam, you have been subjected, I would say all your life, to the republican viewpoint that the British are no more than colonists in Ireland. That isn't the whole case, you must make up your own mind and not be swayed by the rebellious elements around you. The British Army did not kill your father, that I can assure you is the truth."

Once again Tony, recalling his days interviewing criminals, analysed the statement that Rupert had made. If he knew the British Army did not kill Liam's father and he was being honest, then he must know who had killed the father and then no doubt the circumstances of his death, something he had earlier denied. Tony was beginning to wonder about Rupert's honesty and by association Neal's too.

"Prove it to me or this little girl comes to harm."

"Don't make threats Liam, that you can't carry out."

"You forget my heritage, I'm Irish and I hate the British, nothing is beyond me. I want to see proof of how my father died or else she dies."

It was a reaction; any father would do the same. Tony moved forward, only to be held back by Neal grabbing his arm. Holding him back, softly Neal told him, "No, wait."

"I'll kill this little bitch and her blood will be on your hands."

"Liam, listen to me, all we have is an administrative challenge to get you all the paperwork regarding your father's death. It might not be easy, but it's possible. By threatening that young lady, you are using a sledgehammer to crack a walnut. Just release her and we can get this sorted out."

"But then you'll concoct some story and back it up with false paperwork. I'll still be no nearer to the truth."

"Liam, unless I can find the Irishman who killed your father, there is nothing in this world that could convince you that you have the facts. There comes a point when we are dealing with historical accusations that trust has to become a part of the equation."

"There you go again, blaming the Irish for murdering my father, that didn't happen. I'm leaving here with her and you will have forty-eight hours to get me the truth or else I will hurt her."

"Making such a clear threat leaves me with little choice Liam," Rupert stated as he dropped his insulated cup. It hit the gravel and bounced, twice, before the top burst open and the clear liquid spilt over the cold grey stones. Liam's eyes flicked towards the discarded cup.

Tony instantly recognised the sound. A short report that splintered the air, startling the gulls that had settled on the roof. A rifle, high powered. A single shot. Tony instinctively looked around for the source of the noise. As he did so, his peripheral vision picked up Liam's head falling backwards, with a crimson-coloured spout erupting from his head.

Tony turned back to his daughter whose knees seemed to fold, falling away from the grip that Liam once had had on her. She tumbled to the floor, diving forwards, throwing her arms in front of her to break the fall. As she did so, behind her Liam's body spun to his left, arching backwards he fell onto the gravel; his body seeming to jerk and shake as it lay on the cold stones.

Casually Rupert bent down and picked up his insulated cup, looking at it to see if any of the liquid remained. There was just enough for a single mouthful of warming gin and tonic, which relieved some of the tension he felt. Executions never came easily for him, although he never shrank away from his responsibility.

Shaking off Neal's grip Tony ran forward. He did not know if any more bullets were going to be discharged but he ignored the threat, he just needed to scoop his daughter up from the ground and hold her in his arms. He had failed in his role as a father, a parent who protects their children. He wanted to say he was sorry.

With his service revolver drawn, Neal stood beside Rupert and looked around for the gunman who had sent a bullet into the depths of Liam's brain. Primarily he stood beside Rupert to protect and shield him from any potential danger that might still be coming.

"Calm down, Neal, that was our Simon, you may recall he's one of us," Rupert pointed out. "You can put your gun away."

Neal looked curiously at his boss; a hidden sniper had never been part of the plan. Rupert had assured those around him that he intended to take Liam alive and there should be no risk to the daughter. In the briefing prior to the rendezvous, Rupert had been at pains to point out that Liam was no more than a misguided son, who was out of his depth and posed no real threat. There was no evidence to suggest that he had any access to firearms and had never shown any form of violence in the past.

The original plan had been that if Liam was going to leave without releasing Isobel, they would let him drive three quarters of the way along the drive before he would be rammed by a car coming in the opposite way. Another car would follow him out blocking any way he could escape in the van. In the bushes that cloaked the driveway were a squad of special agents who would storm the van, take Isobel out and detain Liam. A simple, safe exercise. A hidden sniper had not been part of the plan, Neal would be the first to point out.

"What's with Simon, the sniper, we never discussed that."

"True, but I am the senior officer in charge, I need to consider all the possible outcomes. For example, if he began to strangle her, or stab her with one of his carpet knives, that van is full of potential weapons. I needed a contingency plan, the man with the high-powered rifle was that plan. I would point out he was threatening her and that it could have been a gun in his pocket that he was holding against her."

"Nothing in our intelligence pointed to the fact that he could get hold of a gun. What would have made you think he had a gun, let alone know how to use it properly. We all discounted it in the briefing."

"Neal, his father was an IRA operative. It could well have been the case that his grandfather or someone in the family held an unregistered weapon, a hidden gun, and he might have had access to it. I could not take that risk. Our intelligence reports, you'll have to agree, are not always one hundred per cent accurate.

"Now let's get father and daughter home and then clear up this mess. There will be other work for us before the day is out."

"Like what?"

"One thing at a time, Neal, I'll tell you when it's appropriate."

"You are the Brigadier, aren't you, and you know a lot more about that boy's father than you have admitted to anyone so far."

"Neal don't question me or my judgement. Yes, I was once known as Brigadier Howard Harvey. I don't have to answer to you for any of my actions. Get the rescued daughter and her father home as I have asked. You will then get this mess sorted out." Rupert nodded towards the body of Liam. "After that I will enlighten you as to what is required to get this whole sorry story concluded once and for all. I'm going to the house to see if they have any gin stashed away."

* * *

"We'll get you home safely," Tony reassured his daughter as he held her as close as he could. They were together in the back seat of the official car as it drove out, away from The Hoo Hundred, carefully past the covered

234

corpse of Liam. They were leaving behind the nightmare they had endured. He could feel her shaking as she sobbed. Isobel had never seen a dead body before, let alone one with a gaping hole in its skull. She had never been held captive before either.

Isobel had never feared so much that she would die alone and away from her parents. In broken emotional phrases she confessed these anxieties to her father whose strong arms assured her that all was going to be well, the danger had passed, and she was now safe. She told him about the moment she was taken. About being left bound and gagged in a strange house, and that she had no idea where it was located. She wondered if anyone even knew she had been taken. She wondered if anyone would be able to try and rescue her. When her father arrived, she felt relieved that all was going to be well. That is until she heard his body tumble to the floor and Liam once again took her away. During that night she had laid sprawled out in the back of his van. She was cold, bitterly cold, hungry and terrified that her father had died in his attempt to save her. Her mother was in prison unable to help. She was alone in the world with a man she did not know, who, as kind as he tried to be, still deprived her of her freedom. The future looked so uncertain. She had cried throughout the night between fitful bouts of sleep.

Tony wiped the tears from her eyes, comforting her again, telling her that they would soon be home, safe and warm and he would cook her whatever she wanted. He was going to spoil her for the next month, such was his relief. And he added a promise of a new dress.

They were driving swiftly along the A2, approaching the M25 interchange when Isobel asked,

"Why do you think he kidnapped me?"

It was a simple, obvious question that Tony had no real answer for. He simply did not know. Was Liam just obsessed with MI5 and assumed that Tony worked for them and would somehow have some influence with them. Finally he answered his daughter honestly.

"I don't know if I am being truthful. Maybe he thought I was someone that I am not. He was a confused young man who, for whatever reason, had no real plan, no real idea of what he was trying to achieve."

"But he did have the same press cutting that you have, you know, the one with the car dealer."

"I know, he showed it to me that day he came around. He seemed obsessed as to why his father was in England. It's a circle I just can't square. In the same way why did Douglas have the cutting and..."

It was the extreme movement of the car that stopped Tony from continuing. Isobel was thrown against him and in turn he was pushed against the door. The car bucked and swerved as it crossed all three lanes of the road causing annoyance to the drivers that it cut across.

"What's up?" Tony asked, as the driver stopped the car abruptly on the hard shoulder. "Does the car have a problem?" he asked. The driver at once turned around holding his finger to his lips, imploring Tony to remain silent. He then bent down and appeared to be writing on a scrap of paper which he then held up for his passengers to read.

'Don't talk, you're in danger, recording being made.'

Once the driver was sure his passengers had understood his warning, he turned the paper over and began writing again.

'You are safe with me. Explanation once we are outside the car. 20mins to our destination.'

This time the driver handed the message to Tony, turned back to the steering wheel and continued the journey.

"Dad?" He stopped Isobel from saying anything else, shaking his head, returning her to silence. He needed to try and comprehend what was happening. A moment ago he had thought he and his daughter were safe, their ordeal over. Now, in the briefest of instants, he had no idea what was going to happen, whether it was good or bad, he prepped himself for whatever was coming next. The quiet gave him the chance to work through his thoughts, none of which made any sense. How can you plan and prepare for the unknown? He would have to wait twenty minutes to wherever they were being driven to.

It soon became clear they were still heading towards Croydon and the general area of where they lived. The roads were familiar so Tony knew where he was, which could be a big advantage if he found himself needing to break away from this puzzling driver. In the end they parked in a small side road about a mile from Tony's house. The driver signalled for them to leave the vehicle and join him on the pavement. Without a word he beckoned them to follow him. They walked possibly ten feet from the car before Tony spoke and demanded an explanation.

"Can it wait another few minutes?" the driver pleaded. "Top of the road we'll go right and then three roads down I have another vehicle. Let's talk when we get there. Trust me, we need to get away from that car." With his head he indicated the black saloon car they had just left.

"Why should I?" Tony stopped walking, holding his daughter. "I have just seen a man be killed in cold blood. What's to say you're not going to take us to some lonely spot and deal out the same fate to us?"

237

The driver huffed, his hands on his hips, his tone was exasperated. "Two things: first, we're in the London Borough of Croydon, there are not many lonely spots in which to kill and dispose of two people, well, none that I know of anyway. Secondly, it was you who contacted me in the first place asking for help. I'm here helping, but I want to get away from that car." This time he pointed back towards the black car to make himself clear. "Because very soon those kind people who, as you say, shot someone in cold blood will realise that their car isn't where it should be. Come on, let's get moving."

They followed him. He looked to be in his late fifties, Tony could not be sure. Tall and thinly developed, he wore an ill-fitting pair of trousers and a jacket that looked far too small for him lengthwise. He was, Tony considered, oddly dressed. Asking for help, he could not recall asking anyone for help, why would he, there was no one he knew to ask. Then the penny dropped.

"Are you Marcus Young, the editor of the Mirror?" he called towards the man leading them along the empty pavements.

"There you go, but it is ex-editor now. Let's get back to my place before we get into a deeper discussion or worse get caught."

Marcus's place turned out to be a motor caravan, which he was very proud of, describing it as a four berth 2014 Adria Matrix Axess M590 SG. All those numbers meant little to Tony or Isobel, who thought it cool when she was told the vehicle had been home to Marcus for the last few years.

"Right, now I know I said that I was going to explain everything to you, but not just yet. To cut a long story short, and partly satisfy your natural curiosity, I followed you this morning on your excursion to the Isle of Grain. I used my motor bike, which usually resides on the back of this van. I left it hidden in bushes not far from that creepy-looking house. If they find it before I can recover it, it will lead them straight to me and by association the two of you. Now, you two sit back and make yourself at home in the back here, while I drive close to that house and recover my bike. Once I've done that. I will find a safe spot to park and then we can have ourselves a bit of a fry up, most likely a stiff drink for us adults and then we can compare notes and hopefully make some sense of what is going on."

Chapter 28

Rupert paused as his personal driver opened the rear door of the black government issue Jaguar XF saloon. He looked across at the activity around Liam's corpse. Three men were roughly manoeuvring it into a body bag. This was not the first time that he had witnessed what some might describe as disgraceful actions. But it was the first time that now, towards the end of his career, he began to wonder what sort of democracy allowed people to be killed at the whim of the state, then the truth wrapped over with rose-tinted paper. Maybe under all democracies lay a government that resembled a dictatorship. Not all were run by a single person, some were democratic dictatorships run by a select few who used their power to stay on, whoever might oppose them. They had the ability to crush any ideas of freedom in its infancy.

If only the public understood the truth. Governments use poverty to suppress parts of the population. Immigration to ensure groups fight amongst themselves. They share their wealth with a small group of valuable, equally powerful people to control any message the media broadcasts. Then to be fully secure in their ivory towers, they dictate how the votes of the people are calculated, ensuring their special version of democracy continues.

Now he was older, Rupert was more cynical than he had ever been. His youthful idealism had faded away. He felt sorry for Liam's mother. She would be told her son had died. There was a department whose sole purpose was to paper over the cracks that other departments had made by eliminating a threat to the status quo. They would find some plausible excuse to offer his mother. Her grief would distract her, she would shed tears and not question what she had been told by the suited official that she was brought up to trust. Or maybe not in her case, being Irish she would have seen at first hand the way governments fight each other at any cost, just to hold power over a population. Rupert knew that the IRA employed similar techniques to maintain its grip on power.

He shook off the dismal thoughts and refocused on his job of protecting those in power, ensuring their safety in the positions they held. He then noticed Neal talking to a man in a white shirt, too little for a chilly day he thought. Rupert's driver waited tolerantly, holding the door while Rupert watched Neal walk towards the car, a frown on his face. Rupert assumed it was not going to be good news.

"The car taking Tony and his daughter home isn't being driven by any of our staff."

"And do we know who might be?"

"No, not at present. The planned driver was told by a man aged about fifty, tall, slightly built, that there was a change in the rota, and he was to wait in the house for further instructions."

"And he swallowed that hook, line and sinker. I'm just glad that the security services employ such gullible staff, they must be hard to find."

Neal ignored the comment. "The car has GPS and voice recording, so we'll have it traced very soon. I have an officer on it as we speak."

"Get in the car," Rupert ordered. Neal felt he was about to get a dressing down, not for the first time, or the last.

In the muffled, warm atmosphere of the car Rupert sounded calm, which was far from what he was feeling. "We're now at a tipping point. From this moment forth, you and one other officer who you trust with your life, will handle future developments. This has gone far enough. You need to locate the father, the daughter, and the rogue driver. Once you have all three of them under your full control, you need to call me and at that point I will make a decision based on the facts at the time. Am I making myself clear?"

"That depends, are you Mr Bell or Brigadier Harvey? And why did you want Liam dead? There was no need to kill him, unless he had touched a nerve from the past which leads directly to you." Neal was confident to confront his boss in the quiet seclusion of the car, away from prying ears he felt he could say it exactly how he saw it. "I imagine that whoever you might have been at the time, you now know exactly how his father was killed and by whom. It might help me if I also knew."

"Trust me, it wouldn't. Get out now and find them."

Standing by the side of a large plant that he could not identify Neal watched the black car whisk Rupert away from the crime scene. As he always did, he let others clear up the mess that he no doubt had a hand in making in the first place.

***

The recording was damming to say the least. Neal listened to it again just to be sure. Tony did after all have the press cutting and no doubt the negatives too, all that Rupert craved and would stop at nothing to retrieve or destroy. Neal had been convinced that they had been destroyed in the fire, but he had now, just as Rupert predicted, been proved wrong. They had recovered Liam's copy which Rupert took sole charge of and left Hundred Hoo with. There was now just the final copy to go. Neal had to find it and he knew what he would have to do in the end.

The real mystery was the driver, who was he and why had he become involved? For Neal that was going to be an answer he would uncover once he had located Tony and his daughter. They were not at home so he needed to find the most likely place they might go to hide away. There was one person, apart from his wife, who knew him and given the right incentive could reveal all. That was how Neal found himself in a police interview room sitting opposite DC Pete Lewer.

"Is this a formal interview? If so, I want a fed rep in the room with me."

"Don't be so daft, it's an informal chat, nothing more than that. I just want to know where Tony might go if he wanted to avoid contact with the world?"

"What sort of stupid question is that? I worked with the guy; I don't know."

"That's not strictly true is it now? You know an awful lot about Tony: his life, his fears, his aspirations, what he does under pressure. You know him very well, better than you make out. And you were once very helpful to him. Remember the boy that ended up under a lorry, Harry Hobbs? I'm sure you do."

"He was cleared, he was never chasing the kid, just flashed his lights and the stupid kid bolted for it."

"I know that, but the family, the Hobbs family, rum personalities all of them, they still wanted revenge for the death of their dear sweet Harry. Didn't they threaten to kill Tony and his family?"

"Yes, there were threats made."

"And Tony and his family were put into police protection. Where did they go?"

"I don't know."

"You do because Tony told me. His superiors expected the family to storm the station the night he was cleared of any wrongdoing. Tony told me that they needed to be out of town fast and Pete came up with a solution. It was your idea, he never actually told me where they went, I didn't ask, never considered it important at the time. Now I'm asking you, where did you send the Vercoe family?"

"I didn't send them anywhere. He was in a state, worried sick about his family, I just reminded him of where we had a colleague's stag do that he arranged. Why does all this matter now?"

"Because Tony thinks he's in danger so I would imagine he might have gone back to the same hidey-hole."

"I don't trust you one little bit, whoever you say you are, I still don't trust you."

"Okay, let's approach this from another angle. Let me suggest to you that you did help Tony hide or suggest a location, like the friend you say you are. The Hobbs family are out for revenge and hear that Pete has hidden the target of their malice. PC Pete who has helped them, the bad guys, out a few times before: withholding evidence, turning a blind eye, in return for financial compensation. I would imagine they wanted to slit your throat as well. But why didn't they?"

Neal paused, wondering if Pete was going to contest any of the allegations. Not that they were groundless accusations, he knew he had been able to draw a picture that resembled the true facts. He almost expected to hear Pete say, 'No comment.'

Neal continued, "I'll suggest to you why they didn't. Because you quickly came up with an excuse that there are better ways to obtain revenge, like getting Tony's wife framed, very cruel. But not as cruel as getting social

244

services on the case, encouraging them to put Isobel into care. Not that they needed much persuasion. Am I right in thinking that Rita is a cousin of Mr Hobbs, she is some sort of blood relation, isn't she? Not that you are going to admit anything to me.

"You know I don't really care what you have done. All I need to do is locate Tony and his daughter. So, I'll ask you one more time before I walk out of here and inform your superiors what I know about you and your involvement with the Hobbs family. Tell me, where would Tony hide?"

"He might not have gone there."

"True, but I must start somewhere. I suspect he doesn't think me intelligent enough to connect the dots, which is ironic as he hasn't worked out that the Hobbs family are getting their own back. Where would he go?"

Neal left the police station with the address. All he needed now was a bit of luck and he would be home and dry.

Chapter 29

It might have been described as a four-berth camper van, but there was not a lot of room around the table, the three of them felt squeezed in. There were no complaints, the sausage, beans, egg and bacon with, what appeared to be an endless supply of toast, was welcomed by Tony and Isobel, neither had eaten properly over the last couple of days. Marcus was more than happy to feed his guests; it was not often he had the chance to entertain. He swung the lush driver's seat around so that he could face father and daughter tucking into a late breakfast. He was happy with just his large mug of coffee.

"I guess you're keen to hear why it took so long to respond to your message."

Tony swallowed a mouthful of beans and answered, "Whatever the reason, you turned up at the right time as far as I can see. I do have just the one question, why your name was on the back of the press cutting that Douglas Wright had?"

"Sit back and I'll explain all, or at least as much as I can work out. It all began for me back in 2017. Douglas turns up at our offices offering what he describes as the scoop of the century. Well, nothing new in that. He wanted five thousand pounds for his story. Of course, we listened, lots of our stories start off the same way. He had photographs of a guy buying the transit van that was used to carry out the mortar attack on Downing Street in 1991."

"What!" Tony spluttered out with his mouth partly full of sausage. "You mean the IRA attack on Downing Street?"

"You didn't know?" Marcus sounded warmly surprised. "The number plate is clear in some of the photographs, I would have thought someone like you would have at least Googled the number if nothing else. Anyway, yes, it was the same van that the IRA modified to send mortar shells towards the cabinet office and nearly succeeded. That was why Douglas thought he had a valuable scoop on his hands. The thing was the attack was twenty-odd years prior to him now standing in the office trying to offer it to me. It was not news, I told him. Although no one had ever been charged in connection with the attack, there was nothing to prove the person buying that van was linked to the IRA. For all I knew he might be some innocent purchaser and the IRA acquired the van later.

"Anyway, Douglas was understandably a little upset, but I had no use for the photographs. I suggested that the security services might still be interested, they would have the resources to possibly link them to their investigations, if they were still investigating. I waved goodbye to Douglas and that was that I thought."

Marcus soothed his throat with coffee before he continued, noting that both Isobel and Tony had finished eating and were now listening intently to his narrative.

"Not long after that, the Manchester Arena Bombing occurred killing all those concert goers. Our security services quickly shared information with their U.S. counterparts. That information was leaked, and the New York Times printed a lot of stuff that the UK would rather have not put into the public domain. The government always like to be in total control, so decided to call a meeting in the days that followed with national newspaper editors, telling us what naughty boys the Americans had been, and that they expected us to behave better. It was a telling-off stroke threat-type meeting. Not that we would take much notice, but the refreshments are always worth going for.

"I digress. After the meeting everyone mingles and has a drink. I begin chatting to this high-ranking civil servant. We talk about terrorism; the threats and the way different groups emerge. Today it is ISIS, yesterday it was the IRA, we wondered who it would be in the future.

"It turned out that he was closely involved with the fight against the IRA, lots of knowledge. I asked if he knew about Douglas and his photographs of the van. He said he hadn't heard of him but was interested. A day or two later I sent him Mr Wright's contact details. Again, I thought no more of it."

"Do you recall who you sent the details to?" Tony asked as he listened attentively to the facts that Marcus was sharing.

"Howard Harvey, the older guy who was there this morning, the same one I met after the meeting. Evidently, he hasn't retired yet. The next stage of this saga happened later that same year, not sure exactly when, it was just a normal day. I was flipping through news stories, ours and our competitors when I read about a man wanted for questioning following a house fire in which his wife was killed. The wanted man, as you know, was Douglas Wright.

"Now to be honest Douglas Wright isn't a rare name, it might have been the same Mr Wright who was selling or trying to sell me photographs, or another one. Even so, I was curious and poked around a bit. It turned out it was the same Douglas Wright. Now you know you get that feeling deep in your stomach, a misgiving, which you try to dismiss. Something made me call Mr Harvey, asking him if he ever got those photographs, the ones with the van. I said I think it's the same bloke who is now wanted by the police

248

in connection with his wife's death. Well, Mr Harvey didn't appear concerned; just said that he had not got around to following up on the contact details and doubted he would now."

Marcus walked past his guests, placed his empty cup in the sink and leaned against it as he continued, "Again, I thought no more of it. There was not much of a story in it for us, so I shelved it. Glad I did because after Christmas, late January 2018, I get the chop. My 'services are no longer required, thank you and goodbye'. The newspaper industry is fickle, so I was not bitter and twisted about it, just supposed there would be other positions for me, oh, how wrong was I.

"Every door I knocked on remained firmly shut. Nothing, not a crumb to be had. Sod it I thought. I used some of my golden goodbye money to buy this little beauty and travelled the length and breadth of the country, acting like a middle-aged hippy as some would describe me, others just called it a mid-life crisis."

Tony gathered the two empty plates and placed them in the sink. He stood alongside Marcus and asked, "Do you think you knowing about the photographs had anything to do with you losing your job?"

"Not at first, I just shrugged my shoulders and got on with my life, no point moping around. Although I did hear a year or so later from one of my contacts. I kept up with some of my contacts in the industry, old habits die hard. I heard that there were rumours about me concerning sniffing nitrates, dressing in leather and enjoying a good beating from a dominatrix, none of which are my idea of a fun night out. But the rumours were enough to make me an outcast from the world of newspapers. Maybe I should have gone for an MP's job." Marcus laughed. "Anyway, yes, I do think my knowledge contributed towards my situation.

"I thought it even more so when I found out through chatting to some journalist friends of mine that I still keep in touch with, that the reporter and the photographer on the original story didn't make old bones. I had glanced at the press cutting when Douglas showed it to me but wanted to refresh my memory. Oddly, there are no file copies anywhere, not at the newspaper office or even at the British Library, odd yet not unheard of. But you do have a copy?"

Tony shrugged his shoulders, explaining he had the press cutting and the photographs hidden away, safely, he hoped, at his home. He gave details of the story or at least the main points of it to give Marcus an idea of the type of person the car dealer was. From there Tony added what he suspected about the car dealer working with George and Douglas to carry out some sort of car crime. Not that he could tie that in with Liam's story. Then he shared what he knew about the office where it appeared Douglas had found the photographs.

"Well, we have some information but not everything, of that, I'm sure," Marcus concluded. "Everyone knows about the bombing. It's the image of two men buying a van that's evidence of something. One of whom could be Liam's father.

"But we can't stay here in this car park for much longer and we can't go to your place just yet. I imagine they're watching it, so I hope the photographs are well hidden. Do you know of anywhere else we could hole up for a day or two?"

"My uncle has a place on the Isle of Sheppey, a small bungalow he has owned for years and years. Has a local man pop in and keep the garden tidy and the place reasonable. I know where the spare key is hidden, so we could go there."

"What about your uncle, where's he living then?"

"He's in his eighties and lives in Spain all the time, he likes the warmth."

"Okay then, give me the address and we'll be on our way. Oh, I'll be stopping on route, you two have eaten me out of camper and home," Marcus chuckled.

Chapter 30

It had been at least twenty years since Neal had visited the Isle of Sheppey. The last time he had driven onto the island he was in search of old road signs that had been left behind when the island went from the grand Municipal Borough of Queenborough-in-Sheppey to be swallowed by Swale Council. That day, he and a fellow enthusiast had found three defunct signs, he wondered if they had finally vanished now.

Today he was in the lead vehicle of a group of three dark-coloured transit vans, each had five men hidden in the back. They were fully armed with automatic weapons, protected with flak jackets, dark balaclavas and helmets with integrated communications.

The convoy drove past Eastchurch towards Leysdown. Neal watched the passing countryside, thinking the island an odd place with its three prisons, numerous caravan parks and a feeling of an area living in the past. Maybe the island status had been a barrier to expansion and development, not a bad thing he thought.

They stopped at a lay-by a few hundred yards from the right turn they planned to take towards the address that Neal had. Their target, a small isolated bungalow was no more than half a mile down the narrow Harty Ferry Road. Neal got out and spoke to each driver in turn ensuring they knew where they were to deposit their human cargo to maximise the containment of the three people they believed were at the address.

Warning each group that the targets in the house were potentially armed and dangerous. To take no chances they had full authority to neutralise any threat. In his mind he

252

hoped that would be the case. If there were to be any detainees from the house, then he knew it would be up to him to deal with them in the fullness of time. He walked back to the leading van, the passing traffic blowing a cool wind across him, driving his hair in different directions. It was always a mystery to him, why traveling at fifty miles an hour in a car seemed to be a slow pace yet walking beside the road where cars were going at that sort of speed, the passing traffic seemed high-speed.

It was quiet in the cab as he indicated that they should move. They soon turned right into Harty Ferry Road, a single-track road. In silence he looked around the open fields, if Tony's trio did run, there were few places they could hide. All too quickly for Neal the small bungalow appeared on the left. It sat in the centre of a parcel of land, square in shape and lawned all around. This allowed the three vans to drive in fast, one to the front, one to the left-hand side and one to the rear. From what Neal saw of the place, there were no windows or doors on the right-hand side, only a decrepit wooden garage that was fixed loosely to the house.

From the instant that the first van slid to a halt at the rear, to the moment that black-clad men threw flash grenades through the window could only have been a matter of seconds, giving those inside no chance to react. Rapidly, men broke through the front door. Others stood guard beside the broken windows and the rear door. Calmly, Neal sat in the comfort of his van watching his troops go about their defined tasks.

Three men broke down the flimsy, aged, wooden front door, throwing a stun grenade ahead of them before they disappeared into the smoke. Neal could see the second van had discharged its load and men stood beside windows in various stances and positions, pre-determined by the training they constantly went through. Although he could not see the group at the rear, he could hear them communicating via his own radio. He heard the shouts, the code words, the short phrases, all planned to deliver clearly and precisely in as short a time as possible. More and more he heard the group that were searching the inside of the premises calling 'clear' as they investigated every room. They had been there no more than three minutes and Neal had a sinking feeling the place was empty. He had thrown the dice and lost. He now needed to think of something else. He needed to find out who the third person was, the man that had driven Tony away. Who was he and why was he helping?

Even before the men in black had finished searching any probable hiding place, Neal was on the phone. He had asked for CCTV from the area around where the official car had been left. There had to be some footage of the three people walking away. He just hoped they had not got straight into a car as that would make things more difficult.

"Have you got anything for me yet?" he asked the voice at the other end.

The reply came back sounding confident, "There's only one camera in the area, it overlooks the entrance to a park, three people matching the descriptions that you gave walked past just a few minutes after the car had stopped. We've looked around but they don't appear on any other cameras, although there are not many at all in the area."

Neal needed inspiration if not a lot of luck, otherwise things would become very difficult for him. Three people walking along the road. They could have slipped into a house anywhere nearby or jumped into another car. But what car, that was the big question.

He tried to think logically. The mysterious driver who highjacked a government car and took Tony and his daughter away, how did he get to the Isle of Grain? There was only one main road onto the island, A228. Neal took a gamble, sometimes that was all that was left to him.

"Target a camera on the A228, log the details of every vehicle that used that road from midnight until noon today. Then find whatever cameras you can around the last sighting of the trio, compare cars and see if there are any matches. Let me know what you find."

Neal wished that something would come out of it or that beyond his wildest hopes Tony was compelled to return home.

***

"This is a long road, but Harty Ferry Road is coming up on the right-hand side," Tony informed Marcus as they travelled along the Leysdown Road, not far from their destination. Isobel was asleep in the back catching up on some of the hours she had missed.

"So how did you find us at that weird house this morning?"

"Bit of luck really. After I got your message on Facebook, I spoke to some of my friends in the newspaper industry, well, at least those who still want to talk to me. Turns out you're a new boy and ex-copper. We'll talk about that another time. You sounded a genuine guy so I thought I'd pop round this morning and see what I could help you with. Thought I'd get there before nine, knowing that most journalists don't emerge from their homes before ten on a good day.

"I parked up my van a little way away, it does tend to stand out, so I used my motor bike. As I arrived, I saw you getting into what was a very official-looking car. I thought

I'd follow out of curiosity and boy did I see that I was dropping myself into a snake pit. I slipped in and thought it might be better to help you out.

"Get your head down, now!" Marcus shouted, using his arm to push Tony's head down below the windscreen. "Keep it down!" he ordered.

From his prone position, Tony sounded muffled as he asked, "What's going on?"

"Quiet!"

There was a tense silence broken only by a disturbed Isobel calling from the back, "What's happening?"

"Everyone shut up and stay out of sight," urged Marcus.

Moments later Marcus spoke to confirm, "Okay, danger over."

Sitting back up in his seat Tony asked, "What did you see? And that's the turn there on the right." He pointed with his finger to emphasise that they were about to pass the turning they wanted.

"We're not going there. "

"Why?"

"I have just seen what looks like a children's presenter, but I know I saw him this morning standing beside Howard Harvey. He was getting into a transit van, one of three in that lay-by back there. I'd put money on it they were about to pay a visit to your uncle's house. Best we don't join them, I think you'll agree. Question is where next?"

Next was parking beside the coastline at Leysdown-on-Sea at a grassy recreation area, where holidaymakers and dog walkers were mingling. The sky had become veiled in a single shade of dark grey with a cold wind blowing off the sea, brushing the low bushes that fenced the car park. Marcus ensured that both of his passengers were at the back of his camper van and well out of sight of any passing motorists. He then started up the vehicle and made his departure from the island. He had no plans to become cornered on an island with so few roads and only one way off.

As he passed Harty Ferry Road, he peered down the narrow road but saw nothing. He also kept his wits about him every time a dark-coloured transit van came near. As he drove, he shouted over the engine noise to his hidden passengers. Together they needed a plan of action. They were being sought for reasons that were not clear, but both Marcus and Tony were convinced that stepping into the arms of Neal was not going to be their best choice.

The only thing they could try was to attempt to understand why the photographs were so important to someone. That someone they felt sure was Howard Harvey, or as he was now known Rupert Bell. He had held a senior position when Marcus spoke to him back in 2017. It was also clear to Marcus that Rupert had a great deal of knowledge and involvement in the Northern Ireland troubles.

Tony pointed out that the order to kill Liam looked likely to have come from Rupert by dropping his coffee mug, sending a signal to a hidden marksman. He allowed it to happen even though Tony did not think that Liam had any intention of hurting Isobel or anyone else. Another victim, Marcus pointed out as he slowly joined the motorway making his way towards London.

They decided they needed to speak to Liam's mother, find out just who her husband was and what their name was before they came to England. That was going to be down to Tony, as he had met and spoken to Liam, he would be better placed to gain her trust. Marcus was going to talk to the car dealer because Marcus had a good knowledge of the bombing and thought he might be able to intimidate the dealer into some sort of confession, or at the very least give up some nugget of information.

They now needed to find somewhere to park that would not attract too much attention. Marcus had just the place in mind. The Abbey Wood Caravan Site, discreet, popular and close to a railway station, perfect, he confessed modestly. Isobel asked what her contribution would be to the mission.

"Sit tight in the camper van," her father told her. She had half-expected that would be her role.

Chapter 31

It was always going to be a risk, Marcus and Tony both agreed, yet it was a risk that they needed to take. Both men assumed and hoped that Liam's home and mother would not be under observation. Even so, Tony approached the street cautiously and walked past the block of flats twice. Looking at every vehicle. Wondering if concealed eyes could be watching the address. His heart was beating rapidly as he rang the doorbell. A small lady opened the door, her grey hair tied back in a bun, her skin wrinkled and dry. Her image was of a woman whose life had been harsher than it was ever meant to be, yet she was still standing, had not given up and would not either. She observed Tony with a distrustful glint in her eye.

"I was talking to Liam yesterday about his father and I wanted to ask a couple more questions."

"I haven't seen Liam in a few days, he often goes off, his job you know, lays carpets for a living."

"Yes, I know, but I thought maybe you could help me. I presume you're the mother he mentioned a few times. I was sorry to hear about his grandfather, your father, loss is always painful."

"Who are you exactly?"

"Well, I'm a reporter for a newspaper in south London, nothing too grand, but I offered to help Liam find out more about his father and the press cutting he was showing everyone. I think I know you've said to him that there's nothing special about it, but I just want to satisfy Liam's curiosity. I just have a couple of quick questions."

"You'd best come in."

The flat was not big by any stretch of the imagination. Tony noticed there were two bedrooms as he followed the little grey-haired lady along the hallway. Liam must have shared one of them with his grandfather for all those years. Everything about the flat was constraining. There was plenty of furniture and oddments around, cluttered but tidy would describe the place Tony thought, as he sat down at the kitchen table.

"There's not much to tell. Liam likes to fantasise about his father. I guess you know he died when Liam was just a young boy." She lit a cigarette without offering one to Tony. Either she assumed he did not smoke, or she was not used to offering her packet to guests. "His father died in the troubles like a lot of good men."

"But the press cutting he showed me, he maintained it was his father and I think he might be right, there is evidence to show that it was."

Mrs Connor blew smoke across the table above Tony's head, she looked serious, almost as if she was not fully engaged with the conversation.

"Why aren't you asking Liam himself?" she asked, her Irish origin still clear in the tone of her voice.

"I think he's busy with work, and I wanted to try and move this forward as quickly as possible." Tony tried, yet utterly failed, sounding like some business consultant who did not know the answer but wanted to sound intelligent.

"My boy's dead, I know it. The minute he told me he wanted to find out the truth about his father I knew he would die. That's exactly what the British did to all the young men who wanted honesty and a better life, they killed them."

"I don't know why you are saying such a thing, as far as I know he is well." Tony knew he was lying, he just wanted to avoid telling her the truth.

"I was washing up the breakfast things this morning and he stood beside me with that sorrowful smile he always used when he knew he had made the wrong decision. He said to me 'Mam, I'm sorry I should have listened to you'. I would have hugged him, but you can't hug those who have passed over. I'm all alone now, no family, no one who will care for me in my old age. I'll pay the price for all the mistakes my menfolk have made. Now what do you want to ask? I am happy to tell you what I know as there is no one left for me to protect."

Tony wanted to hug her, that was what she needed more than anything else, he could see that. She was now a woman alone. Even so, Tony held back on his emotions and coldly asked the questions he wanted the answers to. He had to; he had his own family to protect.

"Was your husband in the IRA?"

She stubbed her cigarette out on a saucer, then laughed.

"How would I know; I was his wife. All I was required to do was give him children and keep house. Politics wasn't for women to get involved with. Although, even if it was frowned upon, I had an opinion. I guess he was part of those rebels, he never told me exactly, but I am sure he was. Late nights away from the house, extra money when none was expected, male friends of his meeting at our house and excluding me from the room. Yes, I imagine he was part of the IRA."

"Yet he never went to England, or so you told your son."

"How would I know? He never told me anything. He was away for days, sometimes weeks, leaving me alone with a new-born laddie and my father. Maybe he did go, I didn't care. Ireland had gone mad back then, families fighting families, communities fighting each other. Secrets and clandestine activities were normal."

"And his death?"

"Ah, his death, execution, truth be known. One night, close to midnight, two men turn up at the door getting us both out of bed. He puts a few clothes on and tells me he must go. Kisses me on the cheek and that's it, he was gone and I never saw him again. Unless you count seeing him in the chapel of rest. He was executed by the IRA, that we all knew. What he had actually done to upset them and be dealt a sentence for a traitor, I have no idea and cared even less. He was no more of a husband to me than the local butcher. I shed only the tears expected of me."

"But why would you come to England?"

"That was my father's idea, Liam's grandfather. The British offered us the start of a new life in Britain, a bit like being offered a home in Berlin during the blitz. Of course, I told them I wanted nothing to do with them, killers that they were and always had been. The British had been ruling Ireland since 1189, why should we embrace the colonialists. But my father said it was the best thing for me, for him and for young Liam. Well, Grandpa knew best for the simple reason he, no doubt, had a better idea of what Liam's dad was up to. Begrudgingly I followed my father and my son, it's what women do, follow our men wherever their stupidity takes us."

The doorbell interrupted their conversation. Tony felt his body tense as he asked, "Are you expecting anyone?"

"I never have visitors; two in one morning, something is going on. You look scared, a bit like my husband used to when the British Army were patrolling the streets. Come with me and I'll show you Liam's bedroom. Have a look around and keep the door closed. It might be for the best."

Sheepishly he followed her and stood in the bedroom as she closed the door. He wondered what sort of life she must have endured to hide someone so readily and naturally.

The bedroom was cramped. Tony stood between the two single beds that were pushed against the wall. There was just one small wardrobe alongside the window. The bed on Tony's right was laden down with clothes, men's clothes. Plain, simple shirts and trousers, socks and pants and a half-full black bag beside them. No doubt, they were Grandfather's clothes being readied for a charity shop or being disposed of. It would have been strange for Liam growing up, sleeping in a room that he had to share with an old man. Privacy was never going to be an option for the young teenage Liam. The bed on his left was tidy and covered with a Star Wars duvet cover. A wad of carpet samples lay on the bed alongside a pair of jeans, which young people called distressed, Tony would have described them as tatty, worn and falling apart. A single poster of Belinda Carlisle was on the wall, Tony wasn't sure if it was Liam or his grandfather who was the fan. That was a mystery he put to one side as he heard the front door open. He listened as Liam's mum greeted her unexpected caller. He heard a male voice that he recognised; it was Neal's.

"Mrs Connor, I have some bad news for you, may I come in?"

"Where're you from?" she asked stubbornly.

"British Intelligence, better known to the public as MI5. It's about your son Liam." He offered her his identification which she ignored.

"What have you done to my son?"

"He was killed as a result of a tragic accident this morning, whilst he was working for us at a location in Kent. Can I come in?"

"The last time the British entered my house they tried to arrest my husband. I've lived through the troubles and if you have anything to say, then say it on my doorstep."

"Mrs Connor, it would be better if I came in and spoke to you." Neal tried to move forward, he did not want to have this discussion where neighbours and passers-by could hear. She stood her ground, denying him entry.

"As you wish. Your son was working at a location in Kent laying carpet when he was struck by a stray bullet from a nearby shooting range. This is a tragic and sad accident that will be fully investigated."

"I saw his spirit this morning. He said he was sorry, but he never told me he was in an accident. He told me he had been killed by the British. They tell us Irish that the Good Friday agreement has brought peace, it hasn't. All it has done is to sweep the violence under the carpet. The Irish are still killing the British and the British are still killing the Irish. Nothing has changed if you live in my world."

The resentment in her voice was obvious to Neal, discussion and sympathy would get him nowhere. But he needed to get some information across the threshold to this aggressive woman.

"As you wish, I will have our undertaker contact you to make what arrangements you wish. We will of course ensure you have no additional expenses. Could I also add and ask that you don't speak to any newspapers. I understand that a certain reporter might try and contact you, someone called Tony Vercoe. He's not to be trusted and might make things difficult for us all."

"I have lived in Northern Ireland for most of my life, under the rule of the British. The great thing about living in England is I can tell you, the British Government, to feck off without the risk of getting arrested or shot. So, feck off." She slammed the door closed.

Mrs Connor opened Liam's bedroom door and looked at Tony standing in the middle of the room. She slumped down on to Liam's bed. "Sounds like you're a threat to them, that makes you a good guy in my books. I'm just sorry I cannot give you any more information, as I said my husband told me very little."

"There's one more thing. What was your surname in Northern Ireland before you changed it when you arrived here."

"That's easy," she replied.

Chapter 32

There were always going to be good days and bad days in any job, that was the nature of paid employment. Some days things went your way, you truly thought you enjoyed your work, then there were the days when nothing seemed to be going right. For Neal today was one of the dark days when through no fault of his own, everything seemed to be going wrong.

Ever since Rupert had dropped his insulated coffee mug with its concealed gin and tonic, followed by the sniper's bullet sailing through the air and into Liam's brain, nothing had gone right.

Somehow Tony and his daughter were allowed to slip out of the protective care of the government. They had proof of three people walking away from the government car, the second male was unidentified so far. Where they went after that was a mystery. Then a raid on a possible location where they might be, turning out to be a total waste of time and energy. Then the visit to Liam's mother. In Neal's mind he had played out the scene as the mother cried and sobbed at the news her son had died. He would help, make tea and comfort her, all very civil. He hoped to ask a few questions about her son and her husband. He hoped to find out something, which was the real cause he was frustrated. It was not so much his inability to locate Tony, more his lack of knowledge as to the reason he was hunting down this ex-policeman.

Given all the technology at his disposal, cameras on almost every street corner, he was no nearer locating Tony or the person helping him. They had to be using some sort of vehicle, he just needed a clue, but that clue was evading him at present.

If things weren't bad enough already for Neal, Rupert walked into his office, slammed the door behind him and sat down with a face that was crimson and flushed with anger.

"You've lost the reporter, haven't you?"

"Mislaid is a better description, it will only be a matter of time before he finds the need to turn his phone on or use a credit card. He is bound to contact his wife in the next few hours to reassure her that he and his daughter are safe."

"And the other man? His personal chauffeur who managed to snatch the interfering reporter out of our hands, have you mislaid him as well?"

"Until I have worked out exactly who he might be, I can neither lose nor mislay him."

"Who do you have working with you on this?"

"No one who needs to know the reason we are seeking to detain the reporter and his daughter. I felt it would be better if any secrets there might be contained between us."

"Sensible and prudent."

"Just one small point. You have kept me in the dark for years. I have no idea just why we are so eager to detain Tony and his daughter and now the unidentified male. I know it relates somehow to some thirty-year-old photographs and the troubles in Northern Ireland. If, in the end, I am required to make sure there's nobody left standing, I would like to know the reason I am required to end someone's life."

"You weren't this concerned when you kicked over a heater and burnt a house down, what has changed?"

It was a fair question. Neal had ensured that the fire took hold, which was what he wanted. Any house fire is dangerous, of that he could not argue. It was just that at the time he was convinced the house was empty. Douglas's car was not outside. He had even rung the doorbell, but no one answered. Then he had broken the lock, stepped inside holding a small paraffin heater that he had modified, lit it, then turned it on its side before swiftly leaving the house. Simple, until he learnt that a woman had died. Why hadn't she answered the door, was she deaf, out of earshot or was the bell just not working? Neal could not ask or ever find out now.

He regretted that day deeply. He had come away believing that the evidence that needed to be wiped out, 'those damn photographs' had been destroyed. They had not.

Now Neal could see that he would be asked to kill a father and his daughter as well as another man he did not even know. It had gone too far just to ask for the photographs back and let's forget about them. An ex-policeman, now a reporter, had witnessed the execution of a young man, he was not going to scuttle away in the shadows and overlook the whole thing.

"I still have a right to know, it might even help me to find them. Why are these photographs so important to you and the government? All I can see is some boring evidence that a man bought a van to bomb Downing Street, hardly any surprise there."

Rupert had relaxed, maybe this was his opportunity to share the secret. It might even help him to sleep at night knowing someone else knew the facts, the dark truths that had to be buried, come what may.

"Maybe this is a good time Neal, just be aware, that once you have let the genie out of the bottle, you will never be able to put him back. Do you want to know the whole story?"

Neal nodded, what could be so toxic after all these years. Cabinet papers are made public after thirty years, no one bats an eyelid then.

"First, let me tell you a story of when I was a boy, a teenager hanging around with friends, getting up to mischief. Thirteen-year-old boys who all thought they were indestructible and acted that way. Smoking, drinking, trying everything we could to prove our worth, including shoplifting.

Not once or twice, but a few times we hit the High Street shops, mooched the aisles of those little shops whose owners could only watch one boy at a time. Easy meat. Looking to see what we could steal, our hearts racing, our senses heightened and our veins full of adrenaline. Better than the booze, better than some of the drugs we tried. I'd see the item that took my fancy, easy enough to pick up, one last look around and it was into my pocket, then move to another part of the shop, fun times. Next off to the local park to compare our loot. I was not the best thief in our gang, but I did try my best, same as I always did.

"But there was one night I got home with my spoils and spread them out on the bed, five items, not worth a lot, but they represented my criminal activities for the day. I looked at them, each one and do you know what I figured out. I didn't really want any of them. None of them were of any worth to me, they were totally useless. I knew I would in a very short time throw them away, just as I was in danger of throwing my life away if I was caught. God, the consequences of that did not bear thinking about.

"I stopped there and then. Never went shoplifting again, even when my friends tried to coerce me, I just stepped away and waited in the park for them to return. I realised that sometimes we do things that seem good at the time, the right thing to do, but in the end a lot of it comes down to peer pressure.

"Thirty years ago, around the time those photographs were taken, I once again yielded to peer pressure because I thought it was going to help me. It didn't, it only left me with a sense of guilt and no one to confess to."

"Your point is?" Neal asked, having been lightly amused as Rupert shared his teenage misdemeanours.

"Thirty years ago, I sat in a meeting with some very powerful men. I felt privileged and a little intimidated being in the same room as these giants of government and I agreed to something which I felt to be right at the time. But it was the worst thing I have ever done."

Chapter 33

The heavy humidity did not make Marcus feel comfortable in the least. He had never coped well with heat at the best of times. Inside a greenhouse designed to hold the high temperature in such a way as to fool the many cacti into behaving as though they were sitting in a desert, was not somewhere Marcus wanted to be. He refused to let the perspiration trickling down his spine put him off asking Mickey questions.

"My missus tells me you're a TV star?"

That was not strictly true as Marcus tried to explain to a wide-eyed Mrs Ross as she answered the door. It was true that Marcus had years ago appeared regularly on a daytime television programme, which took a broad and often humorous look at current news events. She was an avid viewer and had recognised him at once. Without further ado she guided this star of television out of the house and into the greenhouse where she introduced her guest as, 'Marcus Young, from the telly'.

"I have been on the box a few times a while back now. My day job was a newspaper editor. But I'm here to ask you just a few questions, man to man."

Mickey turned back to the cactus he was potting. He liked to avoid answering questions, he knew from experience, how you answer could often get you into trouble.

"If you're not Old Bill, I don't have to answer, do I?" Mickey pointed out arrogantly.

Marcus picked up one of the potted cacti from a shelf in front of him and examined the specimen closely. The tall spiky plant resembled a small under-ripe pineapple with small pink flowers. He turned it round before replacing it and observing, "Mammillaria Sheldonii, ugly little plant with attractive flowers."

The comment caused Mickey to turn back to his guest. "You a cactus fan?"

"I dabbled a few years ago. I found them to be very therapeutic after a long hard day at the office. I lined my windowsills with them. Just sat there in the evening imagining I was in a far-off desert, although I wouldn't be, for the simple reason I hate the sun. But the mental image was relaxing enough."

"Bit of a gardener are you?"

"No, hate gardening. Also, I lived in a flat, hence no garden thankfully, which everyone thinks is odd, given that I was brought up in the country. My father was a local vicar, Sunday services, living in a vicarage, that sort of thing. Always out in the woods or rushing across fields. Yet I prefer the town to live in with the escape of some greenery around the house. Selling a van to the IRA, that was a dangerous thing to do?"

"Ahh, that's what this is all about, that bloody news story. Thirty years ago and still it haunts me. At the time I never knew the Irish guy was IRA, not that it would have stopped me selling him the van, I didn't really care who I sold to. If anyone wanted a vehicle with little or no paperwork, I was their man."

"Euphorbia Obesa," Marcus pointed towards another cactus, a boring green globe, "or the baseball plant, as I recall. When did you learn that the IRA had bought a van from you?"

"Why the questions and why now?"

"Because I want to know what actually happened back then. You're a small spoke in a very large wheel. You, I have little interest in. Although I would imagine the local police would take an interest in you if they knew a little more about your current business associates. George Stevens I hear is one, as well as the deceased Douglas Wright. But I couldn't really care less about that. When did you find out you had supplied the van that the IRA used to bomb Downing Street?"

Mickey took off his rubber gloves placing them carefully on the bench before he knelt and opened a fridge door. He offered a bottle of beer to Marcus who refused. Mickey stood up with his bottle, twisted the top off and took a large swig. "Helps to keep me cool in this atmosphere. I never knew about the IRA connection until Douglas showed me the press cutting. He told me I'd sold the van to the Irish and it was a secret I should keep as the police would be interested to know more about it."

"Was that a threat or a friend helping out?"

"It was a threat, a bloody obvious threat. He told me he was happy to keep quiet, not mention it to anyone if I helped him out."

"Doing what?"

"Once a car dealer always a car dealer. I get friends and family asking if I can get them cars, do them a good deal being in the trade an' all, I help out. I tell George and Douglas the sort of car I'm looking for and they source it. Just good old-fashioned deals between friends, they make a bit, I make a bit, my friends get a good deal, nothing untoward."

"They nick cars to order?"

"I have no idea where they source them. All I know is they give me the car and the paperwork. I pass it on. I am sure they would never dream of stealing a car. But Douglas, thinking he had a hold over me, wanted a bigger slice of the profit margin. He wasn't going to get it."

"You killed him?"

"Don't be stupid, in my world a good beating is one thing, murder is never on my agenda, never has been and never will be. You sure you don't want a beer; you look like you're getting hot."

"No thanks. Back when the article came out, grassing you up as a bent car dealer, I bet you thought that was the end."

"Is that all you're interested in, me selling a van and getting my name in the paper?"

"Yes, I am sure there is something in there which will help me. Run me through your prosecution."

"Well, when I read the paper I thought, that's it, I'll be doing time for this. But in the end, it was all very easy, nothing much happened to me. I got a suspended sentence; I had a good result. I did think it funny at the time that not many local coppers were doing the investigation, I knew a few of them. I was told it was more to do with the way I avoided VAT. Some officials turned up, took what they said was a sample of my records. In the end they did nothing about the VAT. Win, win for me. I can tell you I was relieved."

"You were dealt with during 1990, before the bombing?"

"Yes, I heard about the bomb the following year, didn't we all, but never really took much notice about the van. It was Douglas who pointed out to me that the van I had sold went to the IRA. I have recently remembered it being an Irish guy, but as I say, I sell to anyone. I couldn't afford to be fussy."

"There's no chance you can recall any names from the transaction, is there?"

"It was thirty years ago, John Smith and Paddy McGinty for all I know. Whatever names they gave me at the time would have been false."

The humidity was starting to get to Marcus. He was still perspiring and now he was feeling a little faint, yet still his mind was sifting through the facts. When Mickey was looked into, no one should have known that the van was going to be used for a bombing, so why was Mickey treated so lightly? Was there a connection? His crimes would have carried a jail sentence and his avoidance of VAT would have landed him a hefty bill. It was almost as if someone wanted his case to be kept quiet, tucked under a pile of other stories. Could someone in authority have known that the van was going to be used in the attack? An IRA spy, deep in the heart of MI5. Surely that was not feasible.

***

They sat like any other customers in Costa coffee. One man tapping away at a laptop, the other writing notes on a paper pad. They could have been dealing with customer questions, ordering stock for their business or setting up some entrepreneurial company that was going to make them millions.

Instead, they were hiding, unable to use their mobile phones for fear of being located. Using what little cash they had to avoid their debit cards showing up in some mainframe computer and alerts being sent to notify the authorities of where they were. Today they might be keeping a low profile, but Tony knew that he could not run forever. He had a daughter who needed her education and a chance to grow up and mature. He had a wife in prison who was looking forward to the day that she would leave the cell walls behind and return to her family. Tony knew he had to find a solution and Marcus was doing his best to help him.

If only they could work out what was so special about the photographs.

Now that they had Liam's surname, the one he had when he was born and the one his father used, they stood a chance. Declan MacGabhann, Liam's father, died in 1992. Quietly for fear of being overheard Marcus shared what he had found out about the father online. It contradicted what Liam had suspected.

"According to this news story, Declan MacGabhann was found dead in a ditch in early July 1992. In a style typical of IRA ritual killings, his body was found naked and hooded, showing evidence of beating and a single bullet through the back of his head. Apparently, the IRA tried to justify the murder in a detailed statement outlining the intelligence work Declan had performed and linking him to the murder of a civil servant. The story makes him out to be a spy for the British, which we suspected. When the IRA found him out, they dealt their own form of justice."

"And the civil servant?"

"There's no name here, nothing more about it. At the time in Ireland there were killings left, right and centre, only the more dramatic ones would have warranted more column inches. And if he was a spy for the British Government, then the powers that be wouldn't have wanted too many headlines."

"Yet I am thinking," Tony said, as he vaguely stirred his coffee, "a dead civil servant, could that have been a British civil servant with a connection back to Rupert Bell, or Brigadier Howard Harvey as he was known at the time?"

"Good point," Marcus agreed nodding his head, stirring the theories around in his mind.

"Then if that was Liam's father who popped over to England to buy the van months before the operation was carried out," Tony began, "the authorities might have known about the bombing, mightn't they?"

"They might well have been aware and sent someone over to pull Liam's father out of Ireland back to England and safety. But maybe the civil servant was then caught and killed. The IRA were lying when they stated that it was Liam's father who killed the civil servant and decided to kill Liam's father as a spy."

Stirring his coffee, Marcus applied his own logic as he had throughout his career. "There's a caveat. It depends on whether he was working for the British at the time. He could have been turned into an informant afterwards for all we know. It could even have been the case that his IRA masters told him to buy a van but didn't tell him the whole plan. It was so long ago, it's hard to tie anything down as a hard fact and without hard facts we have little to fight with."

Chapter 34

Being alone was the worst part. She had spent too many hours over the last couple of days in unfamiliar surroundings, first as a hostage strapped to a chair, now ordered to stay in the camper van. She felt she was still imprisoned and longed for the normality of her school, her bedroom. The luxury of going out when she wanted, showering in her own bathroom with her own sponge and the perfumed shower gel her parents had bought for her birthday. And using her phone, that was what she missed the most.

Alone watching boring TV, she could not rid herself of the gruesome image of Liam releasing his grip on her as the blood gushed from his head and splattered down her body. She screamed then and wanted to scream now, but her confinement forced her to be silent, her emotions building within her young body. She wanted sweets, a packet of Haribo, a sugar rush. Or was there something else she could use to divert the painful sensations?

She searched the cupboards. There were not many to look through and she soon found a half-full bottle of red wine. She took a mouthful straight from the bottle. The taste made her cringe and shudder, it also tempted her to try again. It was better the second time around, the third more so. By the fourth she felt calm and looked around for a glass. Then she decided it was not worth it now and continued to drink from the bottle. There was something rebellious about the action that made her believe in herself and that things were not as bad as they might be.

Once it was emptied, she again focused on the Haribo sweets that she craved, and indeed anything else that might distract her from replaying the sound of the bullet cracking the bones in Liam's skull.

She left the confines of the camper van and for a few moments drank in the freedom and fresh air of the outside world. There was a shop nearby which she walked towards and entered; pleased to find it sold a wide assortment of sweets. She picked up what looked like a pretty coloured bag of sweets. She liked pretty bags and was not concerned about what was inside. The wine was starting to cloud her normally discerning taste. As she gripped three Haribo bags, her nostrils detected the warm homely odour of the freshly cooked pies which were residing in a cabinet keeping them warm.

She had to have a Cornish pasty if they had one, she loved them and just hoped that Marcus had some brown sauce back at the camper van. She swayed a little as she pointed out to the shopkeeper the pastry that had taken her fancy.

In front of her on the counter were the objects of her slightly addled desire. Three Haribo bags, one pasty in a brown paper bag and a postcard that she planned to send to her mother. She scrabbled around her pockets to find some money, not that she ever had much on her. Normally she would only use cash as she had always thought it better to be aware of how much you were spending. Credit and debit cards seemed to easily hide and confuse about the amount being spent on them. Her friends called her old-fashioned, she thought she was sensible. With all that had gone on in her life over the last few days, she had run low on cash and so had to offer her debit card to the small terminal. Contactless, so easy, she was always terrible at recalling her PIN. Pleased with herself she walked in an unsteady manner back to the camper van, looking forward to a

Cornish pasty with lashings of brown sauce followed by sweets as she watched more boring TV. She wondered if Marcus had any more wine hidden in the van.

***

"Have you been drinking?" was the first thing that Tony asked his daughter, as he stepped into the van followed by Marcus. He could smell the alcohol on her breath and her speech was not as distinct as it was normally. She could not deny it, she admitted it at once offering her father a sweet as a peace offering.

Not being a parent Marcus saw the funny side, suggesting that given what Isobel had been through a glass of wine was perhaps the best thing for her, adding, "Maybe we should all have a glass or two tonight, I think we could use it."

Tony could see the point Marcus was trying to make. Yes, she had been through, things no teenager should have to endure. The last few years had been traumatic for her. Her mother in prison, her father losing his job, difficult days at school, being kidnapped and then having to watch a man being killed violently. And now she was with her father and a stranger in a mobile home, hiding out from a threat they were sure was there. Considering all that, he was pleased that she had not taken to recreational drugs to try and find some peace.

"I suppose you're right, a glass of red would be good," Tony agreed. "Although I don't think Isobel should have much more if any at all."

"I'll pop to the shop and grab us a bottle as your daughter has cleared out my cellar," Marcus joked seeing the funny side of the situation.

As Marcus opened the door, a gush of cold air blew in clearing Tony's mind. He spoke firmly, "Wait," he instructed Marcus. "Isobel, how did you pay for all this?"

"There was half a bottle of red in the cupboard."

"No, I'm talking about the sweets."

She looked at her father with confusion in her eyes. What did he mean? Was he asking if she stole them? Who did he think she was, a little tipsy maybe, but not dishonest.

"My debit card," she confessed innocently.

Marcus stopped, turned back and closed the door.

Looking at Tony he expressed what both men felt. "Shit!" he exclaimed, "they're bound to be watching her card as well. We'd best get going." He moved towards the driving seat collecting the ignition keys from the table.

"What's 'a matter?" Isobel, still slightly intoxicated, asked, not comprehending what was occurring.

"Don't worry, darling, we just need to get going again." Tony put his arm around the daughter he loved, hoping he could continue to do the same in the coming years. "We need to find somewhere else to stay."

Chapter 35

Ask any red-blooded male, 'Fancy driving fast through traffic with blue lights flashing and a loud two-tone horn blaring, parting the said traffic like the Red Sea?' most would say, 'Yes please'.

Neal was not in that group; in fact, he hated being driven at speed. There were several elements to being propelled in an unmarked car boasting a siren and blue flashing lights, which he disliked. First the noise. The two-tone horns are not in the least tuneful and when you are in the car, they are constant and deafening. All around you, the blue lights are reflecting off other cars, shop windows and buildings, even more so at this time of night. If Neal suffered from epilepsy, he would have by now been convulsing in the passenger seat.

Then the misconception that traffic jumps out of the way when an emergency vehicle approaches, do they heck! To be fair, he saw that most did. Others, though, drove in a lacklustre fashion, unaware of the impatient car behind them that needed to be somewhere else urgently.

Added to that, the speed that the trained drivers sent their cars through traffic, unimaginable gaps between car and traffic islands towards oncoming traffic. The whole experience resulted in him feeling nauseous and wishing that he did not have to get to a mundane camping ground in southeast London in the shortest possible time.

The only redeeming feature of this drive was that he had a lead. Isobel Vercoe had used her debit card at a shop located at the Abbey Wood caravan site. Neal could not imagine Abbey Wood had such a facility, yet he could not deny the fact that was exactly where they were heading. It did also lead onto another possible fact, if she was at a camp site then he could assume her father and the mystery third man were with her. A simple deduction would point out that the three of them were ether under canvas, a little unlikely, or in a camper van of some description. This had encouraged him into asking by phone, as he was being bounced around in the high–speed car, for one of his staff to check all registration numbers entering the Isle of Grain today, picking out those that were registered to a mobile home of any shape or size, including those small, to his mind, useless VW camper vans. The unlucky member of staff was then told to do the same for the Isle of Sheppey and see if there were any matches between the lists. Neal wanted the answer within thirty minutes. He imagined that was going to be a tall order but hoped his diligent employee would think of a quick method.

Luckily for Neal, the employee had the answer within twenty–three minutes as he pointed out to Neal. He had taken the list of all cars entering the Isle of Grain today, then the list of all the cars entering the Isle of Sheppey, compared the two, simple. There were twenty registration plates to run, more than Neal had imagined there might be. Three of the vehicles were camper vans. Using his initiative, not always encouraged in the civil service, he checked the ANPR cameras close to the camp site that he had heard Neal was heading for. There was now just one number left.

"Just text me the bloody index number," Neal shouted over the din of the sirens. "Writing down numbers at speed is not an option for me."

The employee texted the number, waiting in vain for any sort of praise.

Chapter 36

"You're the ex-copper," Marcus pointed out as he guided the camper van into the back streets of Abbey Wood. "What are the chances they have identified this magnificent vehicle with their clever technology?"

It was a critical factor, Tony agreed as he comforted his daughter.

"I'm sorry, Dad, I didn't think." Her voice was racked with guilt.

"It's not a problem. For all we know they might not be tracking any of your cards. And to be honest, it won't be the first time a Vercoe has done something silly under the influence of drink," he joked, hoping to lighten the mood and ease her remorse.

"You make a good point Tony; they might not be tracking her card. But if they are, then they will be on their way. How much do you have in your account Isobel?"

She shrugged her shoulders. "I dunno, about three or four hundred pounds."

"Good, we'll stop at the next cash point we find and take the lot out. If they are tracking your card, then they will not learn much if we do it soon. Also, we'll have cash on us should we need it. I'm sure your dad will pay you back."

All agreed that was a sensible plan. They had nothing to lose, although Tony did suggest that if they were tracking Isobel's card then he might as well use his own at the same machine, they would not learn anything extra. Marcus could see his point, yet felt caution was still a better plan. Using Tony's card would guarantee giving their location away.

"We're only leaving the camping ground as a precaution. There's nothing to suggest at present that they're watching Isobel's bank account," Marcus pointed out.

They stopped in Plumstead High Street, cleared out Isobel's account and continued their journey.

As Marcus made his way back to the A2 trunk road, he asked once again, "You haven't answered me. Do you think they have this vehicle on their radar?"

"Well, I doubt a four-berth caravan on wheels fits their idea of a perfect getaway car. They know where you dumped their car, so maybe in time by crosschecking numbers, they might identify your registration plate. But if they have been tracking Isobel's bank card, then that will be a big clue, they will know we're at a camp site. The site office will have records of our arrival so they will have the information about this vehicle and by now they will have an identity for you."

"OK, for now we could still be under the radar, but for how much longer we can't tell. We need a plan, somewhere we can hole up for a few days," Marcus advised as he manoeuvred along in lane one amongst the lorries and vans travelling towards south Kent.

"George's place," Tony suggested, "where Douglas Wright died. That's the only place I can think of. There's space there to hide your camper, places where we can be out of sight, and he has a natural distrust of authority. He'd be happy to help, I'm sure."

"OK, we'll start there. But first I need to do something."

Marcus pulled off at the next slip road, drove over the motorway and parked up in a quiet corner of the car park which serviced the Black Prince Hotel. He ignored Tony's questions and got out and began fiddling first at the rear of

285

the motorhome and then at the front. Five minutes later he got back into the driver's seat, wiped his hand on an oddment of cloth from the door pocket and started the engine.

"I know you are wondering what I have just done," Marcus said as he left the car park and re-joined the motorway, Kent bound, "and I'm not proud of it. But when travelling the country, I found it a lot easier when going through certain places, such as the Dartford Tunnel to fit false plates on this jalopy to avoid paying the required tolls, most of which are no more than an unofficial tax, lining the pockets of rich companies. Anyway, I thought it might be prudent to change the identity of our transport just in case they have identified me and my mobile home. It seems a small crime in the scheme of things.

"Right, what's the address of this George chap who is going to conceal us outlaws?"

***

"Stand 30, round to the left opposite the toilets," Neal instructed his driver, having gathered the information from the site reception. No longer travelling at break-neck speed, they were now no more than a discreet black car smoothly driving along the tarmac at a leisurely pace avoiding drawing any attention from the campers.

They parked on stand 30, it was empty. Neal banged the dashboard with his fist in frustration and anger. How did they know he was coming for them? Or had they just chosen that moment to leave, even though they had booked for two days? No, they knew somehow.

"What now?" the driver asked, hoping that Neal would say, 'let's have a break'. He was gasping for a cigarette.

Neal ignored the question, instead he called the employee who was still monitoring, among other things,

286

the ANPR cameras. From the conversation Neal learnt that Isobel had again used her card to withdraw three hundred and twenty pounds from a cash dispensing machine in Plumstead. Following that the camper van was pinged by an ANPR camera in lane one of the A2 heading south. That was exactly what Neal wanted to hear. What he did not want to listen to was that his employee had been due to leave the office an hour ago and would very much like to be relieved from duty.

"You stay right where you are, doing what you are doing until I tell you to stand down. Understood?" It was understood, just not welcomed. The driver listening to Neal gave up any hope of having a cigarette.

"Right, let's get back on the road, blue lights till we get to the motorway, then blend in with the rest of the traffic until we catch them up which should not be that hard."

"It's going to be a long night. I need a pee." The driver turned the engine off and made his way to the toilet block. How hard could it be to catch up with a slow-moving camper van, they had a high-powered car with blue lights and sirens plus access to ANPR and CCTV. Neal joined his driver in the urinals, no point being uncomfortable.

***

Marcus was driving steadily along the motorway, Tony, beside him in the passenger seat. Isobel had fallen asleep on the bed at the back of the vehicle. They drove in silence, each man lost in his own thoughts.

Tony began to reflect on what Marcus had said about Mickey, the car dealer, and the veiled threat that Douglas had made to him because he wanted a bigger share of the profit. Money and greed are two vices that often end in death. Part of Tony wanted to believe that MI5 had ended Douglas's life, but that just was not plausible. He was hiding away from them and there was nothing to indicate that they had found him. Was it a coincidence that Douglas ended up with George, both men having an interest in stealing cars, or had there already been a connection between the two? Tony could not square that circle.

He was sure that Mrs Wright had died in a fire that had been deliberately started, not by her husband, but by the national security agents that no doubt had a hand in murdering the reporter and photographer connected to the original story. They would have initiated the career-wrecking tales that plagued Marcus.

The night of the fire Douglas had tickets, he had a passport to leave the country, he could have slipped away, unless he was convinced that government officials would have warned all ports and points of departure. That had to be the reason he stayed in the United Kingdom. He knew the government wanted him dead at all costs. In the end they missed out, someone else had succeeded. But who? That was the question Tony turned over and over in his mind until his thoughts were disrupted when Marcus spoke.

***

The blue lights had been turned off. The siren silenced as they flew along in the fast lane making as much progress as they could, both men peering forward looking for the camper van. The noise of the tyres on the tarmac seemed to reassure Neal that things were going well. His phone rang.

His employee was reporting that they now had the name of the driver. Marcus Young, currently unemployed, was at one time an editor of a national newspaper, no fixed address, contact details are a solicitor's office. Plenty of sleaze on him, the reporter, not the solicitor, one of the reasons that he lost his job and never found employment again. There is an intelligence flag that he might have connections to the IRA.

After what Rupert Bell had confessed to Neal earlier, he thought it strange that an editor that might have links to the IRA had lost his job through sleaze. Something in Neal's logical mind did not fully connect the dots.

"Which intelligence officer added that flag to his file?" It was a natural question in the circumstances.

"Rupert Bell."

It made sense now but was depressing for Neal; he knew that all three of them, once in his grasp, would not be allowed to survive the night.

"By the way," the employee added, "the target has just pinged leaving the motorway at the Black Prince Junction."

"Shit! We've just passed it. Turn around at the next junction," Neal instructed his driver, then asked the man on the other end of the phone, "How long ago did it ping?"

"Seven minutes."

"Why didn't you start with that information you cretin?"

"How am I supposed to prioritise facts when I have no idea what you are working on, plus, I don't work well when I am tired." The protest was blatant.

It might have been obvious, but Neal ignored it.

"Any other pings? Where's he heading now?" The answer came back negative. The employee started to view traffic CCTV from the area to see if he could spot them.

The next junction was for the M25 and was slow and sluggish. Neal did not want to say it, he knew he would hate it, but he had little choice.

"Blues and twos, let's get back to the Black Prince junction as quick as we can."

***

"I have been wondering," Marcus asked, as a large articulated lorry sped past them, the vortex of wind shuddering the camper van. "I'm sure your wife is innocent of any criminal activity and was framed, could that be somehow connected to all this?"

"She was certainly framed; of that I've no doubt. The motive is the part I can't figure out. I'm sure I made a few enemies while I was in the force, but now I'm out, it's hard to get any facts or investigate to the degree required. No one at my station, save for a couple, is willing to help and those I consider to be amenable don't want to risk their own career to help me. But connected to all this, I can't see how it could be, it's only recently the photographs have come to light."

Maybe nothing was related, Marcus supposed, then again maybe everything was, that was the dilemma. The quandary was not unusual territory for Marcus, he had faced many such choices during his time as a newspaper editor. A selection of facts, some would join up for a story, others would be cast aside. Then there was the ever-present danger that the facts you cast aside were the ones that led to an even greater story.

"Okay, let's consider the photographs, including the press cutting and the negatives. All were neatly hidden away in an office, which we know was a part of the National Security Services housing spy masters. Or at least those bods who looked after informants during the Northern Ireland troubles.

"Why hide them in the first place? Why not just leave them in some grey filing cabinet that's locked away or simply destroyed? I'll tell you – they were kept to either provide some sort of insurance for someone or to use for blackmail. The thing is they get forgotten, left behind. So, whoever hid them away either has a bad memory, or they were no longer around to pull them out before the place was refurbished. That leads me to the civil servant who was murdered in Northern Ireland. Could they have been the person to have hidden the photographs...?"

"And Liam's father was being blackmailed, hence him killing the civil servant," Tony interrupted gleefully.

"It makes sense," Marcus agreed. "A civil servant, knowing that Declan McGabhann brought the van used in the mortar bombing, sees it as a way of making money. Or at the very least forcing Declan to do things he was not keen on doing. So Declan kills the civil servant.

"We just need to research and find the name of the actual person that Declan MacGabhann murdered, that will I'm sure reveal all the reasons behind the strange events that are overtaking us. Once we're at George's place we can start digging on the internet."

"As well as ask George a few questions about supplying vehicles to Mickey, which should make him compliant to any of our requests," Tony laughed.

***

To start with they could not move fast, the traffic was thick but as they cajoled drivers to move and shift, a gap gradually opened up. At least, Neal thought, when they did drive at speed no one had a chance to look at the occupants. Now as they edged alongside cars, vans and lorries, Neal felt as though he was in a goldfish bowl. He tried to ignore the curious stares of drivers and passengers.

Before long they were racing once again at high-speed back to the junction. For Neal it was still a discomfort, just a different type of discomfort. This time his phone beeped, a WhatsApp message. Understandably, the employee was done talking to his boss.

'Target in Black Prince car park.'

"What's the silly sod talking about Black Prince car park, I thought it was the junction."

The driver, bored with driving up and down a motorway, shared the local knowledge he had gained over years of working for the department.

"I think he must mean the hotel there; it's called the Black Prince. Well, it used to be called that, I believe it's a Holiday Inn now."

They entered the car park without fanfare, just another car arriving at a hotel. They looked around for the camper van, up and down the lines of parked cars, surveying the area. Nothing.

Neal called back to the office, "We're in the car park, where's he gone now?"

There were a few moments of silence before the reply came, "The target has not left the car park."

"I'm looking for a poxy camper van not the friggin' Tardis," Neal interrupted.

"I know, if you'll just give me a chance. A van looking just like the target left, the plates were different, hence I missed it at first. I think they might have changed their registration plates. The new van has just re-joined the A2 Kent bound. I'm tracking it as best I can."

They left the car park and re-joined the trunk road, Kent bound. The driver wanted to say it was a bit like being in the Keystone Cops but thought better of it.

***

"So what's Rupert's interest in all this? What if the murdered civil servant was blackmailing Declan

292

MacGabhann, who in turn found himself at the wrong end of a gun, doesn't that end the affair?"

"Apparently not," Marcus concluded. "It can only go back to the fact that the UK Government was aware that the bombing was going to take place, they just failed to stop it. It could still prove to be embarrassing even thirty years on, but I would not have thought uncomfortable enough to go on a killing spree. Unless somehow Rupert, who handled Declan MacGabhann, did something to spur the IRA to kill Declan, which might have then left the powers that be knowing the attack was coming, just no idea when it was going to occur."

"But Declan MacGabhann was killed after the bombing, as was the civil servant."

"And Liam maintained that it was the British who killed his father, yet they were sympathetic enough to his family to bring them over here and change their identities. We need to find the identity of that murdered civil servant and what their purpose was."

"Not only that, we need to find the answer before we're apprehended by the authorities."

***

This time Neal decided to keep the phone glued to his ear and ensure that his employee did not slack on the job all the time passing instructions onto his driver.

"Leave at the M25 junction, go towards the Dartford Tunnel." Neal hoped that the traffic had cleared a little since his last visit. Marginally better, at least it would have held Tony and his gang up as well.

"Last CCTV sighting was southbound on the B260 towards Longfield."

All the while Neal had been trying to figure out just where they were going, backwards and forwards, or at least that was how it seemed to be. But he was wrong. Tony and his accomplices had simply pulled over at the Black Prince, changed the number plates and continued southbound towards Kent. They did have a destination in mind. But what was it? If Neal could work that out, he stood a good chance of getting them with or without CCTV.

Longfield rang a bell, he was sure he had been there recently. It came back to him. He had driven through it, on the way to New Ash Green to see George Stevens; the man in the chaotic house. It was where Douglas had been found dead and where Tony had, no doubt, found the photographs. That had to be their destination. It was off the beaten track, plenty of space to hide a camper van. Plus, a host who is not averse to breaking the law. Neal was convinced, he relaxed. At last, he felt back in control of the situation.

Once they were on the B260 and the signs were pointing them in the direction of Longfield, Neal's driver picked up the speed, moving past traffic where he could. To the other road users, he just looked like a mad driver speeding and no doubt they were cursing him. The contact with the office had now slipped into silence, cameras along this stretch of road were few and far between.

They saw it and spoke at the same time to announce what they had spotted; the camper van was ahead of them. There was no other car between them, so they gained quickly on the unsuspecting vehicle.

"How do you want to do this?" the driver asked, settling into a more mundane pace, matching that of the vehicle ahead of him.

The answer did not come at once, Neal was thinking. After a few moments, he answered, "Lights on, then ram it from behind. Catch it on the offside corner, which should push it into the verge, then we'll have them."

"Are you sure we shouldn't wait until we have some sort of back up. If I hit him and I damage this car, we'll be up the creek without a paddle."

"I told you before, no back up, this is a very sensitive operation. Lights, then ram the back. Let's go."

Against his better instincts the driver switched on the blue flashing lights that were located behind the grill of the car. He placed his foot firmly on the accelerator and aimed for the camper van.

***

It was the blue lights reflected in his door mirror that first caught his attention. The strobe effect distracted Marcus for a moment before he came to his senses. The fact that they were being pursued came home to him. What had been talked about was now a reality. The car behind them wanted them stopped, questioned, and Marcus surmised, something even worse could well happen.

"They've got us," was all he said.

Those three words woke Tony up from the doze that he had relaxed into. At once his senses were heightened and his nerve endings prickled with anticipation. He tried to look into the passenger mirror. He did not see the car, just the blue lights reflecting off the hedgerow they were passing.

"Watch out, he'll try and get in front of us, block our route," Tony said, recalling times he had worked in the police force and being in marked cars that drove in front of criminals who had decided not to stop once the blue lights were on. "Put your foot down," he added, encouraging Marcus to speed away from their hunters.

"I'm in a house on wheels which does not behave like a sports car, you'll be surprised to learn, I'm never going to outrun or lose him. We need another plan for when he, in the end, stops us."

"Just keep driving," Tony advised. "All the time we're moving he can only follow or be forced to commit to trying to block our path, which may give us other opportunities. Just keep going for now."

Tony struggled to think. He attempted to imagine what he would have done if he was in the car behind, lights flashing, urging the car in front to stop. An innocent bystander would just stop, a criminal would run, start a chase, neither was an option for them. They would have to stop in the end, then what? Decamp across the fields – pointless. Outrun whoever might be in the car behind, there could be four burly men in the car following them, they would be no match for them. If they could lose the car behind, turn off the main road, then still make their way to George's place, they stood a slim chance. But Tony began to accept that they were not going to lose the car behind, it was like a sports car chasing a transit. There was no way that they could outrun or outmanoeuvre the car behind them.

Facing the stark cold facts, Tony began to wonder just what might happen next. Would they all be taken to some discreet spot, then what, interrogated, questioned? Would they suffer the same fate as Liam? Had they truly uncovered something that warranted their deaths? If he was going to die, then he could accept it, but he would fight to the end, not for himself, but for his daughter, she did not deserve to die, she was a teenager, an innocent victim.

"He's speeding up. I think he's going to ram us." Marcus decided as he watched the car race towards them.

Now Tony began to understand, ramming and stopping the camper van, a police strategy. But why not bring some other cars into the equation, block the van in between three or four other cars, that was the best, most secure option. One lone car striking the camper van did not seem the best solution.

"Get ready, he's going to hit us at a fair pace."

All three occupants prepared themselves for the imminent impact. As Marcus tensed up, he called out, "This is it!"

Then nothing, there was no massive jolt. No lurching of the camper van in one direction or another.

"He's stopped." Marcus glued his eyes to the mirror, not the road in front.

"What?" Tony leaned forward and looked into the nearside mirror. He saw the receding lights flashing, the car stationary in the middle of the road growing smaller as Marcus accelerated as much as the heavy van would allow.

Straight away, Marcus swung the steering wheel right and hurled the van into a small lane and drove as fast as he dared. He was not going to waste this golden opportunity.

***

Neal prepared himself for the impact, he closed his eyes. They were just feet away, another millisecond and there would be a coming together of metal and plastic, a loud noise and the sound of metal bending as his car impacted the van. Instead, there was nothing. Suddenly the car came to a sharp sudden halt, the engine silent. They were straddling the white dotted lines in the middle of the road.

"What the fuck!" Neal shouted as he watched the camper van continue its journey, before turning right down a lane whose entrance was concealed from where he sat in the car.

"What have you stopped for? Get a fucking move on!"

Cautiously the driver turned towards Neal with an awkward look on his face. This was not a conversation he wanted to have.

"I'm sorry, it's the ACB."

"The what?"

"The Active City Brake, it's a safety thing, stops you driving into other cars, rear-ending them at the lights, that sort of thing. I forgot to turn it off," he sheepishly admitted.

"You're telling me because you forgot to turn something off, this car in its wisdom decided that it was dangerous for us to hit the car in front."

"A bit like that, yes."

"You're joking me. This is the nanny state gone mad when a man can't ram the car in front just because his car's computer says so. Can we get the car started again or has this stupid car had enough for the night?"

The driver started the car again, turned off the ACB and accelerated away. In the first instance, he missed the turning that the camper van had taken even though Neal had made it clear, or so he thought, which lane they needed to go down. Neal consoled himself with the fact that it should not be too hard to follow a bloody great big camper van, but he was starting to think it might be trickier than he had at first thought.

***

"I have no idea where I am going or where I am," Marcus admitted as he drove down a selection of narrow lanes, turning left or right depending on where his karma decided it would be good to go.

He also relied on the screen of his sat-nav. Every time he stumbled across a main road, he glanced at the screen

298

looking for a smaller narrow lane that went off it, he would take that road even though he did not know where it might lead. What he did know was that narrow country lanes were less likely to have intrusive cameras watching, spying on passing traffic. He reasoned that that was going to be the only way to lose the black car that had found them. He drove, turning here, turning there, sneaking along lanes where he hoped he would not be confronted by too much oncoming traffic. When he did come up against another car travelling along a narrow lane in the opposite direction, luckily it gave way, reversing to a point where Marcus could squeeze his van past. He smiled, thanked them for their courtesy and continued his flight.

It was a destination that Marcus would never have agreed to if he had known what he had just been told. MI5 paid George a visit. They knew the address and it would be one they would visit in the fullness of time. Marcus wanted somewhere unconnected, somewhere there was no logical association. Maybe earlier he could have suggested a few ideas, but they were no longer an option. They now had his registration number, by now they would know that Marcus Young was in the driving seat. The same Marcus Young who knew about the photographs. The same Marcus Young who they had concocted a series of lies about to send his career into freefall. He was thankful that they had not decided to erase him from the face of the earth. They had let him live then, but perhaps that option was no longer on the table.

"We need a new plan," was all he said to Tony, who looked drawn and worried.

Both adults knew the gravity of their situation. Marcus hoped that Isobel was not so aware, yet she was a sensible teenager and would have very likely seen the signs of two adults with no real idea of what they should do. How many people would know what to do if they were being pursued by officials of Her Majesty's Government, whose sole intent was to ensure that any knowledge they had was never used and the most effective way of ensuring that was to kill you. Where do you go? Who do you see? Life nowadays is based on electronic cards, mobile phones, registration plates, facial recognition. There was no escape from big brother, unless you found a cave in the middle of some desolate landscape and managed to survive on heather and berries. A cave was not going to be an option for the occupants of the motor home.

"We now have another choice to make," Marcus offered to either one of them, knowing that Tony would be the one taking on board what he was saying. "I have about sixty miles of petrol left in the tank. We drive for sixty miles to end up motionless in some place, or we go to a petrol station, fill up and continue running. The downside of the latter is that the CCTV cameras in the station will no doubt be linked in some way to our friends back at MI5, meaning they'll then have a location for us."

Tony groaned, he was tired and feeling desolate, he did not have an answer for any of this. "Get the fuel and take the risk, at least we will have about a half hour start on them if we are quick."

***

They drove past George's house slowly. Neal and his driver peered past the gate into the garden area, there was no sign of the camper van. There was plenty of other debris in the garden, but no indication that Tony and Marcus had arrived at the house. A single light shone out from one of the downstairs windows. Neal could always knock on the door, see what he might shake up. He was also fully aware that if Tony and Marcus were already secreted in the residence, then George would not invite him in and Neal had little legal redress to enter. Not that he was ever bothered about that, but it might just complicate matters even more on this occasion.

If he had to put money on it, Neal would say that Tony and his allies had not arrived yet. He decided he would wait, but not outside, the road was too narrow and they would be obvious. At the top of the road, he had seen a pub which offered a small car park that would give an advantageous view of anyone or anything entering the country lane.

They sat in silence observing the light traffic that passed, paying particular attention to any vehicle that turned into the lane. They had been parked for about thirty minutes and still not seen their target. Neal was on the verge of giving up and knocking on George's door as he had no other ideas when his phone rang.

"They have just filled up at a Shell garage in Orpington, joined the Croydon Road. They have become lax, pinging some cameras, heading towards Hayes Common."

They left the car park in a hurry with both lights and sirens, they did not want to lose their quarry again. Croydon Road, Neal wondered if they were going back to Tony's house, that would be stupid, but not impossible.

As he received updates, Neal plotted their course. He could see the gap shrinking, they were getting closer and closer. In just a few minutes, they would be behind them, this time with the Active City Brake switched off.

"Up ahead." Neal pointed through the windscreen towards the distant white shape that represented their goal. "Let's get it done this time," he pointedly remarked.

Neal's driver swung right to overtake a small hatchback that had seen the lights closing in fast and begun to pull to the left indicating they were letting the speeding car pass. Accidentally the driver of the small hatchback flashed his main headlights at the same time, a common error. What the driver of the small hatchback did not see was the large white truck illegally reversing out into the road.

The lorry driver had done it a hundred times after delivering to this shop. The road was quiet at this time of night, tonight, it was different. Thankfully the little hatchback flashed him and slowed, no doubt allowing him to continue his difficult reversing manoeuvre.

In disbelief, Neal saw the lorry continuing its journey across the path of his car. At the same time his driver swung his steering wheel sharply right and pushed hard on the brakes. Almost out of control, the black car with blue flashing lights mounted the pavement and struck a pedestrian railing, which crumpled under the impact, but not before the right-hand front wing of the car had been torn off.

Without pausing for breath, Neal's driver reversed back onto the road ignoring the lorry, and managed to slip through a small gap that it had left, his focus, as was Neal's, was the camper van that had been tantalisingly close to them. Neal looked as far as he could down the road, the camper van was once more out of sight.

**

"They're back like the proverbial bad penny and they are closing fast," Marcus pointed out as he noticed the blue lights once again in his mirror. He could not be sure that the vehicle travelling towards them contained their pursuers, it could have been any sort of urgent vehicle heading to an incident, but he was erring on the side of caution.

Together Isobel and her father peered into the passenger mirror, they trusted Marcus, but curiosity made them look for themselves.

"Any bright ideas?" Marcus asked. He was adrift in a part of the London suburbs he had rarely visited. Fortunately for them all, Tony and Isobel were more acquainted with the area.

"I'm wondering if we should just stop and decamp, split up and confuse them. There's no way we are going to lose them driving in this thing," Tony advised, inadvertently showing contempt for the living quarters they were being driven around in.

"Can't see that helping, they'll soon flood the area and pick us off. No relations around here by any chance?" Marcus asked hopefully, as the lights began to get closer.

"I've an idea; take the next left after the roundabout." Isobel pointed to a turning that was fast approaching. "Featherbed Lane, about a quarter of a mile up the road there is a small break in the fence, you can get in there and then the area is surrounded by bushes. We might be lucky and lose them."

"Are you sure?" Tony questioned his daughter, wondering just how she knew of such an escape route.

The camper van swung left as Marcus steered it along the road. All of them missed the scene playing out behind them.

"A bit further," Isobel encouraged, looking ahead for the break in the hedge. In the darkness of the unlit road the gap appeared out of nowhere for Marcus. "There!" Isobel shouted and pointed. Marcus stood on the brakes and bounced the van through the narrow open gateway. Isobel jumped out of the van's side door. "Go on about a hundred yards, I'll shut the gate," she ordered.

As instructed, Marcus brought the camper van to a halt amongst bushes and overgrown trees. Turning the lights off, they awaited Isobel's return.

Out of breath, she threw herself into the van. "Gate shut. Hope they just drive on by and not see us."

Tony could no longer stop himself from asking the burning question he wanted to be answered.

"Just how do you know about this little hidey-hole?"

Isabel looked a little embarrassed. She dropped her head to avoid her father's direct gaze before she admitted, "A couple of boyfriends have brought me here in the past. It's discreet and relatively quiet at night."

"Thank God for young love, it might well have saved us," Marcus pointed out. He had a smile on his face, only just discernible to his fellow passengers in the half-light.

"I suppose this isn't the time to show my disapproval, I'll postpone it for another day."

In silence they waited.

***

"Keep going, they can't have gone far," Neal instructed the driver, as he called back to the office, only to be told the camper van had not had any recent camera pings.

Neal opened his window; he was getting both hot and frustrated.

"Okay," he spoke into his mobile, "plot all the cameras around this area and tell me a way that avoids cameras. I'm not sure how they're doing it, but they're missing all the static surveillance that's around. And while you're at it..." He stopped; his eyes had seen the white colour of a large vehicle disappear into the darkness of a left-hand turn that

304

they had just passed. "There, the left we have just passed, it's them. Turn this bloody thing around and get cracking."

His driver stopped the car and tried to change direction. That was easier said than done. The melee of vehicles around the traffic lights they had just gone through only added to the confusion. And the delay caused as drivers tried to work out just what this damaged black car with the blue lights wanted to do exactly. It took a couple of minutes before Neal's driver managed to extract himself from the stream of traffic and drive into Featherbed Lane, blue lights illuminating the shrubbery and trees that lined the narrow country road.

"Slow down and turn the blues off; we don't want to announce our arrival too soon."

The lane was long, reasonably straight and incredibly narrow in places. More than a mile later they arrived at an offset crossroads, close to a vintage pub called the White Bear. They stopped and looked around; the lights of the pub reflected on the junction as customers began to trickle out at the approaching closing time.

Neal sighed again; he was tired. Annoyed he still had not caught Tony, he would have liked to throw something at a brick wall just to hear it break. Instead, he banged the dashboard with his fist.

"I don't suppose you've a powerful torch on your person?"

The driver retrieved one from the boot and checked it worked before handing the large torch to Neal. Then as instructed, he slowly retraced his tracks along Featherbed Lane while Neal scanned each side with a powerful white beam that penetrated the darkness that now fully cloaked the landscape.

They edged along the road, taking their time to examine both sides, or at least the spaces that bordered the road. Occasionally they had to stop to let a car pass them, or they pulled to one side as a vehicle approached them.

They passed an odd assortment of leisure activities: a paint ball warfare site, a horticultural nursery, a forest school, a scout camp, a golf course, all closed for the night. Plus, there was dense woodland that often thinned to reveal an open grass area, before reverting to tall shrubs and finally the trees taking over again.

The contrast between the bright light and the starless night sky was causing Neal's eyes to water. He was exhausted and just wanted to go home. He knew his driver felt the same as did the employee back at the office who was becoming more cantankerous the longer he stayed at work. But he also saw the reason he had to find Tony, Marcus and Isobel. He understood how vitally important locating them was to Rupert and the government that he had sworn to serve and protect.

***

They could see the car moving slowly, the headlights illuminating the gaps between the leaves of the bushes. Like sparkling stars, the lights moved towards the camper van. It was obvious to the trio that the black car was investigating as best it could from a moving car, the space beyond the hedge for any clue. It was getting nearer. Marcus wanted to take a closer look and after isolating the courtesy light he opened the door, darkness remained. Carefully he closed the door behind him and moved a little nearer to the road, crouching down low. He was forming the plan that once they had passed, he could observe them as they proceeded along the lane. He hoped that after they had made one sweep of the lane they would give up and drive away. That would give him the opportunity to return to the camper van and they could make their escape.

Marcus remained on his knees behind a thick bush close to the gate. He watched as the beam of light swung from one side to the other. The car continued past the gate, sweeping the area with the white light, slowly moving on its way. Marcus breathed again, edged a little closer to the road. Then he held his breath as he saw the reversing lights come on and the car began to travel backwards. Instinctively, he moved away from the gate, laying even lower in the damp cold grass. The reversing car went past the wooden gate and then stopped. The mottled light shone through the foliage and Marcus turned to see what they had seen. It was small, insignificant Marcus would have thought, but it had just given up the position of the parked camper van.

***

He might have been tired, fed up and frustrated, but Neal still concentrated on his search. His diligence had paid off.

"Stop! Go back just beyond that wooden gate."

As commanded, the driver reversed, trying to see what Neal had seen. It was not only small and inconsequential, but it was also reflective. An orange strip that stood out behind the bushes. It might be nothing, Neal surmised, it could just be an odd fluorescent strip that had fallen off something. But it was not on the ground and the more he looked the more he could see. A silver chrome reflection and something white behind it. The camper van, what else could it be?

***

Why, Marcus asked himself, what on earth possessed me to put it on in the first place? As if a strip of orange, fluorescent tape would make his home more obvious. It was attached to the bike rack, where he had his motor bike strapped. Maybe he was thinking it would make it clearer that there was something on the rear of the camper van. Whatever he had been thinking, he deeply regretted it now.

He heard the car doors open followed by the footsteps of two men walking across the tarmac towards the gate. One of them leaned over the wooden gate and shone the torch towards the camper van, which was then illuminated by a bright white light. Marcus watched as the other man began to open the gate. It was time to make some choices, hard choices, the consequences of which he did not have time to consider. He stood up, putting himself in the cold beam like some ringmaster in the spotlight. He held his hands up.

"I'm not sure what you guys are after, but I can assure you I've done nothing wrong. I was just getting some fresh air, been on a long drive." He stood, hoping his voice would carry back to the van and act as a warning to Tony and his daughter.

"I know you're Marcus Young, a rogue editor, and a bit of a wanderer since your fall from grace. Are Tony and his daughter with you in that van?" Neal nodded towards the static vehicle. Now that the clouds had shifted it was bathed in delicate moonlight.

"They were with me, but they got out back in Orpington when I filled up, they wanted to go off on their own."

It was possible, yet Neal was sceptical. There would have been no reason for Tony and his daughter to leave and go their own way. It was now his turn to make some hard choices. There was going to be no turning back, he knew what Rupert wanted him to do. It was just how to, the best way. If you were going to kill someone, was now the safest time to do it or was there going to be a better time? A time that would provide him with a possible motive to offer those authorities that investigate crimes.

Standing under the moonlight in an isolated area of greenery seemed to Neal to be a perfect place. Marcus would no doubt be discovered tomorrow by some dog walker going about their innocent trek through the dew-laden grass. The dog would discover the body. The police would be called, the media informed; an investigation started. A man, with a gunshot wound had been found. The police would look at intention and opportunity. Luckily for the local constabulary, MI5 would be able to offer an explanation as they had intelligence on Marcus Young. He had been travelling the country moving drugs around to earn money. No doubt he upset a member of the criminal fraternity and had paid the price. No one would worry if a criminal got killed, the enthusiasm would wane and the death would be just forgotten, shelved, or put on hold.

"Why should I believe you?"

"Because it's the truth."

"Lay face down close to that bush, spreadeagle in fashion, while my colleague searches you for any weapon that you might have concealed."

"I don't have one."

"Maybe, but I want to know for sure. Lay down Mr Young."

Marcus complied and lay on the wet grass that felt cold. He spread his legs wide and stretched out his arms. He waited to be searched. He just hoped that Tony was making a plan to make use, as best he could, of the delay.

Neals's driver moved forward assuming that he was going to have to search this man. But Neal stopped him by holding his arm and he shook his head. Then Neal drew his automatic firearm from his jacket, walked towards Marcus and stood astride the prone man. He held the gun barely an inch from Marcus's head and without any hesitation fired a single shot that went through the skull and out into the soft earth. The body twitched briefly then never moved again.

Neal heard the gasp of astonishment from his colleague. He looked at him and said, "I can't tell you how sensitive this operation is, you now see why we could not ask for back up. Let's check the motorhome, my guess there are two others in there. Best prime your weapon."

***

Tony at once recognised the sound of a single gunshot. The noise echoed and seemed to hang in the air like a warning of the things to come. He jumped into the driver's seat, started the motor, pushed it into gear and released the handbrake, the camper van lurched forward.

"Is there another way out?" Tony asked Isobel as he drove forward without any regard of where they might be going.

"There's a fence up ahead, but no gate."

Tony did not need a gate, he wanted momentum to push through any wooden barrier that he might come up against. The van slewed from left to right as its wheels struggled to grip the soft mud throwing sods and grass upwards and outwards. The engine was revving hard. He saw the break in the hedgerow, a four–bar wooden fence stretched for maybe thirty or forty feet before the hedgerow returned. This was going to be the only chance, the one break that he could escape the soft ground and find the tarmac. He accelerated and aimed for the fence, all he could reasonably manage was an oblique angle, he hoped it would be enough to break the wood and not just scrape along and be deflected back into the field.

The wood cracked and splintered; debris flew in all directions as the camper van ploughed through the fence. Dents in the grill, a broken headlight and a wing mirror tore off as he drove through the fragments of the fence. He was back on the road, driving as fast as the tired motor would let him. They had escaped for the moment, but Tony knew it was only going to be a short respite. He was alone with his daughter and now he knew exactly what was at stake – their lives.

***

The white camper van receding into the distance, moving out of his grasp, was becoming a recurring image for Neal. He and the man with him ran back to their car waiting on the road. By now it was not the only one, there were now two more trying to squeeze past the badly parked black car.

There was no option to go forward, only to reverse a distance back and use the entrance to the golf club to turn around and give chase to Tony. That strategy was quickly scuppered as a pickup truck appeared behind them.

"Get out of our way," Neal shouted from his open door to the heavy-set man in the pickup truck.

The response made it clear that he had no intention of moving for, as he pointed out, 'some dickhead who parked in the middle of the road'.

Neal would have liked to simply point his gun at the driver and tell him to move, he sensibly decided that was not the best option. The truck was then joined by the two drivers who had already tried to squeeze past Neal's black car, decrying the way they had been stopped. Voices were raised, horns were beeped, as intransigence became everyone's standpoint.

In the melee, Neal's phone rang. It was Rupert Bell. As much as he wanted to, Neal could not refuse to answer the call.

"Sir, it's not a good time."

"It never is, is it? I understand that you have been keeping some of our office staff way beyond their allotted finishing time, not good for morale. I assume you have still to make contact with Tony and his daughter?" Rupert did not wait for an answer as he already knew it. "You do realise that Tony left his house this morning to meet with his daughter's abductor. I would very much doubt that he took the photographs that we're so interested in with him. What is that noise in the background, are you at some sort of pub brawl?"

"Issue with traffic," Neal avoided a detailed answer. "You think that the photographs are at his house?"

"I would say it's highly likely," Rupert pointed out. "Leave your driver to sort out the traffic mess, you grab an Uber or something and meet me at Tony's house."

As Neal walked along Featherbed Lane away from the traffic jam that seemed to be increasing by the minute, he searched for a nearby Uber. Why hadn't he thought of that? There would have been no reason for Tony to take the photographs with him earlier. Even though Neal had searched the house as best he could, at the time he was sceptical about them still being in existence, now he knew they were, he would be a lot more thorough in his search.

***

"Do you think they killed Marcus?" Isobel asked. It was not a question she wanted to ask or ever thought she would have to about anyone. Yet after the day's events, she suspected it was true, but she still could not understand why it had to happen.

"After what they did to Liam, I don't think they can take any prisoners."

"Are we next?"

"That depends on what we do and how we do it. First, I think we need to get away from this area, lose ourselves in another city, only then can we plan together. No doubt Marcus will be discovered and they will make up some sort of story. Well at least I still have contacts in the force, we might be able to tip them off, put pressure on them. I don't have a clear plan right now, but I know we need to get back to our house quickly. It's a risk, but a risk we need to take. I have cash there; we need to get other clothes. Then we lose ourselves in the night. It will be hard for a few days, but together we will get through this," he promised, although he was not sure how much he believed in his own words.

"What about Mum? What will she think when she hasn't heard from us for a few days?"

"We'll find a way to get a message to her, and we'll find a way out of the mess we have fallen into."

Cautiously, Tony and Isobel left the van a few streets away from their home. Walking the last quarter of a mile, they studied every parked car they passed. Every person walking on the street they assumed might be an agent. There was the risk that someone would be watching for them as they walked through their front door, but it was a risk that Tony had to take. Risk is in all parts of life; it was just this one had greater consequences.

Isobel set about gathering some items into a holdall: fresh underwear, a warm top, another pair of trainers, some make up, her favourite teddy. Plus, her journal which she had not filled in for many days now. There was a lot to be added. She crushed as much as she could into the bag.

Tony followed a similar pattern in his room. An overnight bag into which he stuffed a random selection of warm clothing. In addition, he took from his bedside drawer an envelope full of twenty-pound notes that he had kept for those times when bank computers failed. He had been caught out once and vowed he would never be caught again. That was an unusual weekend, he and his wife scrabbling around for some cash to buy groceries; modern life relied so much on electronic chips and cables. At the time he also relied on his wife to care for his daughter and look after the house while he was working long hours. The room felt empty without her, just as it had done when she was first imprisoned. He wondered if he would ever be back here in his bedroom with his wife beside him.

He next pulled a brown folder out from under the mattress. The photographs. Those cursed photographs that he wished he had never seen. Why was the government so desperate to recover them that they would kill anyone who was in contact with them? Why kill people when they had no idea as to the significance of the seemingly innocent black-and-white images? Tony thought of Marcus lying cold and lifeless on a patch of wet grass waiting for his body to be discovered. He shrugged off the thought, he needed to survive and take care of his family.

"Come on darling." He urged his daughter to finish her packing quickly. They had been in the house for a little under five minutes, but Tony knew even that might be too long. They ran down the stairs together.

"I've booked an Uber to take us to East Croydon station, from there we can get into London. I know they can't track Ubers easily."

He was reassuring his daughter as he opened the door. Blocking his way were two men, he recognised both of them. The children's TV presenter who had appeared to befriend him to help him find his daughter. Then the other man, Tony knew, drops coffee cups to kill people.

It was the older man who spoke, "Before you leave the country Mr Vercoe, I'd like a quick word. Shall we go inside?"

Chapter 37

Entertaining was something that both Tony and his wife always enjoyed. It was for that reason that when they set about furnishing and decorating their home, they paid special attention to the dining room. By some standards the space might be considered bare. A rectangular table, spacious enough for eight covers, three down each side plus one at either end. The table was made from smoked glass with a shiny chrome frame, nothing too ornate. The room was not the biggest, but they wanted to give a feeling of space. Against the wall opposite the bay window, on one of the short walls was a simple yet practical white cupboard which served the purpose of storing crockery and the cutlery they used for enjoyable dinners with friends. It also held all the trappings including napkins, a candle holder and a vase which Mrs Vercoe would spend a good couple of hours setting with flowers.

Following the modern theme, on each wall but for the bay window, hung a vibrant modern abstract painting. Originals by an artist that no one had ever heard of, although Tony always insisted that one day they might be worth a fortune, much to the amusement of their guests. Dining chairs had light grey material on the seats which were set into chrome frames that matched the table. All in all, it was a dining room that drew compliments from their guests.

Tony looked around the room, it somehow looked different when you were attached to a chair with plastic ties. His hands and legs were bound to the chrome frames. His daughter, equally bound up stared at him with a pleading look in her eyes. She was, not for the first time over the last few days, scared.

"This would have been so much easier if you had handed this envelope over to Neal the very first time you saw him. But reporters are always looking for the story that will make them renowned amongst their peers, even half-baked reporters who were once coppers." Rupert examined the prints. "If you'd handed them over it would have saved you the trouble of getting all these extra prints developed. Bit of a waste, they, along with the negatives, are all going to be destroyed. No trace at all will be left of their existence."

"That doesn't sound encouraging for our longevity," Tony commented, trying to sound as flippant as he could manage under the circumstances. He watched Rupert as he unrolled the negatives, holding them up to the light, squinting, no doubt ensuring they matched the black and white prints that had been discarded on the table. Neal had also placed a small box on the table, which he had opened and was now fussing around with whatever was inside, Tony could not make out exactly what he had in the box. Whatever Neal was doing, it absorbed all his attention. His gun lay on the table close to him. The weapon was small, with what appeared to be a silencer attached to the end of the barrel. Tony hoped that it was not going to scar the glass, his wife would not be pleased to find her table scratched. It was a worry that Tony dismissed from his mind as he wondered how bad the odds were for him and his daughter ever leaving their house alive.

Carefully, Rupert replaced the negatives, the wad of photographs, plus the yellowed press cutting back in the envelope.

"You're right," Rupert spoke, his voice cold and direct. "You will no doubt have noticed that these photographs are very much the kiss of death to anyone who comes even remotely close. They are and always have been very toxic. They hold a secret that can never be revealed."

"If you're going to dispose of us," Tony wanted to avoid the word 'kill', he did not want to spook his daughter, although he guessed that moment had long passed, she was not a stupid girl, she had seen death up close and personal, "then at least you could tell me just why they are so toxic as you put it."

"I could, but then Neal would know the whole story and I would have to kill him as well. I don't kill people, that's not in my job description, thankfully. In the end it's best that you don't know. Are you ready, Neal?"

"You mean I only know part of the story?" Neal asked, a questioning look on his face amplified by his thick glasses.

"You know enough, the last part you don't want to know. Are you ready?" Rupert repeated irritably.

Neal nodded towards Rupert before he returned his attention to his box.

"What I can tell you is that your story is both sad and heart-warming in part," Rupert smiled. "See that gun on the table, that's the very same one that ended the life of your friend Marcus. What might surprise you is that we have already found a quantity of class 'A' drugs on his person. A good old-fashioned drug dealer, who no doubt supplied your wife. This will explain why the gun will be found here in your house along with both of your bodies, having carried out some sort of suicide pact. I guess the premise will be you being an ex-policeman had located the nasty man who sullied your wife with drugs which she could deal in. Sadly, you killed him and unable to bear the consequences decided to take your daughter's life as well as your own. A heart-warming story on some level I imagine." Rupert's face smirked proudly. He liked the synchronicity of the narrative and the events. It was all very plausible.

"But my wife is not, and never has been, a drug dealer."

It was Neal who spoke this time, "You know that; we know that, but the police investigation into the death of a drug dealer and your suicide will only see her criminal record, they'll make the obvious connection." As he finished, Neal moved away from the box, holding in his hand a medical syringe, which he primed whilst moving towards Isobel.

"This fluid, once inside you will not kill you, it sort of knocks you out. Confuses and weakens you. It means that I can put the gun in your hand before it fires. It will look as if you pulled the trigger. It's some form of Valium I believe." He turned to Tony and with an apologetic voice told him that the daughter needed to die first to make it clear that Tony had killed her before taking his own life, murder and death needed a plausible timeline. Neal looked at Isobel, he could see the fear in her eyes, that was to be expected, this poor teenager was about to have her life ended.

"Isobel, what I'm going to do is pull your leggings down so I can put this stuff into your thigh. The last thing I want is my needle getting blocked as I push through the material, or worse leave a tell-tale clue." Neal edged towards her, bending forward to grab the waistband of her leggings.

"You can piss off," she shouted at him.

"Isobel!" Tony berated his daughter; he had not brought her up to use such swear words. Only after he had shouted her name did he realise the stupidity of scolding her.

"At least let me do it myself, remove my leggings and not have your lecherous hands all over me."

Neal stopped, considered the request, then looked at Rupert for some sort of guidance.

"She's a teenager, cut the ties and let her do it herself. But, young lady, do not try anything clever, I can assure you that Neal will not hesitate in hurting you if he has to."

Neal put the syringe down on the table not far from Tony. He pulled a small pen knife from his pocket and knelt, cutting the leg ties first, then stood up and cut the hand ties. Isobel rose from the chair rubbing her wrists. She was about an inch shorter than Neal who impatiently asked her to pull her leggings down. He wanted to get this done, he hated delaying the inevitable, interruptions were only adding to his already taut nerves.

It was the searing pain in his testicles that surprised Neal. He could not, in that fleeting split second, understand why he had such excruciating pain that he was forced to bend forwards. He had not noticed Isobel's knee driving upwards between his legs finding her intended target. Even with her leggings on, Isobel felt Neal's vulnerable genitals being crushed against her knee, reassuring her that she had hit her target without the need even to move her eyes.

Swiftly she followed up her first action with a classic karate move that she had learnt during her lessons. As Neal's body lurched forward, his neck was met by Isobel's straight rigid fingers striking his windpipe with a force that led him to believe she had stabbed him. He tried to override the pain, to force his body to start a defence. He had no time before her fingers were again stabbing his throat forcing his head to move backwards. In mid-movement Isobel, with the palm of her hand, pushed against his skull forcing it hard and firmly onto the table. In the back of her mind, she hoped that the table would not smash, her mother would hate that. The table stayed intact, which enabled her to grab the gun. It was heavier than she thought it might be, but the balancer enabled her to grip it and hold it close to Neal's head. Instinctively, in a fit of self-defence, she squeezed the trigger. At such a close range there was little damage to Neal's head as the bullet passed through his brain and exited beside his ear. Although the gun was silenced, the noise of the glass tabletop shattering was louder than she had expected. She had not thought it through as she watched Neal fall over the broken crystal-like pieces that the table had crumbled into and were now scattered across the carpeted floor that was soaking up his blood. She looked down at the bloodied body and overcame the feeling of nausea she felt welling up inside her.

Regaining her composure, still holding the gun, she looked away and her stare fell upon Rupert. She aimed the gun at his head, then paused, not sure what she should do.

Rupert broke the silence, "If you ever need a job, young lady, I am sure the department would welcome someone with your talent." His voice lacked emotion. He had already disregarded the death of his colleague.

It was her father who intervened, telling her to stop, pause and think of the bigger picture. Together they could get out of this, there was an opportunity to clear this mess up without killing anyone else. He had seen the look of anger in her eyes, which was about to override any of the morals that he had always tried to teach her.

"Dad, you're such an optimist. This bloke kills people without any fear of justice for the law or anyone. Liam was killed, Marcus was killed, and we'll be next unless I end him here and now." Her finger began to tighten on the trigger, she wanted to see this old man dead, that was the only way he would pay for all the wrong he had done.

"Before you pull that trigger," Rupert sounded calm, it was not the first time that he had had a loaded revolver aimed at him, "you need to consider some facts young lady. Point the gun downwards slightly, those triggers can be incredibly sensitive."

She lowered the gun until it was pointing at his abdomen, enough to stop him in his tracks if he lunged at her.

"I know and understand why you want to kill me; I wouldn't blame you in the least. Killing is easy. The thing you need to consider is just how you are going to explain two dead bodies in your house. The bodies of two government officials, one of them a high-ranking official. You might well start citing a jumbled story about old photographs, the IRA and as much as you know, but I can assure you it will not be enough to warrant your freedom. You will, in effect, be in the same position, for the simple reason that there are people still in the government besides me who wish these photographs to go away."

Rupert looked down at the lifeless body of Neal, someone he had always liked. It was a shame that sometimes sacrifices were needed. He continued, "But if you spare me, I have the resources and the influence to clear up this mess and ensure that no criminal charges are laid against you. Young though you are, I am sure that you can appreciate finding someone in the Yellow Pages to take away a body and clear up a crime scene are not two a penny."

Tony, still affixed to the chair, pointed out an obvious question, "As my daughter indicated, how can we trust you when so many people have already had to die because MI5 wanted to cover up the truth? They knew the attack was going to happen but when their informant murdered a civil servant, things became more complex." Tony tried to make it sound as if he knew a lot more than he did, he hoped he was close enough to the facts.

Rupert knew the girl's father had made a valid point. He also knew from what he had said that Tony had no idea of the whole story. He could understand that in their situation, he would not trust him in the slightest. He needed a solution. He was not worried about dying, at his age and in his condition, death was expected, it was just that he did not want to suffer his fate at the barrel of a gun. He wanted to go out in style with a large gin and tonic and possibly a cigar, not that he was a great fan of them, it would just seem the right thing to do when death finally arrived to take his life.

"If that is all you know, then I think we might be able to come up with a compromise that would satisfy us all and get out of this. May I?" He indicated that he wished to sit down on the chair beside him. He did not wait for permission, he never waited for permission, his professional standing did not require him to. He brushed away the glass shards and sat down, loosening his tie, he felt rebellious.

"If you think that a stupid Irish spy is the reason these photographs are important, then you still have a lot to learn. This is my proposal: I will tell you everything there's to know about these photographs, and I will even hand them back to you for safe keeping. The only thing I ask in return, apart from sparing my life, is that you do nothing with them for at least three months from today. In return I will ensure that this mess is cleared up, the body will be gone and managed. There will be no charges against you for anything you might have done in recent days. My offer also includes sourcing a replacement table, I would hate you to end up in your wife's bad books. Do we have an agreement?"

"Why should I trust anything you say given what has gone before?"

"Because the simple alternative is you kill me and you're left with two dead bodies to explain to the police, who, might I point out, are not very friendly to an ex-employee such as yourself."

"Why three months?"

"Hmm, I was afraid you were going to ask that question." Rupert paused, he did not want to admit it, speaking out loud made it real, inescapable. Today he had little choice if he wanted to enjoy a few more gin and tonics. "I have stage four cancer that is being very nasty to my body. I could be spending time going through chemotherapy and having needles stuck into me, which the doctors suggest could add another six to nine months to my life, but I'd rather have three good months than nine feeling like shit. In three months, I will be dead. When that moment comes you can do whatever you like with those photographs that have haunted me for the last thirty years. Plus, if you know the whole story, and I do mean the whole story, then no one can ever silence you because the whole story points to the very centre of the ruling class. Do we have an agreement?"

Tony nodded. "But first release me from this chair," he requested.

Chapter 38

Out of respect for Neal's corpse, they left the dining room and crossed the hall into the lounge. Tony had taken over control of the gun from his daughter and he kept the weapon levelled at Rupert's body as they all sat down.

"I don't suppose you have a gin and tonic to hand, by any chance?" Rupert asked calmly as if they had just had an enjoyable social meal and now the guests were sitting expecting a post-dinner drink.

"None of us are moving until you have told us the whole story, and make sure it is the whole truth and nothing but the truth. You'd best begin," there was tension in Tony's voice, he still had little faith in this man.

"I guess a good place to start would be at the very beginning, which was 1990 before this nightmare began. Back then I was a young man brimming with hope for the future, for my life and the world. I was working for the security services, a glamorous world, or so I thought. At that time, we were still fighting a challenging war against the IRA. My role in that conflict was sitting in a comfortable office in the Kingsway building handling three IRA informants, gathering intelligence from their sources and feeding the information into the high command. Nothing earth shattering, just useful day-to-day knowledge that helped those with a higher status than mine decide what actions might be needed.

"Liam's father, Declan MacGabhann. His surname is Gaelic for Smith, if you didn't know, that interesting yet pointless fact. I digress, Declan, Liam's father was one of those informants that I handled. He had been supplying us with material for about two years, nothing remarkable, oddments of personnel changes, supply lines, various gossip. I imagine he viewed it as some sort of useful second income stream.

"Our ears pricked up when he told us he was being sent to the UK on a special mission which included buying a van. We speculated of course that it could be part of a bombing campaign or moving explosives or arms around. Perhaps even just a simple bank robbery. When he told me what was planned, I felt the hairs on the back of my young neck stand up. The van was going to be a platform from which the IRA were going to launch a mortar attack on Margaret Thatcher, who was at that time Prime Minister. This was something big, and we were already onto them. I just needed more information, date and time of the attack. Declan said he would do his best.

"I was excited, this was going to be my time to shine, cement my credentials to the career ladder and reach the highest level of the office, maybe even Director. I waited for Declan to come up with the details of the IRA plan."

Rupert paused allowing the chance for his listeners to ask questions. They just sat in silence watching him. He drew breath and continued the saga,

"The weeks rolled by and Declan, who by this time had returned to Ireland, had no more information. All we knew was an attack was planned. Then in November of that year, Maggie resigned in tears and John Major took over. We in the department wondered what the IRA might do now, their prime target was no longer in office. We waited.

"Christmas came and went before Declan came back to us. The planned attack was going ahead, but they now were intending to kill the Prime Minister and his whole cabinet. They were going to park the van at the top of Downing Street and fire off the mortars. By this time my seniors, two other men well above me in status in the department, were aware of what was going on. Just the three of us knew and that was how it had to be. I was now at the top table in the department and my ego was going through the roof. A young, inexperienced man with a lot of responsibility. I suggested disrupting the whole operation, but I was told to wait, see if any prominent IRA members became involved.

"In late January 1991, Declan gave me the date, unsurprisingly it coincided with a planned cabinet meeting. The Prime Minister, his cabinet, as well as a range of top civil servants would all be in the same room. I passed all this information on to my senior officer. At the same time, I suggested a planned raid. We knew where the van was being stored, we were also aware of the safe house where the IRA team charged with carrying out the operation were staying and the warehouse where the mortars were. We knew it all. In one fell swoop we would stop an audacious attack at the heart of government. I was told to wait, sit back, do nothing for now, they were seeking guidance from someone higher in the food chain."

As if he was waiting for a commercial break, Rupert paused again. He wanted to ask for a glass of water to soothe his throat. He declined to ask, knowing they would think it was some sort of ruse to take back control of the room. As much as he thought of doing that, there was a part of him that wanted to unburden himself of the whole sorry affair. He continued, "I found myself in a room, a meeting of the great and good to which I had been invited. Two senior departmental heads, who I had been liaising with, plus a Minister of State who I recognised yet had never held a high enough rank to have spoken to. Today was different. They quickly made it clear that the attack should be allowed to go ahead.

"I was flabbergasted, they were going to allow the IRA to drop explosives onto Number Ten. Was the plan to move the cabinet meeting elsewhere, let the IRA bomb an empty room? No, everyone would be in place. I made my opinion clear, maybe I was a little too vocal, but I made my point. They were more controlled in their emotions as they explained their reasoning to me.

"Mortar attacks even by trained professionals with purpose-built equipment are not that accurate. A home-made mortar fired out of the back of a van had little chance of hitting the intended target. By disrupting the attack, it could possibly expose one of our informants, i.e., Declan, who, if he was now being included in high-level operations, could prove to be of great value in the future. Who knows what atrocities the IRA has planned? I still felt they were taking a grave risk with the lives of all those in the cabinet meeting.

"They were forgetting, I was an intelligence officer. Gossip is rife in the civil service and I knew the rumours after the power battles of the last few months that the government minister sitting opposite me, looking very calm, had his eye on the top job, wanted to be the PM. I wondered about his motives yet dismissed them when he assured me that he would also be in the room and was putting his own life on the line. That I couldn't deny.

"Even so, I still tried to argue that we, as a responsible government department, could not be seen to be risking the lives of those who rule us. My ideological, humanitarian reasons fell on deaf ears. I was instructed, in no uncertain terms, that there would be no action taken to stop or hinder the IRA operation.

"I was then told, I could either become part of the mission, or I would be seen as a liability to the department.

Code for my life was being threatened or at the very least my career would be in tatters. The minister added a carrot, he suggested that I would, if I became part of their team, see a rapid profitable rise in my status. I could not beat them, so I thought it made more sense to join them whatever my reservations might be.

"I think, just to cement my involvement in this clandestine operation, I was given a role. Visit the garage where the van was being stored, check the lights, tax, everything else. All this to ensure it was not stopped by any traffic official. The attack must not fail because of a simple traffic stop. I was now part of the whole conspiracy. Just as much as Declan and his IRA compatriots.

"The rest as they say is history. The attack did fail, the shells falling into the garden at the back of Downing Street resulting in a few minor injuries to some people outside. Everyone agreed it was a surprise IRA attack that caught out the security services. If only the truth had been known at the time, I doubt we would be sitting here today. I would certainly not have progressed as far up the ranks of civil servants as I have, in part, thanks to that minister who just happened, along with one other, not to have attended that particular cabinet meeting due to other pressing engagements."

Rupert smiled wryly; he recalled the feeble, yet plausible explanations for those two ministers not being present at that meeting. Under the watchful eye of Tony, Rupert stood up slowly, removed his jacket, folded it neatly and placed it over the back of the chair, he was getting warm. As he sat down Tony spoke, "Who was that cabinet minister who decided against going to the meeting?"

"Naming names to you here and now wouldn't be appropriate. To be fair, it was not a full cabinet meeting, just a meeting of relevant departments to discuss the Gulf War. But when I have passed over to the great pasture in the sky, it will not take a lot of effort for you to compare who was missing and judge who should have been at that meeting. There could have been a legitimate reason for the minister who was aware of the attack not to attend. Dig a little more and make your own decision, I have made mine. All I am giving you here today are the facts, my opinion isn't relevant."

Respectfully, Rupert waited for a follow-up question from Tony, nothing was forthcoming, hence he continued.

"That should have been it, the end of the saga. I was now part of an elite group, my status was assured for the future. I know I should have been stronger, but what if Mr Major had been killed in that attack and another Prime Minister voted in. They all come and go like the tides, the only difference between them is the sort of rubbish they leave on the shore for others to clean up. But I knew what I had done was morally wrong and a bad thing. If I hoped that was the end of the whole sorry affair, I was seriously mistaken.

"In April 1991, just a couple of months after the attack, a newspaper photographer arrives at my office showing me photographs of the IRA buying the van, hoping it would prove to be valuable evidence. Not the biggest problem unless somehow Liam's father was identified and shown to be a UK spy, which could have posed a problem. I fobbed off the photographer with the fact that he should keep this thing quiet until we had investigated, I promised him a good news story at the end of it. Then a complication, I heard the newspaper had published a story about the car dealer way back in late 1990. There was a situation emerging that I needed to get under control quickly.

"Without any delay, I consulted my superiors, the same two men who had instructed me to disregard the date of the mortar attack.

"They made it plain the department had no choice but to act, the risks were too high. Every trace of that story was removed from libraries where we could and then the photographer and reporter were to meet with unfortunate accidents. We had the photographs, the negatives we had contained the story, we were all safe. Being young I thought that not destroying evidence as instructed might give me an edge or at least a lever should I ever need it in the future. That is why I stashed the evidence behind some panelling in our office in Kingsway. With hindsight I think I should have just destroyed it. By Christmas 1991, we had fully secured the story once again."

"You mean you killed two innocent human beings," Tony interrupted with venom in his voice that he did nothing to disguise. "They had done nothing wrong, yet you killed one outright and the other had a slow death in a nursing home. Or were they just collateral damage in your eyes?"

"Exactly, they were innocent victims of the terrorist war that the Irish were inflicting on our country. Think about it for a moment, if this story had become public knowledge at the time, can you imagine what damage it would have done to the UK government? It would have highlighted a power struggle in which one faction was happy to see the other faction killed. Here in the green grass of England we're much more accustomed to bloodless coups. The IRA, apart from purging many of their staff of informers, would no doubt have stepped up their operations, ensuring the authority of the UK government faltered. Yes, they were innocent victims, but their deaths, in my humble opinion, saved the lives of countless others who would have been killed in terror attacks as part of a refreshed and rejuvenated IRA."

"And the others, Mr and Mrs Douglas Wright as well as Marcus Young, did they die for the same reasons? I doubt it, the IRA have long since given up the fight."

"The IRA will never give up the fight, they're just waiting for the optimum moment to strike. But let me continue and you can judge for yourself."

Tony indicated with a casual wave of Neal's weapon that Rupert should continue.

"I was beginning to wonder if somehow the whole operation had been jinxed and one day it would destroy me, for the simple reason, like a recurring nightmare, another problem popped up. Declan, Liam's father, reported that he had been having an affair. I couldn't have cared less, but still he wanted to share details. One of which was the woman was finished with him and ending the affair. I almost yawned at this point; I imagined that two unfaithful people could always find another person to be unfaithful with. It was when he told me that she was going to expose him as a British informant, that my ears pricked up. How did she know? The answer was post–coitus pillow talk.

"If I had my way, we would only employ eunuch informants, but I gather it would be against some employment law. Nevertheless, she knew and was going to pass on the information to the IRA. Declan pleaded for us to pick him and his family up, then bring them to England with a new identity. The alternative for him would be an IRA execution.

"His sexual exploits had put me in a difficult situation. If I brought him back to the UK, the IRA would wonder why, possibly assume he was an informant, check back and see exactly what he had access to, then wonder about the mortar bombing. Potentially this could expose the fact we knew. On the other hand, if I left him to his fate, the IRA would execute him as an informer. You know what I am saying. Which option posed less risk to our government?

"Fortuitously for me I told him to wait a week while I sought advice from my superiors. Poor Declan could not wait that long, he silenced his mistress for good, leaving her in a ditch with a broken neck. It turned out that she was some sort of lower rank officer in the Provisionals and her colleagues were upset and wanted to dig up the truth. I don't know, neither am worried about the whole story or sequence of events that led to Declan being found beside a damp, dark roadside. In a style typical of IRA ritual killings, his body was found in a muddy ditch, naked and hooded, with evidence of beatings and a single bullet through the back of his head. Not a bad result for us, one less finger to be pointed at. There were now just four people in the whole world who knew the true circumstances behind the Downing Street Bombing."

"The woman he murdered, was she also a civil servant?"

"As I recall more of a council employee, nothing as grand as a civil servant. The postscript to Declan's death was that we did, at the request of the grandfather, bring the family over. He had shown concern for the safety of the family. We guessed the IRA were not going to be too interested in the family after Declan's death and they weren't." Rupert smiled in the same way he had done back in 1992 when he had heard that the body of Declan MacGabhann had been found.

"Again, everything went quiet, maybe at last the whole episode was closed and behind me. In July 1996, I was given a prestigious deployment to Cyprus to begin intelligence gathering in support of the USA operation, Desert Strike. Again, I was sending out spies and looking after their needs. I stayed on to work on operation Desert Fox in 1998. Then stayed another three years after that before I was called back to Kingsway and a grand promotion. It was a surprise when I found out the office had been modernised and the panels where I had concealed the evidence was now under another layer of plastic and wood. Still well out of reach, which suited me just fine. I look back at those years as the quiet years, almost forgetting the mortars ever fell, while my career blossomed until soon after the London Olympics, I achieved the heady heights of Assistant Director. I felt I had arrived.

"Yet, unbeknown to me the storm clouds that had first begun back in the nineties started gathering again. It seems strange to me that an error of judgement I made way back then has haunted me ever since. I'll try not to be too melancholy.

"Soon after the Manchester Arena bombing, our department was holding a briefing for national newspaper editors. During the drinks afterwards, I met Marcus Young, an astute young man undoubtedly always on the lookout for a good story. He asked me, having found out I was deeply involved with the war with the IRA, if a Douglas Wright had paid me a visit with some photographs of the IRA buying the van that was used in the Downing Street Bombing." Rupert stopped, smirked and looked down at the floor. "That day I felt I must have committed one of the greatest sins and was being punished by God. The photographs were once again out in the open. I guess Marcus would have told you about our meeting and passed on the contact details for Douglas Wright.

"Before you start jumping to conclusions, we never meant for Mrs Wright to die. We had broken into the house on a couple of occasions and left without finding the photographs that had to be there somewhere. Well Neal was tasked with, when the couple were out, burning the place down. To be fair to Neal, he did honestly believe they had both gone out, as had been the plan, but for some reason they had changed their minds at the last moment and Mrs Wright was alone in the house."

"And Douglas, crushed under a car?"

"You forget, he had absconded. We had no idea where he had escaped to. Only when you, being an upstanding citizen, pointed out to the police that they had incorrectly identified the body under the car, did we hear that our Mr Wright and the photographs had been found. His death is not on my hands."

Tony stood up and walked over to the window, no longer training the weapon on Rupert. He was tired, frustrated and bitter. Lives lost and young lives tainted with the horror of death and the cruelty of humans. All in the name of national security which would be the mitigating circumstances but was a lie.

"All those lives sacrificed just to protect you, a couple of other civil servants and a government minister who I would imagine is long retired."

"Yes, the other three are indeed long retired, although still alive, leaving me the sole guardian of the secret. But I will not be around for much longer. Without a sentry, it will undoubtedly become public. And before you ask why I am sharing all this now, well apart from the obvious fact you will shorten my life even further, is because there's a part of me, no doubt from my strict Catholic childhood upbringing, that makes me a little fearful of how my

335

judgement day might go. Hopefully this final act might allow me some degree of forgiveness when St Peter tallies up my score."

Standing with his back to the window, the dawn sunlight creating a silhouette of the man, Tony spoke solemnly, "I guess you had better make your phone call and get that mess in the other room cleared up."

Epilogue

The fragrance of honeysuckle teased Tony's nostrils. It was an aroma that reminded him of his mother. As he walked across the dew-laden grass he had not noticed any honeysuckle growing anywhere around him, yet the floral scent persisted. Perhaps it was his long-departed mother, visiting him, making sure her boy was taking care of himself. As Tony watched Rupert Bell's coffin descend into the cold damp earth, it was possible it reminded Tony of his own mother's funeral. Back then the graveside was crowded, with friends and family. Today the gathering was sparse, in fact it was nothing like a crowd, a small congregation of six mourners does not constitute a crowd in anyone's imagination. Tony doubted that Rupert would have cared that much. Rupert lived beyond the three months that the doctors had given him. A few days shy of five months, although Tony thought the last three weeks of Rupert's life, in a hospice sedated and motionless would not have counted as living in Rupert's mind.

Tony wondered just how Rupert might be greeted when he stood before the gates of heaven and was interviewed by St Peter. 'The wrong actions justified by the right reasons' was how Rupert planned to plead when he finally met his maker. That much he had admitted to Tony during their discussions in the hospice before the morphine had robbed Rupert of coherent speech.

It could not be denied that Rupert during his career with the British government had stepped over many moral boundaries, which gave him a reputation of being a horrendous man. Tony could only speak as he found, which would have pleased his mother. From the moment that

Tony lowered the gun he had aimed at Rupert, accepting what Rupert was offering, the man's oath was kept.

That night Rupert had installed Tony and his daughter into a very respectable hotel, while the department removed Neal's body, cleared all the damaged furniture, replaced the blood-stained carpet, making good the house to live in again. Not that Tony could ever sit in the dining room without seeing the body sprawled on the floor. In time, they would move house.

By the second night in the hotel Tony had heard that his wife was being released, on the orders of a high court judge, pending a new appeal following the discovery of new evidence. The speed and ease at which some people can undo the decisions of the justice system showed Tony just what real power can do.

One by one the mourners filed past the grave, throwing a clod of damp soil into the void, the dull sound of earth hitting the wooden coffin echoing around the still graveyard. They then walked away leaving Rupert alone in the earth. Janice Vercoe slipped her arm into her husband's, she felt cold, funerals did that to her. His daughter joined her parents holding onto her mother's arm.

"I still find it strange that you forgave him, given all the hideous crimes he carried out." Janice told her husband, an opinion she had often shared with him.

"How do I know that I would not have done the same thing, given the circumstances that he found himself in. We can never stand in anyone's shoes, therefore judging anyone else isn't something I'm qualified to do. He tangled himself into a lie, which he thought he had covered up. Yet each time that lie resurrected itself he could see no escape, so just erased any threat that might have exposed him."

"But with all that you knew he had done, you still trusted him, instead of shooting him there and then..."

Isobel interrupted, "...that's because he knew we were bad-arse dudes who were tough as nails. He stood no chance."

"Clearly." Janice pointed out. "Your counselling sessions are not having the desired effect. I'm just glad the government are paying for them and not us. So why didn't you shoot him?" the question was directed at her husband.

"If I'd have shot him, I would have ended up doing a lot more time that you ever did." He smiled as she playfully punched his side. "I trusted him, that he would keep his word. If he'd have picked up the gun and killed Isobel and me. Well, it would have been tragic for you, but at least Isobel and I would have died being honest and having faith in human nature. Which is something we should never lose sight of.

"I have a family. A loving wife and a wonderful daughter. Rupert had nothing like that, look who is here. Apart from the three of us, who else do you see around? The vicar, he's paid to be here, Rupert's secretary and a junior representative from his old department. No family, no relations. His work was his family. A family that he had no compunction about sanctioning murder for."

Walking carefully between the weather-worn headstones, the Vercoe family made their way back to their car. There was going to be no wake, no family drinks, just the simple service and the burial, which was all that Rupert Bell's life warranted.

The family drove home in silence, each with their thoughts and memories of the last few months. For all she had been through, Isobel seemed to have accepted what had happened to her and what she did to others. Now sitting in the back of the car listening to her music via her headphones, she could have been any teenager. Tony was grateful for that, that she had inner strength, just like her mother.

Tony looked across at his wife as she looked out of the window, watching the suburban houses slide past the window. She too had a strength of character. Knowing you are innocent only to be imprisoned, yet not lose faith that things would come right in the end is a special form of optimism. He could see where Isobel got her strength from. The documents confirming her exoneration arrived just a few days ago. Proving her innocence, letting her now think about building her life again. Although she could never return to the exact person she was before her incarceration, but who could?

But she was now free. In part Tony knew that it was Neal's early doubts that the family he was working alongside did not appear to be the type to deal drugs. As if it was a hobby, he started to dig around to see what he could find. It was his initial scepticism about Janice's drug conviction that provided Rupert with the evidence to put before a High Court Judge, with whom he had a good working relationship. It's not what you know it's who you know. That enabled Janice to leave prison and return to her family.

Neal was one of those humans, who would never kill a spider, would fight against injustice, yet could kill another human being in cold blood without a second thought. For all the thanks Tony had for Neal, he could still never forgive him for killing Marcus.

Once Neal's suspicions and evidence were placed before Detective Constable Pete Lewer, it did not take long for the corrupt police officer to accept the inevitable and cooperate with the investigation. Senior officers had reviewed almost all his cases, finding evidence of corruption and fraud. In the end they charged him and he was found guilty on all counts. He has now taken up residence in a cell block, where he is desperate to hide his former profession from his fellow inmates.

For Rita, in the end there were not any charges that could easily be brought against her, but not for the want of trying. The only consequence of her enthusiastic pursuit of a care order for Isobel was losing her job. That disappointed Tony and did nothing to suppress the rage his wife felt about the vindictive social worker. Justice comes in all shapes and sizes.

Ironically, the investigation team around Pete Lewer put a lot of resources into the death of Douglas Wright. Tony was questioned several times, as was George, who did not take kindly to that part of the process of taking down a bent copper. As for George's business arrangement with Mickey, the powers that be decided that to pursue their crimes might expose the establishment to a scrutiny it did not welcome. Much to George's relief.

In the end the conclusion was that Douglas had died as a result of his own negligence having drunk too much whisky and deciding it was a good idea to do some work under the car. Even now, as Tony pulled up at his home, with its for-sale sign attached to the front wall, Tony harboured his doubts as to just how Douglas met his fate.

As Tony opened the door to his house, walked along the hall past the door where a murder had taken place, he recalled he had a choice. Rupert was now dead and Tony had a story that could tear the establishment apart. He now had to decide, what he should do with all that information.

"Tony," Janice called from the kitchen, "tea or coffee?"

Some choices, Tony thought, were easier than others.

Author Notes

The story you have just read is a work of fiction. I have sprinkled some facts into it, the bombing of Downing Street for example, as well as the IRA execution.

If you search online: 'IRA Mortar Attack Downing Street', you will see that the attack was overall unsuccessful. The bombers failed in wiping out the Cabinet who were meeting at the time. But that is not the whole story.

If you dig deeper, behind the headlines, you will discover that it was not a full Cabinet meeting. It was a meeting of various ministers in connection with the ongoing Gulf War; two members were unable to attend.

Following the attack, military experts praised– if that is the right word –the incident. During an interview Peter Gurney, head of the Explosives Section of the Anti–Terrorist Branch, gave his opinion of the attack.

'It was a remarkably good aim if you consider that the bomb was fired 250 yards with no direct line of sight. Technically, it was quite brilliant and I'm sure that many army crews if given a similar task, would be very pleased to drop a bomb that close. You've got to park the launch vehicle in an area which is guarded by armed men, and you've got less than a minute to do it. I was very, very surprised at how good it was. If the angle of fire had been moved about five or ten degrees, then those bombs would actually have impacted on Number Ten.'

The operation was not a spontaneous attack, far from it. The Ford Transit was purchased the previous year, as the original target had been Margaret Thatcher. It was prepared for the mortar attack, then dramatically Mrs

Thatcher left office and the IRA's original target was no longer in place, which would explain the extended period between the van's purchase and deployment.

The story of Liam's father is loosely based on a triple execution that the IRA carried out in July 1992. In an unusual statement, the IRA admitted the killings stating that the three were informers, who had, as a trio, killed the lover of one of the men. A lover who was planning to expose their connection to the UK government.

As for the two ministers who should have been at the meeting on the morning of the mortar attack. I'll let you Google search that one. As I said at the very start, this story is fiction.

Acknowledgements

My research for Caught on Camera has brought me into contact with several interesting people, all of whom have guided me through the creation of this story. Some have asked to remain anonymous. You know who you are and thank you.

I owe a special thanks to Dave Aldrich, Retired Fire Officer, London Fire Brigade. He taught me a lot about the way firefighters react and then fight house fires, such as the one in which Mrs Wright died.

My wife deserves a medal for not only listening to my broad list of conspiracy theories, but also assisting me pick my way through thirty-year-old press cuttings. Before helping me focus my abstract thoughts into a readable story.

Then the brave souls who read through the draft story, offered up their honest opinion, suggesting improvements, as well as words of wisdom and support. In no particular order: Angela, Claire, Jean, Irene, Pete, Brian, Anthony, Andy and Gavan. I thank you all.

To you, the reader, I hope you have enjoyed this tale. I would love to hear what you thought of the story, good or bad, as I know I can't please everyone. You can let me know your opinion of the book either via an Amazon or a Goodreads review or simply leave a message on my Facebook page. www.facebook.com/adrianspaldingbooks.

You can also keep up to date with my future publications by joining my mailing list (there is a free gift on offer!) via my website: www.adrianspalding.co.uk

Until the next time, all the best, Adrian.

tabslaig & yahoo.co.uk